WILLA CATHER was born in Winchester, Virginia, in 1873. Her family moved to Nebraska before she was ten. She learned both Latin and Greek during her teens, and graduated from the University of Nebraska in 1895. She then taught high school, worked for the Pittsburgh *Leader*, and spent a good deal of time traveling. *The Troll Garden* (1905) was her first volume of short stories, and was followed by her appointment as associate editor of *McClure's Magazine*. She continued in this position for six years, but resigned in 1912 because she felt that the work for the magazine was interfering with her writing. In *O Pioneers!* (1913), a novel, she used typically American material with unusual depth and beauty. *My Ántonia* (1918), *A Lost Lady* (1923), *The Professor's House* (1925), and *Death Comes for the Archbishop* (1927) are considered to be among her best novels. She lived in New York for many years and was a familiar figure in intellectual and literary circles. *The Old Beauty and Others*, a collection of short stories, was published posthumously in 1948—a year after the author's death.

Willa Cather

24 Stories

Selected and
with an Introduction by
Sharon O'Brien

A MERIDIAN CLASSIC

NEW AMERICAN LIBRARY

NEW YORK

PUBLISHER'S NOTE

NAL BOOKS ARE AVAILABLE AT QUANTITY DISCOUNTS
WHEN USED TO PROMOTE PRODUCTS OR SERVICES.
FOR INFORMATION PLEASE WRITE TO PREMIUM MARKETING DIVISION,
NEW AMERICAN LIBRARY, 1633 BROADWAY,
NEW YORK, NEW YORK 10019.

Introduction copyright © 1987 by Sharon O'Brien

MERIDIAN CLASSIC TRADEMARK REG. U.S. PAT OFF. AND FOREIGN COUNTRIES
REGISTERED TRADEMARK—MARCA REGISTRADA
HECHO EN WINNIPEG, CANADA

SIGNET, SIGNET CLASSIC, MENTOR, ONYX, PLUME, MERIDIAN and NAL BOOKS are published by NAL PENGUIN INC., 1633 Broadway, New York, New York 10019

Library of Congress Cataloging-in-Publication Data

Cather, Willa, 1873–1947.
  Willa Cather—24 stories.

  I. O'Brien, Sharon. II. Title. III. Title: Willa Cather—twenty four stories.
PS3505.A87A6   1988   813'.52   87-20387
ISBN 0-452-00874-3 (pbk.)

First Printing, January, 1988

1 2 3 4 5 6 7 8 9

PRINTED IN CANADA

Contents

INTRODUCTION

We think of Willa Cather as a novelist—as the author of *O Pioneers!* (1913), *My Ántonia* (1918), *Death Comes for the Archbishop* (1927). Perhaps we might also remember her as the author of one gemlike short story—"Paul's Case" (1905)—and wonder why she, unlike her contemporaries Fitzgerald and Faulkner, did not do more in this genre. Yet Willa Cather began her literary apprenticeship with the short story and continued to be a prolific writer of short fiction throughout her long career. She had been writing short stories for almost twenty years before she completed her first novel (*Alexander's Bridge* [1912]), publishing over forty stories in various periodicals as well as a book of short ficiton, *The Troll Garden* (1905). Even after Cather defined herself as a novelist with *O Pioneers!*, she continued to write short fiction: two collections were published during her lifetime (*Youth and the Bright Medusa* [1920], *Obscure Destinies* [1932]) and one posthumously (*The Old Beauty and Others* [1948]), and several uncollected stories appeared in national publications.

Perhaps because her earliest stories were not reviewed, thus allowing her to enjoy the delights of publication without the disadvantages of public criticism, Cather often used the short story as the realm for experimentation and exploration, later reworking the advances she made in this genre in her novels. In her early fiction she played with point of view and narrative structure: in "A Tale of the White Pyramid" (1892) and "On the Gulls' Road" (1908) she first created the reflective (and perhaps untrustworthy) narrator whom we later see as Jim Burden in *My Ántonia*. Later, in "Coming, Aphrodite!" (1920) she produced the most erotic passages in all of her fiction, daringly suggesting the power of desire that underlay her creative process, while in "Old Mrs. Harris" (1932), her most autobiographical work, she reveals the mature writer's understanding of her grandmother's and mother's contributions to her artistic and professional life, an understanding that ultimately led to *Sapphira and the Slave Girl* (1940).

When Cather was arranging the official Library Edition of her work in the late 1930s, she honored the short fiction she had published during her novelist's career by including *Youth and the Bright Medusa* and *Obscure Destinies*, but she entirely eliminated the uncollected short stories she had published during her lengthy apprenticeship. Writing literary critic Edward Wagenknecht in 1938, Cather used the metaphor of Robert Frost's apple picker to describe the mature artist's view of her early fiction. Some apples were worth preserving, she wrote, but others—the immature or imperfect fruit—should be left to decay in obscurity. So eager was she to dissociate herself from her unwelcome literary progeny that she even disclaimed sole authorship of some of her earliest fiction, telling Wagenknecht that some stories had been partially written by college mentors, a claim that has been effectively disputed by Mildred Bennett.

It is understandable that Cather would want to detach herself from her early short stories. Like many writers, the accomplished author was embarrassed by the beginner's stylistic and technical misadventures. Cather particularly did not like to be reminded that many of her early stories were imitative and derivative. "It is not always easy for the inexperienced writer to distinguish between his own material and that which he would like to make his own," she explained in her 1922 preface to *Alexander's Bridge;* as the literary acolyte eager to "follow the masters"—in particular, her mentor Henry James—she felt she had strained and falsified her literary voice. But at other times Cather attributed the inadequacies of her first fiction to its source in deeply felt emotions. Because it was "hard to write about the things that are near to your heart," she told an interviewer in 1913, she had been forced to find "self-protection" by trying to "distort and disguise" the "personal feeling" that had inspired her work. In another interview she similarly condemned her early stories as "bald, clumsy, and emotional."

As these contradictory assessments suggest, Cather's early stories were both artificial and authentic, self-concealing and self-revealing. Although of uneven quality, the short stories Cather wrote between 1893 and 1912 are important documents in charting her literary evolution, revealing the psychological conflicts as well as the technical deficiences she overcame before giving birth to her novelist's voice in *O Pioneers!* Her later characterization of this fiction as both imitative and emotional reflects the tension the beginning writer experienced between what she called "disclosure" and "concealment": how could she draw deeply on the self, tapping profound and perhaps unconscious energies, and yet control, shape, and transform this material without distorting or denying the private sources of her art?

This is a pressing question for all writers, of course, and yet the young Cather found it particularly troubling. Having come of age at a time when lesbianism was emerging as a social category and sexual identity, Cather could not regard her close female friendships with the unselfconsciousness that would have been possible twenty or thirty years earlier. As she wrote to her college friend Louise Pound, it was unfair that an affection like theirs should be deemed unnatural. Hence Cather knew that she could not draw directly on her love for women in her fiction, and yet she believed that the "power of loving" was the woman writer's only creative resource. How could the writer both reveal and conceal?

Moreover, as a woman writer who at first firmly associated the highest creative power with masculinity—who advised women writers to attempt "manly battle yarns" if they wished to escape their inferior status—the young Cather faced a potentially debilitating conflict as she began to write: that between gender and vocation. Even her imitative short stories are of interest to us, for they show the woman writer trying to borrow literary identity and authority from the male-dominated literary tradition. Perhaps, Cather thought, if she spoke in the cultivated cadences of Henry James and placed her characters in the drawing room, she might achieve the power and status she desired.

But this solution could not be a permanent one, for it required Cather to reject both her womanhood and her Western roots. Eventually she would speak in her own voice in *O Pioneers!*, the novel in which she both takes what she called the "road home" to her Nebraska past and creates a strong female hero who is not masculine. And yet we see signs of this creative emergence in the short stories that Cather later sought to deny and to suppress. Anticipations of the mature fiction can be glimpsed in her early work, from "Peter" (1892), her first published story, to "The Bohemian Girl" (1912), the polished and powerful story that immediately preceded *O Pioneers!*

To read Cather's short stories chronologically, as they are arranged in this edition, is thus to see not only a writer's gradual mastery of a craft but also to see a woman writer's gradual attainment of literary identity and authority as she freed herself from conventional Victorian definitions of gender. Doing so enabled her to follow Sarah Orne Jewett's wise advice when she became a novelist: "Of course, one day you will write about your own country. In the meantime, get all you can. One must know the world *so well* before one can know the parish."

*   *   *

In tracing Cather's evolution as a short story writer, we can best understand the connections between her life and her art by considering her stories in three groupings: those published during her college years at the University of Nebraska (1892–96); those published during her Pittsburgh decade as magazine editor, newspaperwoman, and high school teacher (1896–1906); and those published during her years at *McClure's* magazine, first as staff member and then as managing editor (1906–12). "Every artist makes himself born," Harsanyi observes to Thea Kronborg in *The Song of the Lark*. "Your mother did not bring anything into the world to play piano. You must bring that into the world yourself." Drawing on all the short fiction Cather published during the twenty years between 1892 and 1912 (with the exception of the stories collected in *The Troll Garden*), I have selected those stories that reveal Cather's struggle to be mother to her own art, to give birth to herself as a writer.

"All students imitate," Cather commented in 1925, "and I began by imitating Henry James. He was the most interesting American who was writing at the time, and I strove laboriously to pattern after him." But the mature author's memory was not quite accurate. The college student began her career as a fiction writer not by imitating James but by attempting to draw on her own knowledge of Nebraska—its landscape, its culture, its immigrant farmers. "Peter" (1892), her first published story, describes the plight of a Bohemian immigrant farmer, a musician who cannot adapt either to the harsh Nebraska landscape or to the entrepreneurial spirit exemplified by his aggressive and successful son. Cather ends her story with an understated and moving description of Peter's suicide, drawing on a story she had heard from her Nebraska neighbors and anticipating her portrayal of the death of Mr. Shimerda in *My Ántonia*. In other college stories—"Lou the Prophet" (1892), "The Clemency of the Court" (1893), "On the Divide" (1896)—Cather likewise draws on her Nebraska past in portraying displaced, lonely, and marginal figures.

In "The Elopement of Allen Poole" (1893) she went back even further, relying on her memories of her childhood home in Virginia's Shenandoah Valley, a region to which she would not return as a novelist until *Sapphira and the Slave Girl*.

Of course in portraying these misfits and rebels, Cather was also drawing, in part, on herself—the defiant teenager who masqueraded as "William Cather, jr." before an audience of disapproving Red Cloud townsfolk because she needed to dramatize fiercely her refusal to accept the domestic role Victorian America assigned to women. Hence these early stories are not sufficiently detached from the young writer's emotional and psychological preoccupations to exist as independent fictions, unlike the major novels that also arose from her Nebraska memories. The college writer's difficulty in transforming life into art is most dramatically evident in "A Tale of the White Pyramid" (1892), seemingly the most imitative of her first stories but in fact the most self-revealing. Set in ancient Egypt—a setting Cather knew only from her reading— the story's preoccupation with entombment, concealment, and repression reveals the central literary and psychological dilemma she experienced in beginning to write fiction. If the writer cannot draw on the inner, the secret, and the passionate, but must enclose this realm just as the pyramid of the title encases the king's body and the story's narrator hides a "mystery," she may find herself silenced and her creativity as concealed—or, perhaps, as dead—as the body in the tomb.

And yet, partly because she was speaking in the conventional accents of the day, Cather was not silenced. In the summer of 1896 she moved to Pittsburgh, where she took over the editorship of the *Home Monthly*, a woman's magazine pledged to provide its female audience with wholesome "entertainment for the idle hour." In her memoir *Willa Cather Living*, Edith Lewis, Cather's friend and mate for almost forty years, lamented that in the stories she wrote for the *Home Monthly* Cather could not develop her gifts as an "original writer" because she was forced to conform to the requirements for formulaic popular fiction. But this is not quite so. During her tenure at the *Home Monthly*, Cather began to manipulate subtly the conventions of popular fiction in order to tell, for the first time, the stories of gifted or assertive women. At the same time that she was praising Kipling as a "manly" and virile writer and celebrating the brutal power of football, Cather was beginning to shed male identification in stories like "Tommy, the Unsentimental" (1896) and "Nanette: An Aside" (1897) (which was later reworked as "A Singer's Romance" [1900]). The latter two stories demonstrate the impact that opera singers had on Cather at this time; the women who dominated the stage with their powerful soprano voices suggested to her that femininity and creativity might be compatible and helped her to envision and to develop her own writer's voice, a connection dramatically evident in *The Song of the Lark* (1915).

Cather's difficulties in becoming a writer were not merely literary and social. As an aesthetically crude but psychologically important *Home Monthly* story reveals, she would have to resolve the conflicts created by the mother–daughter bond—in particular, to develop an identity as daughter both separate from and attached to her mother—if she were to become an artist. In "The Burglar's Christmas" (1896) Cather unconsciously demonstrates the allure and danger of a child's return to a seductive and overpowering mother (a subject she had also approached, although in disguised fashion, in "The Clemency of the Court" and "The Elopement of Allen Poole"), foreshadowing the plot she would eventually control brilliantly in *My Ántonia* and *A Lost Lady*.

Cather left her post at the *Home Monthly* after a year, and soon secured another job on the telegraph desk of the Pittsburgh *Leader*. She continued to publish short fiction even while her energies were drained by the demands of newspaper work, but her writing did not really flourish until 1901, when she took a new job as a high school teacher and simultaneously moved in with Pittsburgh socialite Isabelle McClung and her family. This important move had both psychological and aesthetic resonance for Cather, who was ending a rootless existence and beginning both a lifelong love affair and a five-year period of emotional well-being and literary productivity. Although some of the short stories she wrote during this period are indistinguishable from the magazine fiction of the day, others reflect her continuing struggle to create an authentic voice and anticipate her literary emergence in *O Pioneers!*, in particular "Eric Hermannson's Soul" (1900) and "The Treasure of Far Island" (1902).

Of these Pittsburgh stories, the one that most fully foreshadows the novelist's accomplishments is "The Sentimentality of William Tavener" (1900), an unpretentious, beautifully crafted short story embodying the truth of Cather's oft-quoted statement: "Life began for me when I ceased to admire and began to remember." Cather wrote this story several years before meeting writer Sarah Orne Jewett, but since she had read *The Country of the Pointed Firs* by this time, it is possible that Jewett's local-color fiction had suggested a way for her to make use of her rural background more sympathetically than she had in the bitter stories of her college years. Of course, her increasing distance from Nebraska in time and place also allowed her to view her Midwestern heritage less critically. Drawing unostentatiously on her Nebraska past and possibly also on a family story, in "Sentimentality" Cather made use of her grandparents' and parents' history of emigration from Virginia to Nebraska in writing a simple, unaffected short story that illuminates the drama in the lives of ordinary people. "Sentimentality" further suggests the possibility missing in Cather's earlier work: if she turned to her own past and her own memories, she could find a heritage of female creativity and self-expression. Here she grants the power of verbal expression to the farm woman; the taciturn husband is a "man of silence," while his wife, who can "talk in prayer meeting as fluently as a man," possesses a "gift of speech."

But the advance represented by "The Sentimentality of William Tavener" was temporary. Although Cather was beginning to find her own voice as a writer during her Pittsburgh years (as we can also see from stories in *The Troll Garden* like "A Wagner Matinee" and "Paul's Case"), once she moved to New York in 1906 to begin work for S. S. McClure and *McClure's* magazine, her short fiction became increasingly Jamesian. Having moved closer to Eastern centers of art and culture, Cather became increasingly anxious to please the literary establishment, and she sought authority by adopting James as her literary father. Publishing four Jamesian stories in 1907, Cather found her control over language and speech waning as her voice became absorbed by her master's. Here is a representative example of the wooden, convoluted dialogue she uses in "The Willing Muse":

> I don't believe he even knew where he stood; the thing had gone so, seemed to answer the purpose so wonderfully well, and there was never anything that one could really put one's finger on—except all of it.

Cather would later say that a young writer "must care vitally, fiercely, absurdly about the trickery and the arrangement of words, the beauty and power of phrases." But the Jamesian stories published during her *McClure's* years—with one important exception—do not show the "beauty and power" of her own voice. That exception is "The Namesake" (1907), an interesting and important story that simultaneously reveals Cather's subservience to James and anticipates her literary breakthrough in *O Pioneers!* The story begins and ends with a Jamesian frame: seven American art students are gathered in the Paris studio of the great sculptor Lyon Hartwell. In telling his expatriate audience the secret of his creative power, however, Hartwell reveals the non-Jamesian view of creativity to which Cather was moving: art has its source in American soil, American history, and American lives. Only when the sculptor returns to his native Pennsylvania and feels "the pull of race and blood and kindred" does his imagination come to life.

Just as "The Namesake" hints at Cather's desire to break free from her Jamesian frame, so it suggests her gradual shift from male to female identification. On the surface, the story defines creative power as masculine, forging a link between the sculptor and his namesake soldier–uncle killed in the Civil War—a literary reflection of Cather's own fictive bond with her maternal uncle William Seibert Boak, whose namesake she imagined herself to be. But "The Namesake" also contains a subtext in which femininity and creativity are allied, for on a deeper level Hartwell owes his discovery of his creative force to the women who have preserved his uncle's memory.

In associating Hartwell's artistic birth with a legacy passed down by his female relatives, Cather anticipates her meeting with Sarah Orne Jewett a year later; the brief friendship the two women enjoyed until Jewett's death in 1909 was a turning point in Cather's literary life. Writing to Jewett in 1908, Cather confessed her fears of literary inadequacy and her despair that her creative powers were being drained by her demanding and exhausting work at *McClure's*. In her loving and encouraging replies, Jewett offered Cather both praise and kindly criticism, reassuring her of her literary promise yet warning her that if she did not find her own "quiet centre of life" her gifts might not mature as they should. Reassured and strengthened, Cather sent Jewett two short stories that drew more deeply on her own material than had her Jamesian efforts: "The Enchanted Bluff" (1909), a sketch derived from memories of her Nebraska childhood, and "On the Gulls' Road," a reworking of the mother–child story so central to her creative imagination. Although Jewett gently chided Cather for her "masquerade" in the latter story—choosing a male narrator to express love for a beautiful, maternal woman when a "woman could have loved her just as well"—her heartfelt praise for "On the Gulls' Road" reassured Cather that she was proceeding in the right direction. "It makes me the more sure that you are far on your road toward a fine and long story of very high class," Jewett wrote encouragingly.

Jewett's death in 1909 was a terrible blow to Cather: the person who most believed in her literary destiny was gone, and she published no short stories in 1910. But Jewett had become a permanent resident of Cather's imagination and memory, and throughout 1910 and 1911 she made several pilgrimages to Jewett's home in South Berwick, Maine. After one visit she felt a particular urgency to commit herself full-time to writing. "The old house had stirred something up," she told her friend Elizabeth Sergeant. "It was as if Miss Jewett's spirit, which filled the place, had warned her that time was flying." After receiving this warning, Cather wrote "The Joy of Nelly Deane" (1911), a story that shows the impact of Jewett's legacy: not only does Cather dispense with her Jamesian voice in returning to Nebraska subject matter, but she also envisions creative power as female; the story's heroine Nelly is a gifted singer. Jewett's harmonious uniting of "woman" and "writer" in her life and work had helped Cather to integrate these seemingly opposed identities, and this reconciliation gave her new confidence and direction as a writer.

But Jewett's legacy was only a partial one. She herself had made her accomplishments in the short story, not the novel. In 1911 Cather was beginning to aspire to this more elevated—and in her view still masculine—genre. During that year she wrote *Alexander's Bridge* (1912), her first novel, but it represents a return to her Jamesian apprenticeship in style and setting. Yet *Alexander's Bridge* also demonstrates Cather's impatience with her subservience to masculine models, symbolized when the hero's lengthy and ambitious bridge crumbles into the St. Lawrence.

In the fall of 1911 Cather decided to take a risk. She obtained a leave of absence from *McClure's* and went with Isabelle McClung to Cherry Valley, a small village near

Cooperstown, New York. There she spent several blissful months resting, walking, and writing; there she produced the "fine and long" story for which Jewett had hoped, "The Bohemian Girl" (1912). A story in the same vein as *O Pioneers!*, "The Bohemian Girl" was "different from anything she'd ever written," Cather confided to Elizabeth Sergeant. "She was convinced that no magazine would consider it. But she liked it herself." What was so different about "The Bohemian Girl"?

Although Cather had drawn on her Nebraska past before, "The Bohemian Girl" differs from her earlier short stories, as she had thought; her use of Nebraska materials is both more compassionate and more thickly textured than in her previous fiction. A closer relative of *O Pioneers!* or *My Ántonia* than of "Peter" or "The Enchanted Bluff," the story is about the immigrant groups who settled the Nebraska plains (here Scandinavian and Bohemian); it places individuals against the backdrop of family and community rituals; and like Cather's major novels, it suggests the profound interrelationships between people and the land. Looking back on her native material with both detachment and sympathy, Cather tells the story of adulterous lovers who break free from social and familial confinements to create new lives and new selves. Both a love story and a story about risk, change, and self-renewal, "The Bohemian Girl" reflects Cather's decision to let her fiction take a new direction, a literary advance that paradoxically was also the "road home" to the material she had been given by her own past. In doing so, she was at last receiving the inheritance of female creativity passed down by women who performed domestic roles, as we can see in this passage describing the dignity, power, and artistry in farm women's lives and work:

> They were a fine company of old women, and a Dutch painter would have loved to find them there together, where the sun made bright patches on the floor and sent long, quivering shafts of gold through the dusky shade up among the rafters. There were fat, rosy old women who

looked hot in their best black dresses; spare, alert old women with brown, dark-veined hands; and several of almost heroic frame. . . . In reality he fell into amazement when he thought of the Herculean labors those fifteen pairs of hands had performed: of the cows they had milked, the butter they had made, the gardens they had planted, the children and grandchildren they had tended, the brooms they had worn out, the mountains of food they had cooked. It made him dizzy.

So in this volume we leave Cather at the point of transition in her literary career: the year is 1912, and she is thirty-eight years old. After finishing "The Bohemian Girl" she spent several months in the Southwest, a liberating sojourn that contributed to her literary birth in *O Pioneers!*, which she completed shortly after her return to the East. But even Cather's discovery of her novelist's voice reveals the centrality of the short story to her artistic development: *O Pioneers!* came into being when, with a "sudden inner explosion," Cather realized that two short stories belonged together. Reading her early fiction in this volume, we are then tracing the evolution of a novelist whose imagination was continually nourished by the short story, the genre that most dramatically tells the story of her emergence as woman and writer.

—SHARON O'BRIEN
August 1987
Carlisle, Pennsylvania

Willa Cather

24 Stories

Peter

"No, Antone, I have told thee many times, no, thou shalt not sell it until I am gone."

"But I need money; what good is that old fiddle to thee? The very crows laugh at thee when thou art trying to play. Thy hand trembles so thou canst scarce hold the bow. Thou shalt go with me to the Blue to cut wood tomorrow. See to it thou art up early."

"What, on the Sabbath, Antone, when it is so cold? I get so very cold, my son, let us not go tomorrow."

"Yes, tomorrow, thou lazy old man. Do not I cut wood upon the Sabbath? Care I how cold it is? Wood thou shalt cut, and haul it too, and as for the fiddle, I tell thee I will sell it yet." Antone pulled his ragged cap down over his low heavy brow, and went out. The old man drew his stool up nearer the fire, and sat stroking his violin with trembling fingers and muttering, "Not while I live, not while I live."

Five years ago they had come here, Peter Sadelack, and his wife, and oldest son Antone, and countless smaller Sadelacks, here to the dreariest part of southwestern Nebraska, and had taken up a homestead. Antone was the acknowledged master of the premises, and people said he was a likely youth, and would do well. That he was mean and untrustworthy every one knew, but that made little difference. His corn was better tended than any in the county, and his wheat always yielded more than other men's.

1

Of Peter no one knew much, nor had any one a good word to say for him. He drank whenever he could get out of Antone's sight long enough to pawn his hat or coat for whiskey. Indeed there were but two things he would not pawn, his pipe and his violin. He was a lazy, absentminded old fellow, who liked to fiddle better than to plow, though Antone surely got work enough out of them all, for that matter. In the house of which Antone was master there was no one, from the little boy three years old, to the old man of sixty, who did not earn his bread. Still people said that Peter was worthless, and was a great drag on Antone, his son, who never drank, and was a much better man than his father had ever been. Peter did not care what people said. He did not like the country, nor the people, least of all he liked the plowing. He was very homesick for Bohemia. Long ago, only eight years ago by the calendar, but it seemed eight centuries to Peter, he had been a second violinist in the great theatre at Prague. He had gone into the theatre very young, and had been there all his life, until he had a stroke of paralysis, which made his arm so weak that his bowing was uncertain. Then they told him he could go. Those were great days at the theatre. He had plenty to drink then, and wore a dress coat every evening, and there were always parties after the play. He could play in those days, ay, that he could! He could never read the notes well, so he did not play first; but his touch, he had a touch indeed, so Herr Mikilsdoff, who led the orchestra, had said. Sometimes now Peter thought he could plow better if he could only bow as he used to. He had seen all the lovely women in the world there, all the great singers and the great players. He was in the orchestra when Rachel played, and he heard Liszt play when the Countess d'Agoult sat in the stage box and threw the master white lilies. Once, a French woman came and played for weeks, he did not remember her name now. He did not remember her face very well either, for it changed so, it was never twice the same. But the beauty of it, and the great hunger men felt at the sight of it, that he remembered. Most of all he remembered her voice. He did not know French, and could not understand a word she said, but it seemed to him that she must be talking the music of Chopin. And her voice, he thought he should know that in the other world. The last night she played a play in which a man touched her arm, and she stabbed him. As Peter sat among the smoking gas jets down below the footlights with his fiddle on his knee, and looked up at her, he thought he would like to die too, if he could touch her arm once, and have her stab him so. Peter went home to his wife very drunk that night. Even in those days he was a foolish fellow, who cared for nothing but music and pretty faces.

It was all different now. He had nothing to drink and little to eat, and here, there was nothing but sun, and grass, and sky. He had forgotten almost everything, but some things he remembered well enough. He loved his violin and the holy Mary, and above all else he feared the Evil One, and his son Antone.

The fire was low, and it grew cold. Still Peter sat by the fire remembering. He dared not throw more cobs on the fire; Antone would be angry. He did not want to cut wood tomorrow, it would be Sunday, and he wanted to go to mass. Antone might let him do that. He held his violin under his wrinkled chin, his white hair fell over it, and he began to play "Ave Maria." His hand shook more than ever before, and at last refused to work the bow at all. He sat stupefied for a while, then arose, and taking his violin with him, stole out into the old sod stable. He took Antone's shotgun down from its peg, and loaded it by the moonlight which streamed in through the door. He sat down on the dirt floor, and leaned back against the dirt wall. He heard the wolves howling in the distance, and the night wind screaming as it swept over the snow. Near him he heard the regular breathing of the horses in the dark. He put his crucifix above his heart, and folding his hands said brokenly all the Latin he had ever known, "*Pater noster, qui in coelum est.*" Then he raised his head and sighed, "Not one kreutzer will Antone pay them to pray for my soul, not one kreutzer, he is so careful of his money, is Antone, he does not waste it in drink, he is a better man than I, but hard sometimes. He works the girls too hard, women were not made to work so. But he shall not sell thee, my fiddle, I can play thee no more, but they shall not part us. We have seen it all together, and we will forget it together, the French woman and all." He held his fiddle under his chin a moment, where it had lain so often, then put it across his knee and broke it through the middle. He pulled off his old boot, held the gun between his knees with the muzzle against his forehead, and pressed the trigger with his toe.

In the morning Antone found him stiff, frozen fast in a pool of blood. They could not straighten him out enough to fit a coffin, so they buried him in a pine box. Before the funeral Antone carried to town the fiddlebow which Peter had forgotten to break. Antone was very thrifty, and a better man than his father had been.

Lou, the Prophet

It had been a very trying summer to every one, and most of all to Lou. He had been in the West for seven years, but he had never quite gotten over his homesickness for Denmark. Among the northern people who emigrate to the great west, only the children and the old people ever long much for the lands they have left over the water. The men only know that in this new land their plow runs across the field tearing up the fresh, warm earth, with never a stone to stay its course. That if they dig and delve the land long enough, and if they are not compelled to mortgage it to keep body and soul together, some day it will be theirs, their very own. They are not like the southern people; they lose their love for their fatherland quicker and have less of sentiment about them. They have to think too much about how they shall get bread to care much what soil gives to them. But among even the most blunted, mechanical people, the youths and the aged always have a touch of romance in them.

Lou was only twenty-two; he had been but a boy when his family left Denmark, and had never ceased to remember it. He was a rather simple fellow, and was always considered less promising than his brothers; but last year he had taken up a claim of his own and made a rough dugout upon it and he lived there all alone. His life was that of many another young man in our country. He rose early in the morning, in the summer just before daybreak;

in the winter, long before. First he fed his stock, then himself, which was a much less important matter. He ate the same food at dinner that he ate at breakfast, and the same at supper that he ate at dinner. His bill of fare never changed the year round; bread, coffee, beans and sorghum molasses, sometimes a little salt pork. After breakfast he worked until dinner time, ate, and then worked again. He always went to bed soon after the sunset, for he was always tired, and it saved oil. Sometimes, on Sundays, he would go over home after he had done his washing and house cleaning, and sometimes he hunted. His life was as sane and as uneventful as the life of his plow horses, and it was as hard and thankless. He was thrifty for a simple, thickheaded fellow, and in the spring he was to have married Nelse Sorenson's daughter, but he had lost all his cattle during the winter, and was not so prosperous as he had hoped to be; so, instead she married her cousin, who had an "eighty" of his own. That hurt Lou more than anyone ever dreamed.

A few weeks later his mother died. He had always loved his mother. She had been kind to him and used to come over to see him sometimes, and shake up his hard bed for him, and sweep, and make his bread. She had a strong affection for the boy, he was her youngest, and she always felt sorry for him; she had danced a great deal before his birth, and an old woman in Denmark had told her that was the cause of the boy's weak head.

Perhaps the greatest calamity of all was the threatened loss of his corn crop. He had bought a new corn planter on time that spring, and had intended that his corn should pay for it. Now, it looked as though he would not have corn enough to feed his horses. Unless rain fell within the next two weeks, his entire crop would be ruined; it was half gone now. All these things together were too much for poor Lou, and one morning he felt a strange loathing for the bread and sorghum which he usually ate as mechanically as he slept. He kept thinking about the strawberries he used to gather on the mountains after the snows were gone, and the cold water in the mountain streams. He felt hot someway, and wanted cold water. He had no well, and he hauled his water from a neighbor's well every Sunday, and it got warm in the barrels those hot summer days. He worked at his haying all day; at night, when he was through feeding, he stood a long time by the pig stye with a basket on his arm. When the moon came up, he sighed restlessly and tore the buffalo pea flowers with his bare toes. After a while, he put his basket away and went into the hot, close, little dugout. He did not sleep well, and he dreamed a horrible dream. He thought he saw the Devil and all his angels in the air holding back the rain clouds, and they loosed all the damned in Hell, and they came, poor tortured things, and drank up whole clouds of rain. Then he thought a strange light shone from the south, just over the river bluffs, and the clouds parted, and Christ and all his angels were descending. They were coming, coming, myriads and myriads of them, in a great blaze of glory. Then he felt something give way in his poor, weak head, and with a cry of pain he awoke. He lay shuddering a long time in the dark, then got up and lit his lantern and took from the shelf his mother's Bible. It opened of itself at Revelation, and Lou began to read, slowly indeed, for it was hard work for him. Page by page, he read those burning, blinding, blasting words, and they seemed to shrivel up his poor brain altogether. At last the book slipped from his hands and he sank down upon his knees in prayer, and stayed so until the dull gray dawn stole over the land and he heard the pigs clamoring for their feed.

He worked about the place until noon, and then prayed and read again. So he went on several days, praying and reading and fasting, until he grew thin and haggard. Nature did not comfort him any, he knew nothing about nature, he had never seen her; he had only stared into a black plow furrow all his life. Before, he had only seen in the wide, green lands and the open blue the possibilities of earning his bread; now, he only saw in them a great world ready for the judgment, a funeral pyre ready for the torch.

One morning, he went over to the big prairie dog town, where several little Danish boys herded their fathers' cattle. The boys were very fond of Lou; he never teased them as the other men did, but used to help them with their cattle, and let them come over to his dugout to make sorghum taffy. When they saw him coming, they ran to meet him and asked him where he had been all these days. He did not answer their questions, but said: "Come into the cave, I want to see you."

Some six or eight boys herded near the dog town every summer, and by their combined efforts they had dug a cave in the side of a high bank. It was large enough to hold them all comfortably, and high enough to stand in. There the boys used to go when it rained or when it was cold in the fall. They followed Lou silently and sat down on the floor. Lou stood up and looked tenderly down into the little faces before him. They were old-faced little fellows, though they were not over twelve or thirteen years old, hard work matures boys quickly.

"Boys," he said earnestly, "I have found out why it don't rain, it's because of the sins of the world. You don't know how wicked the world is, it's all bad, all, even Denmark. People have been sinning a long time, but they won't much longer. God has been watching and watching for thousands of years, and filling up the phials of wrath, and now he is going to pour out his vengeance and let Hell loose upon the world. He is burning up our corn now, and worse things will happen; for the sun shall be as sackcloth, and the moon shall be like blood, and the stars of heaven shall fall, and the heavens shall part like a scroll, and the mountains shall be moved out of their places, and the great day of his wrath shall come, against which none may stand. Oh, boys! the floods and the flames shall come down upon us together and the whole world shall perish." Lou paused for breath, and the little boys gazed at him in wonder. The sweat was running down his haggard face, and his eyes were staring wildly. Presently, he resumed in a softer tone, "Boys, if you want rain, there is only one way to get it, by prayer. The people of the world won't pray, perhaps if they did God would not hear them, for they are so wicked; but he will hear you, for you are little children and are likened unto the kingdom of heaven, and he loved ye."

Lou's haggard, unshaven face bent toward them and his blue eyes gazed at them with terrible earnestness.

"Show us how, Lou," said one little fellow in an awed whisper. Lou knelt down in the cave, his long, shaggy hair hung down over his face, and his voice trembled as he spoke:

"Oh God, they call thee many long names in thy book, thy prophets; but we are only simple folk, the boys are all little and I am weak headed ever since I was born, therefore, let us call thee Father, for thy other names are hard to remember. O Father, we are so thirsty, all the world is thirsty; the creeks are all dried up, and the river is so low that the fishes die and rot in it; the corn is almost gone; the hay is light; and even the little flowers are no more beautiful. O God! our corn may yet be saved. O, give us rain! Our corn means so much to us, if it fails, all our pigs and cattle will die, and we ourselves come very near it; but if you do not send rain, O Father, and if the end is indeed come, be merciful to thy great, wicked world. They do many wrong things, but I think they forget thy word, for it is a long book to remember, and some are little and some are born weak headed, like me, and some are born very strong headed, which is near as bad. Oh, forgive them their abominations in all the world, both in Denmark and here, for the fire hurts so, O God! Amen."

The little boys knelt and each said a few blundering words. Outside, the sun shone brightly and the cattle nibbled at the short, dry grass, and the hot wind blew through the shriveled corn; within the cave, they knelt as many another had knelt before them, some in temples, some in prison cells, some in the caves of earth, and One, indeed, in the garden, praying for the sin of the world.

The next day, Lou went to town, and prayed in the streets. When the people saw his emaciated frame and wild eyes, and heard his wild words, they told the sheriff to do his duty, the man must be mad. Then Lou ran away; he ran for miles, then walked and limped and stumbled on, until he reached the cave; there the boys found him in the morning. The officials hunted him for days, but he hid in the cave, and the little Danes kept his secret well. They shared their dinners with him, and prayed with him all day long. They had always liked him, but now they would have gone straight through fire for him, any one of them, they almost worshipped him. He had about him that mysticism which always appeals so quickly to children. I have always thought that bear story which the Hebrews used to tell their children very improbable. If it was true, then I have my doubts about the prophet; no one in the world will hoot at insincere and affected piety sooner than a child, but no one feels the true prophetic flame quicker, no one is more readily touched by simple goodness. A very young child can tell a sincere man better than any phrenologist.

One morning, he told the boys that he had had another "true dream." He was not going to die like other men, but God was going to take him to himself as he was. The end of the world was close at hand, too very close. He prayed more than usual that day, and when they sat eating their dinner in the sunshine, he suddenly sprang to his feet and stared wildly south, crying, "See, see, it is the great light! the end comes!! and they do not know it; they will keep on sinning, I must tell them, I must!"

"No, no, Lou, they will catch you; they are looking for you, you must not go!"

"I must go, my boys; but first let me speak once more to you. Men would not heed me, or believe me, because my head is weak, but you have always believed in me, that God has revealed his word to me, and I will pray God to take you to himself quickly, for ye are worthy. Watch and pray always, boys, watch the light over the bluffs, it is breaking, breaking, and shall grow brighter. Goodbye, my boys, I must leave ye in the world yet awhile." He kissed them all tenderly and blessed them, and started south. He walked at first, then he ran, faster and faster he went, all the while shouting at the top of his voice, "The sword of the Lord and of Gideon!"

The police officers heard of it, and set out to find him. They hunted the country over and even dragged the river, but they never found him again, living or dead. It is thought that he was drowned and the quicksands of the river sucked his body under. But the little Dane boys in our country firmly believe that he was translated like Enoch of old. On stormy nights, when the great winds sweep down from the north they huddle together in their beds and fancy that in the wind they still hear that wild cry, "The sword of the Lord and of Gideon."

A Tale of
the White Pyramid

(I, Kakau, son of Ramenka, high priest of Phtahah [Ptah] in the great temple at Memphis, write this, which is an account of what I, Kakau, saw on the first day of my arrival in Memphis, and the first day of my sojourn in the home of Rui, my uncle, who was a priest of Phtahah before me.)

As I drew near the city the sun hung hot over the valley which wound like a green thread toward the south. On either side the river lay the fields of grain, and beyond was the desert of yellow sand which stretched away to where the low line of Libyan hills rose against the sky. The heat was very great, and the breeze scarce stirred the reeds which grew in the black mud down where the Nile, like a great tawny serpent, crept lazily away through the desert. Memphis stood as silent as the judgment hall of Osiris. The shops and even the temples were deserted, and no man stirred in the streets save the watchmen of the city. Early in the morning the people had arisen and washed the ashes from their faces, shaved their bodies, taken off the robes of mourning, and had gone out into the plain, for the seventy-two days of mourning were now over.

Senefrau the first, Lord of the Light and Ruler of the Upper and Lower Kingdoms, was dead and gathered unto his fathers. His body had passed into the hands of the embalmers, and lain for the allotted seventy days in niter, and had been wrapped in gums and spices and white linen and placed in a golden mummy case, and today it was to be placed in the stone sarcophagus in the white pyramid, where it was to await its soul.

Early in the morning, when I came unto the house of my uncle, he took me in his chariot and drove out of the city into the great plain which is north of the city, where the pyramid stood. The great plain was covered with a multitude of men. There all the men of the city were gathered together, and men from all over the land of Khem. Here and there were tethered many horses and camels of those who had come from afar. The army was there, and the priesthood, and men of all ranks; slaves, and swineherds, and the princes of the people. At the head of the army stood a tall dark man in a chariot of ivory and gold, speaking with a youth who stood beside the chariot.

"It is Kufu, the king," said Rui, "men say that before the Nile rises again he will begin to build a pyramid, and that it will be such a one as men have never seen before, nor shall we afterwards."

"Who is he that stands near unto the king, and with whom the king speaks?" I asked. Then there came a cloud upon the face of Rui, the brother of my father, and he answered and said unto me:

"He is a youth of the Shepherd people of the north, he is a builder and has worked upon the tomb. He is cunning of hand and wise of heart, and Kufu has shown him great favor, but the people like him not, for he is of the blood of strangers."

I spoke no more of the youth, for I saw that Rui liked him not, but my eyes were upon him continually, for I had seen no other man like unto him for beauty of face or of form.

After a time it came to pass that the great tumult ceased throughout the plain, and the words of men died upon their lips. Up from the shore of the sacred lake wound the funeral procession toward the tomb, and by the Lord of Truth I then thought the glory of Isis could be no grander. There were boys clad in white and wreathed with lotus flowers, and thousands of slaves clad in the skins of leopards, bearing bread and wine and oil, and carrying the images of the gods. There were maidens, bands of harpers and of musicians, and the captives which the king had taken in war leading tigers and lions of the desert. There was the sacred ark drawn by twenty white oxen, and there were many priests, and the guards of the king, and the sacred body of Senefrau, borne by carriers. After the body of the king came all the women of his household, beating their hearts, and weeping bitterly. As the train approached men fell upon their faces and prayed to Phtahah, the Great South Wall, and Kufu bowed his head. At the foot of the pyramid the train halted, and the youths clothed in white, and the priests, and those who bore the body began to ascend the pyramid, singing as they went:

> *Enter into thy rest, oh Pharaoh!*
> *Enter into thy kingdom.*
> *For the crown of the two lands was heavy,*
> *And thy head was old,*
> *And thou hast laid it aside forever.*
> *Thy two arms were weak,*
> *And the scepter was a great weight,*
> *And thou hast put it from thee.*
> *Enter thou into thy new reign,*
> *Longer than the eternities.*
> *Darkness shall be thy realm, O King,*
> *And sleep thy minion.*
> *The chariots of Ethiopia shall surround thee no more,*
> *Nor the multitudes of the mighty encompass thee in battle,*
> *For thou, being dead, art become as a god;*
> *Good thou knowest, oh king;*
> *And evil has been nigh unto thee,*
> *Yet neither approach thee now,*
> *For thou art dead, and like unto the gods.*

They bore him down into the pyramid, and left him to sleep, and to wait. Then I saw a multitude of men gather about a great white stone that lay at the base of the tomb, and I questioned Rui concerning it, and he answered me:

"This pyramid as thou seest opens not at the side, but from the top down. That great slab of stone is to cover the top of the tomb. See, even now the workmen spread mortar upon the top of the tomb, and fasten ropes about the great stone to lift it into place. Neith grant that they harm not the stone, for it has taken a thousand men ten years to cut and polish it and to bring it thither."

I saw slaves bending over the great stone, fastening about it ropes which hung from the great pulleys built upon the shafts which rose from the upper stage of the pyramid. While they did this, companies of slaves began to ascend the sides of the tomb, each company with its master. The men were all fashioned like the men of the north, and their strength was like ribbed steel, for these were the mightiest men in Egypt. After a time there was silence in the plain. The slaves took hold of the ropes that swung from the pulleys, and every voice was hushed. It was as still without the pyramid as it was within. At last the sound of the Sistrum broke the stillness, the master builders waved their lashes, and the two thousand slaves who were upon the pyramid set their feet firmly upon the polished stone and threw the weight of their bodies upon the ropes. Slowly, slowly, amid the creaking and groaning of the ropes, the great stone left the earth. The musicians played and the people shouted, for never before in all Egypt had so great a stone been raised. But suddenly the shouting ceased, and the music was hushed, and a stillness like the sleep of Nut fell over the plain. All the people gazed upward, and the heart of Khem grew sick as they looked. The great stone had risen halfway, the lifting ropes were firm as the pillars of heaven, but one of the ropes which held the stone in place gave way and stretched, and the great stone which was the pride of the land, was settling at one end and slipping from its fastenings. The slaves crouched upon the pyramid, the builders spoke no word, and the people turned their eyes from the stone, that they might not see it fall. As I looked up, I saw a man running rapidly along the tier of the pyramid opposite the rocking stone. I knew his face to be the face of the stranger whom I saw speaking with the king. He threw off his garments as he ran, and at the edge of the stone tier he paused for a moment, he crouched low, gathering all his strength, then suddenly straightening his body he threw back his head and shot straight forward, like an arrow shot from the bow, over eighteen cubits, and fell lightly upon his feet on the uppermost end of the stone. He stood with both hands clenched at his side, his right foot a little before his left, erect and fair as the statue of Houris [Horus], watching the farther end of the stone. For a little the stone stood still, then swung back and lay evenly as when all was well, and then the end upon which the youth stood, sank. He thrust his right foot further forward, his toes clinging to the polished stone, and clasping his hands about his waist above the hips, slowly bowed his great frame forward. The stone slab felt its master and swung slowly back, and again the end on which the youth stood was uppermost. So he stood, his dusky limbs showing clear against the white stone, his every muscle quivering, the sweat pouring from his body, swaying the great stone. The great white desert seemed to rock and sway, the sun grew hotter and stood still in heaven, the sky and the sea of faces seemed to whirl and reel, then blend into one awful face, grinning horribly. The slaves, not daring to breathe, crouched upon the tomb, the multitude stood still and gazed upward, and earth and heaven and men were as dumb as if the gods had smitten them mad with thunder. Then a great cry rang out:

"In the name of Phtahah and of your fathers' souls, pull!"

It was the voice of Kufu. Slowly, like men awakened from a dream, the slaves drew up that swinging stone, and he stood upon it. Below the king stood, his hands clutching the front of his chariot, and his eyes strained upon the stone. When the slab reached the top of the shaft on which the pulley hung, it was swung back over the pyramid, and the descent began. The slaves, sick with fear, lost control of it, and the great stone plunged down faster and faster. I wondered if the mortar spread upon the top was thick enough to break its fall. Just as it struck the top in safety, he who stood upon it, gathering all his strength leaped high into air to break the shock and fell motionless upon the stone. Then such a cry as went up, never before roused old Nilus from his dreams, or made the walls of the city to tremble. They bore him down from the tomb and placed him in the chariot of the king. Then the king's trumpeter sounded, and then Kufu spake:

"We have this day seen a deed the like of which we have never seen before, neither have our fathers told us of such a thing. Know, men of Egypt that he, the Shepherd stranger, who has risen upon the swinging stone, shall build the great pyramid, for he is worthy in my sight. The king has said."

Then the people cheered, but their faces were dark. And the charioteer of the king lashed his horses across the plain toward the city.

Of the great pyramid and of the mystery thereof, and of the strange builder, and of the sin of the king, I may not speak, for my lips are sealed.

The Elopement
of Allen Poole

I

"Seein' yo' folks ain't willin', sweetheart, I tell yo' there hain't no other way."

"No, I reckon there hain't." She sighed and looked with a troubled expression at the thin spiral of blue smoke that curled up from a house hidden behind the pine trees.

"Besides, I done got the license now, an' told the preacher we was comin'. Yo' ain't goin' back on me now, Nell?"

"No, no, Allen, of course I hain't, only—" her mouth quivered a little and she still looked away from him. The man stood uneasily, his hands hanging helplessly at his side, and watched her. As he saw the color leave her cheeks and her eyes fill up, he began to fear lest he might lose her altogether, and he saw that something must be done. Rousing himself he went up to her, and taking her hand drew himself up to the full height of his six feet.

"See here, Nell, I hain't goin' to make yo' leave yo' folks, I hain't got no right to. Yo' kin come with me, or bide with 'em, jist as yo' choose, only fo' Gawd's sake tell me now, so if yo' won't have me I kin leave yo'."

The girl drew close to him with that appealing gesture of a woman who wants help or strength from some one, and laid her face on his arm.

"I want yo', Allen, yo' know that. I hain't feelin' bad to

18

go, only I do hate to wear that dress mighty bad. Yo'
know Pap bought it fo' me to wear to the Bethel camp-
meetin'. He got real silk ribbon fo' it, too, jist after he
sold the sheep, yo' know. It seems real mean to run away
in it."

"Don't wear it then, I kin get yo' plenty o' dresses,
wear what yo' got on, yo' surely purty enough fo' me that
way."

"No, I must wear it, cause I ain't got nothin' else good
enough to marry yo' in. But don't lets talk about it no mo'
dear. What time yo' goin' to come tonight?"

"Bout ten o'clock I reckon. I better not come too early,
yo' folks might hear me. I lay I won't go fer away today,
them revenue fellers is lookin' fo' me purty sharp."

"I knowed they would be, I knowed it all along. I wish
yo' wouldn't still no mo'. I jist am scared to death now all
the time fo' fear they'll ketch yo'. Why don't yo' quit
stillin' now, Allen?"

"Law me, honey! there hain't no harm in it. I jist makes
a little fo' the camp-meetin's."

"I don't keer 'bout the harm, it's yo' I'm feerd fo'."

"Don't yo' worry 'bout me. I kin give 'em the slip. I'll
be here tonight at ten o'clock if all the revenue officers in
the country are after me. I'll come down here by the big
chistnut an' whistle. What shall I whistle, anyhow, so yo'
kin know it's me?"

" 'Nelly Bly,' course," she whispered, blushing.

"An' yo'll come to me, sho?"

Her only answer was to draw his big, blonde head
down to her and hold it against her cheek.

"I must go now, Allen, mammy will be lookin' fo' me
soon." And she slipped from his arms and ran swiftly up
the steep path toward the house.

Allen watched her disappear among the pines, and
then threw himself down beside a laurel bush and clasping his hands under his head began to whistle softly. It
takes a man of the South to do nothing perfectly, and
Allen was as skilled in that art as were any of the F. F.

V.'s who wore broadcloth. It was the kind of a summer morning to encourage idleness. Behind him were the sleepy pine woods, the slatey ground beneath them strewn red with slippery needles. Around him the laurels were just blushing into bloom. Here and there rose tall chestnut trees with the red sumach growing under them. Down in the valley lay the fields of wheat and corn, and among them the creek wound between its willow-grown banks. Across it was the old, black, creaking foot-bridge which had neither props nor piles, but was swung from the arms of a great sycamore tree. The reapers were at work in the wheat fields; the mowers swinging their cradles and the binders following close behind. Along the fences companies of bare-footed children were picking berries. On the bridge a lank youth sat patiently fishing in the stream where no fish had been caught for years. Allen watched them all until a passing cloud made the valley dark, then his eyes wandered to where the Blue Ridge lay against the sky, faint and hazy as the mountains of Beulah Land.

Allen still whistled lazily as he lay there. He was noted for his whistling. He was naturally musical, but on Limber Ridge the mouth organ and jews harp are considered the only thoroughly respectable instruments, and he preferred whistling to either. He could whistle anything from "Champagne Charley" to the opera airs he heard the city folks playing in the summer at the Springs. There was a marvelous sweet and mellow quality about that chirp of his, like the softened fire of the famous apple brandy he made from his little still in the mountains. The mountain folk always said they could tell Allen Poole's whiskey or his whistle wherever they found them. Beyond his music and his brandy and his good heart there was not much to Allen. He was never known to do any work except to pour apples into his still and drink freely of the honied fire which came out of the worm. As he said himself, between his still and the women and the revenue officers he had scarcely time to eat. The officers of the law hated him because they knew him to be an incorrigible "moonshiner," yet never could prove anything against him. The women all loved him because he was so big and blue-eyed and so thoroughly a man. He was happy enough and good natured enough; still it was no wonder that old Sargent did not want his daughter to marry the young man, for making whiskey on one's own hook and one's own authority is not a particularly safe or honorable business. But the girl was willing and Allen was very much so, and they had taken matters into their own hands and meant to elope that night. Allen was not thinking very seriously about it. He never took anything very seriously. He was just thinking that the dim blueness of the mountains over there was like her eyes when they had tears in them, and wondering why it was that when he was near her he always felt such an irresistible impulse to pick her up and carry her. When he began to get hungry he arose and yawned and began to stroll lazily down the mountain side, his heavy boot heels cutting through the green moss and craunching the soft slate rock underneath, whistling "My Bonnie Lies Over the Ocean" as he went.

II

It was about nine o'clock that evening when Allen crossed the old foot-bridge and started down the creek lane toward the mountain. He kept carefully in the shadow of the trees, for he had good cause to fear that night. There was a little frown on his face, for when he got home at noon he found his shanty in confusion; the revenue officer had been there and had knocked the still to pieces and chopped through the copper worm with an ax. Even the winning of his sweetheart could not quite make up for the loss of his still.

The creek lane, hedged on either side by tall maples, ran by a little graveyard. It was one of those little family burying grounds so common in the south, with its white headstones, tall, dark cedars, and masses of rosemary, myrtle and rue. Allen, like all the rest of the Mountain men, was superstitious, and ordinarily he would have hurried past, not anxious to be near a graveyard after night. But now he went up and leaned on the stone fence, and looked over at the headstones which marked the sunken graves. Somehow he felt more pity for them than fear of them that night. That night of all nights he was so rich in hope and love, lord of so much life, that he wished he could give a little of it to those poor, cold, stiff fellows shut up down there in their narrow boxes with prosy scripture text on their coffin plates, give a little of the warm blood that tingled through his own veins, just enough, perhaps, to make them dream of love. He sighed as he went on, leaving them to their sleep and their understanding.

He turned aside into a road that ran between the fields. The red harvest moon was just rising; on one side of the road the tall, green corn stood whispering and rustling in the moonrise, sighing fretfully now and then when the hot south breeze swept over it. On the other side lay the long fields of wheat where the poppies drooped among the stubble and the sheaves gave out that odor of indescribable richness and ripeness which newly cut grain always has. From the wavering line of locust trees the song of the whip-poor-will throbbed through the summer night. Above it all were the dark pine-clad mountains, in the repose and strength of their immortality.

The man's heart went out to the heart of the night, and he broke out into such a passion of music as made the singer in the locusts sick with melody. As he went on, whistling, he suddenly heard the beat of a horse's feet upon the road, and silenced his chirping.

"Like as not it's them government chaps," he muttered.

A cart came around the bend in the road, Allen saw two men in it and turned aside into the corn field, but he was too late, they had already seen him. One of them raised his pistol and shouted, "Halt!"

But Allen knew too well who they were, and did not stop. The officer called again, and then fired. Allen stopped a moment, clutched the air above his head, cried "My Gawd!" and then ran wildly on. The officer was not a bad fellow, only young and a little hot headed, and that agonized cry took all the nerve out of him, and he drove back toward town to get the ringing sound out of his ears.

Allan ran on, plunging and floundering through the corn like some wounded animal, tearing up stalk after stalk as he clutched it in his pain. When he reached the foot of the mountain he started up, dragging himself on by the laurel and sumach bushes. When his legs failed him he used his hands and knees, wrenching the vines and saplings to pieces and tearing the flesh on [his] hands as he pulled himself up. At last he reached the chestnut tree and sank with a groan upon the ground. But he rose again muttering to himself: "She'd be skeered to death if she seen me layin' down."

He braced himself against the tree, all blood and dirt as he was, his wedding clothes torn and soiled, and drawing his white lips up in the old way he whistled for his love:

Nelly Bly shuts her eye when she goes to sleep,
But in the morning when she wakes then they begin to peep.
Hi Nelly! Ho Nelly! listen unto me,
I'll sing for you, I'll play for you a charming melody.

He had not long to wait. She came softly through the black pines, holding her white dress up carefully from the dewy grass, with the moonlight all about her in a halo, like a little Madonna of the hills. She slipped up to him and leaned her cheek upon his breast.

"Allen, my own boy! Why yo' all wet, Oh it's blood! it's blood! have they hurt yo' honey, have they hurt yo'?"

He sank to the ground, saying gently, "I'm afeerd they've done fo' me this time, sweetheart. It's them damned revenue men."

"Let me call Pap, Allen, he'll go fo' the doctor, let me go, Allen, please."

"No, yo' shan't leave me. It ain't fo' many minutes, a doctor won't do no good. Stay with me Nell, stay with me, I'm afeerd to be alone."

She sat down and drew his head on her knee and leaned her face down to his.

"Take keer, darlin', yo' goin' to git yo' dress all bloody, yo' nice new frock what yo' goin' to wear to the Bethel picnic."

"Oh, Allen! there ain't no Bethel picnic no more, nor nothin' but yo'. Oh my boy! my boy!" and she rocked herself over him as a mother does over a little baby that is in pain.

"It's mighty hard to lose yo', Nell, but maybe it's best. Maybe if I'd lived an' married yo' I might a' got old an' cross an' used to yo' some day, an' might a' swore at you an' beat yo' like the mountain folks round here does, an' I'd sooner die now, while I love yo' better'n anything else in Gawd's world. Yo' like me, too, don't yo' dear?"

"Oh Allen! more'n I ever knowed, more'n I ever knowed."

"Don't take on so, honey. Yo' will stay with me to-night? Yo' won't leave me even after I'm dead? Yo' know we was to be married an' I was to have yo' tonight. Yo' won't go way an' leave me the first night an' the last, will yo' Nell?"

The girl calmed herself for his sake and answered him steadily: "No, Allen. I will set an' hold yo' till mornin' comes. I won't leave yo'."

"Thank yo'. Never mind, dear, the best thing in livin' is to love hard, and the best thing in dyin' is to die game; an' I've done my best at both. Never mind."

He drew a long sigh, and the rest was silence.

The Clemency
of the Court

"Damn you! What do you mean by giving me hooping like that?"

Serge Povolitchky folded his big workworn hands and was silent. That helpless, doglike silence of his always had a bad effect on the guard's temper, and he turned on him afresh.

"What do you mean by it, I say? Maybe you think you are some better than the rest of us; maybe you think you are too good to work. We'll see about that."

Serge still stared at the ground, muttering in a low, husky voice, "I could make some broom, I think. I would try much."

"O, you would, would you? So you don't try now? We will see about that. We will send you to a school where you can learn to hoop barrels. We have a school here, a little, dark school, a night school, you know, where we teach men a great many things."

Serge looked up appealingly into the man's face and his eyelids quivered with terror, but he said nothing, so the guard continued:

"Now I'll sit down here and watch you hoop them barrels, and if you don't do a mighty good job, I'll report you to the warden and have you strung up as high as a rope can twist."

Serge turned to his work again. He did wish the guard would not watch him; it seemed to him that he could

25

hoop all right if he did not feel the guard's eye on him all
the time. His hands had never done anything but dig and
plow and they were so clumsy he could not make them
do right. The guard began to swear and Serge trembled so
he could scarcely hold his hammer. He was very much
afraid of the dark cell. His cell was next to it and often at
night he had heard the men groaning and shrieking when
the pain got bad, and begging the guards for water. He
heard one poor fellow get delirious when the rope cut and
strangled him, and talk to his mother all night long, begging her not to hug him so hard, for she hurt him.

The guard went out and Serge worked on, never even
stopping to wipe the sweat from his face. It was strange
he could not hoop as well as the other men, for he was as
strong and stalwart as they, but he was so clumsy at it.
He thought he could work in the broom room if they
would only let him. He had handled straw all his life, and
it would seem good to work at the broom corn that had
the scent of outdoors about it. But they said the broom
room was full. He felt weak and sick all over, someway.
He could not work in the house, he had never been
indoors a whole day in his life until he came here.

Serge was born in the western part of the State, where
he did not see many people. His mother was a handsome
Russian girl, one of a Russian colony that a railroad had
brought West to build grades. His father was supposed to
be a railroad contractor, no one knew surely. At any rate
by no will of his own or wish of his own, Serge existed.
When he was a few months old, his mother had drowned
herself in a pond so small that no one ever quite saw how
she managed to do it.

Baba Skaldi, an old Russian woman of the colony, took
Serge and brought him up among her own children. A
hard enough life he had of it with her. She fed him what
her children would not eat, and clothed him in what her
children would not wear. She used to boast to *baba* Konach
that she got a man's work out of the young rat. There was
one pleasure in Serge's life with her. Often at night after

she had beaten him and he lay sobbing on the floor in the corner, she would tell her children stories of Russia. They were beautiful stories, Serge thought. In spite of all her cruelty he never quite disliked *baba* Skaldi because she could tell such fine stories. The story told oftenest was one about her own brother. He had done something wrong, Serge could never make out just what, and had been sent to Siberia. His wife had gone with him. The *baba* told all about the journey to Siberia as she had heard it from returned convicts; all about the awful marches in the mud and ice, and how on the boundary line the men would weep and fall down and kiss the soil of Russia. When her brother reached the prison, he and his wife used to work in the mines. His wife was too good a woman to get on well in the prison, the *baba* said, and one day she had been knouted to death at the command of an officer. After that her husband tried in many ways to kill himself, but they always caught him at it. At last, one night, he bit deep into his arm and tore open the veins with his teeth and bled to death. The officials found him dead with his teeth still set in his lacerated arm.

When she finished the little boys used to cry out at the awfulness of it, but their mother would soothe them and tell them that such things could not possibly happen here, because in this country the State took care of people. In Russia there was no State, only the great Tzar. Ah, yes, the State would take care of the children! The *baba* had heard a Fourth-of-July speech once, and she had great ideas about the State.

Serge used to listen till his eyes grew big, and play that he was that brother of the *baba*'s and that he had been knouted by the officials and that was why his little legs smarted so. Sometimes he would steal out in the snow in his bare feet and take a sunflower stalk and play he was hunting bears in Russia, or would walk about on the little frozen pond where his mother had died and think it was the Volga. Before his birth his mother used to go off alone and sit in the snow for hours to cool the fever in her head

and weep and think about her own country. The feeling
for the snow and the love for it seemed to go into the
boy's blood, somehow. He was never so happy as when
he saw the white flakes whirling.

When he was twelve years old a farmer took him to
work for his board and clothes. Then a change came into
Serge's life. That first morning [as] he stood, awkward
and embarrassed, in the Davis kitchen, holding his hands
under his hat and shuffling his bare feet over the floor, a
little yellow cur came up to him and began to rub its nose
against his leg. He held out his hand and the dog licked
it. Serge bent over him, stroking him and calling him
Russian pet names. For the first time in his lonely, loveless life, he felt that something liked him.

The Davises gave him enough to eat and enough to
wear and they did not beat him. He could not read or talk
English, so they treated him very much as they did the
horses. He stayed there seven years because he did not
have sense enough to know that he was utterly miserable
and could go somewhere else, and because the Slavonic
instinct was in him to labor and keep silent. The dog was
the only thing that made life endurable. He called the dog
Matushka, which was the name by which he always
thought of his mother. He used to go to town sometimes,
but he did not enjoy it, people frightened him so. When
the town girls used to pass him dressed in their pretty
dresses with their clean, white hands, he thought of his
bare feet and his rough, tawny hair and his ragged overalls, and he would slink away behind his team with
Matushka. On the coldest winter nights he always slept in
the barn with the dog for a bedfellow. As he and the dog
cuddled up to each other in the hay, he used to think
about things, most often about Russia and the State. Russia must be a fine country but he was glad he did not live
there, because the State was much better. The State was
so very good to people. Once a man came there to get
Davis to vote for him, and he asked Serge who his father
was. Serge said he had none. The man only smiled and

said, "Well, never mind, the State will be a father to you, my lad, and a mother."

Serge had a vague idea that the State must be an abstract thing of some kind, but he always thought of her as a woman with kind eyes, dressed in white with a yellow light about her head, and a little child in her arms, like the picture of the virgin in the church. He always took off his hat when he passed the court house in town, because he had an idea that it had something to do with the State someway. He thought he owed the State a great deal for something, he did not know what; that the State would do something great for him some day, because he had no one else. After his chores he used to go and sit down in the corral with his back against the wire fence and his chin on his knees and look at the sunset. He never got much pleasure out of it, it was always like watching something die. It made him feel desolate and lonesome to see so much sky, yet he always sat there, irresistibly fascinated. It was not much wonder that his eyes grew dull and his brain heavy, sitting there evening after evening with his dog, staring across the brown, windswept prairies that never lead anywhere, but always stretch on and on in a great yearning for something they never reach. He liked the plains because he thought they must be like the Russian steppes, and because they seemed like himself, always lonely and empty-handed.

One day when he was helping Davis top a haystack, Davis got angry at the dog for some reason and kicked at it. Serge threw out his arm and caught the blow himself. Davis, angrier than before, caught the hatchet and laid the dog's head open. He threw down the bloody hatchet and, telling Serge to go clean it, he bent over his work. Serge stood motionless, as dazed and helpless as if he had been struck himself. The dog's tail quivered and his legs moved weakly, its breath came through its throat in faint, wheezing groans and from its bleeding head its two dark eyes, clouded with pain, still looked lovingly up at him. He dropped on his knees beside it and lifted its poor head

against his heart. It was only for a moment. It laid its paw
upon his arm and then was still. Serge laid the dog gently
down and rose. He took the bloody hatchet and went up
behind his master. He did not hurry and he did not falter.
He raised the weapon and struck down, clove through the
man's skull from crown to chin, even as the man had
struck the dog. Then he went to the barn to get a shovel
to bury the dog. As he passed the house, the woman
called out to him to tell her husband to come to dinner.
He answered simply, "He will not come to dinner today. I
killed him behind the haystack."

She rushed from the house with a shriek and when she
caught sight of what lay behind the haystack, she started
for the nearest farm house. Serge went to the barn for the
shovel. He had no consciousness of having done wrong.
He did not even think about the dead man. His heart
seemed to cling to the side of his chest, the only thing he
had ever loved was dead. He went to the haymow where
he and Matushka slept every night and took a box from
under the hay from which he drew a red silk handkerchief, the only "pretty thing," and indeed, the only handkerchief he had ever possessed. He went back to the
haystack and never once glancing at the man, took the
dog in his arms.

There was one spot on the farm that Serge liked. He
and Matushka used often to go there on Sundays. It was a
little, marshy pool, grown up in cattails and reeds with a
few scraggy willows on the banks. The grass used to be
quite green there, not red and gray like the buffalo grass.
Then he carried Matushka. He laid him down and began
to dig a grave under the willows. The worst of it was that
the world went on just as usual. The winds were laughing
away among the rushes, sending the water slapping against
the banks. The meadow larks sang in the corn field and
the sun shone just as it did yesterday and all the while
Matushka was dead and his own heart was breaking in
his breast. When the hole was deep enough, he took the
handkerchief from his pocket and tied it neatly about poor

Matushka's mangled head. Then he pulled a few wild roses and laid them on its breast and fell sobbing across the body of the little yellow cur. Presently he saw the neighbors coming over the hill with Mrs. Davis, and he laid the dog in the grave and covered him up.

About his trial Serge remembered very little, except that they had taken him to the court house and he had not found the State. He remembered that the room was full of people, and some of them talked a great deal, and that the young lawyer who defended him cried when his sentence was read. That lawyer seemed to understand it all, about Matushka and the State, and everything. Serge thought he was the handsomest and most learned man in the world. He had fought day and night for Serge, without sleeping and almost without eating. Serge could always see him as he looked when he paced up and down the platform, shaking the hair back from his brow and trying to get it through the heads of the jurymen that love was love, even if it was for a dog. The people told Serge that his sentence had been commuted from death to imprisonment for life by the clemency of the court, but he knew well enough that it was by the talk of that lawyer. He had not deserted Serge after the trial even, he had come with him to the prison and had seen him put on his convict clothing.

"It's the State's badge of knighthood, Serge," he said, bitterly, touching one of the stripes. "The old emblem of the royal garter, to show that your blood is royal."

Just as the six o'clock whistle was blowing, the guard returned.

"You are to go to your cell tonight, and if you don't do no better in the morning, you are to be strung up in the dark cell, come along."

Serge laid down his hammer and followed him to his cell. Some of the men made little bookshelves for their cells and pasted pictures on the walls. Serge had neither books nor pictures, and he did not know how to ask for any, so his cell was bare. The cells were only six by four, just a little larger than a grave.

As a rule, the prisoners suffered from no particular cruelty, only from the elimination of all those little delicacies that make men men. The aim of the prison authorities seemed to be make everything unnecessarily ugly and repulsive. The little things in which fine feeling is most truly manifest received no respect at all. Serge's bringing up had been none of the best, but it took him some time to get used to eating without knife or fork the indifferent food thrust in square tin bowls under the door of his cell. Most of the men read at night, but he could not read, so he lay tossing on his iron bunk, wondering how the fields were looking. His greatest deprivation was that he could not see the fields. The love of the plains was strong in him. It had always been so, ever since he was a little fellow, when the brown grass was up to his shoulders and the straw stacks were the golden mountains of fairyland. Men from the cities on the hills never understand this love, but the men from the plain country know what I mean. When he had tired himself out with longing, he turned over and fell asleep. He was never impatient, for he believed that the State would come some day and explain, and take him to herself. He watched for her coming every day, hoped for it every night.

In the morning the work went no better. They watched him all the time and he could do nothing. At noon they took him into the dark cell and strung him up. They put his arms behind him and tied them together, then passed the rope about his neck, drawing [his] arms up as high as they could be stretched, so that if he let them "sag" he would strangle, and so they left him. The cell was perfectly bare and was not long enough for a man to lie at full length in. The prisoners were told to stand up, so Serge stood. At night his arms were let down long enough for him to eat his bread and water, then he was roped up again. All night long he stood there. By the end of the next day the pain in his arms was almost unendurable.

They were paralyzed from the shoulder down so that the guard had to feed him like a baby. The next day and the next night and the next day he lay upon the floor of the cell, suffering as though every muscle were being individually wrenched from his arms. He had not been out of the bare cell for four days. All the ventilation came through some little auger holes in the door and the heat and odor were becoming unbearable. He had thought on the first night that the pain would kill him before morning, but he had endured over eighty-four hours of it and when the guard came in with his bread and water he found him lying with his eyes closed and his teeth set on his lip. He roused him with a kick and held the bread and water out to him, but Serge took only the water.

"Rope too tight?" growled the guard. Serge said nothing. He was almost dead now and he wanted to finish for he could not hoop barrels.

"Gittin so stuck up you can't speak, are you? Well, we'll just stretch you up a bit tighter." And he gave the stick in the rope another vicious twist that almost tore the arms from their sockets and sent a thrill of agony through the man's whole frame. Then Serge was left alone. The fever raged in his veins and about midnight his thirst was intolerable. He lay with his mouth open and his tongue hanging out. The pain in his arms made his whole body tremble like a man with a chill. He could no longer keep his arms up and the ropes were beginning to strangle him. He did not call for help. He had heard poor devils shriek for help all night long and get no relief. He suffered, as the people of his mother's nation, in hopeless silence. The blood of the serf was in him, blood that has cowered beneath the knout for centuries and uttered no complaint. Then the State would surely come soon, she would not let them kill him. His mother, the State!

He fell into a half stupor. He dreamed about what the *baba* used to tell about the bargemen in their bearskin coats coming down the Volga in the spring when the ice had broken up and gone out; about how the wolves used to howl and follow the sledges across the snow in the starlight. That cold, white snow, that lay in ridges and banks! He thought he felt it in his mouth and he awoke and found himself licking the stone floor. He thought how lovely the plains would look in the morning when the sun was up; how the sunflowers would shake themselves in the wind, how the corn leaves would shine and how the cobwebs would sparkle all over the grass and the air would be clear and blue, the birds would begin to sing, the colts would run and jump in the pasture and the black bull would begin to bellow for his corn.

The rope grew tighter and tighter. The State must come soon now. He thought he felt the dog's cold nose against his throat. He tried to call its name, but the sound only came in an inarticulate gurgle. He drew his knees up to his chin and died.

And so it was that this great mother, the State, took this willful, restless child of hers and put him to sleep in her bosom.

On the Divide

Near Rattlesnake Creek, on the side of a little draw, stood Canute's shanty. North, east, south, stretched the level Nebraska plain of long rust-red grass that undulated constantly in the wind. To the west the ground was broken and rough, and a narrow strip of timber wound along the turbid, muddy little stream that had scarcely ambition enough to crawl over its black bottom. If it had not been for the few stunted cottonwoods and elms that grew along its banks, Canute would have shot himself years ago. The Norwegians are a timber-loving people, and if there is even a turtle pond with a few plum bushes around it they seem irresistibly drawn toward it.

As to the shanty itself, Canute had built it without aid of any kind, for when he first squatted along the banks of Rattlesnake Creek there was not a human being within twenty miles. It was built of logs split in halves, the chinks stopped with mud and plaster. The roof was covered with earth and was supported by one gigantic beam curved in the shape of a round arch. It was almost impossible that any tree had ever grown in that shape. The Norwegians used to say that Canute had taken the log across his knee and bent it into the shape he wished. There were two rooms, or rather there was one room with a partition made of ash saplings interwoven and bound together like big straw basket work. In one corner there was a cook stove, rusted and broken. In the other a bed made of unplaned planks and poles. It was fully eight feet long, and upon it was a heap of dark bed clothing. There was a chair and a bench of colossal proportions. There was an ordinary kitchen cupboard with a few cracked dirty dishes in it, and beside it on a tall box a tin washbasin. Under the bed was a pile of pint flasks, some broken, some whole, all empty. On the wood box lay a pair of shoes of almost incredible dimensions. On the wall hung a saddle, a gun, and some ragged clothing, conspicuous among which was a suit of dark cloth, apparently new, with a paper collar carefully wrapped in a red silk handkerchief and pinned to the sleeve. Over the door hung a wolf and a badger skin, and on the door itself a brace of thirty or forty snake skins whose noisy tails rattled ominously every time it opened. The strangest thing in the shanty were the wide window sills. At first glance they looked as though they had been ruthlessly hacked and mutilated with a hatchet, but on closer inspection all the notches and holes in the wood took form and shape. There seemed to be a series of pictures. They were, in a rough way, artistic, but the figures were heavy and labored, as though they had been cut very slowly and with very awkward instruments. There were men plowing with little horned imps sitting on their shoulders and on their horses' heads. There were men praying with a skull hanging over their heads and little demons behind them mocking their attitudes. There were men fighting with big serpents, and skeletons dancing together. All about these pictures were blooming vines and foliage such as never grew in this world, and coiled among the branches of the vines there was always the scaly body of a serpent, and behind every flower there was a serpent's head. It was a veritable Dance of Death by one who had felt its sting. In the wood box lay some boards, and every inch of them was cut up in the same manner. Sometimes the work was very rude and careless, and looked as though the hand of the workman had trembled. It would sometimes have been hard to distinguish the men from their evil genuises but for one fact, the men were always grave and were either toiling or praying, while the devils were always smiling and dancing. Several of these boards had been split for kindling and it was evident that the artist did not value his work highly.

It was the first day of winter on the Divide. Canute stumbled into his shanty carrying a basket of cobs, and after filling the stove, sat down on a stool and crouched his seven foot frame over the fire, staring drearily out of the window at the wide gray sky. He knew by heart every individual clump of bunch grass in the miles of red shaggy prairie that stretched before his cabin. He knew it in all the deceitful loveliness of its early summer, in all the bitter barrenness of its autumn. He had seen it smitten by all the plagues of Egypt. He had seen it parched by drought, and sogged by rain, beaten by hail, and swept by fire, and in the grasshopper years he had seen it eaten as bare and clean as bones that the vultures had left. After the great fires he had seen it stretch for miles and miles, black and smoking as the floor of hell.

He rose slowly and crossed the room, dragging his big feet heavily as though they were burdens to him. He looked out the window into the hog corral and saw the pigs burying themselves in the straw before the shed. The leaden gray clouds were beginning to spill themselves, and the snow-flakes were settling down over the white leprous patches of frozen earth where the hogs had gnawed even the sod away. He shuddered and began to walk, trampling heavily with his ungainly feet. He was the wreck of ten winters on the Divide and he knew what they meant. Men fear the winters of the Divide as a child fears night or as men in the North Seas fear the still dark cold of the polar twilight.

His eyes fell upon his gun, and he took it down from the wall and looked it over. He sat down on the edge of his bed and held the barrel towards his face, letting his forehead rest upon it, and laid his finger on the trigger. He was perfectly calm, there was neither passion nor despair in his face, but the thoughtful look of a man who is considering. Presently he laid down the gun, and reaching into the cupboard, drew out a pint bottle of raw white alcohol. Lifting it to his lips, he drank greedily. He washed his face in the tin basin and combed his rough hair and shaggy blond beard. Then he stood in uncertainty before the suit of dark clothes that hung on the wall. For the fiftieth time he took them in his hands and tried to summon courage to put them on. He took the paper collar that was pinned to the sleeve of the coat and cautiously slipped it under his rough beard, looking with timid expectancy into the cracked, splashed glass that hung over the bench. With a short laugh he threw it down on the bed, and pulling on his old black hat, he went out, striking off across the level.

It was a physical necessity for him to get away from his cabin once in a while. He had been there for ten years, digging and plowing and sowing, and reaping what little the hail and the hot winds and the frosts left him to reap. Insanity and suicide are very common things on the Divide. They come on like an epidemic in the hot wind season. Those scorching dusty winds that blow up over the bluffs from Kansas seem to dry up the blood in men's veins as they do the sap in the corn leaves. Whenever the yellow scorch creeps down over the tender inside leaves about the ear, then the coroners prepare for active duty; for the oil of the country is burned out and it does not take long for the flame to eat up the wick. It causes no great sensation there when a Dane is found swinging to his own windmill tower, and most of the Poles after they have become too careless and discouraged to shave themselves keep their razors to cut their throats with.

It may be that the next generation on the Divide will be very happy, but the present one came too late in life. It is useless for men that have cut hemlocks among the mountains of Sweden for forty years to try to be happy in a country as flat and gray and as naked as the sea. It is not easy for men that have spent their youths fishing in the

Northern seas to be content with following a plow, and men that have served in the Austrian army hate hard work and coarse clothing and the loneliness of the plains, and long for marches and excitement and tavern company and pretty barmaids. After a man has passed his fortieth birthday it is not easy for him to change the habits and conditions of his life. Most men bring with them to the Divide only the dregs of the lives that they have squandered in other lands and among other peoples.

Canute Canuteson was as mad as any of them, but his madness did not take the form of suicide or religion but of alcohol. He had always taken liquor when he wanted it, as all Norwegians do, but after his first year of solitary life he settled down to its steadily. He exhausted whisky after a while, and went to alcohol, because its effects were speedier and surer. He was a big man with a terrible amount of resistant force, and it took a great deal of alcohol even to move him. After nine years of drinking, the quantities he could take would seem fabulous to an ordinary drinking man. He never let it interfere with his work, he generally drank at night and on Sundays. Every night, as soon as his chores were done, he began to drink. While he was able to sit up he would play on his mouth harp or hack away at his window sills with his jackknife. When the liquor went to his head he would lie down on his bed and stare out of the window until he went to sleep. He drank alone and in solitude not for pleasure or good cheer, but to forget the awful loneliness and level of the Divide. Milton made a sad blunder when he put mountains in hell. Mountains postulate faith and aspiration. All mountain peoples are religious. It was the cities and the plains that, because of their utter lack of spirituality and the mad caprice of their vice, were cursed of God.

Alcohol is perfectly consistent in its effects upon man. Drunkenness is merely an exaggeration. A foolish man drunk becomes maudlin; a bloody man, vicious; a coarse man, vulgar. Canute was none of these, but he was morose and gloomy, and liquor took him through all the hells of Dante. As he lay on his giant's bed all the horrors of this world and every other were laid bare to his chilled senses. He was a man who knew no joy, a man who toiled in silence and bitterness. The skull and the serpent were always before him, the symbols of eternal futileness and of eternal hate.

When the first Norwegians near enough to be called neighbors came, Canute rejoiced, and planned to escape from his bosom vice. But he was not a social man by nature and had not the power of drawing out the social side of other people. His new neighbors rather feared him because of his great strength and size, his silence and his lowering brows. Perhaps, too, they knew that he was mad, mad from the eternal treachery of the plains, which every spring stretch green and rustle with the promises of Eden, showing long grassy lagoons full of clear water and cattle whose hoofs are stained with wild roses. Before autumn the lagoons are dried up, and the ground is burnt dry and hard until it blisters and cracks open.

So instead of becoming a friend and neighbor to the men that settled about him, Canute become a mystery and a terror. They told awful stories of his size and strength and of the alcohol he drank. They said that one night, when he went out to see to his horses just before he went to bed, his steps were unsteady and the rotten planks of the floor gave way and threw him behind the feet of a fiery young stallion. His foot was caught fast in the floor, and the nervous horse began kicking frantically. When Canute felt the blood trickling down into his eyes from a scalp wound in his head, he roused himself from his kingly indifference, and with the quiet stoical courage of a drunken man leaned forward and wound his arms about the horse's hind legs and held them against his breast with crushing embrace. All through the darkness and cold of the night he lay there, matching strength against strength. When little Jim Peterson went over the next morning at four o'clock to go with him to the Blue to cut wood, he found him so, and the horse was on its foreknees, trembling and whinnying with fear. This is the story the Norwegians tell of him, and if it is true it is no wonder that they feared and hated this Holder of the Heels of Horses.

One spring there moved to the next "eighty" a family that made a great change in Canute's life. Ole Yensen was too drunk most of the time to be afraid of any one, and his wife Mary was too garrulous to be afraid of any one who listened to her talk, and Lena, their pretty daughter, was not afraid of man nor devil. So it came about that Canute went over to take his alcohol with Ole oftener than he took it alone. After a while the report spread that he was going to marry Yensen's daughter, and the Norwegian girls began to tease Lena about the great bear she was going to keep house for. No one could quite see how the affair had come about, for Canute's tactics of courtship were somewhat peculiar. He apparently never spoke to her at all: he would sit for hours with Mary chattering on one side of him and Ole drinking on the other and watch Lena at her work. She teased him, and threw flour in his face and put vinegar in his coffee, but he took her rough jokes with silent wonder, never even smiling. He took her to church occasionally, but the most watchful and curious people never saw him speak to her. He would sit staring at her while she giggled and flirted with the other men.

Next spring Mary Lee went to town to work in a steam laundry. She came home every Sunday, and always ran across to Yensens to startle Lena with stories of ten cent theatres, firemen's dances, and all the other esthetic delights of metropolitan life. In a few weeks Lena's head was completely turned, and she gave her father no rest until he let her go to town to seek her fortune at the ironing board. From the time she came home on her first visit she began to treat Canute with contempt. She had bought a plush cloak and kid gloves, had her clothes made by the dressmaker, and assumed airs and graces that made the other women of the neighborhood cordially detest her. She generally brought with her a young man from town who waxed his mustache and wore a red necktie, and she did not even introduce him to Canute.

The neighbors teased Canute a good deal until he knocked one of them down. He gave no sign of suffering from her neglect except that he drank more and avoided the other Norwegians more carefully than ever. He lay around in his den and no one knew what he felt or thought, but little Jim Peterson, who had seen him glowering at Lena in church one Sunday when she was there with the town man, said that he would not give an acre of his wheat for Lena's life or the town chap's either; and Jim's wheat was so wondrously worthless that the statement was an exceedingly strong one.

Canute had bought a new suit of clothes that looked as nearly like the town man's as possible. They had cost him half a miller crop; for tailors are not accustomed to fitting giants and they charge for it. He had hung those clothes in his shanty two months ago and had never put them on, partly from fear of ridicule, partly from discouragement, and partly because there was something in his own soul that revolted at the littleness of the device.

Lena was at home just at this time. Work was slack in the laundry and Mary had not been well, so Lena stayed at home, glad enough to get an opportunity to torment Canute once more.

She was washing in the side kitchen, singing loudly as she worked. Mary was on her knees, blacking the stove and scolding violently about the young man who was coming out from town that night. The young man had committed the fatal error of laughing at Mary's ceaseless babble and had never been forgiven.

"He is no good, and you will come to a bad end by running with him! I do not see why a daughter of mine should act so. I do not see why the Lord should visit such a punishment upon me as to give me such a daughter. There are plenty of good men you can marry."

Lena tossed her head and answered curtly, "I don't happen to want to marry any man right away, and so long as Dick dresses nice and has plenty of money to spend, there is no harm in my going with him."

"Money to spend? Yes, and that is all he does with it I'll be bound. You think it very fine now, but you will change your tune when you have been married five years and see your children running naked and your cupboard empty. Did Anne Hermanson come to any good end by marrying a town man?"

"I don't know anything about Anne Hermanson, but I know any of the laundry girls would have Dick quick enough if they could get him."

"Yes, and a nice lot of store clothes huzzies you are too. Now there is Canuteson who has an 'eighty' proved up and fifty head of cattle and—"

"And hair that ain't been cut since he was a baby, and a big dirty beard, and he wears overalls on Sundays, and drinks like a pig. Besides he will keep. I can have all the fun I want, and when I am old and ugly like you he can have me and take care of me. The Lord knows there ain't nobody else going to marry him."

Canute drew his hand back from the latch as though it were red hot. He was not the kind of man to make a good eavesdropper, and he wished he had knocked sooner. He pulled himself together and struck the door like a battering ram. Mary jumped and opened it with a screech.

"God! Canute, how you scared us! I thought it was crazy Lou—he has been tearing around the neighborhood trying to convert folks. I am afraid as death of him. He ought to be sent off, I think. He is just as liable as not to kill us all, or burn the barn, or poison the dogs. He has been worrying even the poor minister to death, and he laid up with the rheumatism, too! Did you notice that he was too sick to preach last Sunday? But don't stand there in the cold—come in. Yensen isn't here, but he just went over to Sorenson's for the mail; he won't be gone long. Walk right in the other room and sit down."

Canute followed her, looking steadily in front of him and not noticing Lena as he passed her. But Lena's vanity would not allow him to pass unmolested. She took the wet sheet she was wringing out and cracked him across the face with it, and ran giggling to the other side of the room. The blow stung his cheeks and the soapy water flew in his eyes, and he involuntarily began rubbing them with his hands. Lena giggled with delight at his discomfiture, and the wrath in Canute's face grew blacker than ever. A big man humiliated is vastly more undignified than a little one. He forgot the sting of his face in the bitter consciousness that he had made a fool of himself. He stumbled blindly into the living room, knocking his head against the door jamb because he forgot to stoop. He dropped into a chair behind the stove, thrusting his big feet back helplessly on either side of him.

Ole was a long time in coming, and Canute sat there, still and silent, with his hands clenched on his knees, and the skin of his face seemed to have shriveled up into little wrinkles that trembled when he lowered his brows. His life had been one long lethargy of solitude and alcohol, but now he was awakening, and it was as when the dumb stagnant heat of summer breaks out into thunder.

When Ole came staggering in, heavy with liquor, Canute rose at once.

"Yensen," he said quietly, "I have come to see if you will let me marry your daughter today."

"Today!" gasped Ole.

"Yes, I will not wait until tomorrow, I am tired of living alone."

Ole braced his staggering knees against the bedstead, and stammered eloquently: "Do you think I will marry my daughter to a drunkard? a man who drinks raw alcohol? a man who sleeps with rattlesnakes? Get out of my house or I will kick you out for your impudence." And Ole began looking anxiously for his feet.

Canute answered not a word, but he put on his hat and went out into the kitchen. He went up to Lena and said without looking at her, "Get your things on and come with me!"

The tone of his voice startled her, and she said angrily, dropping the soap, "Are you drunk?"

"If you do not come with me, I will take you—you had better come," said Canute quietly.

She lifted a sheet to strike him, but he caught her arm roughly and wrenched the sheet from her. He turned to the wall and took down a hood and shawl that hung there, and began wrapping her up. Lena scratched and fought like a wild thing. Ole stood in the door, cursing, and Mary howled and screeched at the top of her voice. As for Canute, he lifted the girl in his arms and went out of the house. She kicked and struggled, but the helpless wailing of Mary and Ole soon died away in the distance, and her face was held down tightly on Canute's shoulder so that she could not see whither he was taking her. She was conscious only of the north wind whistling in her ears, and of rapid steady motion and of a great breast that heaved beneath her in quick, irregular breaths. The harder she struggled the tighter those iron arms that had held the heels of horses crushed about her, until she felt as if they would crush the breath from her, and lay still with fear. Canute was striding across the level fields at a pace at which man never went before, drawing the stinging north wind into his lungs in great gulps. He walked with his eyes half closed and looking straight in front of him, only lowering them when he bent his head to blow away the snow-flakes that settled on her hair. So it was that Canute took her to his home, even as his bearded barbarian ancestors took the fair frivolous women of the South in their hairy arms and bore them down to their war ships. For ever and anon the soul becomes weary of the conventions that are not of it, and with a single stroke shatters the civilized lies with which it is unable to cope, and the strong arm reaches out and takes by force what it cannot win by cunning.

When Canute reached his shanty he placed the girl upon a chair, where she sat sobbing. He stayed only a few minutes. He filled the stove with wood and lit the lamp, drank a huge swallow of alcohol and put the bottle in his pocket. He paused a moment, staring heavily at the weeping girl, then he went off and locked the door and disappeared in the gathering gloom of the night.

Wrapped in flannels and soaked with turpentine, the little Norwegian preacher sat reading his Bible, when he heard a thundering knock at his door, and Canute entered, covered with snow and with his beard frozen fast to his coat.

"Come in, Canute, you must be frozen," said the little man, shoving a chair towards his visitor.

Canute remained standing with his hat on and said quietly, "I want you to come over to my house tonight to marry me to Lena Yensen."

"Have you got a license, Canute?"

"No, I don't want a license. I want to be married."

"But I can't marry you without a license, man. It would not be legal."

A dangerous light came in the big Norwegian's eyes. "I want you to come over to my house to marry me to Lena Yensen."

"No, I can't, it would kill an ox to go out in a storm like this, and my rheumatism is bad tonight."

"Then if you will not go I must take you," said Canute with a sigh.

He took down the preacher's bearskin coat and bade him put it on while he hitched up his buggy. He went out and closed the door softly after him. Presently he returned and found the frightened minister crouching before the fire with his coat laying beside him. Canute helped him put it on and gently wrapped his head in his big muffler. Then he picked him up and carried him out and placed him in his buggy. As he tucked the buffalo robes around him he said: "Your horse is old, he might flounder or lose his way in this storm. I will lead him."

The minister took the reins feebly in his hands and sat shivering with the cold. Sometimes when there was a lull in the wind, he could see the horse struggling through the snow with the man plodding steadily beside him. Again the blowing snow would hide them from him altogether. He had no idea where they were or what direction they were going. He felt as though he were being whirled away in the heart of the storm, and he said all the prayers he knew. But at last the long four miles were over, and Canute set him down in the snow while he unlocked the door. He saw the bride sitting by the fire with her eyes red and swollen as though she had been weeping. Canute placed a huge chair for him, and said roughly,

"Warm yourself."

Lena began to cry and moan afresh, begging the minister to take her home. He looked helplessly at Canute. Canute said simply,

"If you are warm now, you can marry us."

"My daughter, do you take this step of your own free will?" asked the minister in a trembling voice.

"No sir, I don't, and it is disgraceful he should force me into it! I won't marry him."

"Then, Canute, I cannot marry you," said the minister, standing as straight as his rheumatic limbs would let him.

"Are you ready to marry us now, sir?" said Canute, laying one iron hand on his stooped shoulder. The little preacher was a good man, but like most men of weak body he was a coward and had a horror of physical suffering, although he had known so much of it. So with many qualms of conscience he began to repeat the marriage service. Lena sat sullenly in her chair, staring at the fire. Canute stood beside her, listening with his head bent reverently and his hands folded on his breast. When the little man had prayed and said amen, Canute began bundling him up again.

"I will take you home, now," he said as he carried him out and placed him in his buggy, and started off with him through the fury of the storm, floundering among the snow drifts that brought even the giant himself to his knees.

After she was left alone, Lena soon ceased weeping.

She was not of a particularly sensitive temperament, and had little pride beyond that of vanity. After the first bitter anger wore itself out, she felt nothing more than a healthy sense of humiliation and defeat. She had no inclination to run away, for she was married now, and in her eyes that was final and all rebellion was useless. She knew nothing about a license, but she knew that a preacher married folks. She consoled herself by thinking that she had always intended to marry Canute someday, anyway.

She grew tried of crying and looking into the fire, so she got up and began to look about her. She had heard queer tales about the inside of Canute's shanty, and her curiosity soon got the better of her rage. One of the first things she noticed was the new black suit of clothes hanging on the wall. She was dull, but it did not take a vain woman long to interpret anything so decidedly flattering, and she was pleased in spite of herself. As she looked through the cupboard, the general air of neglect and discomfort made her pity the man who lived there.

"Poor fellow, no wonder he wants to get married to get somebody to wash up his dishes. Batchin's pretty hard on a man."

It is easy to pity when once one's vanity has been tickled. She looked at the window sill and gave a little shudder and wondered if the man were crazy. Then she sat down again and sat a long time wondering what her Dick and Ole would do.

"It is queer Dick didn't come right over after me. He surely came, for he would have left town before the storm began and he might just as well come right on as go back. If he'd hurried he would have gotten here before the preacher came. I suppose he was afraid to come, for he knew Canuteson could pound him to jelly, the coward!" Her eyes flashed angrily.

The weary hours wore on and Lena began to grow horribly lonesome. It was an uncanny night and this was an uncanny place to be in. She could hear the coyotes howling hungrily a little way from the cabin, and more terrible still were all the unknown noises of the storm. She remembered the tales they told of the big log overhead and she was afraid of those snaky things on the window sills. She remembered the man who had been killed in the draw, and she wondered what she would do if she saw crazy Lou's white face glaring into the window. The rattling of the door became unbearable, she thought the latch must be loose and took the lamp to look at it. Then for the first time she saw the ugly brown snake skins whose death rattle sounded every time the wind jarred the door.

"Canute, Canute!" she screamed in terror.

Outside the door she heard a heavy sound as of a big dog getting up and shaking himself. The door opened and Canute stood before her, white as a snow drift.

"What is it?" he asked kindly.

"I am cold," she faltered.

He went out and got an armful of wood and a basket of cobs and filled the stove. Then he went out and lay in the snow before the door. Presently he heard her calling again.

"What is it?" he said, sitting up.

"I'm so lonesome, I'm afraid to stay in here all alone."

"I will go over and get your mother." And he got up.

"She won't come."

"I'll bring her," said Canute grimly.

"No, no. I don't want her, she will scold all the time."

"Well, I will bring your father."

She spoke again and it seemed as though her mouth was close up to the key hole. She spoke lower than he had ever heard her speak before, so low that he had to put his ear up to the lock to hear her.

"I don't want him either, Canute—I'd rather have you."

For a moment she heard no noise at all, then something like a groan. With a cry of fear she opened the door, and saw Canute stretched in the snow at her feet, his face in his hands, sobbing on the door step.

A Night
at Greenway Court

I, Richard Morgan, of the town of Winchester, county of Frederick, of the Commonwealth of Virginia, having been asked by my friend Josiah Goodrich, who purports making a history of this valley, to set down all I know concerning the death of M. Philip Marie Maurepas, a gentleman, it seems, of considerable importance in his own country, will proceed to do so briefly and with what little skill I am master of.

The incident which I am about to relate occurred in my early youth, but so deeply did it fix itself upon my memory that the details are as clear as though it had happened but yesterday. Indeed, of all the stirring events that have happened in my time, those nights spent at Greenway Court in my youth stand out most boldly in my memory. It was, I think, one evening late in October, in the year 1752, that my Lord Fairfax sent his man over to my father's house at Winchester to say that on the morrow his master desired my company at the Court. My father, a prosperous tobacco merchant, greatly regretted that I should be brought up in a new country, so far from the world of polite letters and social accomplishments, and contrived that I should pass much of my leisure in the company of one of the most gracious gentlemen and foremost scholars of his time, Thomas, Lord Fairfax. Accordingly, I was not surprised at my lord's summons. Late in the afternoon of the following day I rode over to the Court, and was first shown into my lord's private office, where for some time we discussed my lord's suit, then pending with the sons of Joist Hite, concerning certain lands beyond the Blue Ridge, then held by them, which my lord claimed through the extension of his grant from the crown. Our business being dispatched, he said:

"Come, Richard, in the hall I will present you to some gentlemen who will entertain you until supper time. There is a Frenchman stopping here, M. Maurepas, a gentleman of most engaging conversation. The Viscount Chillingham you will not meet until later, as he has gone out with the hounds."

We crossed the yard and entered the hall where the table was already laid with my lord's silver platters and thin glass goblets, which never ceased to delight me when I dined with him, and though since, in London, I have drunk wine at a king's table, I have seen none finer. At the end of the room, by the fire place, sat two men over their cards. One was a clergyman, whom I had met before, the other a tall spare gentleman whom my lord introduced as M. Philip Marie Maurepas. As I sat down, the gentleman addressed me in excellent English. The bright firelight gave me an excellent opportunity for observing this man, which I did, for with us strangers were too few not to be of especial interest, and in a way their very appearance spoke to us of an older world beyond the seas for which the hearts of all of us still hungered.

He was, as I have said, a tall man, narrow chested and with unusually long arms. His forehead was high and his chin sharp, his skin was dark, tanned, as I later learned, by his long service in the Indes. He had a pair of restless black eyes and thin lips shaded by a dark mustache. His hair was coal black and grew long upon his shoulders; later I noticed that it was slightly touched with gray. His dress had once been fine, but had seen considerable service and was somewhat the worse for the weather. He wore breeches of dark blue velvet and leather leggins. His shirt and vest were dark red and had once been worked with gold.

In his belt he wore a long knife with a slender blade and a handle of gold curiously worked in the form of a serpent, with eyes of pure red stones which sparkled mightily in the firelight. I must confess that in the very appearance of this man there was something that both interested and attracted me, and I fell to wondering what strange sights those keen eyes of his had looked upon.

"M. Maurepas intends spending the winter in our wilderness, Richard, and I fear he will find that our woods offer a cold welcome to a stranger."

"Well, my lord, all the more to my taste. Having seen how hot the world can be, I am willing to see how cold."

"To see that, sir," said I, "you should go to Quebec where I have been with trappers. There I have thrown a cup full of water in the air and seen it descend solid ice."

"I fear it will be cold enough here for my present attire," said he laughing, "yet it may be that I will taste the air of Quebec before quitting this wilderness of yours."

My lord then excused himself and withdrew, leaving me alone with the gentlemen.

"Come join me in a game of hazard, Master Morgan; it is yet half an hour until supper time," said the clergyman, who had little thought for anything but his cards and his dinner.

"And I will look at the portraits; you have fleeced me quite enough for one day, good brother of the Church. I have nothing left but my diamond that I cut from the hand of a dead Rajpoot, finger and all, and it is a lucky stone, and I have no mind to lose it."

"With your permission, M. Maurepas, I will look at the portraits with you, as I have no mind to play tonight; besides I think this is the hour for Mr. Courtney's devotions," said I, for I had no liking for the fat churchman. He, like so many of my lord's guests, was in a sense a refugee from justice; having fallen into disgrace with the heads of the English church, he had fled to our country and sought out Lord Fairfax, whose door was closed against no man. He had been there then three months, dwelling in shameful idleness, one of that band of renegades who continually ate at my lord's table and hunted with his dogs and devoured his substance, waiting for some turn of fortune, like the suitors in the halls of Penelope. So we left the clergyman counting his gains and repaired to the other end of the hall, where, above the mahogany bookcases, the portraits hung. Of these there were a considerable number, and I told the Frenchman the names of as many as I knew. There was my lord's father and mother, and his younger brother, to whom he had given his English estate. There was his late majesty George I, and old Fernando Fairfax. Hanging under the dark picture of the king he had deposed and yet loved was Fernando's son, fighting Thomas Fairfax, third Lord and Baron of Cameron, the great leader of the commoners with Cromwell, who rode after Charles at Heyworth Moor and thrust the people's petition in the indignant monarch's saddle bow; who defeated the king's forces at Naseby, and after Charles was delivered over to the commissioners of Parliament, met him at Nottingham and kissed his fallen sovereign's hand, refusing to sit in judgment over God's anointed.

Among these pictures there was one upon which I had often gazed in wonderment. It was the portrait of a lady, holding in her hand a white lily. Some heavy instrument had been thrust through the canvas, marring the face beyond all recognition, but the masses of powdered hair, and throat and arms were enough to testify to the beauty of the original. The hands especially were of surpassing loveliness, and the thumb was ornamented with a single emerald, as though to call attention to its singular perfection. The costume was the court dress of the then present reign, and with the eagerness of youthful imagination I had often fancied that could that picture speak it might tell something of that upon which all men wondered; why, in the prime of his manhood and success at court, Lord Fairfax had left home and country, friends, and all that men hold dear, renounced the gay society in which he had shone and his favorite pursuit of letters, and buried himself in the North American wilderness. Upon this canvas the Frenchman's eye was soon fixed.

"And this?" he asked.

"I do not know, sir; of that my lord has never told me."

"Well, let me see; what is a man's memory good for, if not for such things? I must have seen those hands before, and that coronet."

He looked at it closely and then stood back and looked at it from a distance. Suddenly an exclamation broke from him, and a sharp light flashed over his features.

"Ah, I thought so! So your lord has never told you of this, *parbleau, il a beaucoup de cause*! Look you, my boy, that emerald is the only beautiful thing that ever came out of Herrenhausen—that, and she who wears it. Perhaps you will see that emerald, too, some day; how many and how various they will yet be, God alone knows. How long, O Lord, how long? as your countrymen say."

So bitter was his manner that I was half afraid, yet had a mind to question him, when my lord returned. He brought with him a young man of an appearance by no means distinguished, yet kindly and affable, whom he introduced as the Viscount Chillingham.

"You've a good country here, Master Norton, and better sport than we, for all our game laws. Hang laws, I say, they're naught but a trouble to them that make 'em and them that break 'em, and it's little good they do any of us. My lord, you must sell me your deer hound, Fanny, I want to take her home with me, and show 'em what your dogs are made of over here."

"You are right welcome to her, or any of the pack."

At this juncture my lord's housekeeper, Mistress Crawford, brought in the silver candlesticks, and the servants smoking dishes of bear's meat and venison, and many another delicacy for which my lord's table was famous, besides French wines and preserved cherries from his old estates in England.

The viscount flung himself into his chair, still flushed from his chase after the hounds, and stretched his long limbs.

"This is a man's life you have here, my lord. I tell you, you do well to be away from London now; it's as dull there as Mr. Courtney's church without its spiritual pastor."

The clergyman lifted his eyes from his venison long enough to remark slyly, "Or as Hampton Court without its cleverest gamester," at which the young man reddened under his fresh coat of tan, for he had been forced to leave England because of some gaming scandal which cast grave doubts upon his personal honor.

The talk drifted to the death of the queen of Denmark, the king's last visit to Hanover, and various matters of court gossip. Of these the gentlemen spoke freely, more freely, perhaps, than they would have dared do at home. As I have said, my lord's guests were too often gentlemen who had left dark histories behind them, and had fled into the wilds where law was scarce more than a name and man had to contend only with the savage condition of nature, and a strong arm stood in better stead than a tender conscience. I have met many a strange man at Greenway Court, men who had cheated at play, men who had failed in great political plots, men who fled from a debtor's prison, and men charged with treason, and with a price upon their heads. For in some respects Lord Fairfax was a strangely conservative man, slow to judge and slow to anger, having seen much of the world, and thinking its conditions hard and its temptations heavy, deeming, I believe, all humanity more sinned against than sinning. And yet I have seldom known his confidence to be misplaced or his trust to be ill repaid. Whatever of information I may have acquired in my youth, I owe to the conversation of these men, for about my lord's board exiles and outlaws of all nations gathered, and unfolded in the friendly solitude of the wilderness plots and intrigues then scarce known in Europe.

On all the matters that were discussed the Frenchman

seemed the best versed man present, even touching the most minute details of the English court. At last the viscount, who was visibly surprised, turned upon him sharply.

"Have you been presented at court, monsieur?"

"Not in England, count, but I have seen something of your kind in Hanover; there, I think, on the banks of the stupid Leine, is his proper court, and 'tis there he sends the riches of your English. But in exchange I hear that he has brought you his treasure of Herrenhausen in her private carriage with a hundred postilions to herald her advent."

His eyes were fixed keenly on my lord's face, but Fairfax only asked coldly:

"And where, monsieur, have you gained so perfect a mastery of the English tongue?"

"At Madras, your lordship, under Bourdonnais, where I fought your gallant countrymen, high and low, for the empire of the Indes. They taught me the sound of English speech well enough, and the music of English swords."

"Faith," broke in the viscount, "then they taught you better than they know themselves, though it's their mother tongue. You've seen hot service there, I warrant?"

"Well, what with English guns sweeping our decks by sea, and the Indian sun broiling our skin by land, and the cholera tearing our entrails, we saw hot service indeed."

"Were you in the Indian service after the return of Governor Bourdonnais to France, M. Maurepas?"

"After his return to the Bastille, you mean, my lord. Yes, I was less fortunate than my commander. There are worse prisons on earth than the Bastille, and Madras is one of them. When France sends a man to the Indes she has no intention he shall return alive. How I did so is another matter. Yes, I served afterward under Dupleix, who seized Bourdonnais' troops as well as his treasure. I was with him in the Deccan when he joined his troops with Murzapha Jung against the Nabob of the Carnatic, and white men were set to fight side by side with heathen. And I say to you, gentlemen, that the bravest man in all that mêlée was the old Nabob himself. He was a hundred and seven years old, and he had been a soldier from his mother's knee. He was mounted on the finest elephant in the Indian army, and he led his soldiers right up into the thick of the fight in full sweep of the French bullets, ordering his body-guard back and attended only by his driver. And when he saw his old enemy, Tecunda Sahib, in the very midst of the French guards, he ordered his driver to up and at him, and he prodded the beast forward with his own hand. When the beast came crashing through our lines a bullet struck the old man in the breast, but still he urged him on. And when the elephant was stopped the driver was gone and the old Nabob was stone dead, sitting bolt upright in his curtained cage with a naked scimitar in his hand, ready for his vengeance. And I tell ye now, gentlemen, that I for one was right sorry that the bullet went home, for I am not the man who would see a brave soldier balked of his revenge."

It is quite impossible with the pen to give any adequate idea of the dramatic manner in which he related this. I think it stirred the blood of more than one of us. The viscount struck the table with his hand and cried:

"That's talking, sir; you see the best of life, you French. As for us, we are so ridden by kingcraft and statecraft we are as good as dead men. Between Walpole and the little German we have forgot the looks of a sword, and we never hear a gun these times but at the christening of some brat or other."

The clergyman looked up reproachfully from his preserved cherries, and Lord Fairfax, who seldom suffered any talk that savored of disloyalty, rose to his feet and lifted his glass.

"Gentlemen, the king's health."

"The king's health," echoed we all rising. But M. Maurepas sat stiff in his chair, and his glass stood full beside him. The viscount turned upon him fiercely.

"Monsieur, you do not drink the king's health?"

"No, sir; your king, nor my king, nor no man's king. I

have no king. May the devil take them one and all! and that's my health to them."

"Monsieur," cried my lord sternly, "I am surprised to hear a soldier of the king of France speak in this fashion."

"Yes, my lord, I have been a soldier of the king, and I know the wages of kings. What were they for Bourdonnais, the bravest general who ever drew a sword? The Bastille! What were they for all my gallant comrades? Cholera, massacre, death in the rotting marshes of Pondicherry. *Le Diable!* I know them well; prison, the sword, the stake, the recompense of kings." He laughed terribly and struck his forehead with his hand.

"Monsieur," said my lord, "It may be that you have suffered much, and for that reason only do I excuse much that you say. Human justice is often at fault, and kings are but human. Nevertheless, they are ordained of heaven, and so long as there is breath in our bodies we owe them loyal service."

The Frenchman rose and stood, his dark eyes flashing like coals of fire and his hands trembling as he waved them in the air. And methought the prophets of Israel must have looked so when they cried out unto the people, though his words were as dark blasphemy as ever fell from human lips.

"I tell you, sir, that the day will come and is now at hand when there will be no more kings. When a king's blood will be cheaper than pothouse wine and flow as plentifully. When crowned heads will pray for a peasant's cap, and princes will hide their royal lineage as lepers hide their sores. Ordained of God! Look you, sir, there is a wise man of France, so wise indeed that he dares not dwell in France, but hides among the Prussians, who says that there is no God! No Jehovah with his frying pan of lost souls! That it is all a tale made up by kings to terrify their slaves; that instead of God making kings, the kings made God."

We were all struck with horror and the viscount rose to his feet again and threw himself into an attitude of attack, while Mr. Courtney, whose place it was to speak, cowered in his seat and continued to look wistfully at the cherries.

"Stop, sir," bawled the viscount, "we have not much faith left in England, thanks to such as Mr. Courtney here, but we've enough still to fight for. Little George may have his faults, but he's a brave man and a soldier. Let us see whether you can be as much."

But the Frenchman did not so much as look at him. He was well sped with wine, and in his eyes there was a fierce light as of some ancient hatred woke anew. Staggering down the hall he pointed to the canvas which had so interested him in the afternoon.

"My lord, I wonder at you, that you should dare to keep that picture here, though three thousand miles of perilous sea, and savagery, and forests, and mountains impassable lie between you and Hampton Court. If you are a man, I think you have no cause to love the name of king. Yet, is not your heart as good as any man's, and will not your money buy as many trinkets? I tell you, this wilderness is not dark enough to hide that woman's face! And she carries a lily in her hand, the lilies of Herrenhausen! *Justice de Dieu—*" but he got no further, for my lord's hand had struck him in the mouth.

It came about so quickly that even then it was but a blur of sudden action to me. We sprang between them, but Fairfax had no intention of striking twice.

"We can settle this in the morning, sir," he said quietly. As he turned away M. Maurepas drew himself together with the litheness of a cat, and before I could catch his arm he had seized the long knife from his belt and thrown it after his host. It whizzed past my lord and stuck quivering in the oak wainscoating, while the man who threw it sank upon the floor a pitiable heap of intoxication. My lord turned to his man, who still stood behind his chair. "Henry, call me at five; at six I shall kill a scoundrel."

With that he left us to watch over the drunken slumbers of the Frenchman.

In the morning they met on the level stretch before the court. At my lord's request I stood as second to M. Maurepas. My principal was much shaken by his debauch of last night, and I thought when my lord looked upon him he was already dead. For in Lord Fairfax's face was a purpose which it seemed no human will could thwart. Never have I seen him look the noble, Christian gentleman as he looked it then. Just as the autumn mists were rising from the hills, their weapons crossed, and the rising sun shot my lord's blade with fire until it looked the sword of righteousness indeed. It lasted but a moment. M. Maurepas, so renowned in war and gallantry, who had been the shame of two courts and the rival of two kings, fell, unknown and friendless, in the wilderness.

Two years later, after I had been presented and, through my father, stood in favor at court, I once had the honor to dine with his majesty at Hampton Court. At his right sat a woman known to history only too well; still brilliant, still beautiful, as she was unto the end. By her side I was seated. When the dishes were removed, as we sat over our wine, the king bade me tell him some of the adventures that had befallen in my own land.

"I can tell you, your majesty, how Lord Fairfax fought and killed M. Maurepas about a woman's picture."

"That sounds well, tell on," said the monarch in his heavy accent.

Then upon my hand under a table I felt a clasp, cold and trembling. I glanced down and saw there a white hand of wondrous beauty, the thumb ornamented with a single emerald. I sat still in amazement, for the lady's face was smiling and gave no sign.

The king clinked his glass impatiently with his nail.

"Well, go on with your story. Are we to wait on you all day?"

Again I felt that trembling pressure in mute entreaty on my hand.

"I think there is no story to tell, your majesty."

"And I think you are very stupid young man," said his majesty testily, as he rose from the table.

"Perhaps he is abashed," laughed my lady, but her bosom heaved with a deep sigh of relief.

So my day of royal favor was a short one, nor was I sorry, for I had kept my friend's secret and shielded a fair lady's honor, which are the two first duties of a Virginian.

Tommy
the Unsentimental

"Your father says he has no business tact at all, and of course that's dreadfully unfortunate."

"Business," replied Tommy, "he's a baby in business; he's good for nothing on earth but to keep his hair parted straight and wear that white carnation in his buttonhole. He has 'em sent down from Hastings twice a week as regularly as the mail comes, but the drafts he cashes lie in his safe until they are lost, or somebody finds them. I go up occasionally and send a package away for him myself. He'll answer your notes promptly enough, but his business letters—I believe he destroys them unopened to shake the responsibility of answering them."

"I am at a loss to see how you can have such patience with him, Tommy, in so many ways he is thoroughly reprehensible."

"Well, a man's likeableness don't depend at all on his virtues or acquirements, nor a woman's either, unfortunately. You like them or you don't like them, and that's all there is to it. For the why of it you must appeal to a higher oracle than I. Jay is a likeable fellow, and that's his only and sole acquirement, but after all it's a rather happy one."

"Yes, he certainly is that," replied Miss Jessica, as she deliberately turned off the gas jet and proceeded to arrange her toilet articles. Tommy watched her closely and then turned away with a baffled expression.

Needless to say, Tommy was not a boy, although her keen gray eyes and wide forehead were scarcely girlish, and she had the lank figure of an active half grown lad. Her real name is Theodosia, but during Thomas Shirley's frequent absences from the bank she had attended to his business and correspondence signing herself "T. Shirley," until everyone in Southdown called her "Tommy." That blunt sort of familiarity is not unfrequent in the West, and is meant well enough. People rather expect some business ability in a girl there, and they respect it immensely. That, Tommy undoubtedly had, and if she had not, things would have gone at sixes and sevens in the Southdown National. For Thomas Shirley had big land interests in Wyoming that called him constantly from home, and his cashier, little Jay Ellington Harper, was, in the local phrase, a weak brother in the bank. He was the son of a friend of old Shirley's, whose papa had sent him West, because he had made a sad mess of his college career, and had spent too much money and gone at too giddy a pace down East. Conditions changed the young gentleman's life, for it was simply impossible to live either prodigally or rapidly in Southdown, but they could not materially affect his mental habits or inclinations. He was made cashier of Shirley's bank because his father bought in half the stock, but Tommy did his work for him.

The relation between these two young people was peculiar; Harper was, in his way, very grateful to her for keeping him out of disgrace with her father, and showed it by a hundred little attentions which were new to her and much more agreeable than the work she did for him was irksome. Tommy knew that she was immensely fond of him, and she knew at the same time that she was thoroughly foolish for being so. As she expressed it, she was not of his sort, and never would be. She did not often take pains to think but when she did she saw matters pretty clearly, and she was of a peculiarly unfeminine mind that could not escape meeting and acknowledging a logical conclusion. But she went on liking Jay Ellington

Harper, just the same. Now Harper was the only foolish man of Tommy's acquaintance. She knew plenty of active young business men and sturdy ranchers, such as one meets about live western towns, and took no particular interest in them, probably just because they were practical and sensible and thoroughly of her own kind. She knew almost no women, because in those days there were few women in Southdown who were in any sense interesting, or interested in anything but babies and salads. Her best friends were her father's old business friends, elderly men who had seen a good deal of the world, and who were very proud and fond of Tommy. They recognized a sort of squareness and honesty of spirit in the girl that Jay Ellington Harper never discovered, or, if he did, knew too little of its rareness to value highly. Those old speculators and men of business had always felt a sort of responsibility for Tom Shirley's little girl, and had rather taken her mother's place, and been her advisers on many points upon which men seldom feel at liberty to address a girl.

She was just one of them; she played whist and billiards with them, and made their cocktails for them, not scorning to take one herself occasionally. Indeed, Tommy's cocktails were things of fame in Southdown, and the professional compounders of drinks always bowed respectfully to her as though acknowledging a powerful rival.

Now all these things displeased and puzzled Jay Ellington Harper, and Tommy knew it full well, but clung to her old manner of living with a stubborn pertinacity, feeling somehow that to change would be both foolish and disloyal to the Old Boys. And as things went on, the seven Old Boys made greater demands upon her time than ever, for they were shrewd men, most of them, and had not lived fifty years in this world without learning a few things and unlearning many more. And while Tommy lived on in the blissful delusion that her role of indifference was perfectly played and without a flaw, they suspected how things were going and were perplexed as to the outcome. Still, their confidence was by no means shaken, and as Joe Elsworth said to Joe Sawyer one evening at billiards, "I think we can pretty nearly depend on Tommy's good sense."

There were too wise to say anything to Tommy, but they said just a word or two to Thomas Shirley, Sr., and combined to make things very unpleasant for Mr. Jay Ellington Harper.

At length their relations with Harper became so strained that the young man felt it would be better for him to leave town, so his father started him in a little bank of his own up in Red Willow. Red Willow, however, was scarcely a safe distance, being only some twenty-five miles north, upon the Divide, and Tommy occasionally found excuse to run up on her wheel to straighten out the young man's business for him. So when she suddenly decided to go East to school for a year, Thomas, Sr., drew a sigh of great relief. But the seven Old Boys shook their heads; they did not like to see her gravitating toward the East; it was a sign of weakening, they said, and showed an inclination to experiment with another kind of life, Jay Ellington Harper's kind.

But to school Tommy went, and from all reports conducted herself in a most seemly manner; made no more cocktails, played no more billiards. She took rather her own way with the curriculum, but she distinguished herself in athletics, which in Southdown counted for vastly more than erudition.

Her evident joy on getting back to Southdown was appreciated by everyone. She went about shaking hands with everybody, her shrewd face, that was so like a clever wholesome boy's, held high with happiness. As she said to old Joe Elsworth one morning, when they were driving behind his stud through a little thicket of cottonwood scattered along the sun-parched bluffs, "It's all very fine down East there, and the hills are great, but one gets mighty homesick for this sky, the old intense blue of it, you know. Down there the skies are all pale and smoky.

And this wind, this hateful, dear, old everlasting wind that comes down like the sweep of cavalry and is never tamed or broken, O Joe, I used to get hungry for this wind! I couldn't sleep in that lifeless stillness down there."

"How about the people, Tom?"

"O, they are fine enough folk, but we're not their sort, Joe, and never can be."

"You realize that, do you, fully?"

"Quite fully enough, thank you, Joe." She laughed rather dismally, and Joe cut his horse with the whip.

The only unsatisfactory thing about Tommy's return was that she brought with her a girl she had grown fond of at school, a dainty, white, languid bit of a thing, who used violet perfumes and carried a sunshade. The Old Boys said it was a bad sign when a rebellious girl like Tommy took to being sweet and gentle to one of her own sex, the worst sign in the world.

The new girl was no sooner in town than a new complication came about. There was no doubt of the impression she made on Jay Ellington Harper. She indisputably had all those little evidences of good breeding that were about the only things which could touch the timid, harassed young man who was so much out of his element. It was a very plain case on his part, and the souls of the seven were troubled within them. Said Joe Elsworth to the other Joe, "The heart of the cad is gone out to the little muff, as is right and proper and in accordance with the eternal fitness of things. But there's the other girl who has the blindness that may not be cured, and she gets all the rub of it. It's no use, I can't help her, and I am going to run down to Kansas City for awhile. I can't stay here and see the abominable suffering of it." He didn't go, however.

There was just one other person who understood the hopelessness of the situation quite as well as Joe, and that was Tommy. That is, she understood Harper's attitude. As to Miss Jessica's she was not quite so certain, for Miss Jessica, though pale and languid and addicted to sunshades, was a maiden most discreet. Conversations on the subject usually ended without any further information as to Miss Jessica's feelings, and Tommy sometimes wondered if she were capable of having any at all.

At last the calamity which Tommy had along foretold descended upon Jay Ellington Harper. One morning she received a telegram from him begging her to intercede with his father; there was a run on his bank and he must have help before noon. It was then ten thirty, and the one sleepy little train that ran up to Red Willow daily had crawled out of the station an hour before. Thomas Shirley, Sr., was not at home.

"And it's a good thing for Jay Ellington he's not, he might be more stony hearted than I," remarked Tommy, as she closed the ledger and turned to the terrified Miss Jessica. "Of course we're his only chance, no one else would turn their hand over to help him. The train went an hour ago and he says it must be there by noon. It's the only bank in the town, so nothing can be done by telegraph. There is nothing left but to wheel for it. I may make it, and I may not. Jess, you scamper up to the house and get my wheel out, the tire may need a little attention. I will be along in a minute."

"O, Theodosia, can't I go with you? I must go!"

"You go! Oh, yes, of course, if you want to. You know what you are getting into, though. It's twenty-five miles uppish grade and hilly, and only an hour and a quarter to do it in."

"Oh, Theodosia, I can do anything now!" cried Miss Jessica, as she put up her sunshade and fled precipitately. Tommy smiled as she began cramming bank notes into a canvas bag. "May be you can, my dear, and may be you can't."

The road from Southdown to Red Willow is not by any means a favorite bicycle road; it is rough, hilly and climbs from the river bottoms up to the big Divide by a steady up grade, running white and hot through the scorched corn fields and grazing lands where the long-horned Texan cattle browse about in the old buffalo wallows. Miss Jessica soon found that with the pedaling that had to be done there was little time left for emotion of any sort, or little sensibility for anything but the throbbing, dazzling heat that had to be endured. Down there in the valley the distant bluffs were vibrating and dancing with the heat, the cattle, completely overcome by it, had hidden under the shelving banks of the "draws" and the prairie dogs had fled to the bottom of their holes that are said to reach to water. The whirr of the seventeen-year locust was the only thing that spoke of animation, and that ground on as if only animated and enlivened by the sickening, destroying heat. The sun was like hot brass, and the wind that blew up from the south was hotter still. But Tommy knew that wind was their only chance. Miss Jessica began to feel that unless she could stop and get some water she was not much longer for this vale of tears. She suggested this possibility to Tommy, but Tommy only shook her head, "Take too much time," and bent over her handle bars, never lifting her eyes from the road in front of her. It flashed upon Miss Jessica that Tommy was not only very unkind, but that she sat very badly on her wheel and looked aggressively masculine and professional when she bent her shoulders and pumped like that. But just then Miss Jessica found it harder than ever to breathe, and the bluffs across the river began doing serpentines and skirt dances, and more important and personal considerations occupied the young lady.

When they were fairly over the first half of the road, Tommy took out her watch. "Have to hurry up, Jess. I can't wait for you."

"O, Tommy, I can't," panted Miss Jessica, dismounting and sitting down in a little heap by the roadside. "You go on, Tommy, and tell him—tell him I hope it won't fail, and I'd do anything to save him."

By this time the discreet Miss Jessica was reduced to tears, and Tommy nodded as she disappeared over the hill laughing to herself. "Poor Jess, anything but the one thing he needs. Well, your kind have the best of it generally, but in little affairs of this sort my kind come out rather strongly. We're rather better at them than at dancing. It's only fair, one side shouldn't have all."

Just at twelve o'clock, when Jay Ellington Harper, his collar crushed and wet about his throat, his eyeglass dimmed with perspiration, his hair hanging damp over his forehead, and even the ends of his moustache dripping with moisture, was attempting to reason with a score of angry Bohemians, Tommy came quietly through the door, grip in hand. She went straight behind the grating, and standing screened by the bookkeeper's desk, handed the bag to Harper and turned to the spokesman of the Bohemians.

"What's all this business mean, Anton? Do you all come to bank at once nowadays?"

"We want 'a money, want 'a our money, he no got it, no give it," bawled the big beery Bohemian.

"O, don't chaff 'em any longer, give 'em their money and get rid of 'em, I want to see you," said Tommy carelessly, as she went into the consulting room.

When Harper entered half an hour later, after the rush was over, all that was left of his usual immaculate appearance was his eyeglass and the white flower in his buttonhole.

"This has been terrible," he gasped. "Miss Theodosia, I can never thank you."

"No," interrupted Tommy. "You never can, and I don't want any thanks. It was rather a tight place, though, wasn't it? You looked like a ghost when I came in. What started them?"

"How should I know? They just came down like the wolf on the fold. It sounded like the approach of a ghost dance."

"And of course you had no reserve? O, I always told you this would come, it was inevitable with your charming methods. By the way, Jess sends her regrets and says she would do anything to save you. She started out with me, but she has fallen by the wayside. O, don't be alarmed, she is not hurt, just winded. I left her all bunched up by the road like a little white rabbit. I think the lack of romance in the escapade did her up about as much as anything; she is essentially romantic. If we had been on fiery steeds bespattered with foam I think she would have made it, but a wheel hurt her dignity. I'll tend bank; you'd better get your wheel and go and look her up and comfort her. And as soon as it is convenient, Jay, I wish you'd marry her and be done with it, I want to get this thing off my mind."

Jay Ellington Harper dropped into a chair and turned a shade whiter.

"Theodosia, what do you mean? Don't you understand what I said to you last fall, the night before you went to school? Don't you remember what I wrote you—"

Tommy sat down on the table beside him and looked seriously and frankly into his eyes.

"Now, see here, Jay Ellington, we have been playing a nice little game, and now it's time to quit. One must grow up sometime. You are horribly wrought up over Jess, and why deny it? She's your kind, and clean daft about you, so there is only one thing to do. That's all."

Jay Ellington wiped his brow, and felt unequal to the situation. Perhaps he really came nearer to being moved down to his stolid little depths than he ever had before. His voice shook a good deal and was very low as he answered her.

"You have been very good to me, I don't believe any woman could be at once so kind and clever. You almost made a man of even me."

"Well, I certainly didn't succeed. As to being good to you, that's rather a break, you know; I am amiable, but I am only flesh and blood after all. Since I have known you I have not been at all good, in any sense of the word, and I suspect I have been anything but clever. Now, take mercy upon Jess—and me—and go. Go on, that ride is beginning to tell on me. Such things strain one's nerve. . . . Thank Heaven he's gone at last and had sense enough not to say anything more. It was growing rather critical. As I told him I am not at all superhuman."

After Jay Ellington Harper had bowed himself out, when Tommy sat alone in the darkened office, watching the flapping blinds, with the bank books before her, she noticed a white flower on the floor. It was the one Jay Ellington Harper had worn in his coat and had dropped in his nervous agitation. She picked it up and stood holding it a moment, biting her lip. Then she dropped it into the grate and turned away, shrugging her thin shoulders.

"They are awful idiots, half of them, and never think of anything beyond their dinner. But O, how we do like 'em!"

The Burglar's Christmas

Two very shabby looking young men stood at the corner of Prairie Avenue and Eightieth Street, looking despondently at the carriages that whirled by. It was Christmas Eve, and the streets were full of vehicles; florists' wagons, grocers' carts and carriages. The streets were in that half-liquid, half-congealed condition peculiar to the streets of Chicago at that season of the year. The swift wheels that spun by sometimes threw the slush of mud and snow over the two young men who were talking on the corner.

"Well," remarked the elder of the two, "I guess we are at our rope's end, sure enough. How do you feel?"

"Pretty shaky. The wind's sharp tonight. If I had had anything to eat I mightn't mind it so much. There is simply no show. I'm sick of the whole business. Looks like there's nothing for it but the lake."

"O, nonsense, I thought you had more grit. Got anything left you can hock?"

"Nothing but my beard, and I am afraid they wouldn't find it worth a pawn ticket," said the younger man ruefully, rubbing the week's growth of stubble on his face.

"Got any folks anywhere? Now's your time to strike 'em if you have."

"Never mind if I have, they're out of the question."

"Well, you'll be out of it before many hours if you don't make a move of some sort. A man's got to eat. See here, I am going down to Longtin's saloon. I used to play the

72

banjo in there with a couple of coons, and I'll bone him for some of his free-lunch stuff. You'd better come along, perhaps they'll fill an order for two."

"How far down is it?"

"Well, it's clear downtown, of course, 'way down on Michigan avenue."

"Thanks, I guess I'll loaf around here. I don't feel equal to the walk, and the cars—well, the cars are crowded." His features drew themselves into what might have been a smile under happier circumstances.

"No, you never did like street cars, you're too aristocratic. See here, Crawford, I don't like leaving you here. You ain't good company for yourself tonight."

"Crawford? O, yes, that's the last one. There have been so many I forget them."

"Have you got a real name, anyway?"

"O, yes, but it's one of the ones I've forgotten. Don't you worry about me. You go along and get your free lunch. I think I had a row in Longtin's place once. I'd better not show myself there again." As he spoke the young man nodded and turned slowly up the avenue.

He was miserable enough to want to be quite alone. Even the crowd that jostled by him annoyed him. He wanted to think about himself. He had avoided this final reckoning with himself for a year now. He had laughed it off and drunk it off. But now, when all those artificial devices which are employed to turn our thoughts into other channels and shield us from ourselves had failed him, it must come. Hunger is a powerful incentive to introspection.

It is a tragic hour, that hour when we are finally driven to reckon with ourselves, when every avenue of mental distraction has been cut off and our own life and all its ineffaceable failures closes about us like the walls of that old torture chamber of the Inquisition. Tonight, as this man stood stranded in the streets of the city, his hour came. It was not the first time he had been hungry and desperate and alone. But always before there had been

some outlook, some chance ahead, some pleasure yet
untasted that seemed worth the effort, some face that he
fancied was, or would be, dear. But it was not so tonight.
The unyielding conviction was upon him that he had
failed in everything, had outlived everything. It had been
near him for a long time, that Pale Spectre. He had caught
its shadow at the bottom of his glass many a time, at the
head of his bed when he was sleepless at night, in the
twilight shadows when some great sunset broke upon
him. It had made life hateful to him when he awoke in the
morning before now. But now it settled slowly over him,
like night, the endless Northern nights that bid the sun
a long farewell. It rose up before him like granite. From
this brilliant city with its glad bustle of Yuletide he was
shut off as completely as though he were a creature of
another species. His days seemed numbered and done,
sealed over like the little coral cells at the bottom of the
sea. Involuntarily he drew that cold air through his lungs
slowly, as though he were tasting it for the last time.

Yet he was but four and twenty, this man—he looked
even younger—and he had a father some place down East
who had been very proud of him once. Well, he had
taken his life into his own hands, and this was what he
had made of it. That was all there was to be said. He
could remember the hopeful things they used to say about
him at college in the old days, before he had cut away and
begun to live by his wits, and he found courage to smile
at them now. They had read him wrongly. He knew now
that he never had the essentials of success, only the superficial agility that is often mistaken for it. He was tow
without the tinder, and he had burnt himself out at other
people's fires. He had helped other people to make it win,
but he himself—he had never touched an enterprise that
had not failed eventually. Or, if it survived his connection
with it, it left him behind.

His last venture had been with some ten-cent specialty
company, a little lower than all the others, that had gone
to pieces in Buffalo, and he had worked his way to Chi-

cago by boat. When the boat made up its crew for the outward voyage, he was dispensed with as usual. He was used to that. The reason for it? O, there are so many reasons for failure! His was a very common one.

As he stood there in the wet under the street light he drew up his reckoning with the world and decided that it had treated him as well as he deserved. He had overdrawn his account once too often. There had been a day when he thought otherwise; when he had said he was unjustly handled, that his failure was merely the lack of proper adjustment between himself and other men, that some day he would be recognized and it would all come right. But he knew better than that now, and he was still man enough to bear no grudge against any one—man or woman.

Tonight was his birthday, too. There seemed something particularly amusing in that. He turned up a limp little coat collar to try to keep a little of the wet chill from his throat, and instinctively began to remember all the birthday parties he used to have. He was so cold and empty that his mind seemed unable to grapple with any serious question. He kept thinking about gingerbread and frosted cakes like a child. He could remember the splendid birthday parties his mother used to give him, when all the other little boys in the block came in their Sunday clothes and creaking shoes, with their ears still red from their mother's towel, and the pink and white birthday cake, and the stuffed olives and all the dishes of which he had been particularly fond, and how he would eat and eat and then go to bed and dream of Santa Claus. And in the morning he would awaken and eat again, until by night the family doctor arrived with his castor oil, and poor William used to dolefully say that it was altogether too much to have your birthday and Christmas all at once. He could remember, too, the royal birthday suppers he had given at college, and the stag dinners, and the toasts, and the music, and the good fellows who had wished him happiness and really meant what they said.

And since then there were other birthday suppers that he could not remember so clearly; the memory of them was heavy and flat, like cigarette smoke that has been shut in a room all night, like champagne that has been a day opened, a song that has been too often sung, an acute sensation that has been overstrained. They seemed tawdry and garish, discordant to him now. He rather wished he could forget them altogether.

Whichever way his mind now turned there was one thought that it could not escape, and that was the idea of food. He caught the scent of a cigar suddenly, and felt a sharp pain in the pit of his abdomen and a sudden moisture in his mouth. His cold hands clenched angrily, and for a moment he felt that bitter hatred of wealth, of ease, of everything that is well fed and well housed that is common to starving men. At any rate he had a right to eat! He had demanded great things from the world once: fame and wealth and admiration. Now it was simply bread—and he would have it! He looked about him quickly and felt the blood begin to stir in his veins. In all his straits he had never stolen anything, his tastes were above it. But tonight there would be no tomorrow. He was amused at the way in which the idea excited him. Was it possible there was yet one more experience that would distract him, one thing that had power to excite his jaded interest? Good! he had failed at everything else, now he would see what his chances would be as a common thief. It would be amusing to watch the beautiful consistency of his destiny work itself out even in that role. It would be interesting to add another study to his gallery of futile attempts, and then label them all: "the failure as a journalist," "the failure as a lecturer," "the failure as a business man," "the failure as a thief," and so on, like the titles under the pictures of the Dance of Death. It was time that Childe Roland came to the dark tower.

A girl hastened by him with her arms full of packages. She walked quickly and nervously, keeping well within the shadow, as if she were not accustomed to carrying bundles and did not care to meet any of her friends. As she crossed the muddy street, she made an effort to lift her skirt a little, and as she did so one of the packages slipped unnoticed from beneath her arm. He caught it up and overtook her. "Excuse me, but I think you dropped something."

She started, "O, yes, thank you, I would rather have lost anything than that."

The young man turned angrily upon himself. The package must have contained something of value. Why had he not kept it? Was this the sort of thief he would make? He ground his teeth together. There is nothing more maddening than to have morally consented to crime and then lack the nerve force to carry it out.

A carriage drove up to the house before which he stood. Several richly dressed women alighted and went in. It was a new house, and must have been built since he was in Chicago last. The front door was open and he could see down the hallway and up the staircase. The servant had left the door and gone with the guests. The first floor was brilliantly lighted, but the windows upstairs were dark. It looked very easy, just to slip upstairs to the darkened chambers where the jewels and trinkets of the fashionable occupants were kept.

Still burning with impatience against himself he entered quickly. Instinctively he removed his mud-stained hat as he passed quickly and quietly up the stair case. It struck him as being a rather superfluous courtesy in a burglar, but he had done it before he had thought. His way was clear enough, he met no one on the stairway or in the upper hall. The gas was lit in the upper hall. He passed the first chamber door through sheer cowardice. The second he entered quickly, thinking of something else lest his courage should fail him, and closed the door behind him. The light from the hall shone into the room through the transom. The apartment was finished richly enough to justify his expectations. He went at once to the dressing case. A number of rings and small trinkets lay in a silver tray. These he put hastily in his pocket. He opened the upper drawer and found, as he expected, several leather cases. In the first he opened was a lady's watch, in the second a pair of old-fashioned bracelets; he seemed to dimly remember having seen bracelets like them before, somewhere. The third case was heavier, the spring was much worn, and it opened easily. It held a cup of some kind. He held it up to the light and then his strained nerves gave way and he uttered a sharp exclamation. It was the silver mug he used to drink from when he was a little boy.

The door opened, and a woman stood in the doorway facing him. She was a tall woman, with white hair, in evening dress. The light from the hall streamed in upon him, but she was not afraid. She stood looking at him a moment, then she threw out her hand and went quickly toward him.

"Willie, Willie! Is it you?"

He struggled to loose her arms from him, to keep her lips from his cheek. "Mother—you must not! You do not understand! Oh, my God, this is worst of all!" Hunger, weakness, cold, shame, all came back to him, and shook his self-control completely. Physically he was too weak to stand a shock like this. Why could it not have been an ordinary discovery, arrest, the station house and all the rest of it. Anything but this! A hard dry sob broke from him. Again he strove to disengage himself.

"Who is it says I shall not kiss my son? Oh, my boy, we have waited so long for this! You have been so long in coming, even I almost gave you up."

Her lips upon his cheek burnt him like fire. He put his hand to his throat, and spoke thickly and incoherently: "You do not understand. I did not know you were here. I came here to rob—it is the first time—I swear it—but I am a common thief. My pockets are full of your jewels now. Can't you hear me? I am a common thief!"

"Hush, my boy, those are ugly words. How could you rob your own house? How could you take what is your own? They are all yours, my son, as wholly yours as my great love—and you can't doubt that, Will, do you?"

That soft voice, the warmth and fragrance of her person stole through his chill, empty veins like a gentle stimulant. He felt as though all his strength were leaving him and even consciousness. He held fast to her and bowed his head on her strong shoulder, and groaned aloud.

"O, mother, life is hard, hard!"

She said nothing, but held him closer. And O, the strength of those white arms that held him! O, the assurance of safety in that warm bosom that rose and fell under his cheek! For a moment they stood so, silently. Then they heard a heavy step upon the stair. She led him to a chair and went out and closed the door. At the top of the staircase she met a tall, broad-shouldered man, with iron gray hair, and a face alert and stern. Her eyes were shining and her cheeks on fire, her whole face was one expression of intense determination.

"James, it is William in there, come home. You must keep him at any cost. If he goes this time, I go with him. O, James, be easy with him, he has suffered so." She broke from a command to an entreaty, and laid her hand on his shoulder. He looked questioningly at her a moment, then went in the room and quietly shut the door.

She stood leaning against the wall, clasping her temples with her hands and listening to the low indistinct sound of the voices within. Her own lips moved silently. She waited a long time, scarcely breathing. At last the door opened, and her husband came out. He stopped to say in a shaken voice,

"You go to him now, he will stay. I will go to my room. I will see him again in the morning."

She put her arm about his neck, "O, James, I thank you, I thank you! This is the night he came so long ago, you remember? I gave him to you then, and now you give him back to me!"

"Don't, Helen," he muttered. "He is my son, I have never forgotten that. I failed with him. I don't like to fail, it cuts my pride. Take him and make a man of him." He passed on down the hall.

She flew into the room where the young man sat with his head bowed upon his knee. She dropped to her knees beside him. Ah, it was so good to him to feel those arms again!

"He is so glad, Willie, so glad! He may not show it, but he is as happy as I. He never was demonstrative with either of us, you know."

"O, my God, he was good enough," groaned the man. "I told him everything, and he was good enough. I don't see how either of you can look at me, speak to me, touch me." He shivered under her clasp again as when she had first touched him, and tried weakly to throw her off.

But she whispered softly,

"This is my right, my son."

Presently, when he was calmer, she rose. "Now, come with me into the library, and I will have your dinner brought there."

As they went downstairs she remarked apologetically, "I will not call Ellen tonight; she has a number of guests to attend to. She is a big girl now, you know, and came out last winter. Besides, I want you all to myself tonight."

When the dinner came, and it came very soon, he fell upon it savagely. As he ate she told him all that had transpired during the years of his absence, and how his father's business had brought them there. "I was glad when we came. I thought you would drift West. I seemed a good deal nearer to you here."

There was a gentle unobtrusive sadness in her tone that was too soft for a reproach.

"Have you everything you want? It is a comfort to see you eat."

He smiled grimly, "It is certainly a comfort to me. I have not indulged in this frivolous habit for some thirty-five hours."

She caught his hand and pressed it sharply, uttering a quick remonstrance.

"Don't say that! I know, but I can't hear you say it—it's too terrible! My boy, food has choked me many a time when I have thought of the possibility of that. Now take the old lounging chair by the fire, and if you are too tired to talk, we will just sit and rest together."

He sank into the depths of the big leather chair with the lions' heads on the arms, where he had sat so often in the days when his feet did not touch the floor and he was half afraid of the grim monsters cut in the polished wood. That chair seemed to speak to him of things long forgotten. It was like the touch of an old familiar friend. He felt a sudden yearning tenderness for the happy little boy who had sat there and dreamed of the big world so long ago. Alas, he had been dead many a summer, that little boy!

He sat looking up at the magnificent woman beside him. He had almost forgotten how handsome she was; how lustrous and sad were the eyes that set under that serene brow, how impetuous and wayward the mouth even now, how superb the white throat and shoulders! Ah, the wit and grace and fineness of this woman! He remembered how proud he had been of her as a boy when she came to see him at school. Then in the deep red coals of the grate he saw the faces of other women who had come since then into his vexed, disordered life. Laughing faces, with eyes artifically bright, eyes without depth or meaning, features without the stamp of high sensibilities. And he had left this face for such as those!

He sighed restlessly and laid his hand on hers. There seemed refuge and protection in the touch of her, as in the old days when he was afraid of the dark. He had been in the dark so long now, his confidence was so thoroughly shaken, and he was bitterly afraid of the night and of himself.

"Ah, mother, you make other things seem so false. You must feel that I owe you an explanation, but I can't make any, even to myself. Ah, but we make poor exchanges in life. I can't make out the riddle of it all. Yet there are things I ought to tell you before I accept your confidence like this."

"I'd rather you wouldn't, Will. Listen: Between you and me there can be no secrets. We are more alike than other people. Dear boy, I know all about it. I am a woman, and circumstances were different with me, but we are of one blood. I have lived all your life before you. You have never had an impulse that I have not known, you have never touched a brink that my feet have not trod. This is your birthday night. Twenty-four years ago I foresaw all this. I was a young woman then and I had hot battles of my own, and I felt your likeness to me. You were not like other babies. From the hour you were born you were restless and discontented, as I had been before you. You used to brace your strong little limbs against mine and try to throw me off as you did tonight. Tonight you have come back to me, just as you always did after you ran away to swim in the river that was forbidden you, the river you loved because it was forbidden. You are tired and sleepy, just as you used to be then, only a little older and a little paler and a little more foolish. I never asked you where you had been then, nor will I now. You have come back to me, that's all in all to me. I know your every possibility and limitation, as a composer knows his instrument."

He found no answer that was worthy to give to talk like this. He had not found life easy since he had lived by his wits. He had come to know poverty at close quarters. He had known what it was to be gay with an empty pocket, to wear violets in his buttonhole when he had not breakfasted, and all the hateful shams of the poverty of idleness. He had been a reporter on a big metropolitan daily, where men grind out their brains on paper until they have not one idea left—and still grind on. He had worked in a real estate office, where ignorant men were swindled. He had sung in a comic opera chorus and played Harris in an *Uncle Tom's Cabin* company, and edited a socialist weekly. He had been dogged by debt and hunger and grinding poverty, until to sit here by a warm fire without concern as to how it would be paid for seemed unnatural.

He looked up at her questioningly. "I wonder if you know how much you pardon?"

"O, my poor boy, much or little, what does it matter? Have you wandered so far and paid such a bitter price for knowledge and not yet learned that love has nothing to do with pardon or forgiveness, that it only loves, and loves—and loves? They have not taught you well, the women of your world." She leaned over and kissed him, as no woman had kissed him since he left her.

He drew a long sigh of rich content. The old life, with all its bitterness and useless antagonism and flimsy sophistries, its brief delights that were always tinged with fear and distrust and unfaith, that whole miserable, futile, swindled world of Bohemia seemed immeasurably distant and far away, like a dream that is over and done. And as the chimes rang joyfully outside and sleep pressed heavily upon his eyelids, he wondered dimly if the Author of this sad little riddle of ours were not able to solve it after all, and if the Potter would not finally mete out his all comprehensive justice, such as none but he could have, to his Things of Clay, which are made in his own patterns, weak or strong, for his own ends; and if some day we will not awaken and find that all evil is a dream, a mental distortion that will pass when the dawn shall break.

Nanette: An Aside

Of course you do not know Nanette. You go to hear Tradutorri, go every night she is in the cast perhaps, and rave for days afterward over her voice, her beauty, her power, and when all is said the thing you most admire is a something which has no name, the indescribable quality which is Tradutorri herself. But of Nanette, the preserver of Madame's beauty, the mistress of Madame's finances, the executrix of Madame's affairs, the power behind the scenes, of course you know nothing.

It was after twelve o'clock when Nanette entered Madame's sleeping apartments at the Savoy and threw up the blinds, for Tradutorri always slept late after a performance. Last night it was *Cavalleria Rusticana*, and Santuzza is a trying role when it is enacted not merely with the emotions but with the soul, and it is this peculiar soul-note that has made Tradutorri great and unique among the artists of her generation.

"Madame has slept well, I hope?" inquired Nanette respectfully, as she presented herself at the foot of the bed.

"As well as usual, I believe," said Tradutorri rather wearily. "You have brought my breakfast? Well, you may put it here and put the ribbons in my gown while I eat. I will get up afterward."

Nanette took a chair by the bed and busied herself with a mass of white tulle.

"We leave America next week, Madame?"

"Yes, Friday; on the *Paris*," said Madame, absently glancing up from her strawberries. "Why, Nanette, you are crying! One would think you had sung 'Voi lo sapete' yourself last night. What is the matter, my child?"

"O, it is nothing worthy of Madame's notice. One is always sorry to say good bye, that is all."

"To one's own country, perhaps, but this is different. You have no friends here; pray, why should you be sorry to go?"

"Madame is mistaken when she says I have no friends here."

"Friends! Why, I thought you saw no one. Who, for example?"

"Well, there is a gentleman—"

"Bah! Must there always be a 'gentleman,' even with you? But who is this fellow? Go on!"

"Surely Madame has noticed?"

"Not I; I have noticed nothing. I have been very absentminded, rather ill, and abominably busy. Who is it?"

"Surely Madame must have noticed Signor Luongo, the head waiter?"

"The tall one, you mean, with the fine head like poor Sandro Salvini's? Yes, certainly I have noticed him; he is a very impressive piece of furniture. Well, what of him?"

"Nothing, Madame, but that he is very desirous that I should marry him."

"Indeed! And you?"

"I could wish for no greater happiness on earth, Madame."

Tradutorri laid a strawberry stem carefully upon her plate.

"Um-m-m, let me see; we have been here just two months and this affair has all come about. You have profited by your stage training, Nanette."

"O, Madame! Have you forgotten last season? We stopped here for six weeks then."

"The same 'gentleman' for two successive seasons? You

are very disappointing, Nanette. You have not profited by
your opportunities after all."

"Madame is pleased to jest, but I assure her that it is a
very serious affair to me."

"O, yes, they all are. *Affaires très sérieux.* That is scarcely
an original remark, Nanette. I think I remember having
made it once myself."

The look of bitter unbelief that Nanette feared came over
Madame's face. Presently, as Nanette said nothing, Tradutorri spoke again.

"So you expect me to believe that this is really a serious
matter?"

"No, Madame," said Nanette quietly. "He believes it
and I believe. It is not necessary that any one else should."

Madame glanced curiously at the girl's face, and when
she spoke again it was in a different tone.

"Very well: I do not see any objection. I need a man. It
is not a bad thing to have your own porter in London,
and after our London engagement is over we will go
directly to Paris. He can take charge of my house there,
my present steward is not entirely satisfactory, you know.
You can spend the summer together there and doubtless
by next season you can endure to be separated from him
for a few months. So stop crying and send this statuesque
signor to me tomorrow, and I will arrange matters. I want
you to be happy, my girl—at least to try."

"Madame is good—too good, as always. I know your
great heart. Out of your very compassion you would
burden yourself with this man because I fancy him, as
you once burdened yourself with me. But that is impossible, Madame. He would never leave New York. He will
have his wife to himself or not at all. Very many professional people stay here, not all like Madame, and he has
his prejudices. He would never allow me to travel, not
even with Madame. He is very firm in these matters."

"O, ho! So he has prejudices against our profession,
this *garçon*? Certainly you have contrived to do the usual

thing in a very usual manner. You have fallen in with a man who objects to your work."

Tradutorri pushed the tray away from her and lay down laughing a little as she threw her arms over her head.

"You see, Madame, that is where all the trouble comes. For of course I could not leave you."

Tradutorri looked up sharply, almost pleadingly, into Nanette's face.

"Leave me? Good Heavens, no. Of course you can not leave me. Why who could ever learn all the needs of my life as you know them? What I may eat and what I may not, when I may see people and when they will tire me, what costumes I can wear and at what temperature I can have my baths. You know I am as helpless as a child in these matters. Leave me? The possibility has never occurred to me. Why, girl, I have grown fond of you! You have come entirely into my life. You have been my confidante and friend, the only creature I have trusted these last ten years. Leave me? I think it would break my heart. Come, brush out my hair, I will get up. The thing is impossible!"

"So I told him, Madame," said Nanette tragically. "I said to him: 'Had it pleased Heaven to give me a voice I should have given myself wholly to my art, without one reservation, without one regret, as Madame has done. As it is, I am devoted to Madame and her art as long as she has need of me.' Yes, that is what I said."

Tradutorri looked gravely at Nanette's face in the glass. "I am not at all sure that either I or my art are worth it, Nanette."

II

Tradutorri had just returned from her last performance in New York. It had been one of those eventful nights when the audience catches fire and drives a singer to her best, drives her beyond herself until she is greater than she knows or means to be. Now that it was over she was utterly exhausted and the life-force in her was low.

I have said she is the only woman of our generation who sings with the soul rather than the senses, the only one indeed since Malibran, who died of that prodigal expense of spirit. Other singers there are who feel and vent their suffering. Their methods are simple and transparent: they pour out their self-inflicted anguish and when it is over they are merely tired as children are after excitement. But Tradutorri holds back her suffering within herself; she suffers as the flesh and blood women of her century suffer. She is intense without being emotional. She takes this great anguish of hers and lays it in a tomb and rolls a stone before the door and walls it up. You wonder that one woman's heart can hold a grief so great. It is this stifled pain that wrings your heart when you hear her, that gives you the impression of horrible reality. It is this too, of which she is slowly dying now.

See, in all great impersonation there are two stages. One in which the object is the generation of emotional power; to produce from one's own brain a whirlwind that will sweep the commonplaces of the world away from the naked souls of men and women and leave them defenseless and strange to each other. The other is the conservation of all this emotional energy; to bind the whirlwind down within one's straining heart, to feel the tears of many burning in one's eyes and yet not to weep, to hold all these chaotic faces still and silent within one's self until out of this tempest of pain and passion there speaks the still, small voice unto the soul of man. This is the theory of "repression." This is classical art, art exalted, art deified. And of all the mighty artists of her time Tradutorri is the only woman who has given us art like this. And now she is dying of it, they say.

Nanette was undoing Madame's shoes. She had put the mail silently on the writing desk. She had not given it to her before the performance as there was one of those blue letters from Madame's husband, written in an unsteady hand with the postmark of Monte Carlo, which always made Madame weep and were always answered by large drafts. There was also another from Madame's little crippled daughter hidden away in a convent in Italy.

"I will see to my letters presently, Nanette. With me news is generally bad news. I wish to speak with you tonight. We leave New York in two days, and the glances of this signor statuesque of yours are more than I can endure. I feel a veritable *mère Capulet*."

"Has he dared to look impertinently at Madame? I will see that this is stopped."

"You think that you could be really happy with this man, Nanette?"

Nanette was sitting upon the floor with the flowers from Madame's corsage in her lap. She rested her sharp little chin on her hand.

"Is any one really happy, Madame? But this I know, that I could endure to be very unhappy always to be with him." Her saucy little French face grew grave and her lips trembled.

Madame Tradutorri took her hand tenderly.

"Then if you feel like that I have nothing to say. How strange that this should come to you, Nanette; it never has to me. Listen: Your mother and I were friends once when we both sang in the chorus in a miserable little theatre in Naples. She sang quite as well as I then, and she was a handsome girl and her future looked brighter than mine. But somehow in the strange lottery of art I rose and she went under with the wheel. She had youth, beauty, vigor, but was one of the countless thousands who fail. When I found her years afterward, dying in a charity hospital in Paris, I took you from her. You were scarcely ten years old then. If you had sung I should have given you the best instruction; as it was I was only able to save you from that most horrible of fates, the chorus. You have been with me so long. Through all my troubles you were the one person who did not change toward me. You have become indispensable to me, but I am no longer so to you. I have inquired as to the reputation of this signor of yours from the proprietors of the house and I find it excellent. Ah, Nanette, did you really think I could stand between you and happiness? You have been a good girl, Nanette. You have stayed with me when we did not stop at hotels like this one, and when your wages were not paid you for weeks together."

"Madame, it is you who have been good! Always giving and giving to a poor girl like me with no voice at all. You know that I would not leave you for anything in the world but this."

"Are you sure you can be happy so? Think what it means! No more music, no more great personages, no more plunges from winter to summer in a single night, no more Russia, no more Paris, no more Italy. Just a little house somewhere in a strange country with a man who may have faults of his own, and perhaps little children growing up about you to be cared for always. You have been used to changes and money and excitement, and those habits of life are hard to change, my girl."

"Madame, you know how it is. One sees much and stops at the best hotels, and goes to the best milliners— and yet one is not happy, but a stranger always. That is, I mean—"

"Yes, I know too well what you mean. Don't spoil it now you have said it. And yet one is not happy! You will not be lonely, you think, all alone in this big strange city, so far from our world?"

"Alone! Why, Madame, Arturo is here!"

Tradutorri looked wistfully at her shining face.

"How strange that this should come to you, Nanette. Be very happy in it, dear. Let nothing come between you and it; no desire, no ambition. It is not given to every one. There are women who wear crowns who would give them for an hour of it."

"O, Madame, if I could but see you happy before I leave you!"

"Hush, we will not speak of that. When the flowers

thrown me in my youth shall live again, or when the dead crater of my own mountain shall be red once more—then, perhaps. Now go and tell your lover that the dragon has renounced her prey."

"Madame, I rebel against this loveless life of yours! You should be happy. Surely with so much else you should at least have that."

Tradutorri pulled up from her dressing case the score of the last great opera written in Europe which had been sent her to originate the title role.

"You see this, Nanette? When I began life, between me and this lay everything dear in life—every love, every human hope. I have had to bury what lay between. It is the same thing florists do when they cut away all the buds that one flower may blossom with the strength of all. God is a very merciless artist, and when he works out his purposes in the flesh his chisel does not falter. But no more of this, my child. Go find your lover. I shall undress alone tonight. I must get used to it. Good night, my dear. You are the last of them all, the last of all who have brought warmth into my life. You must let me kiss you tonight. No, not that way—on the lips. Such a happy face tonight, Nanette! May it be so always!"

After Nanette was gone Madame put her head down on her dressing case and wept, those lonely tears of utter wretchedness that a homesick girl sheds at school. And yet upon her brow shone the coronet that the nations had given her when they called her queen.

Eric Hermannson's Soul

It was a great night at the Lone Star schoolhouse—a night when the Spirit was present with power and when God was very near to man. So it seemed to Asa Skinner, servant of God and Free Gospeller. The schoolhouse was crowded with the saved and sanctified, robust men and women, trembling and quailing before the power of some mysterious psychic force. Here and there among this cowering, sweating multitude crouched some poor wretch who had felt the pangs of an awakened conscience, but had not yet experienced that complete divestment of reason, that frenzy born of a convulsion of the mind, which, in the parlance of the Free Gospellers, is termed "the Light." On the floor before the mourners' bench lay the unconscious figure of a man in whom outraged nature had sought her last resort. This "trance" state is the highest evidence of grace among the Free Gospellers, and indicates a close walking with God.

Before the desk stood Asa Skinner, shouting of the mercy and vengeance of God, and in his eyes shone a terrible earnestness, an almost prophetic flame. Asa was a converted train gambler who used to run between Omaha and Denver. He was a man made for the extremes of life; from the most debauched of men he had become the most ascetic. His was a bestial face, a face that bore the stamp of Nature's eternal injustice. The forehead was low, projecting over the eyes, and the sandy hair was plastered down over it and then brushed back at an abrupt right angle. The chin was heavy, the nostrils were low and wide, and the lower lip hung loosely except in his moments of spasmodic earnestness, when it shut like a steel trap. Yet about those coarse features there were deep, rugged furrows, the scars of many a hand-to-hand struggle with the weakness of the flesh, and about that drooping lip were sharp, strenuous lines that had conquered it and taught it to pray. Over those seamed cheeks there was a certain pallor, a grayness caught from many a vigil. It was as though, after Nature had done her worst with that face, some fine chisel had gone over it, chastening and almost transfiguring it. Tonight, as his muscles twitched with emotion, and the perspiration dropped from his hair and chin, there was a certain convincing power in the man. For Asa Skinner was a man possessed of a belief, of that sentiment of the sublime before which all inequalities are leveled, that transport of conviction which seems superior to all laws of condition, under which debauchees have become martyrs; which made a tinker an artist and a camel-driver the founder of an empire. This was with Asa Skinner tonight, as he stood proclaiming the vengeance of God.

It might have occurred to an impartial observer that Asa Skinner's God was indeed a vengeful God if he could reserve vengeance for those of his creatures who were packed into the Lone Star schoolhouse that night. Poor exiles of all nations; men from the south and the north, peasants from almost every country of Europe, most of them from the mountainous, night-bound coast of Norway. Honest men for the most part, but men with whom the world had dealt hardly; the failures of all countries, men sobered by toil and saddened by exile, who had been driven to fight for the dominion of an untoward soil, to sow where others should gather, the advance guard of a mighty civilization to be.

Never had Asa Skinner spoken more earnestly than now. He felt that the Lord had this night a special work for him to do. Tonight Eric Hermannson, the wildest lad on all the Divide, sat in his audience with a fiddle on his knee, just as he had dropped in on his way to play for some dance. The violin is an object of particular abhorrence to the Free Gospellers. Their antagonism to the church organ is bitter enough, but the fiddle they regard as a very incarnation of evil desires, singing forever of worldly pleasures and inseparably associated with all forbidden things.

Eric Hermannson had long been the object of the prayers of the revivalists. His mother had felt the power of the Spirit weeks ago, and special prayer-meetings had been held at her house for her son. But Eric had only gone his ways laughing, the ways of youth, which are short enough at best, and none too flowery on the Divide. He slipped away from the prayer-meetings to meet the Campbell boys in Genereau's saloon, or hug the plump little French girls at Chevalier's dances, and sometimes, of a summer night, he even went across the dewy cornfields and through the wild-plum thicket to play the fiddle for Lena Hanson, whose name was a reproach through all the Divide country, where the women are usually too plain and too busy and too tired to depart from the ways of virtue. On such occasions Lena, attired in a pink wrapper and silk stockings and tiny pink slippers, would sing to him, accompanying herself on a battered guitar. It gave him a delicious sense of freedom and experience to be with a woman who, no matter how, had lived in big cities and knew the ways of town folk, who had never worked in the fields and had kept her hands white and soft, her throat fair and tender, who had heard great singers in Denver and Salt Lake, and who knew the strange language of flattery and idleness and mirth.

Yet, careless as he seemed, the frantic prayers of his mother were not altogether without their effect upon Eric. For days he had been fleeing before them as a criminal from his pursuers, and over his pleasures had fallen the shadow of something dark and terrible that dogged his steps. The harder he danced, the louder he sang, the more was he conscious that this phantom was gaining upon him, that in time it would track him down. One Sunday afternoon, late in the fall, when he had been drinking beer with Lena Hanson and listening to a song which made his cheeks burn, a rattlesnake had crawled out of the side of the sod house and thrust its ugly head in under the screen door. He was not afraid of snakes, but he knew enough of Gospellism to feel the significance of the reptile lying coiled there upon her doorstep. His lips were cold when he kissed Lena goodbye, and he went there no more.

The final barrier between Eric and his mother's faith was his violin, and to that he clung as a man sometimes will cling to his dearest sin, to the weakness more precious to him than all his strength. In the great world beauty comes to men in many guises, and art in a hundred forms, but for Eric there was only his violin. It stood, to him, for all the manifestations of art; it was his only bridge into the kingdom of the soul.

It was to Eric Hermannson that the evangelist directed his impassioned pleading that night.

"*Saul, Saul, why persecutest thou me?* Is there a Saul here tonight who has stopped his ears to that gentle pleading, who has thrust a spear into that bleeding side? Think of it, my brother; you are offered this wonderful love and you prefer the worm that dieth not and the fire which will not be quenched. What right have you to lose one of God's precious souls? *Saul, Saul, why persecutest thou me?*"

A great joy dawned in Asa Skinner's pale face, for he saw that Eric Hermannson was swaying to and fro in his seat. The minister fell upon his knees and threw his long arms over his head.

"O my brothers! I feel it coming, the blessing we have prayed for. I tell you the Spirit is coming! Just a little more prayer, brothers, a little more zeal, and he will be here. I can feel his cooling wing upon my brow. Glory be to God forever and ever, amen!"

The whole congregation groaned under the pressure of this spiritual panic. Shouts and hallelujahs went up from every lip. Another figure fell prostrate upon the floor. From the mourners' bench rose a chant of terror and rapture:

> "Eating honey and drinking wine,
>   *Glory to the bleeding Lamb!*
> I am my Lord's and he is mine,
>   *Glory to the bleeding Lamb!*"

The hymn was sung in a dozen dialects and voiced all the vague yearning of these hungry lives, of these people who had starved all the passions so long, only to fall victims to the basest of them all, fear.

A groan of ultimate anguish rose from Eric Hermannson's bowed head, and the sound like the groan of a great tree when it falls in the forest.

The minister rose suddenly to his feet and threw back his head, crying in a loud voice:

"*Lazarus, come forth!* Eric Hermannson, you are lost, going down at sea. In the name of God, and Jesus Christ his Son, I throw you the life line. Take hold! Almighty God, my soul for his!" The minister threw his arms out and lifted his quivering face.

Eric Hermannson rose to his feet; his lips were set and the lightning was in his eyes. He took his violin by the neck and crushed it to splinters across his knee, and to Asa Skinner the sound was like the shackles of sin broken audibly asunder.

II

For more than two years Eric Hermannson kept the austere faith to which he had sworn himself, kept it until a girl from the East came to spend a week on the Nebraska Divide. She was a girl of other manners and conditions, and there were greater distances between her life and Eric's than all the miles which separated Rattlesnake

Creek from New York City. Indeed, she had no business to be in the West at all; but ah! across what leagues of land and sea, by what improbable chances, do the unrelenting gods bring to us our fate!

It was in a year of financial depression that Wyllis Elliot came to Nebraska to buy cheap land and revisit the country where he had spent a year of his youth. When he had graduated from Harvard it was still customary for moneyed gentlemen to send their scapegrace sons to rough it on ranches in the wilds of Nebraska or Dakota, or to consign them to a living death in the sagebrush of the Black Hills. These young men did not always return to the ways of civilized life. But Wyllis Elliot had not married a half-breed, nor been shot in a cowpunchers' brawl, nor wrecked by bad whisky, nor appropriated by a smirched adventuress. He had been saved from these things by a girl, his sister, who had been very near to his life ever since the days when they read fairy tales together and dreamed the dreams that never come true. On this, his first visit to his father's ranch since he left it six years before, he brought her with him. She had been laid up half the winter from a sprain received while skating, and had had too much time for reflection during those months. She was restless and filled with a desire to see something of the wild country of which her brother had told her so much. She was to be married the next winter, and Wyllis understood her when she begged him to take her with him on this long, aimless jaunt across the continent, to taste the last of their freedom together. It comes to all women of her type—that desire to taste the unknown which allures and terrifies, to run one's whole soul's length out to the wind—just once.

It had been an uneventful journey. Wyllis somehow understood that strain of gypsy blood in his sister, and he knew where to take her. They had slept in sod houses on the Platte River, made the acquaintance of the personnel of a third-rate opera company on the train to Deadwood, dined in a camp of railroad constructors at the world's end beyond New Castle, gone through the Black Hills on horseback, fished for trout in Dome Lake, watched a dance at Cripple Creek, where the lost souls who hide in the hills gathered for their besotted revelry. And now, last of all, before the return to thraldom, there was this little shack, anchored on the windy crest of the Divide, a little black dot against the flaming sunsets, a scented sea of cornland bathed in opalescent air and blinding sunlight.

Margaret Elliot was one of those women of whom there are so many in this day, when old order, passing, giveth place to new; beautiful, talented, critical, unsatisfied, tired of the world at twenty-four. For the moment the life and people of the Divide interested her. She was there but a week; perhaps had she stayed longer, that inexorable ennui which travels faster even than the Vestibule Limited would have overtaken her. The week she tarried there was the week that Eric Hermannson was helping Jerry Lockhart thresh; a week earlier or a week later, and there would have been no story to write.

It was on Thursday and they were to leave on Saturday. Wyllis and his sister were sitting on the wide piazza of the ranchhouse, staring out into the afternoon sunlight and protesting against the gusts of hot wind that blew up from the sandy riverbottom twenty miles to the southward.

The young man pulled his cap lower over his eyes and remarked:

"The wind is the real thing; you don't strike it anywhere else. You remember we had a touch of it in Algiers and I told you it came from Kansas. It's the keynote of this country."

Wyllis touched her hand that lay on the hammock and continued gently:

"I hope it's paid you, Sis. Roughing it's dangerous business; it takes the taste out of things."

She shut her fingers firmly over the brown hand that was so like her own.

"Paid? Why, Wyllis, I haven't been so happy since we were children and were going to discover the ruins of

Troy together some day. Do you know, I believe I could just stay on here forever and let the world go on its own gait. It seems as though the tension and strain we used to talk of last winter were gone for good, as though one could never give one's strength out to such petty things any more."

Wyllis brushed the ashes of his pipe away from the silk handkerchief that was knotted about his neck and stared moodily off at the skyline.

"No, you're mistaken. This would bore you after a while. You can't shake the fever of the other life. I've tried it. There was a time when the gay fellows of Rome could trot down into the Thebaid and burrow into the sandhills and get rid of it. But it's all too complex now. You see we've made our dissipations so dainty and respectable that they've gone further in than the flesh, and taken hold of the ego proper. You couldn't rest, even here. The war cry would follow you."

"You don't waste words, Wyllis, but you never miss fire. I talk more than you do, without saying half so much. You must have learned the art of silence from these taciturn Norwegians. I think I like silent men."

"Naturally," said Wyllis, "since you have decided to marry the most brilliant talker you know."

Both were silent for a time, listening to the sighing of the hot wind though the parched morning-glory vines. Margaret spoke first.

"Tell me, Wyllis, were many of the Norwegians you used to know as interesting as Eric Hermannson?"

"Who, Siegfried? Well, no. He used to be the flower of the Norwegian youth in my day, and he's rather an exception, even now. He has retrograded, though. The bonds of the soil have tightened on him, I fancy."

"Siegfried? Come, that's rather good, Wyllis. He looks like a dragon-slayer. What is it that makes him so different from the others? I can talk to him; he seems quite like a human being."

"Well," said Wyllis, meditatively, "I don't read Bourget

as much as my cultured sister, and I'm not so well up in analysis, but I fancy it's because one keeps cherishing a perfectly unwarranted suspicion that under that big, hulking anatomy of his, he may conceal a soul somewhere. *Nicht wahr?*"

"Something like that," said Margaret, thoughtfully, "except that it's more than a suspicion, and it isn't groundless. He has one, and he makes it known, somehow, without speaking."

"I always have my doubts about loquacious souls," Wyllis remarked, with the unbelieving smile that had grown habitual with him.

Margaret went on, not heeding the interruption. "I knew it from the first, when he told me about the suicide of his cousin, the Bernstein boy. That kind of blunt pathos can't be summoned at will in anybody. The earlier novelists rose to it, sometimes, unconsciously. But last night when I sang for him I was doubly sure. Oh, I haven't told you about that yet! Better light your pipe again. You see, he stumbled in on me in the dark when I was pumping away at that old parlor organ to please Mrs. Lockhart. It's her household fetish and I've forgotten how many pounds of butter she made and sold to buy it. Well, Eric stumbled in, and in some inarticulate manner made me understand that he wanted me to sing for him. I sang just the old things, of course. It's queer to sing familiar things here at the world's end. It makes one thing how the hearts of men have carried them around the world, into the waste of Iceland and the jungles of Africa and the islands of the Pacific. I think if one lived here long enough one would quite forget how to be trivial, and would read only the great books that we never get time to read in the world, and would remember only the great music, and the things that are really worth while would stand out clearly against that horizon over there. And of course I played the intermezzo from *Cavalleria Rusticana* for him; it goes rather better on an organ than most things do. He shuffled his feet and twisted his big hands up into knots and blurted out that he didn't know there was any music like that in the world. Why, there were tears in his voice, Wyllis! Yes, like Rossetti, I *heard* his tears. Then it dawned upon me that it was probably the first good music he had ever heard in all his life. Think of it, to care for music as he does and never to hear it, never to know that it exists on earth! To long for it as we long for other perfect experiences that never come. I can't tell you what music means to that man. I never saw any one so susceptible to it. It gave him speech, he became alive. When I had finished the intermezzo, he began telling me about a little crippled brother who died and whom he loved and used to carry everywhere in his arms. He did not wait for encouragement. He took up the story and told it slowly, as if to himself, just sort of rose up and told his own woe to answer Mascagni's. It overcame me."

"Poor devil," said Wyllis, looking at her with mysterious eyes, "and so you've given him a new woe. Now he'll go on wanting Grieg and Schubert the rest of his days and never getting them. That's a girl's philanthropy for you!"

Jerry Lockhart came out of the house screwing his chin over the unusual luxury of a stiff white collar, which his wife insisted upon as a necessary article of toilet while Miss Elliot was at the house. Jerry sat down on the step and smiled his broad, red smile at Margaret.

"Well, I've got the music for your dance, Miss Elliot. Olaf Oleson will bring his accordion and Mollie will play the organ, when she isn't lookin' after the grub, and a little chap from Frenchtown will bring his fiddle—though the French don't mix with the Norwegians much."

"Delightful! Mr. Lockhart, the dance will be the feature of our trip, and it's so nice of you to get it up for us. We'll see the Norwegians in character at last," cried Margaret, cordially.

"See here, Lockhart, I'll settle with you for backing her in this scheme," said Wyllis, sitting up and knocking the ashes out of his pipe. "She's done crazy things enough on this trip, but to talk of dancing all night with a gang of half-mad Norwegians and taking the carriage at four to catch the six o'clock train out of Riverton—well, it's tommy-rot, that's what it is!"

"Wyllis, I leave it to your sovereign power of reason to decide whether it isn't easier to stay up all night than to get up at three in the morning. To get up at three, think what that means! No, sir, I prefer to keep my vigil and then get into a sleeper."

"But what do you want with the Norwegians? I thought you were tired of dancing."

"So I am, with some people. But I want to see a Norwegian dance, and I intend to. Come, Wyllis, you know how seldom it is that one really wants to do anything nowadays. I wonder when I have really wanted to go to a party before. It will be something to remember next month at Newport, when we have to and don't want to. Remember your own theory that contrast is about the only thing that makes life endurable. This is my party and Mr. Lockhart's; your whole duty tomorrow night will consist in being nice to the Norwegian girls. I'll warrant you were adept enough at it once. And you'd better be very nice indeed, for if there are many such young Valkyries as Eric's sister among them, they would simply tie you up in a knot if they suspected you were guying them."

Wyllis groaned and sank back into the hammock to consider his fate, while his sister went on.

"And the guests, Mr. Lockhart, did they accept?"

Lockhart took out his knife and began sharpening it on the sole of his plowshoe.

"Well, I guess we'll have a couple dozen. You see it's pretty hard to get a crowd together here any more. Most of 'em have gone over to the Free Gospellers, and they'd rather put their feet in the fire than shake 'em to a fiddle."

Margaret made a gesture of impatience. "Those Free Gospellers have just cast an evil spell over this country, haven't they?"

"Well," said Lockhart, cautiously, "I don't just like to pass judgment on any Christian sect, but if you're to know the chosen by their works, the Gospellers can't make a very proud showin', an' that's a fact. They're responsible for a few suicides, and they've sent a good-sized delegation to the state insane asylum, an' I don't see as they've made the rest of us much better than we were before. I had a little herdboy last spring, as square a little Dane as I want to work for me, but after the Gospellers got hold of him and sanctified him, the little beggar used to get down on his knees out on the prairie and pray by the hour and let the cattle get into the corn, an' I had to fire him. That's about the way it goes. Now there's Eric; that chap used to be a hustler and the spryest dancer in all this section—called all the dances. Now he's got no ambition and he's glum as a preacher. I don't suppose we can even get him to come in tomorrow night."

"Eric? Why, he must dance, we can't let him off," said Margaret, quickly. "Why, I intend to dance with him myself!"

"I'm afraid he won't dance. I asked him this morning if he'd help us out and he said, 'I don't dance now, any more,' " said Lockhart, imitating the labored English of the Norwegian.

" 'The Miller of Hofbau, the Miller of Hofbau, O my Princess!' " chirped Wyllis, cheerfully, from his hammock.

The red on his sister's cheek deepened a little, and she laughed mischievously. "We'll see about that, sir. I'll not admit that I am beaten until I have asked him myself."

Every night Eric rode over to St. Anne, a little village in the heart of the French settlement, for the mail. As the road lay through the most attractive part of the Divide country, on several occasions Margaret Elliot and her brother had accompanied him. Tonight Wyllis had business with Lockhart, and Margaret rode with Eric, mounted on a frisky little mustang that Mrs. Lockhart had broken to the sidesaddle. Margaret regarded her escort very much as she did the servant who always accompanied her on long rides at home, and the ride to the village was a silent one. She was occupied with thoughts of another world,

and Eric was wrestling with more thoughts than had ever
been crowded into his head before. He rode with his eyes
riveted on that slight figure before him, as though he
wished to absorb it through the optic nerves and hold it in
his brain forever. He understood the situation perfectly.
His brain worked slowly, but he had a keen sense of the
values of things. This girl represented an entirely new
species of humanity to him, but he knew where to place
her. The prophets of old, when an angel first appeared
unto them, never doubted its high origin.

Eric was patient under the adverse conditions of his life,
but he was not servile. The Norse blood in him had not
entirely lost its self-reliance. He came of a proud fisher
line, men who were not afraid of anything but the ice and
the devil, and he had prospects before him when his
father went down off the North Cape in the long Arctic
night, and his mother, seized by a violent horror of seafar-
ing life, had followed her brother to America. Eric was
eighteen then, handsome as young Siegfried, a giant in
stature, with a skin singularly pure and delicate, like a
Swede's; hair as yellow as the locks of Tennyson's amo-
rous Prince, and eyes of a fierce, burning blue, whose
flash was most dangerous to women. He had in those
days a certain pride of bearing, a certain confidence of
approach, that usually accompanies physical perfection. It
was even said of him then that he was in love with life,
and inclined to levity, a vice most unusual on the Divide.
But the sad history of those Norwegian exiles, transplanted
in an arid soil and under a scorching sun, had repeated
itself in his case. Toil and isolation had sobered him, and
he grew more and more like the clods among which he
labored. It was as though some red-hot instrument had
touched for a moment those delicate fibers of the brain
which respond to acute pain or pleasure, in which lies the
power of exquisite sensation, and had seared them quite
away. It is a painful thing to watch the light die out of the
eyes of those Norsemen, leaving an expression of impene-
trable sadness, quite passive, quite hopeless, a shadow

that is never lifted. With some this change comes almost at once, in the first bitterness of homesickness, with others it comes more slowly, according to the time it takes each man's heart to die.

Oh, those poor Northmen of the Divide! They are dead many a year before they are put to rest in the little graveyard on the windy hill where exiles of all nations grow akin.

The peculiar species of hypochondria to which the exiles of his people sooner or later succumb had not developed in Eric until that night at the Lone Star schoolhouse, when he had broken his violin across his knee. After that, the gloom of his people settled down upon him, and the gospel of maceration began its work. *"If thine eye offend thee, pluck it out,"* et cetera. The pagan smile that once hovered about his lips was gone, and he was one with sorrow. Religion heals a hundred hearts for one that it embitters, but when it destroys, its work is quick and deadly, and where the agony of the cross has been, joy will not come again. This man understood things literally: one must live without pleasure to die without fear; to save the soul it was necessary to starve the soul.

The sun hung low above the cornfields when Margaret and her cavalier left St. Anne. South of the town there is a stretch of road that runs for some three miles through the French settlement, where the prairie is as level as the surface of a lake. There the fields of flax and wheat and rye are bordered by precise rows of slender, tapering Lombard poplars. It was a yellow world that Margaret Elliot saw under the wide light of the setting sun.

The girl gathered up her reins and called back to Eric, "It will be safe to run the horses here, won't it?"

"Yes, I think so, now," he answered, touching his spur to his pony's flank. They were off like the wind. It is an old saying in the West that newcomers always ride a horse or two to death before they get broken in to the country. They are tempted by the great open spaces and try to outride the horizon, to get to the end of something.

Margaret galloped over the level road, and Eric, from behind, saw her long veil fluttering in the wind. It had fluttered just so in his dreams last night and the night before. With a sudden inspiration of courage he overtook her and rode beside her, looking intently at her half-averted face. Before, he had only stolen occasional glances at it, seen it in blinding flashes, always with more or less embarrassment, but now he determined to let every line of it sink into his memory. Men of the world would have said that it was an unusual face, nervous, finely cut, with clear, elegant lines that betokened ancestry. Men of letters would have called it a historic face, and would have conjectured at what old passions, long asleep, what old sorrows forgotten time out of mind, doing battle together in ages gone, had curved those delicate nostrils, left their unconscious memory in those eyes. But Eric read no meaning in these details. To him this beauty was something more than color and line; it was a flash of white light, in which one cannot distinguish color because all colors are there. To him it was a complete revelation, an embodiment of those dreams of impossible loveliness that linger by a young man's pillow on midsummer nights; yet, because it held something more than the attraction of health and youth and shapeliness, it troubled him, and in its presence he felt as the Goths before the white marbles in the Roman Capitol, not knowing whether they were men or gods. At times he felt like uncovering his head before it, again the fury seized him to break and despoil, to find the clay in this spirit-thing and stamp upon it. Away from her, he longed to strike out with his arms, and take and hold; it maddened him that this woman whom he could break in his hands should be so much stronger than he. But near her, he never questioned this strength; he admitted its potentiality as he admitted the miracles of the Bible; it enervated and conquered him. Tonight, when he rode so close to her that he could have touched her, he knew that he might as well reach out his hand to take a star.

Margaret stirred uneasily under his gaze and turned questioningly in her saddle.

"This wind puts me a little out of breath when we ride fast," she said.

Eric turned his eyes away.

"I want to ask you if I go to New York to work, if I may-be hear music like you sang last night? I been a purty good hand to work," he asked, timidly.

Margaret looked at him with surprise, and then, as she studied the outline of his face, pityingly.

"Well, you might—but you'd lose a good deal else. I shouldn't like you to go to New York—and be poor, you'd be out of atmosphere, some way," she said, slowly. Inwardly she was thinking: *There he would be altogether sordid, impossible—a machine who would carry one's trunks upstairs, perhaps. Here he is every inch a man, rather picturesque; why is it?* "No," she added aloud, "I shouldn't like that."

"Then I not go," said Eric, decidedly.

Margaret turned her face to hide a smile. She was a trifle amused and a trifle annoyed. Suddenly she spoke again.

"But I'll tell you what I do want you to do, Eric. I want you to dance with us tomorrow night and teach me some of the Norwegian dances; they say you know them all. Won't you?"

Eric straightened himself in his saddle and his eyes flashed as they had done in the Lone Star schoolhouse when he broke his violin across his knee.

"Yes, I will," he said, quietly, and he believed that he delivered his soul to hell as he said it.

They had reached the rougher country now, where the road wound through a narrow cut in one of the bluffs along the creek, when a beat of hoofs ahead and the sharp neighing of horses made the ponies start and Eric rose in his stirrups. Then down the gulch in front of them and over the steep city banks thundered a herd of wild ponies, nimble as monkeys and wild as rabbits, such as horse-traders drive east from the plains of Montana to sell in the farming country. Margaret's pony made a shrill sound, a neigh that was almost a scream, and started up the clay bank to meet them, all the wild blood of the range breaking out in an instant. Margaret called to Eric just as he threw himself out of the saddle and caught her pony's bit. But the wiry little animal had gone made and was kicking and biting like a devil. Her wild brothers of the range were all about her, neighing, and pawing the earth, and striking her with their forefeet and snapping at her flanks. It was the old liberty of the range that the little beast fought for.

"Drop the reins and hold tight!" Eric called, throwing all his weight upon the bit, struggling under those frantic forefeet that now beat at his breast, and now kicked at the wild mustangs that surged and tossed about him. He succeeded in wrenching the pony's head toward him and crowding her withers against the clay bank, so that she could not roll.

"Hold tight, tight!" he shouted again, launching a kick at a snorting animal that reared back against Margaret's saddle. If she should lose her courage and fall now, under those hoofs—He struck out again and again, kicking right and left with all his might. Already the negligent drivers had galloped into the cut, and their long quirts were whistling over the heads of the herd. As suddenly as it had come, the struggling, frantic wave of wild life swept up out of the gulch and on across the open prairie, and with a long despairing whinny of farewell the pony dropped her head and stood trembling in her sweat, shaking the foam and blood from her bit.

Eric stepped close to Margaret's side and laid his hand on her saddle. "You are not hurt?" he asked, hoarsely. As he raised his face in the soft starlight she saw that it was white and drawn and that his lips were working nervously.

"No, no, not at all. But you, you are suffering; they struck you!" she cried in sharp alarm.

He stepped back and drew his hand across his brow.

"No, it is not that," he spoke rapidly now, with his

hands clenched at his side. "But if they had hurt you, I would beat their brains out with my hands, I would kill them all. I was never afraid before. You are the only beautiful thing that has ever come close to me. You came like an angel out of the sky. You are like the music you sing, you are like the stars and the snow on the mountains where I played when I was a little boy. You are like all that I wanted once and never had, you are all that they have killed in me. I die for you tonight, tomorrow, for all eternity. I am not a coward; I was afraid because I love you more than Christ who died for me, more than I am afraid of hell, or hope for heaven. I was never afraid before. If you had fallen—oh, my God!" he threw his arms out blindly and dropped his head upon the pony's mane, leaning limply against the animal like a man struck by some sickness. His shoulders rose and fell perceptibly with his labored breathing. The horse stood cowed with exhaustion and fear. Presently Margaret laid her hand on Eric's head and said gently:

"You are better now, shall we go on? Can you get your horse?"

"No, he has gone with the herd. I will lead yours, she is not safe. I will not frighten you again." His voice was still husky, but it was steady now. He took hold of the bit and tramped home in silence.

When they reached the house, Eric stood stolidly by the pony's head until Wyllis came to lift his sister from the saddle.

"The horses were badly frightened, Wyllis. I think I was pretty thoroughly scared myself," she said as she took her brother's arm and went slowly up the hill toward the house. "No, I'm not hurt, thanks to Eric. You must thank him for taking such good care of me. He's a mighty fine fellow. I'll tell you all about it in the morning, dear. I was pretty well shaken up and I'm going right to bed now. Good night."

When she reached the low room in which she slept, she sank upon the bed in her riding dress face downward.

"Oh, I pity him! I pity him!" she murmured, with a long sigh of exhaustion. She must have slept a little. When she rose again, she took from her dress a letter that had been waiting for her at the village post office. It was closely written in a long, angular hand, covering a dozen pages of foreign note paper, and began:

My Dearest Margaret: If I should attempt to say *how like a winter hath thine absence been*, I should incur the risk of being tedious. Really, it takes the sparkle out of everything. Having nothing better to do, and not caring to go anywhere in particular without you, I remained in the city until Jack Courtwell noted my general despondency and brought me down here to his place on the sound to manage some open-air theatricals he is getting up. *As You Like It* is of course the piece selected. Miss Harrison plays Rosalind. I wish you had been here to take the part. Miss Harrison reads her lines well, but she is either a maiden-all-forlorn or a tomboy; insists on reading into the part all sorts of deeper meanings and highly colored suggestions wholly out of harmony with the pastoral setting. Like most of the professionals, she exaggerates the emotional element and quite fails to do justice to Rosalind's facile wit and really brilliant mental qualities. Gerard will do Orlando, but rumor says he is *épris* of your sometime friend, Miss Meredith, and his memory is treacherous and his interest fitful.

My new pictures arrived last week on the *Gascogne*. The Puvis de Chavannes is even more beautiful than I thought it in Paris. A pale dream-maiden sits by a pale dream-cow and a stream of anemic water flows at her feet. The Constant, you will remember, I got because you admired it. It is here in all its florid splendor, the whole dominated by a glowing sensuosity. The drapery of the female figure is as wonderful as you said; the fabric all barbaric pearl and gold, painted with an easy, effortless voluptuosness, and that white, gleaming line of African coast in the background recalls memories of you very precious to me. But it is useless to deny that Constant irritates me. Though I cannot prove the charge against him, his brilliancy always makes me suspect him of cheapness.

Here Margaret stopped and glanced at the remaining pages of this strange love-letter. They seemed to be filled chiefly with discussions of pictures and books, and with a slow smile she laid them by.

She rose and began undressing. Before she lay down she went to open the window. With her hand on the sill, she hesitated, feeling suddenly as though some danger were lurking outside, some inordinate desire waiting to spring upon her in the darkness. She stood there for a long time, gazing at the infinite sweep of the sky.

"Oh, it is all so little, so little there," she murmured. "When everything else is so dwarfed, why should one expect love to be great? Why should one try to read highly colored suggestions into a life like that? If only I could find one thing in it all that mattered greatly, one thing that would warm me when I am alone! Will life never give me that one great moment?"

As she raised the window, she heard a sound in the plum bushes outside. It was only the house-dog roused from his sleep, but Margaret started violently and trembled so that she caught the foot of the bed for support. Again she felt herself pursued by some overwhelming longing, some desperate necessity for herself, like the outstretching of helpless, unseen arms in the darkness, and the air seemed heavy with sighs of yearning. She fled to her bed with the words, "I love you more than Christ, who died for me!" ringing in her ears.

III

About midnight the dance at Lockhart's was at its height. Even the old men who had come to "look on" caught the spirit of revelry and stamped the floor with the vigor of old Silenus. Eric took the violin from the Frenchman, and Minna Oleson sat at the organ, and the music grew more and more characteristic—rude, half mournful music, made up of the folksongs of the North, that the villagers sing through the long night in hamlets by the sea, when they are thinking of the sun, and the spring, and the fishermen so long away. To Margaret some of it sounded like Grieg's *Peer Gynt* music. She found something irresistibly infectious in the mirth of these people who were so seldom merry, and she felt almost one of them. Something seemed struggling for freedom in them tonight, something of the joyous childhood of the nations which exile had not killed. The girls were all boisterous with delight. Pleasure came to them but rarely, and when it came, they caught at it wildly and crushed its fluttering wings in their strong brown fingers. They had a hard life enough, most of them. Torrid summers and freezing winters, labor and drudgery and ignorance, were the portion of their girlhood; a short wooing, a hasty, loveless marriage, unlimited maternity, thankless sons, premature age and ugliness, were the dower of their womanhood. But what matter? Tonight there was hot liquor in the glass and hot blood in the heart; tonight they danced.

Tonight Eric Hermannson had renewed his youth. He was no longer the big, silent Norwegian who had sat at Margaret's feet and looked hopelessly into her eyes. Tonight he was a man, with a man's rights and a man's power. Tonight he was Siegfried indeed. His hair was yellow as the heavy wheat in the ripe of summer, and his eyes flashed like the blue water between the ice packs in the North Seas. He was not afraid of Margaret tonight, and when he danced with her he held her firmly. She was tired and dragged on his arm a little, but the strength of the man was like an all-pervading fluid, stealing through her veins, awakening under her heart some nameless, unsuspected existence that had slumbered there all these years and that went out through her throbbing finger-tips to his that answered. She wondered if the hoydenish blood of some lawless ancestor, long asleep, were calling out in her tonight, some drop of a hotter fluid that the centuries had failed to cool, and why, if this curse were in her, it had not spoken before. But was it a curse, this awakening, this wealth before undiscovered, this music set free? For the first time in her life her heart held something stronger than herself, was not this worth while? Then she ceased to wonder. She lost sight of the lights and the faces, and the music was drowned by the beating of her own arteries. She saw only the blue eyes that flashed above her, felt only the warmth of that throbbing hand which held hers and which the blood of his heart fed. Dimly, as in a dream, she saw the drooping shoulders, high white forehead and tight, cynical mouth of the man she was to marry in December. For an hour she had been crowding back the memory of that face with all her strength.

"Let us stop, this is enough," she whispered. His only answer was to tighten the arm behind her. She sighed and let that masterful strength bear her where it would. She forgot that this man was little more than a savage, that they would part at dawn. The blood has no memories, no reflections, no regrets for the past, no consideration of the future.

"Let us go out where it is cooler," she said when the music stopped; thinking, *I am growing faint here, I shall be all right in the open air*. They stepped out into the cool, blue air of the night.

Since the older folk had begun dancing, the young Norwegians had been slipping out in couples to climb the windmill tower into the cooler atmosphere, as is their custom.

"You like to go up?" asked Eric, close to her ear.

She turned and looked at him with suppressed amusement. "How high is it?"

"Forty feet, about. I not let you fall." There was a note of irresistible pleading in his voice, and she felt that he tremendously wished her to go. Well, why not? This was a night of the unusual, when she was not herself at all, but was living an unreality. Tomorrow, yes, in a few hours, there would be the Vestibule Limited and the world.

"Well, if you'll take good care of me. I used to be able to climb, when I was a little girl."

Once at the top and seated on the platform, they were silent. Margaret wondered if she would not hunger for that scene all her life, through all the routine of the days to come. Above them stretched the great Western sky, serenely blue, even in the night, with its big, burning stars, never so cold and dead and far away as in denser atmospheres. The moon would not be up for twenty minutes yet, and all about the horizon, that wide horizon, which seemed to reach around the world, lingered a pale, white light, as of a universal dawn. The weary wind brought up to them the heavy odors of the cornfields. The music of the dance sounded faintly from below. Eric leaned on his elbow beside her, his legs swinging down on the ladder. His great shoulders looked more than ever like those of the stone Doryphorus, who stands in his perfect, reposeful strength in the Louvre, and had often made her wonder if such men died forever with the youth of Greece.

"How sweet the corn smells at night," said Margaret nervously.

"Yes, like the flowers that grow in paradise, I think."

She was somewhat startled by this reply, and more startled when this taciturn man spoke again.

"You go away tomorrow?"

"Yes, we have stayed longer than we thought to now."

"You not come back any more?"

"No, I expect not. You see, it is a long trip halfway across the continent."

"You soon forget about this country, I guess." It seemed to him now a little thing to lose his soul for this woman, but that she should utterly forget this night into which he threw all his life and all his eternity, that was a bitter thought.

"No, Eric, I will not forget. You have all been too kind to me for that. And you won't be sorry you danced this one night, will you?"

"I never be sorry. I have not been so happy before. I not be so happy again, ever. You will be happy many nights yet, I only this one. I will dream sometimes, maybe."

The mighty resignation of his tone alarmed and touched her. It was as when some great animal composes itself for death, as when a great ship goes down at sea.

She sighed, but did not answer him. He drew a little closer and looked into her eyes.

"You are not always happy, too?" he asked.

"No, not always, Eric; not very often, I think."

"You have a trouble?"

"Yes, but I cannot put it into words. Perhaps if I could do that, I could cure it."

He clasped his hands together over his heart, as children do when they pray, and said falteringly, "If I own all the world, I give him you."

Margaret felt a sudden moisture in her eyes, and laid her hand on his.

"Thank you, Eric; I believe you would. But perhaps even then I should not be happy. Perhaps I have too much of it already."

She did not take her hand away from him; she did not dare. She sat still and waited for the traditions in which she had always believed to speak and save her. But they were dumb. She belonged to an ultra-refined civilization which tries to cheat nature with elegant sophistries. Cheat nature? Bah! One generation may do it, perhaps two, but the third—Can we ever rise above nature or sink below her? Did she not turn on Jerusalem as upon Sodom, upon St. Anthony in his desert as upon Nero in his seraglio? Does she not always cry in brutal triumph: "I am here still, at the bottom of things, warming the roots of life; you cannot starve me nor tame me nor thwart me; I made the world, I rule it, and I am its destiny."

This woman, on a windmill tower at the world's end with a giant barbarian, heard that cry tonight, and she was afraid! Ah! the terror and the delight of that moment when first we fear ourselves! Until then we have not lived.

"Come, Eric, let us go down; the moon is up and the music has begun again," she said.

He rose silently and stepped down upon the ladder, putting his arm about her to help her. That arm could have thrown Thor's hammer out in the cornfields yonder, yet it scarcely touched her, and his hand trembled as it had done in the dance. His face was level with hers now and the moonlight fell sharply upon it. All her life she had searched the faces of men for the look that lay in his eyes. She knew that that look had never shone for her before, would never shine for her on earth again, that such love comes to one only in dreams or in impossible places like this, unattainable always. This was Love's self, in a moment it would die. Stung by the agonized appeal that emanated from the man's whole being, she leaned forward and laid her lips on his. Once, twice and again she heard the deep respirations rattle in his throat while she held them there, and the riotous force under her heart became an engulfing weakness. He drew her up to him until he felt all the resistance go out of her body, until every nerve relaxed and yielded. When she drew her face back from his, it was white with fear.

"Let us go down, oh, my God! let us go down!" she muttered. And the drunken stars up yonder seemed reeling to some appointed doom as she clung to the rounds of the ladder. All that she was to know of love she had left upon his lips.

"The devil is loose again," whispered Olaf Oleson, as he saw Eric dancing a moment later, his eye blazing.

But Eric was thinking with an almost savage exultation of the time when he should pay for this. Ah, there would be no quailing then! If ever a soul went fearlessly, proudly down to the gates infernal, his should go. For a moment he fancied he was there already, treading down the tempest of flame, hugging the fiery hurricane to his breast. He wondered whether in ages gone, all the countless years of sinning in which men had sold and lost and flung their souls away, any man had ever so cheated Satan, had ever bartered his soul for so great a price.

It seemed but a little while till dawn.

The carriage was brought to the door and Wyllis Elliot and his sister said goodbye. She could not meet Eric's eyes as she gave him her hand, but as he stood by the horse's head, just as the carriage moved off, she gave him one swift glance that said, "I will not forget." In a moment the carriage was gone.

Eric changed his coat and plunged his head into the water tank and went to the barn to hook up his team. As he led his horses to the door, a shadow fell across his path, and he saw Skinner rising in his stirrups. His rugged face was pale and worn with looking after his wayward flock, with dragging men into the way of salvation.

"Good morning, Eric. There was a dance here last night?" he asked, sternly.

"A dance? Oh, yes, a dance," replied Eric, cheerfully.

"Certainly you did not dance, Eric?"

"Yes, I danced. I danced all the time."

The minister's shoulders drooped, and an expression of profound discouragement settled over his haggard face. There was almost anguish in the yearning he felt for his soul.

"Eric, I didn't look for this from you. I thought God had set his mark on you if he ever had on any man. And it is for things like this that you set your soul back a thousand years from God. O foolish and perverse generation!"

Eric drew himself up to his full height and looked off to where the new day was gilding the corn-tassels and flooding the uplands with light. As his nostrils drew in the breath of the dew and the morning, something from the only poetry he had ever read flashed across his mind, and he murmured, half to himself, with dreamy exultation:

" 'And a day shall be as a thousand years, and a thousand years as a day.' "

The Sentimentality of William Tavener

It takes a strong woman to make any sort of success of living in the West, and Hester undoubtedly was that. When people spoke of William Tavener as the most prosperous farmer in McPherson County, they usually added that his wife was a "good manager." She was an executive woman, quick of tongue and something of an imperatrix. The only reason her husband did not consult her about his business was that she did not wait to be consulted.

It would have been quite impossible for one man, within the limited sphere of human action, to follow all Hester's advice, but in the end William usually acted upon some of her suggestions. When she incessantly denounced the "shiftlessness" of letting a new threshing machine stand unprotected in the open, he eventually built a shed for it. When she sniffed contemptuously at his notion of fencing a hog corral with sod walls, he made a spiritless beginning on the structure—merely to "show his temper," as she put it—but in the end he went off quietly to town and bought enough barbed wire to complete the fence. When the first heavy rains came on, and the pigs rooted down the sod wall and made little paths all over it to facilitate their ascent, he heard his wife relate with relish the story of the little pig that built a mud house, to the minister at the dinner table, and William's gravity never relaxed for an instant. Silence, indeed, was William's refuge and his strength.

William set his boys a wholesome example to respect their mother. People who knew him very well suspected that he even admired her. He was a hard man towards his neighbors, and even towards his sons: grasping, determined and ambitious.

There was an occasional blue day about the house when William went over the store bills, but he never objected to items relating to his wife's gowns or bonnets. So it came about that many of the foolish, unnecessary little things that Hester bought for boys, she had charged to her personal account.

One spring night Hester sat in a rocking chair by the sitting room window, darning socks. She rocked violently and sent her long needle vigorously back and forth over her gourd, and it took only a very casual glance to see that she was wrought up over something. William sat on the other side of the table reading his farm paper. If he had noticed his wife's agitation, his calm, clean-shaven face betrayed no sign of concern. He must have noticed the sarcastic turn of her remarks at the supper table, and he must have noticed the moody silence of the older boys as they ate. When supper was but half over little Billy, the youngest, had suddenly pushed back his plate and slipped away from the table, manfully trying to swallow a sob. But William Tavener never heeded ominous forecasts in the domestic horizon, and he never looked for a storm until it broke.

After supper the boys had gone to the pond under the willows in the big cattle corral, to get rid of the dust of plowing. Hester could hear an occasional splash and a laugh ringing clear through the stillness of the night, as she sat by the open window. She sat silent for almost an hour reviewing in her mind many plans of attack. But she was too vigorous a woman to be much of a strategist, and she usually came to her point with directness. At last she cut her thread and suddenly put her darning down, saying emphatically:

"William, I don't think it would hurt you to let the boys go to that circus in town tomorrow."

William continued to read his farm paper, but it was not Hester's custom to wait for an answer. She usually divined his arguments and assailed them one by one before he uttered them.

"You've been short of hands all summer, and you've worked the boys hard, and a man ought use his own flesh and blood as well as he does his hired hands. We're plenty able to afford it, and it's little enough our boys ever spend. I don't see how you can expect 'em to be steady and hard workin', unless you encourage 'em a little. I never could see much harm in circuses, and our boys have never been to one. Oh, I know Jim Howley's boys get drunk an' carry on when they go, but our boys ain't that sort, an' you know it, William. The animals are real instructive, an' our boys don't get to see much out here on the prairie. It was different where we were raised, but the boys have got no advantages here, an' if you don't take care, they'll grow up to be greenhorns."

Hester paused a moment, and William folded up his paper, but vouchsafed no remark. His sisters in Virginia had often said that only a quiet man like William could ever have lived with Hester Perkins. Secretly, William was rather proud of his wife's "gift of speech," and of the fact that she could talk in prayer meeting as fluently as a man. He confined his own efforts in that line to a brief prayer at Covenant meetings.

Hester shook out another sock and went on.

"Nobody was ever hurt by goin' to a circus. Why, law me! I remember I went to one myself once, when I was little. I had most forgot about it. It was over at Pewtown, an' I remember how I had set my heart on going. I don't think I'd ever forgiven my father if he hadn't taken me, though that red clay road was in a frightful way after the rain. I mind they had an elephant and six poll parrots, an' a Rocky Mountain lion, an' a cage of monkeys, an' two camels. My! but they were a sight to me then!"

Hester dropped the black sock and shook her head and smiled at the recollection. She was not expecting anything from William yet, and she was fairly startled when he said gravely, in much the same tone in which he announced the hymns in prayer meeting:

"No, there was only one camel. The other was a dromedary."

She peered around the lamp and looked at him keenly.

"Why, William, how come you to know?"

William folded his paper and answered with some hesitation, "I was there, too."

Hester's interest flashed up. "Well, I never, William! To think of my finding it out after all these years! Why, you couldn't have been much bigger'n our Billy then. It seems queer I never saw you when you was little, to remember about you. But then you Back Creek folks never have anything to do with us Gap people. But how come you to go? Your father was stricter with you than you are with your boys."

"I reckon I shouldn't 'a gone," he said slowly, "but boys will do foolish things. I had done a good deal of fox hunting the winter before, and father let me keep the bounty money. I hired Tom Smith's Tap to weed the corn for me, an' I slipped off unbeknownst to father an' went to the show."

Hester spoke up warmly: "Nonsense, William! It didn't do you no harm, I guess. You was always worked hard enough. It must have been a big sight for a little fellow. That clown must have just tickled you to death."

William crossed his knees and leaned back in his chair.

"I reckon I could tell all that fool's jokes now. Sometimes I can't help thinkin' about 'em in meetin' when the sermon's long. I mind I had on a pair of new boots that hurt me like the mischief, but I forgot all about 'em when that fellow rode the donkey. I recall I had to take them boots off as soon as I got out of sight o' town, and walked home in the mud barefoot."

"O poor little fellow!" Hester ejaculated, drawing her chair nearer and leaning her elbows on the table. "What cruel shoes they did use to make for children. I remember

I went up to Back Creek to see the circus wagons go by. They came down from Romney, you know. The circus men stopped at the creek to water the animals, an' the elephant got stubborn an' broke a big limb off the yellow willow tree that grew there by the toll house porch, an' the Scribners were 'fraid as death he'd pull the house down. But this much I saw him do; he waded in the creek an' filled his trunk with water and squirted it in at the window and nearly ruined Ellen Scribner's pink lawn dress that she had just ironed an' laid out on the bed ready to wear to the circus."

"I reckon that must have been a trial to Ellen," chuckled William, "for she was mighty prim in them days."

Hester drew her chair still nearer William's. Since the children had begun growing up, her conversation with her husband had been almost wholly confined to questions of economy and expense. Their relationship had become purely a business one, like that between landlord and tenant. In her desire to indulge her boys she had unconsciously assumed a defensive and almost hostile attitude towards her husband. No debtor ever haggled with his usurer more doggedly than did Hester with her husband in behalf of her sons. The strategic contest had gone on so long that it had almost crowded out the memory of a closer relationship. This exchange of confidences tonight, when common recollections took them unawares and opened their hearts, had all the miracle of romance. They talked on and on; of old neighbors, of old familiar faces in the valley where they had grown up, of long forgotten incidents of their youth—weddings, picnics, sleighing parties and baptizings. For years they had talked of nothing else but butter and eggs and the prices of things, and now they had as much to say to each other as people who meet after a long separation.

When the clock struck ten, William rose and went over to his walnut secretary and unlocked it. From his red leather wallet he took out a ten dollar bill and laid it on the table beside Hester.

"Tell the boys not to stay late, an' not to drive the horses hard," he said quietly, and went off to bed.

Hester blew out the lamp and sat still in the dark a long time. She left the bill lying on the table where William had placed it. She had a painful sense of having missed something, or lost something; she felt that somehow the years had cheated her.

The little locust trees that grew by the fence were white with blossoms. Their heavy odor floated in to her on the night wind and recalled a night long ago, when the first whippoorwill of the Spring was heard, and the rough, buxom girls of Hawkins Gap had held her laughing and struggling under the locust trees, and searched in her bosom for a lock of her sweetheart's hair, which is supposed to be on every girl's breast when the first whippoorwill sings. Two of those same girls had been her bridesmaids. Hester had been a very happy bride. She rose and went softly into the room where William lay. He was sleeping heavily, but occasionally moved his hand before his face to ward off the flies. Hester went into the parlor and took the piece of mosquito net from the basket of wax apples and pears that her sister had made before she died. One of the boys had brought it all the way from Virginia, packed in a tin pail, since Hester would not risk shipping so precious an ornament by freight. She went back to the bedroom and spread the net over William's head. Then she sat down by the bed and listened to his deep, regular breathing until she heard the boys returning. She went out to meet them and warn them not to waken their father.

"I'll be up early to get your breakfast, boys. Your father says you can go to the show." As she handed the money to the eldest, she felt a sudden throb of allegiance to her husband and said sharply, "And you be careful of that, an' don't waste it. Your father works hard for his money."

The boys looked at each other in astonishment and felt that they had lost a powerful ally.

A Singer's Romance

The rain fell in torrents and the great stream of people which poured out of the Metropolitan Opera House stagnated about the doors and seemed effectually checked by the black line of bobbing umbrellas on the sidewalk. The entrance was fairly blockaded, and the people who were waiting for carriages formed a solid phalanx, which the more unfortunate opera goers, who had to depend on street cars no matter what the condition of the weather, tried to break through in vain. There was much shouting of numbers and hurrying of drivers, from whose oilcloth-covered hats the water trickled in tiny streams, quite as though the brims had been curved just to accommodate it. The wind made the management of the hundreds of umbrellas difficult, and they rose and fell and swayed about like toy balloons tugging at their moorings. At the stage entrance there was less congestion, but the confusion was not proportionally small, and Frau Selma Schumann was in no very amiable mood when she was at last told that her carriage awaited her. As she stepped out of the door, the wind caught the black lace mantilla wound about her head and lifted it high in the air in such a ludicrous fashion that the substantial soprano cut a figure much like a malicious Beardsley poster. In her frantic endeavor to replace her sportive headgear, she dropped the little velvet bag in which she carried her jewel case. A young man stationed by the door darted forward and snatched it up from the sidewalk, uncovered his head and returned the bag to her with a low bow. He was a tall man, slender and graceful, and he looked as dark as a Spaniard in the bright light that fell upon him from the doorway. His curling black hair would have been rather long even for a tenor, and he wore a dark mustache. His face had that oval contour, slightly effeminate, which belongs to the Latin races. He wore a long black ulster and held in his hand a wide-brimmed, black felt hat. In his buttonhole was a single red carnation. Frau Schumann took the bag with a radiant smile, quite forgetting her ill humor. "I thank you, sir," she said graciously. But the young man remained standing with bared head, never raising his eyes. "Merci, Monsieur," she ventured again, rather timidly, but his only recognition was to bow even lower than before, and Madame hastened to her carriage to hide her confusion from her maid, who followed close behind. Once in the carriage, Madame permitted herself to smile and to sigh a little in the darkness, and to wonder whether the disagreeable American prima donna, who manufactured gossip about every member of the company, had seen the little episode of the jewel bag. She almost hoped she had.

This Signorino's reserve puzzled her more than his persistence. This was the third time she had given him an opportunity to speak, to make himself known, and the third time her timid advance had been met by silence and downcast eyes. She was unable to comprehend it. She had been singing in New York now eight weeks, and since the first week this dark man, clad in black, had followed her like a shadow. When she and Annette walked in the park, they always encountered him on one of the benches. When she went shopping, he sauntered after them on the other side of the street. She continually encountered him in the corridors of her hotel; when she entered the theatre he was always stationed near the stage door, and when she came out again, he was still at his post. One evening, just to assure herself, she had gone to the Opera House when she was not in the cast, and, as she had hoped, the dark Signor was absent. He had grown so familiar to her that she knew the outline of his head and shoulders a square away, and in the densest crowd her eyes instantly singled him out. She looked for him so constantly that she knew she would miss him if he should not appear. Yet he made no attempt whatever to address her. Once, when he was standing near her in the hotel corridor, she made pointless and incoherent inquiries about directions from the bell boy, in the hope that the young man would volunteer information, which he did not. On another occasion, when she found him smoking a cigarette at the door of the Holland as she went out into a drizzling rain, she had feigned impossible difficulties in raising her umbrella. He did, indeed, raise it for her, and bowing passed quickly down the street. Madame had begun to feel like a very bold and forward woman, and to blush guiltily under the surveillance of her maid. By every doorstep, at every corner, wherever she turned, whenever she looked out of a window, she encountered always the dark Signorino, with his picturesque face and Spanish eyes, his broad-brimmed black felt hat set at an angle on his glistening black curls, and the inevitable red carnation in his buttonhole.

When they arrived at the hotel Antoinette went to the office to ask for Madame's mail, and returned to Madame's rooms with a letter which bore the familiar post mark of Monte Carlo. This threw Madame into an honest German rage, refreshing to witness, and she threw herself into a chair and wept audibly. The letter was from her husband, who spent most of his time and her money at the Casino, and who continually sent urgent letters for re-enforcement.

"It's too much, 'Toinette, too much," she sobbed. "He says he must have money to pay his doctor. Why I have sent him money enough to pay the doctor bills of the royal family. Here am I singing three and four nights a week—no, I will not do it."

But she ended by sitting down at her desk and writing

out a check, with which she enclosed very pointed advice, and directed it to the suave old gentleman at Monte Carlo.

Then she permitted 'Toinette to shake out her hair, and became lost in the contemplation of her own image in the mirror. She had to admit that she had grown a trifle stout, that there were many fine lines about her mouth and eyes, and little wrinkles on her forehead that had defied the arts of massage. Her blonde hair had lost its luster and was somewhat deadened by the heat of the curling iron. She had to hold her chin very high indeed in order not to have two, and there were little puffy places under her eyes that told of her love for pastry and champagne. Above her own face in the glass she saw the reflection of her maid's. Pretty, slender 'Toinette, with her satin-smooth skin and rosy cheeks and little pink ears, her arched brows and long black lashes and her coil of shining black hair. 'Toinette's youth and freshness irritated her tonight: She could not help wondering—but then this man was probably a man of intelligence, quite proof against the charm of mere prettiness. He was probably, she reflected, an artist like herself, a man who revered her art, and art, certainly, does not come at sixteen. Secretly, she wondered what 'Toinette thought of this dark Signorino whom she must have noticed by this time. She had great respect for 'Toinette's opinion. 'Toinette was by no means an ordinary ladies' maid, and Madame had grown to regard her as a companion and confidante. She was the child of a French opera singer who had been one of Madame's earliest professional friends and who had come to an evil end and died in a hospital, leaving her young daughter wholly without protection. As the girl had no vocal possibilities, Madame Schumann had generously rescued her from the awful fate of the chorus by taking her into her service.

"You have been contented here, 'Toinette? You like America, you will be a little sorry to leave?" asked Madame as she said good night.

"Oh, yes, Madame, I should be sorry," returned 'Toinette.

"And so shall I," said Madame softly, smiling to herself.

'Toinette lingered a moment at the door; "Madame will have nothing to eat, no refreshment of any kind?"

"No, nothing tonight, 'Toinette."

"Not even the very smallest glass of champagne?"

"No, no, nothing," said Madame impatiently.

'Toinette turned out the light and left her in bed, where she lay awake for a long time, indulging in luxurious dreams.

In the morning she awoke long before it was time for 'Toinette to bring her coffee, and lay still, with her eyes closed, while the early rumble of the city was audible through the open window.

Selma Schumann was a singer without a romance. No one felt the incongruity of this more than she did, yet she had lived to the age of two-and-forty without ever having known an *affaire de coeur*. After her debut in grand opera she had married her former singing teacher, who at once decided that he had already done quite enough for his wife and the world in the placing and training of that wonderful voice, and lived in cheerful idleness, gambling her earnings with the utmost complacency, and when her reproaches grew too cutting, he would respectfully remind her that he had enlarged her upper register four tones, and in so doing had fulfilled the whole duty of man. Madame had always been industrious and an indefatigable student. She could sing a large repertoire at the shortest notice, and her good nature made her invaluable to managers. She lacked certainly, that poignant individuality which alone secures great eminence in the world of art, and no one ever went to the opera solely because her name was on the bill. She was known as a thoroughly "competent" artist, and as all singers know, that means a thankless life of underpaid drudgery. Her father had been a professor of etymology in a German university and she had inherited something of his taste for grubbing and had been measurably happy in her work. She practiced incessantly and skimped herself and saved money and dutifully supported her husband, and surely such virtue should bring its own reward. Yet when she saw other women in the company appear in a new tiara of diamonds, or saw them snatch notes from the hands of messenger boys, or take a carriage full of flowers back to the hotel with them, she had felt ill used, and had wondered what that other side of life was like. In short, from the wastes of this humdrum existence which seems so gay to the uninitiated, she had wished for a romance. Under all her laborious habits and thrift and economy there was left enough of the unsatisfied spirit of youth for that.

Since the shadow of the dark Signorino had fallen across her path, the routine of her life hitherto as fixed as that of the planets or of a German housewife, had become less rigid and more variable. She had decided that she owed it to her health to walk frequently in the park, and to sleep later in the morning. She had spent entire afternoons in dreamful idleness, whereas she should have been struggling with the new roles she was to sing in London. She had begun to pay the most scrupulous attention to her toilettes, which she had begun to neglect in the merciless routine of her work. She was visited by many *massageurs*, for she discovered that her figure and skin had been allowed to take care of themselves and had done it ill. She thought with bitter regret that a little less economy and a little more care might have prevented a wrinkle. One great sacrifice she made. She stopped drinking champagne. The sole one of the luxuries of life she had permitted herself was that of the table. She had all her countrywomen's love for good living, and she had indulged herself freely. She had known for a long time that champagne and sweets were bad for her complexion, and that they made her stout, but she had told herself that it was little enough pleasure she had at best.

But since the appearance of the dark Signorino, all this had been changed, and it was by no means an easy sacrifice.

Madame waited a long time for her coffee, but 'Toinette

did not appear. Then she rose and went into her reception room, but no one was there. In the little music room next door she heard a low murmur of voices. She parted the curtains a little, and saw 'Toinette with both her hands clasped in the hands of the dark Signorino.

"But Madame," 'Toinette was saying, "she is so lonely, I cannot find the heart to tell her that I must leave her."

"Ah," murmured the Signorino, and his voice was as caressing as Madame had imagined it in her dreams, "she has been like a mother to you, the Madame, she will be glad of your happiness."

When Selma Schumann reached her own room again she threw herself on her bed and wept furiously. Then she dried her eyes and railed at Fortune in deep German polysyllables, gesturing like an enraged Valkyrie.

Then she ordered her breakfast—and a quart of champagne.

The Professor's Commencement

The professor sat at his library table at six o'clock in the morning. He had risen with the sun, which is up betimes in June. An uncut volume of *Huxley's Life and Letters* lay open on the table before him, but he tapped the pages absently with his paper knife and his eyes were fixed unseeingly on the St. Gaudens medallion of Stevenson on the opposite wall. The professor's library testified to the superior quality of his taste in art as well as to his wide and varied scholarship. Only by a miracle of taste could so unpretentious a room have been made so attractive; it was as dainty as a boudoir and as original in color scheme as a painter's studio. The walls were hung with photographs of the works of the best modern painters—Burne-Jones, Rossetti, Corot, and a dozen others. Above the mantel were delicate reproductions in color of some of Fra Angelico's most beautiful paintings. The rugs were exquisite in pattern and color, pieces of weaving that the Professor had picked up himself in his wanderings in the Orient. On close inspection, however, the contents of the bookshelves formed the most remarkable feature of the library. The shelves were almost equally apportioned to the accommodation of works on literature and science, suggesting a form of bigamy rarely encountered in society. The collection of works of pure literature was wide enough to include nearly all the major languages of modern Europe, besides the Greek and Roman classics.

To an interpretive observer nearly everything that was to be found in the Professor's library was represented in his personality. Occasionally, when he read Hawthorne's "Great Stone Face" with his classes, some clear-sighted student wondered whether the man ever realized how completely he illustrated the allegory in himself. The Professor was truly a part of all that he had met, and he had managed to meet most of the good things that the mind of man had desired. In his face there was much of the laborious precision of the scientist and not a little of Fra Angelico and of the lyric poets whose influence had prolonged his youth well into the fifties. His pupils always remembered the Professor's face long after they had forgotten the things he had endeavored to teach them. He had the bold, prominent nose and chin of the oldest and most beloved of American actors, and the high, broad forehead which Nature loves to build about her finely adjusted minds. The grave, large outlines of his face were softened by an infinite kindness of mouth and eye. His mouth, indeed, was as sensitive and mobile as that of a young man, and, given certain passages from *Tristran and Isolde* or certain lines from Heine, his eyes would flash out at you like wet cornflowers after a spring shower. His hair was very thick, straight, and silver white. This, with his clear skin, gave him a somewhat actor-like appearance. He was slight of build and exceedingly frail, with delicate, sensitive hands curving back at the finger-ends, with dark purple veins showing prominently on the back. They were exceedingly small, white as a girl's, and well kept as a pianist's.

As the Professor sat caressing his Huxley, a lady entered. "It is half past six, Emerson, and breakfast will be served at seven." Anyone would have recognized her as the Professor's older sister, for she was a sort of simplified and expurgated edition of himself, the more alert and masculine character of the two, and the scholar's protecting angel. She wore a white lace cap on her head and a knitted shawl about her shoulders. Though she had been a widow for twenty-five years and more, she was always called Miss Agatha Graves. She scanned her brother critically and having satisfied herself that his linen was immaculate and his white tie a fresh one, she remarked, "You were up early this morning, even for you."

"The roses never have the fragrance that they have in the first sun, they give out their best then," said her brother nodding toward the window where the garden roses thrust their pink heads close to the screen as though they would not be kept outside. "And I have something on my mind, Agatha," he continued, nervously fingering the sandalwood paper-cutter, "I feel distraught and weary. You know how I shrink from changes of any sort, and this—why this is the most alarming thing that has ever confronted me. It is absolutely cutting my life off at the stalk, and who knows whether it will bud again?"

Miss Agatha turned sharply about from the window where she had been standing, and gravely studied her brother's drooping shoulders and dejected figure

"There you go at your old tricks, Em," she remonstrated. "I have heard many kinds of ability attributed to you, but to my mind no one has ever put his finger on the right spot. Your real gift is for getting all the possible pain out of life, and extracting needless annoyance from commonplace and trivial things. Here you have buried yourself for the best part of your life in that high school, for motives Quixotic to an absurdity. If you had chosen a university I should not complain, but in that place all your best tools have rusted. Granted that you have done your work a little better than the people about you, it's no great place in which to excel—a city high school where failures in every trade drift to teach the business they cannot make a living by. Now it is time that you do something to justify the faith your friends have always had in you. You owe something to them and to your own name."

"I have builded myself a monument more lasting than brass," quoted the Professor softly, balancing the tips of his slender fingers together.

"Nonsense, Emerson!" said Miss Agatha impatiently. "You are a sentimentalist and your vanity is that of a child. As for those slovenly persons with offensive manners whom you call your colleagues, do you fancy they appreciate you? They are as envious as green gourds and their mouths pucker when they pay you compliments. I hope you are not so unsophisticated as to believe all the sentimental twaddle of your old students. When they want recommendations to some school board, or run for a city office and want your vote, they come here and say that you have been the inspiration of their lives, and I believe in my heart that you are goose enough to accept it all."

"As for my confrères," said the Professor smiling, "I have no doubt that each one receives in the bosom of his family exactly the same advice that you are giving me. If there dwell an appreciated man on earth I have never met him. As for the students, I believe I have, to some at least, in a measure supplied a vital element that their environment failed to give them. Whether they realize this or not is of slight importance; it is in the very nature of youth to forget its sources, physical and mental alike. If one labors at all in the garden of youth, it must be free from the passion of seeing things grow, from an innate love of watching the strange processes of the brain under varying influences and limitations. He gets no more thanks than the novelist gets from the character he creates, nor does he deserve them. He has the whole human comedy before him in embryo, the beginning of all passions and all achievements. As I have often told you, this city is a disputed strategic point. It controls a vast manufacturing region given over to sordid and materialistic ideals. Any work that has been done here for æsthetics cannot be lost. I suppose we shall win in the end, but the reign of Mammon has been long and oppressive. You remember when I was a boy working in the fields how we used to read Bunyan's *Holy War* at night? Well, I have always felt very much as though I were keeping the Ear Gate of the town of Mansoul, and I know not whether the Captains who succeed me be trusty or no."

Miss Agatha was visibly moved, but she shook her head. "Well, I wish you had gone into the church, Emerson. I respect your motives, but there are more tares than wheat in your crop, I suspect."

"My dear girl," said the Professor, his eye brightening, "that is the very reason for the sowing. There is a picture by Vedder of the Enemy Sowing Tares at the foot of the cross, and his seeds are golden coins. That is the call to arms; the other side never sleeps; in the theatres, in the newspapers, in the mills and offices and coal fields, by day and by night the enemy sows tares."

As the Professor slowly climbed the hill to the high school that morning, he indulged in his favorite fancy, that the old grey stone building was a fortress set upon the dominant acclivity of that great manufacturing city, a stronghold of knowledge in the heart of Mammon's kingdom, a Pharos to all those drifting, storm-driven lives in the valley below, where mills and factories thronged, blackening the winding shores of the river, which was dotted with coal barges and frantic, puffing little tugs. The high school commanded the heart of the city, which was like that of any other manufacturing town—a scene of bleakness and naked ugliness and of that remorseless desolation which follows upon the fiercest lust of man. The beautiful valley, where long ago two limpid rivers met at the foot of wooded heights, had become a scorched and blackened waste. The river banks were lined with bellowing mills which broke the silence of the night with periodic crashes of sound, filled the valley with heavy carboniferous smoke, and sent the chilled products of their red forges to all parts of the known world—to fashion railways in Siberia, bridges in Australia, and to tear the virgin soil of Africa. To the west, across the river, rose the steep bluffs, faintly etched through the brown smoke, rising five hundred feet, almost as sheer as a precipice, traversed by cranes and inclines and checkered by winding yellow paths like sheep trails which led to the wretched habitations clinging to the face of the cliff, the lairs of the vicious and the poor, miserable rodents of civilization. In the middle of the stream, among the tugs and barges, were the dredging boats, hoisting muck and filth from the clogged channel. It was difficult to believe that this was the shining river which tumbles down the steep hills of the lumbering district, odorous of wet spruce logs and echoing the ring of axes and the song of the raftsmen, come to this black ugliness at last, with not one throb of its woodland passion and bright vehemence left.

For thirty years the Professor's classroom had overlooked this scene which caused him unceasing admiration and regret. For thirty years he had cried out against the image set up there as the Hebrew prophets cried out against the pride and blind prosperity of Tyre. Nominally he was a professor of English Literature, but his real work had been to try to secure for youth the rights of youth; the right to be generous, to dream, to enjoy; to feel a little the seduction of the old Romance, and to yield a little. His students were boys and girls from the factories and offices, destined to return thither, and hypnotized by the glitter of yellow metal. They were practical, provident, unimaginative, and mercenary at sixteen. Often, when some lad was reading aloud in the classroom, the puffing of the engines in the switch yard at the foot of the hill would drown the verse and the young voice entirely, and the Professor would murmur sadly to himself: "Not even this respite is left to us; even here the voice of youth is drowned by the voice of the taskmaster that waits for them all impatiently enough."

Never had his duty seemed to call him so urgently as on this morning when he was to lay down his arms. As he entered the building he met the boys carrying palms up into the chapel for class-day exercises, and it occurred to him for the first time that this was his last commencement, a commencement without congratulations and without flowers. When he went into the chapel to drill the seniors on their commencement orations, he was unable to fix his mind upon his work. For thirty years he had heard youth say exactly the same thing in the same place; had heard young men swear fealty to the truth, pay honor to the pursuit of noble pleasures, and pledge themselves "to follow knowledge like a sinking star beyond the utmost bound of human thought." How many, he asked himself, had kept their vows? He could remember the occasion of his own commencement in that same chapel; the story that every senior class still told the juniors, of the Professor's humiliation and disgrace when, in attempting to recite "Horatius at the Bridge," he had been unable to recall one word of the poem following

> Then out spake bold Horatius
> The Captain of the gate;

and after some moments of agonizing silence he had shame-facedly left the platform. Even the least receptive of the Professor's students realized that he had risen to a much higher plane of scholarship than any of his colleagues, and they delighted to tell his story of the frail, exquisite, little man whom generations of students had called "the bold Horatius."

All the morning the Professor was busy putting his desk and bookcases in order, impeded by the painful consciousness that he was doing it for the last time. He made many trips to the window and often lapsed into periods of idleness. The room had been connected in one way and another with most of his intellectual passions, and was as full of sentimental associations for him as the haunts of his courtship days are to a lover. At two o'clock he met his last class, which was just finishing *Sohrab and Rustum*, and he was forced to ask one of the boys to read and interpret the majestic closing lines on the "shorn and parceled Oxus." What the boy's comment was the Professor never knew, he felt so close a kinship to that wearied river that he sat stupefied, with his hand shading his eyes and his fingers twitching. When the bell rang announcing the end of the hour he felt a sudden pain clutch his heart; he had a vague hope that the students would gather around his desk to discuss some point that youth loves to discuss, as they often did, but their work was over and they hurried out, eager for their freedom, while the professor sat helplessly watching them.

That evening a banquet was given to the retiring professor in the chapel, but Miss Agatha had to exert all her native power of command to induce him to go. He had come home so melancholy and unnerved that after laying out his dress clothes she literally had to put them on him. When he was in his shirt sleeves and Miss Agatha had carefully brushed his beautiful white hair and arranged his tie, she wheeled him sharply about and retreated to a chair.

"Now, Emerson, say your piece," she commanded.

Plucking up his shirt sleeves and making sure of his cuffs, the Professor began valiantly:

> "Lars Porsena of Clusium,
> By the Nine Gods he swore . . ."

It was all Miss Agatha's idea. After the invitations to the banquet were out and she discovered that half-a-dozen of the Professor's own classmates and many of his old students were to be present, she divined that it would be a tearful and depressing occasion. Emerson, she knew, was an indifferent speaker when his heart was touched, so she had decided that after a silence of thirty-five years Horatius should be heard from. The idea of correcting his youthful failure in his old age had rather pleased the Professor on the whole, and he had set to work to memorize Lord Macaulay's lay, rehearsing in private to Miss Agatha, who had drilled him for that fatal exploit of his commencement night.

After this dress rehearsal the Professor's spirits rose, and during the carriage ride he even made several feeble efforts to joke with his sister. But later in the evening when he sat down at the end of the long table in the dusky chapel, green with palms for commencement week, he fell into deep depression. The guests chattered and boasted and gossiped, but the guest of honor sat silent, staring at the candles. Beside him sat old Fairbrother, of the Greek department, who had come into the faculty in the fifth year of Graves's professorship, and had married a pretty senior girl who had rejected Graves's timid suit. She had been dead this many a year; since his bereavement lonely old Fairbrother had clung to Graves, and now the Professor felt a singular sense of support in his presence.

The Professor tried to tell himself that now his holiday time had come, and that he had earned it; that now he could take up the work he had looked forward to and prepared for for years, his History of Modern Painting, the Italian section of which was already practically complete. But his heart told him that he had no longer the strength to take up independent work. Now that the current of young life had cut away from him and into a new channel, he felt like a ruin of some extinct civilization, like a harbor from which the sea has receded. He realized that he had been living by external stimulation from the warm young blood about him, and now that it had left him, all his decrepitude was horribly exposed. All those hundreds of thirsty young lives had drunk him dry. He compared himself to one of those gigantic colossi of antique lands, from which each traveller has chipped a bit of stone until only a mutilated torso is left.

He looked reflectively down the long table, picking out the faces of his colleagues here and there, souls that had toiled and wrought and thought with him, that simple, unworldly sect of people he loved. They were still discussing the difficulties of the third conjugation, as they had done there for twenty years. They were cases of arrested development, most of them. Always in contact with immature minds, they had kept the simplicity and many of the callow enthusiasms of youth. Those facts and formulae which interest the rest of the world for but a few years at most, were still the vital facts of life for them.

They believed quite sincerely in the supreme importance of quadratic equations, and the rule for the special verbs that govern the dative was a part of their decalogue. And he himself—what had he done with the youth, the strength, the enthusiasm and splendid equipment he had brought there from Harvard thirty years ago? He had come to stay but a little while—five years at the most, until he could save money enough to defray the expense of a course in some German university. But then the battle had claimed him; the desire had come upon him to bring some message of repose and peace to the youth of this work-driven, joyless people, to cry the name of beauty so loud that the roar of the mills could not drown it. Then the reward of his first labors had come in the person of his one and only genius; his restless, incorrigible pupil with the gentle eyes and manner of a girl, at once timid and utterly reckless, who had seen even as Graves saw; who had suffered a little, sung a little, struck the true lyric note, and died wretchedly at three-and-twenty in his master's arms, the victim of a tragedy as old as the world and as grim as Samson, the Israelite's.

He looked about at his comrades and wondered what they had done with their lives. Doubtless they had deceived themselves as he had done. With youth always about them, they had believed themselves of it. Like the monk in the legend they had wandered a little way into the wood to hear the bird's song—the magical song of youth so engrossing and so treacherous, and they had come back to their cloister to find themselves old men— spent warriors who could only chatter on the wall, like grasshoppers, and sigh at the beauty of Helen as she passed.

The toasts were nearly over, but the Professor had heard none of the appreciative and enthusiastic things that his students and colleagues had said of him. He read a deeper meaning into this parting than they had done and his thoughts stopped his ears. He heard Miss Agatha clear her throat and caught her meaning glance. Realizing that everyone was waiting for him, he blinked his eyes like a man heavy with sleep and arose.

"How handsome he looks," murmured the woman looking at his fine old face and silver hair. The Professor's remarks were as vague as they were brief. After expressing his thanks for the honor done him, he stated that he had still some work to finish among them, which had been too long incomplete. Then with as much of his schoolboy attitude as he could remember, and a smile on his gentle lips, he began his

> "Lars Porsena of Clusium,
>   By the Nine Gods he swore
> That the noble house of Tarquin
>   Should suffer wrong no more."

A murmur of laughter ran up and down the long table, and Dr. Maitland, the great theologian, who had vainly tried to prompt his stage-struck fellow graduate thirty-five years ago, laughed until his nose glasses fell off and dangled across his black waistcoat. Miss Agatha was highly elated over the success of her idea, but the Professor had no heart in what he was doing, and the merriment rather hurt him. Surely this was a time for silence and reflection, if ever such time was. Memories crowded upon him faster than the lines he spoke, and the warm eyes turned upon him, full of pride and affection for their scholar and their "great man," moved him almost beyond endurance.

> "—the Consul's brow was sad
> And the Consul's speech was low,"

he read, and suited the action marvellously to the word. His eyes wandered to the chapel rostrum. Thirty-five years ago he had stood there repeating those same lines, a young man, resolute and gifted, with the strength of Ulysses and the courage of Hector, with the kingdoms of the earth and the treasures of the ages at his feet, and the singing rose in his heart; a spasm of emotion contracted the old man's vocal cords.

"Outspake the bold Horatius,
The Captain of the gate,"

he faltered;——his white hand nervously sought his collar, then the hook on his breast where his glasses usually hung, and at last tremulously for his handkerchief; then with a gesture of utter defeat, the Professor sat down. There was a tearful silence; white handkerchiefs fluttered down the table as from a magician's wand, and Miss Agatha was sobbing. Dr. Maitland arose to his feet, his face distorted between laughter and tears. "I ask you all," he cried, "whether Horatius has any need to speak, for has he not kept the bridge these thirty years? God bless him!"

"It's all right, so don't worry about it, Emerson," said Miss Agatha as they got into the carriage. "At least they were appreciative, which is more than I would have believed."

"Ah, Agatha," said the Professor, wiping his face wearily with his crumpled handkerchief, "I am a hopeless dunce, and you ought to have known better. If you could make nothing of me at twenty, you showed poor judgment to undertake it at fifty-five. I was not made to shine, for they put a woman's heart in me."

The Treasure of
Far Island

> Dark brown is the river,
>   Golden is the sand;
> It flows along forever,
>   With trees on either hand.
> —*Robert Louis Stevenson.*

I

Far Island is an oval sand bar, half a mile in length and perhaps a hundred yards wide, which lies about two miles up from Empire City in a turbid little Nebraska river. The island is known chiefly to the children who dwell in that region, and generation after generation of them have claimed it; fished there, and pitched their tents under the great arched tree, and built camp fires on its level, sandy outskirts. In the middle of the island, which is always above water except in flood time, grow thousands of yellow-green creek willows and cottonwood seedlings, brilliantly green, even when the hottest winds blow, by reason of the surrounding moisture. In the summer months, when the capricious stream is low, the children's empire is extended by many rods, and a long irregular beach of white sand is exposed along the east coast of the island, never out of the water long enough to acquire any vegetation, but dazzling white, ripple marked, and full of possibilities for the imagination. The island is No-Man's-

143

Land; every summer a new chief claims it and it has been called by many names; but it seemed particularly to belong to the two children who christened it Far Island, partially because they were the original discoverers and claimants, but more especially because they were of that favored race whom a New England sage called the true land-lords and sea-lords of the world.

One afternoon, early in June, the Silvery Beaches of Far Island were glistening in the sun like pounded glass, and the same slanting yellow rays that scorched the sand beat upon the windows of the passenger train from the East as it swung into the Republican Valley from the uplands. Then a young man dressed in a suit of gray tweed changed his seat in order to be on the side of the car next the river. When he crossed the car several women looked up and smiled, for it was with a movement of boyish abandon and an audible chuckle of delight that he threw himself into the seat to watch for the shining curves of the river as they unwound through the trees. He was sufficiently distinguished in appearance to interest even tired women at the end of a long, sultry day's travel. As the train rumbled over a trestle built above a hollow grown up with sunflowers and ironweed, he sniffed with delight the rank odor, familiar to the prairie-bred man, that is exhaled by such places as evening approaches. "Ha," he murmured under his breath, "there's the white chalk cliff where the Indians used to run the buffalo over Bison Leap—we kids called it—the remote sea wall of the boy world. I'm getting home sure enough. And heavens! there's the island, Far Island, the Ultima Thule; and the arched tree, and Spy Glass Hill, and the Silvery Beaches; my heart's going like a boy's. 'Once on a day he sailed away, over the sea to Skye.' "

He sat bolt upright with his lips tightly closed and his chest swelling, for he was none other than the original discoverer of the island, Douglass Burnham, the playwright—our only playwright, certain critics contend—and, for the first time since he left it a boy, he was coming home. It was only twelve years ago that he had gone away, when Pagie and Temp and Birkner and Shorty Thompson had stood on the station siding and waved him goodbye, while he shut his teeth to keep the tears back; and now the train bore him up the old river valley, though the meadows where he used to hunt for cattails, along the streams where he had paddled his canvas boat, and past the willow-grown island where he had buried the pirate's treasure—a man with a man's work done and the world well in hand. Success had never tasted quite so sweet as it tasted then. The whistle sounded, the brakemen called Empire City, and Douglass crossed to the other side of the car and looked out toward the town, which lay half a mile up from the station on a low range of hills, half hidden by the tall cottonwood trees that still shaded its streets. Down the curve of the track he could see the old railroad "eating house," painted the red Burlington color; on the hill above the town the standpipe towered up from the treetops. Douglass felt the years dropping away from him. The train stopped. Waiting on the platform stood his father and a tall spare man, with a straggling colorless beard, whose dejected stoop and shapeless hat and ill-fitting clothes were in themselves both introduction and biography. The narrow chest, long arms, and skinny neck were not to be mistaken. It was Rhinehold Birkner, old Rhine who had not been energetic enough to keep up his father's undertaking business, and who now sold sewing machines and parlor organs in a feeble attempt to support an invalid wife and ten children, all colorless and narrow chested like himself. Douglass sprang from the platform and grasped his father's hand.

"Hello, father, hello, Rhine, where are the other fellows? Why, that's so, you must be the only one left. Heavens! how we *have* scattered. What a lot of talking we two have got before us."

Probably no event had transpired since Rhine's first baby was born that had meant so much to him as Douglass's return, but he only chuckled, putting his limp, rough hand into the young man's smooth, warm one, and ventured.

"Jest the same old coon, Doug."

"How's mother, father?" Douglass asked as he hunted for his checks.

"She's well, son, but she thought she couldn't leave supper to come down to meet you. She has been cooking pretty much all day and worrying for fear the train would be late and your supper would spoil."

"Of course she has. When I am elected to the Academy mother will worry about my supper." Douglass felt a trifle nervous and made a dash for the shabby little street car which ever since he could remember had been drawn by mules that wore jingling bells on their collars.

A silence settled down over the occupants of the car as the mules trotted off. Douglass felt that his father stood somewhat in awe of him, or at least in awe of that dread Providence which ordered such dark things as that a hard-headed, money-saving real-estate man should be the father of a white-fingered playwright who spent more on his fads in a year than his father had saved by the thrift of a lifetime. All the hundred things Douglass had had to say seemed congested upon his tongue, and though he had a good measure of that cheerful assurance common to young people whom the world has made much of, he felt a strange embarrassment in the presence of this angular gray-whiskered man who used to warm his jacket for him in the hayloft.

His mother was waiting for him under the bittersweet vines on the porch, just where she had always stood to greet him when he came home for his college vacations, and, as Douglass had lived in a world where the emotions are cultivated and not despised, he was not ashamed of the lump that rose in his throat when he took her in his arms. She hurried him out of the dark into the parlor lamplight and looked him over from head to foot to assure herself that he was still the handsomest of men, and then she told him to go into her bedroom to wash his face for supper. She followed him, unable to take her eyes from this splendid creature whom all the world claimed but who was only hers after all. She watched him take off his coat and collar, rejoicing in the freshness of his linen and the whiteness of his skin; even the color of his silk suspenders seemed a matter of importance to her.

"Douglass," she said impressively, "Mrs. Governor gives a reception for you tomorrow night, and I have promised her that you will read some selections from your plays."

This was a matter which was very near Mrs. Burnham's heart. Those dazzling first nights and receptions and author's dinners which happened out in the great world were merely hearsay, but it was a proud day when her son was held in honor by the women of her own town, of her own church; women she had shopped and marketed and gone to sewing circle with, women whose cakes and watermelon pickles won premiums over hers at the county fair.

"Read?" ejaculated Douglass, looking out over the towel and pausing in his brisk rubbing, "why, mother, dear, I can't read, not any more than a John rabbit. Besides, plays aren't meant to be read. Let me give them one of my old stunts; 'The Polish Boy' or 'Regulus to the Carthaginians.' "

"But you must do it, my son; it won't do to disappoint Mrs. Governor. Margie was over this morning to see about it. She has grown into a very pretty girl." When his mother spoke in that tone Douglass acquiesced, just as naturally as he helped himself to her violet water, the same kind, he noticed, that he used to covertly sprinkle on his handkerchief when he was primping for Sunday school after she had gone to church.

"Mrs. Governor still leads the pack, then? What a civilizing influence she has been in this community. Taught most of us all the manners we ever knew. Little Margie has grown up pretty, you say? Well, I should never have thought it. How many boys have I slugged for yelling

'Reddy, go dye your hair green' at her. She was not an indifferent slugger herself and never exactly stood in need of masculine protection. What a wild Indian she was! Game, clear through, though! I never found such a mind in a girl. But *is* she a girl? I somehow always fancied she would grow up a man—and a ripping fine one. Oh, I see you are looking at me hard! No, mother, the girls don't trouble me much." His eyes met hers laughingly in the glass as he parted his hair. "You spoiled me so outrageously that women tell me frankly I'm a selfish cad and they will have none of me."

His mother handed him his coat with a troubled glance. "I was afraid, my son, that some of those actresses—"

The young man laughed outright. "Oh, never worry about them, mother. Wait till you've seen them at rehearsals in soiled shirtwaists wearing out their antiques and doing what they call 'resting' their hair. Poor things! They have to work too hard to bother about being attractive."

He went out into the dining room where the table was set for him just as it had always been when he came home on that same eight o'clock train from college. There were all his favorite viands and the old family silver spread on the white cloth with the maidenhair fern pattern, under the soft lamplight. It had been years since he had eaten by the mild light of a kerosene lamp. By his plate stood his own glass that his grandmother had given him with "For a Good Boy" ground on the surface which was dewy from the ice within. The other glasses were unclouded and held only fresh water from the pump, for his mother was very economical about ice and held the most exaggerated views as to the pernicious effects of ice water on the human stomach. Douglass only got it because he was the first dramatist of the country and a great man. When he decided that he would like a cocktail and asked for whiskey, his mother dealt him out a niggardly tablespoonful, saying, "That's as much as you ought to have at your age, Douglass." When he went out into the kitchen to greet the old servant and get some ice for his drink, his mother hurried after him crying with solicitude.

"I'll get the ice for you, Douglass. Don't you go into the refrigerator; you always leave the ice uncovered and it wastes."

Douglass threw up his hands, "Mother, whatever I may do in the world I shall never be clever enough to be trusted with that refrigerator. 'Into all the chambers of the palace mayest thou go, save into this thou shalt not go.' " And now he knew he was at home, indeed, for his father stood chuckling in the doorway, washing his hands from the milking, and the old servant threw her apron over her head to stifle her laughter at this strange reception of a celebrity. The memory of his luxurious rooms in New York, where he lived when he was an artist, faded dim; he was but a boy again in his father's house and must not keep supper waiting.

The next evening Douglass with resignation accompanied his father and mother to the reception given in his honor. The town had advanced somewhat since his day; and he was amused to see his father appear in an apology for a frock coat and a black tie, such as Kentucky politicians wear. Although people wore frock coats nowadays they still walked to receptions, and as Douglass climbed the hill the whole situation struck him as farcical. He dropped his mother's arm and ran up to the porch with his hat in his hand, laughing. "Margie!" he called, intending to dash through the house until he found her. But in the vestibule he bumped up against something large and splendid, then stopped and caught his breath. A woman stood in the dark by the hall lamp with a lighted match in her hand. She was in white and very tall. The match burned but a moment; a moment the light played on her hair, red as Etruscan gold and piled high above the curve of the neck and head; a moment upon the oval chin, the lips curving upward and red as a crimson cactus flower; the deep, gray, fearless eyes; the white shoulders framed about with darkness. Then the match went out, leaving Douglass to wonder whether, like Anchises, he had seen the vision that should forever blind him to the beauty of mortal women.

"I beg your pardon," he stammered, backing toward the door, "I was looking for Miss Van Dyck. Is she—" Perhaps it was a mere breath of stifled laughter, perhaps it was a recognition by some sense more trustworthy than sight and subtler than mind; but there seemed a certain familiarity in the darkness about him, a certain sense of the security and peace which one experiences among dear and intimate things, and with widening eyes he said softly,

"Tell me, is this Margie?"

There was just a murmur of laughter from the tall, white figure. "I was going to be presented to you in the most proper form, and now you've spoiled it all. How are you, Douglass, and did you get a whipping this time? You've played hooky longer than usual. Ten years, isn't it?" She put out her hand in the dark and he took it and drew it through his arm.

"No, I didn't get a whipping, but I may get worse. I wish I'd come back five years ago. I would if I had known," he said promptly.

The reading was just as stupid as he had said it would be, but his audience enjoyed it and he enjoyed his audience. There was the old deacon who had once caught him in his watermelon patch and set the dog on him; the president of the W.C.T.U., with her memorable black lace shawl and cane, who still continued to send him temperance tracts, mindful of the hundredth sheep in the parable; his old Sunday school teacher, a good man of limited information who never read anything but his Bible and *Teacher's Quarterly*, and who had once hung a cheap edition of *Camille* on the church Christmas tree for Douglass, with an inscription on the inside to the effect that the fear of the Lord is the beginning of Wisdom. There was the village criminal lawyer, one of those brilliant wrecks sometimes found in small towns, who, when he was so drunk he could not walk, used to lie back in his office chair and read Shakespeare by the hour to a little barefoot boy. Next him sat the rich banker who used to offer the boys a quarter to hitch up his horse for him, and then drive off, forgetting all about the quarter. Then there were fathers and mothers of Douglass's old clansmen and vassals who were scattered all over the world now. After the reading Douglass spent half an hour chatting with nice tiresome old ladies who reminded him of how much he used to like their teacakes and cookies, and answering labored compliments with genuine feeling. Then he went with a clear conscience and light heart whither his eyes had been wandering ever since he had entered the house.

"Margie, I needn't apologize for not recognizing you, since it was such an involuntary compliment. However did you manage to grow up like this? Was it boarding school that did it? I might have recognized you with your hair down, and oh, I'd know you anywhere when you smile! The teeth are just the same. Do you still crack nuts with them?"

"I haven't tried it for a long time. How remarkably little the years change you, Douglass. I haven't seen you since the night you brought out *The Clover Leaf*, and I heard your curtain speech. Oh, I was very proud of our Pirate Chief!"

Douglass sat down on the piano stool and looked searchingly into her eyes, which met his with laughing frankness.

"What! you were in New York then and didn't let me know? There was a day when you wouldn't have treated me so badly. Didn't you want to see me just a little bit—out of curiosity?"

"Oh, I was visiting some school friends who said it would be atrocious to bother you, and the newspapers were full of interesting details about your being so busy that you ate and got shaved at the theatre. Then one's time isn't one's own when one is visiting, you know."

She saw the hurt expression on his face and repented, adding gayly, "But I may as well confess that I kept a sharp lookout for you on the street, and when I did meet you you didn't know me."

"And you didn't stop me? That's worse yet. How in Heaven's name was I to know you? Accost a goddess and say, 'Oh yes, you used to be a Pirate Chief and wear a butcher knife in your belt.' But I hadn't grown into an Apollo, save the mark! and you knew me well enough. I couldn't have passed you like that in a strange land."

"No, you do your duty by your countrymen, Douglass. You haven't grown haughty. One by one our old towns-people go out to see the world and bring us back tales of your glory. What unpromising specimens have you not dined and wined in New York! Why even old Skin Jackson, when he went to New York to have his eyes treated, you took to the Waldorf and to the Player's Club, where he drank with the Immortals. How do you have the courage to do it? *Did* he wear those dreadful gold nugget shirt studs that he dug up in Colorado when we were young?"

"Even the same, Margie, and he scored a hit with them. But you are dodging the point. When and where did you see me in New York?"

"Oh, it was one evening when you were crossing Madison Square. You were probably going to the theatre for Flashingham and Miss Grew were with you and you seemed in a hurry." Margie wished now that she had not mentioned the incident. "I remember that was the time I so deeply offended your mother on my return by telling her that Miss Grew had announced her engagement to you. How did it come out? She certainly did announce it."

"Doubtless, but it was entirely a misunderstanding on the lady's part. We never were anything of the sort," said Douglass impatiently. "That is a disgusting habit of Edith's; she announces a new engagement every fortnight as mechanically as the butler announces dinner. About once a month she calls the dear Twelfth Night girls together to a solemn high tea and gently breaks the news of a new engagement, and they kiss and cry over her and say the things they have said a dozen times before and go away tittering. Why she has been engaged to every society chap in New York and to the whole Milton family, with the possible exception of Sir Henry, and her papa has cabled his blessing all over the known world to her. But it is a waste of time to talk about such nonsense; don't let's," he urged.

"I think it is very interesting; I don't indulge in weekly engagements myself. But there is one thing I want to know, Douglass; I want to know how you did it."

"Did what?"

Margie threw out her hands with an impetuous gesture. "Oh, all of it, all the wonderful things you have done. You remember that night when we lay on the sand bar—"

"The Uttermost Desert," interrupted Douglass softly.

"Yes, the Uttermost Desert, and in the light of the driftwood fire we planned the conquest of the world? Well, other people plan, too, and fight and suffer and fail the world over, and a very few succeed at the bitter end when they are old and it is no longer worth while. But you have done it as they used to do it in the fairy tales, without soiling your golden armor, and I can't find one line in your face to tell me that you have suffered or found life bitter to your tongue. How have you cheated fate?"

Douglass looked about him and saw that the guests had thronged about the punchbowl, and his mother, beaming in her new black satin, was relating touching incidents of his infancy to a group of old ladies. He leaned forward, clasped his hands between his knees, and launched into an animated description of how his first play, written at college, had taken the fancy of an old school friend of his father's who had turned manager. The second, a political farce, had put him fairly on his feet. Then followed his historical drama, *Lord Fairfax*, in which he had at first failed completely. He told her of those desperate days in

New York when he would draw his blinds and work by lamplight until he was utterly exhausted, of how he fell ill and lost the thread of his play and used to wander about the streets trying to beat it out of the paving stones when the very policemen who jostled him on the crossings knew more about *Lord Fairfax* than he.

As he talked he felt the old sense of power, lost for many years; the power of conveying himself wholly to her in speech, of awakening in her mind every tint and shadow and vague association that was in his at the moment. He quite forgot the beauty of the woman beside him in the exultant realization of comradeship, the egotistic satisfaction of being wholly understood. Suddenly he stopped short.

"Come, Margie, you're not playing fair, you're telling me nothing about yourself. What plays have you been playing? Pirate or enchanted princess or sleeping beauty or Helen of Troy, to the disaster of men?"

Margie sighed as she awoke out of the fairyland. Doug's tales were as wonderful as ever.

"Oh, I stopped playing long ago. I have grown up and you have not. Some one has said that is wherein geniuses are different; they go on playing and never grow up. So you see you're only a case of arrested development, after all."

"I don't believe it, you play still, I can see it in your eyes. And don't say genius to me. People say that to me only when they want to be disagreeable or tell me how they would have written my plays. The word is my bogie. But tell me, are the cattails ripe in the Salt Marshes, and will your mother let you wade if the sun is warm, and do the winds still smell sharp with salt when they blow through the mists at night?"

"Why, Douglass, did the wind always smell salty to you there too? It does to me yet, and you know there isn't a particle of salt there. Why did we ever name them the Salt Marshes?"

"Because they *were* the Salt Marshes and couldn't have

had any other name any more than the Far Island could. I went down to those pestiferous Maremma marshes in Italy to see whether they would be as real as our marshes, but they were not real at all; only miles and miles of bog. And do the nightingales still sing in the grove?"

"Yes. Other people call them ring doves—but they still sing there."

"And you still call them nightingales to yourself and laugh at the density of big people?"

"Yes, sometimes."

Later in the evening Douglass found another opportunity, and this time he was fortunate enough to encounter Margie alone as she was crossing the veranda.

"Do you know why I have come home in June, instead of July as I had intended, Margie? Well, sit down and let me tell you. They don't need you in there just now. About a month ago I changed my apartment in New York, and as I was sorting over my traps I came across a box of childish souvenirs. Among them was a faded bit of paper on which a map was drawn with elaborate care. It was the map of an island with curly blue lines all around it to represent water, such as we used always to draw around the continents in our geography class. On the west coast of the island a red sword was sticking upright in the earth. Beneath this scientific drawing was an inscription to the effect that *'whoso should dig twelve paces west of the huge fallen tree, in direct line with the path made by the setting sun on the water on the tenth day of June, should find the great treasure and his heart's desire!'* "

Margie laughed and applauded gently with her hands. "And so you have come to dig for it; some two thousand miles almost. There's a dramatic situation for you. I have my map still, and I've often contemplated going down to Far Island and digging, but it wouldn't have been fair, for the treasure was really yours, after all."

"Well, you are going now, and on the tenth day of June, that's next Friday, for that's what I came home for, and I had to spoil the plans and temper of a manager and all his company to do it."

"Nonsense, there are too many mosquitoes on Far Island and I mind them more than I used to. Besides there are no good boats like the *Jolly Roger* nowadays."

"We'll go if I have to build another *Jolly Roger*. You can't make me believe you are afraid of mosquitoes. I know too well the mettle of your pasture. Please do, Margie, please." He used his old insidious coaxing tone.

"Douglass, you have made me do dreadful things enough by using that tone of voice to me. I believe you used to hypnotize me. Will you never, never grow up?"

"Never so long as there are pirate's treasures to dig for and you will play with me, Margie. Oh, I wish I had some of the cake that Alice ate in Wonderland and could make you a little girl again."

That night, after the household was asleep, Douglass went out for a walk about the old town, treading the ways he had trod when he was a founder of cities and a leader of hosts. But he saw few of the old landmarks, for the blaze of Etruscan gold was in his eyes, and he felt as a man might feel who in some sleepy humdrum Italian village had unearthed a new marble goddess, as beautiful as she of Milo; and he felt as a boy might feel who had lost all his favorite marbles and his best pea shooter and the dog that slept with him, and had found them all again. He tried to follow, step by step, the wonderful friendship of his childhood.

A child's normal attitude toward the world is that of the artist, pure and simple. The rest of us have to do with the solids of this world, whereas only their form and color exist for the painter. So, in every wood and street and building there are things, not seen of older people at all, which make up their whole desirableness or objectionableness to children. There are maps and pictures formed by cracks in the walls of bare and unsightly sleeping chambers which make them beautiful; smooth places on the lawn where the grass is greener than anywhere else and which are good to sit upon; trees which are valuable by reason of the peculiar way in which the branches grow, and certain spots under the scrub willows along the creek which are in a manner sacred, like the sacrificial groves of the Druids, so that a boy is almost afraid to walk there. Then there are certain carpets which are more beautiful than others, because with a very little help from the imagination they become the rose garden of the Thousand and One Nights; and certain couches which are peculiarly adapted for playing Sindbad in his days of ease, after the toilsome voyages were over. A child's standard of value is so entirely his own, and his peculiar part and possessions in the material objects around him are so different from those of his elders, that it may be said his rights are granted by a different lease. To these two children the entire external world, like the people who dwelt in it, had been valued solely for what they suggested to the imagination, and people and places alike were merely stage properties, contributing more or less to the intensity of their inner life.

II

"Green leaves a-floating
   Castles of the foam,
Boats of mine a-boating
   When will all come home?"

sang Douglass as they pulled from the mill wharf out into the rapid current of the river, which that morning seemed the most beautiful and noble of rivers, an enchanted river flowing peacefully out of Arcady with the Happy Isles somewhere in the distance. The ripples were touched with silver and the sky was as blue as though it had been made today; the cow bells sounded faintly from the meadows along the shore like the bells of fairy cities ringing on the day the prince errant brought home his bride; the meadows that sloped to the water's edge were the greenest in all the world because they were the meadows of the long ago; and the flowers that grew there were the freshest and sweetest of growing things because once, long ago in the golden age, two children had gathered other flowers like them, and the beauties of vanished summers were everywhere. Douglass sat in the end of the boat, his back to the sun and his straw hat tilted back on his head, pulling slowly and feeling that the day was fine rather than seeing it; for his eyes were fixed upon his helmsman in the other end of the boat, who sat with her hat in her lap, shading her face with a white parasol, and her wonderful hair piled high on her head like a helmet of gleaming bronze.

Of all the possessions of their childhood's Wonderland, Far Island had been dearest; it was graven on their hearts as Calais was upon Mary Tudor's. Long before they had set foot upon it the island was the goal of their loftiest ambitions and most delightful imaginings. They had wondered what trees grew there and what delightful spots were hidden away under the matted grapevines. They had even decided that a race of kindly dwarfs must inhabit it and had built up a civilization and historic annals for these imaginary inhabitants, surrounding the sand bar with all the mystery and enchantment which was attributed to certain islands of the sea by the mariners of Greece. Douglass and Margie had sometimes found it expedient to admit other children into their world, but for the most part these were but hewers of wood and drawers of water, who helped to shift the scenery and construct the balcony and place the king's throne, and were no more in the atmosphere of the play than were the supers who watched Mr. Keane's famous duel with Richmond. Indeed Douglass frequently selected the younger and more passive boys for his vassals on the principle that they did as they were bid and made no trouble. But there is something of the explorer in the least imaginative of boys, and when Douglass came to the building of his famous boat, the *Jolly Roger*, he found willing hands to help him. Indeed the sawing and hammering, the shavings and cut fingers and blood blisters fell chiefly to the lot of dazzled lads who claimed no part in the craft, and who gladly trotted and sweated for their board and keep in this fascinating play world which was so much more exhilarating than any they could make for themselves.

"Think of it, Margie, we are really going back to the island after so many years, just you and I, the captain and his mate. Where are the other gallant lads that sailed with us then?"

"Where are the snows of yester' year?" sighed Margie softly. "It is very sad to grow up."

"Sad for them, yes. But we have never grown up, you know, we have only grown more considerate of our complexions," nodding at the parasol. "What a little mass of freckles you used to be, but I liked you freckled, too. Let me see: old Temp is commanding a regiment in the Philippines, and Bake has a cattle ranch in Wyoming, Mac is a government clerk in Washington, Jim keeps his father's hardware store, poor Ned and Shorty went down in a catboat on the Hudson while they were at college (I went out to hunt for the bodies, you know), and old Rhine is selling sewing machines; he never did get away at all, did he?"

"No, not for any length of time. You know it used to frighten Rhine to go to the next town to see a circus. He went to Arizona once for his lungs, but his family never could tell where he was for he headed all his letters 'Empire City, Nebraska,' for habit."

"Oh, that's delightful, Margie, you must let me use that. Rhine would carry Empire City through Europe with him and never know he was out of it. Have I told you about Pagie? Well, you know Pagie is travelling for a New York tailoring house and I let his people make some clothes for me that I had to give to Flashingham's valet. When he first came to town he tried to be gay, with his fond mother's prayers still about him, a visible nimbus, and the Sunday school boy written all over his open countenance and downy lip and large, white butter teeth.

But I know, at heart, he still detested naughty words and whiskey made him sick. One day I was standing at the Hoffman House bar with some fellows, when a slender youth, who looked like a nice girl masquerading as a rake, stepped up and ordered a claret and seltzer. The whine was unmistakable. I turned and said, even before I had looked at him squarely, 'Oh, Pagie! if your mother saw you here!' "

"Poor Pagie! I'll warrant he would rather have had bread and sugar. Do you remember how, at the Sunday school concerts on Children's Day, you and Pagie and Shorty and Temp used to stand in a row behind the flower-wreathed pulpit rail, all in your new round-about suits with large silk bows tied under your collars, your hands behind you, and assure us with sonorous voices that you would come rejoicing bringing in the sheaves? Somehow, even then, I never doubted that you would do it."

The keel grated on the sand and Douglass sprang ashore and gave her his hand.

"Descend, O Miranda, upon your island! Do you know, Margie, it makes me seem fifteen again to feel this sand crunching under my feet. I wonder if I ever again shall feel such a thrill of triumph as I felt when I first leaped upon this sand bar? None of my first nights have given me anything like it. Do you remember *really*, and did you feel the same?"

"Of course I remember, and I knew that you were playing a double rôle that day, and that you were really the trail-breaker and world-finder inside of the pirate all the while. Here are the same ripple marks on the Silvery Beaches, and here is the great arched tree, let's run for it." She started fleetly across the glittering sand and Douglass fell behind to watch with immoderate joy that splendid, generous body that governed itself so well in the open air. There was a wholesomeness of the sun and soil in her that was utterly lacking in the women among whom he had lived for so long. She had preserved that strength of arm and freedom of limb that had made her so fine a playfellow, and which modern modes of life have well-nigh robbed the world of altogether. Surely, he thought, it was like that that Diana's women sped after the stag down the slopes of Ida, with shouting and bright spear. She caught an overhang branch and swung herself upon the embankment and, leaning against the trunk of a tree, awaited him flushed and panting, her bosom rising and falling with her quick drawn breaths.

"Why did you close the tree behind you, Margie? I have always wanted to see just how Dryads keep house," he exclaimed, brushing away a dried leaf that had fallen on her shoulder.

"Don't strain your inventive powers to make compliments, Douglass; this is your vacation and you are to rest your imagination. See, the willows have scarcely grown at all. I'm sure we shall hear Pagie whimpering over there on the Uttermost Desert where we marooned him, or singing hymns to keep up his courage. Now for the Huge Fallen Tree. Do you suppose the floods have moved it?"

They struck through the dense willow thicket, matted with fragrant wild grapevines which Douglass beat down with his spade, and came upon the great white log, the bleached skeleton of a tree, and found the cross hacked upon it, the rough gashes of the hatchet now worn smooth by the wind and rain and the seething of spring freshets. Near the cross were cut the initials of the entire pirate crew; some of them were cut on gravestones now. The scrub willows had grown over the spot where they had decided the treasure must lie, and together they set to work to break them away. Douglass paused more than once to watch the strong young creature beside him, outlined against the tender green foliage, reaching high and low and snapping the withes where they were weakest. He was still wondering whether it was not all a dream picture, and was half afraid that his man would call him

to tell him that some piqued and faded woman was awaiting him at the theatre to quarrel about her part.

"Still averse to manual labor, Douglass?" she laughed
as she turned to bend a tall sapling. "The most remarkable thing about your enthusiasm was that you had only
to sing of the glories of toil to make other people do all the
work for you."

"No, Margie, I was thinking very hard indeed—about
the Thracian women when they broke the boughs where-
with they flayed unhappy Orpheus."

"Now, Douglass, you'll spoil the play. A sentimental
pirate is impossible. Pagie was a sentimental pirate and
that was what spoiled him. A little more of this and I will
maroon you upon the Uttermost Desert."

Douglass laughed and settled himself back among the
green boughs and gazed at her with the abandoned admiration of an artist contemplating a masterpiece.

When they came to the digging of the treasure a little
exertion was enough to unearth what had seemed hidden
so fabulously deep in olden time. The chest was rotten
and fell apart as the spade struck it, but the glass jar was
intact, covered with sand and slime. Douglass spread his
handkerchief upon the sand and weighted the corners
down with pebbles and upon it poured the treasure of Far
Island. There was the manuscript written in blood, a con-
fession of fantastic crimes, and the Spaniard's heart in a
bottle of alcohol, and Temp's Confederate bank notes,
damp and grewsome to the touch, and Pagie's rare tobacco tags, their brilliant colors faded entirely away, and
poor Shorty's bars of tinfoil dull and eaten with rust.

"And, Douglass," cried Maggie, "there is your father's
silver ring that was made from a nugget; he whipped you
for burying it. You remember it was given to a Christian
knight by an English queen, and when he was slain before Jerusalem a Saracen took it and we killed the Saracen
in the desert and cut off his finger to get the ring. It is
strange how those wild imaginings of ours seem, in retro-
spect, realities, things that I actually lived through. I sup-

pose that in cold fact my life was a good deal like that of other little girls who grow up in a village; but whenever I look back on it, it is all exultation and romance—sea fights and splendid galleys and Roman triumphs and brilliant caravans winding through the desert."

"To people who live by imagination at all, that is the only life that goes deep enough to leave memories. We were artists in those days, creating for the day only; making epics sung once and then forgotten, building empires that set with the sun. Nobody worked for money then, and nobody worked for fame, but only for the joy of the doing. Keats said the same thing more elegantly in his May Day Ode, and we were not so unlike those Hellenic poets who were content to sing to the shepherds and forget and be forgotten, 'rich in the simple worship of a day.' "

"Why, Douglass," she cried as she bent her face down to the little glass jar, "it was really our childhood that we buried here, never guessing what a precious thing we were putting under the ground. That was the real treasure of Far Island, and we might dig up the whole island for it but all the king's horses and all the king's men could not bring it back to us. That voyage we made to bury our trinkets, just before you went away to school, seems like unconscious symbolism, and somehow it stands out from all the other good times we knew then as the happiest of all." She looked off where the setting sun hung low above the water.

"Shall I tell you why, Margie? That was the end of our childhood, and there the golden days died in a blaze of glory, passed in music out of sight. That night, after our boat had drifted away from us, when we had to wade down the river hand in hand, we two, and the noises and the coldness of the water frightened us, and there were quicksands and sharp rocks and deep holes to shun, and terrible things lurking in the woods on the shore, you cried in a different way from the way you sometimes cried when you hurt yourself, and I found that I loved you afraid better than I had ever loved you fearless, and in that moment we grew up, and shut the gates of Eden behind us, and our empire was at an end."

"And now we are only kings in exile," sighed Margie softly, "who wander back to look down from the mountain tops upon the happy land we used to rule."

Douglass took her hand gently; "If there is to be any Eden on earth again for us, dear, we must make it with our two hearts."

There was a sudden brightness of tears in her eyes, and she drew away from him. "Ah, Douglass, you are determined to spoil it all. It is you who have grown up and taken on the ways of the world. The play is at an end for me." She tried to rise, but he held her firmly.

"From the moment I looked into your eyes in the vestibule that night we have been parts of the same dream again. Why, Margie, we have more romance behind us than most men and women ever live."

Margie's face grew whiter, but she pushed his hand away and the look in her eyes grew harder. "This is only a new play, Douglass, and you will weary of it tomorrow. I am not so good at playing as I used to be. I am no longer content with the simple worship of a day."

In her touch, in her white face, he divined the greatness of what she had to give. He bit his lip and answered, "I think you owe me more confidence than that, if only for the sake of those days when we trusted each other entirely."

She turned with a quick flash of remorseful tenderness, as she used to do when she hurt him at play. "I only want to keep you from hurting us both, Douglass. We neither of us could go on feeling like this. It's only the dregs of the old enchantment. Things have always come easily to you, I know, for at your birth nature and fortune joined to make you great. But they do not come so to me; I should wake and weep."

"Then weep, my princess, for I will wake you now!"

The fire and fancy that had so bewitched her girlhood

that no other man had been able to dim the memory of it came furiously back upon her, with arms that were new and strange and strong, and with tenderness stranger still in this wild fellow of dreams and jests; and all her vows never to grace another of his Roman triumphs were forgotten.

"You are right, Margie; the pirate play is ended and the time has come to divide the prizes, and I choose what I chose fifteen years ago. Out of the spoils of a lifetime of crime and bloodshed I claimed only the captive princess, and I claim her still. I have sought the world over for her, only to find her at last in the land of lost content."

Margie lifted her face from his shoulder, and, after the manner of women of her kind, she played her last card rhapsodically. "And she, O Douglass! the years she has waited have been longer than the waiting of Penelope, and she has woven a thousand webs of dreams by night and torn them asunder by day, and looked out across the Salt Marshes for the night train, and still you did not come. I was only your pensioner like Shorty and Temp and the rest, and I could not play anything alone. You took my world with you when you went and left me only a village of mud huts and loneliness."

As her eyes and then her lips met his in the dying light, he knew that she had caught the spirit of the play, and that she would ford the river by night with him and never be afraid.

The locust chirped in the thicket; the setting sun threw a track of flame cross the water; the willows burned with fire and were not consumed; a glory was upon the sand and the river and upon the Silvery Beaches; and these two looked about over God's world and saw that it was good. In the western sky the palaces of crystal and gold were quenched in night, like the cities of old empires; and out of the east rose the same moon that has glorified all the romances of the world—that lighted Paris over the blue Ægean and the feet of young Montague to the Capulets' orchard. The dinner hour in Empire City was long past, but the two upon the island wist naught of these things, for they had become as the gods, who dwell in their golden houses, recking little of the woes and labors of mortals, neither heeding any fall of rain or snow.

The Namesake

Seven of us, students, sat one evening in Hartwell's studio on the Boulevard St. Michel. We were all fellow-countrymen, one from New Hampshire, one from Colorado, another from Nevada, several from the farmlands of the Middle West, and I myself from California. Lyon Hartwell, though born abroad, was simply, as every one knew, "from America." He seemed, almost more than any other one living man, to mean all of it—from ocean to ocean. When he was in Paris, his studio was always open to the seven of us who were there that evening, and we intruded upon his leisure as often as we thought permissible.

Although we were within the terms of the easiest of all intimacies, and although the great sculptor, even when he was more than usually silent, was at all times the most gravely cordial of hosts, yet, on that long remembered evening, as the sunlight died on the burnished brown of the horse chestnuts below the windows, a perceptible dullness yawned through our conversation.

We were, indeed, somewhat low in spirit, for one of our number, Charley Bentley, was leaving us indefinitely, in response to an imperative summons from home. Tomorrow his studio, just across the hall from Hartwell's, was to pass into other hands, and Bentley's luggage was even now piled in discouraged resignation before his door. The various bales and boxes seemed literally to weigh upon us as we sat in his neighbor's hospitable rooms, drearily putting in the time until he should leave us to catch the ten o'clock express for Dieppe.

The day we had got through very comfortably, for Bentley made it the occasion of a somewhat pretentious luncheon at Maxim's. There had been twelve of us at table, and the two young Poles were so thirsty, the Gascon so fabulously entertaining, that it was near upon five o'clock when we put down our liqueur glasses for the last time, and the red, perspiring waiter, having pocketed the reward of his arduous and protracted services, bowed us affably to the door, flourishing his napkin and brushing back the streaks of wet, black hair from his rosy forehead. Our guests having betaken themselves belated to their respective engagements, the rest of us returned with Bentley—only to be confronted by the depressing array before his door. A glance about his denuded room had sufficed to chill the glow of the afternoon, and we fled across the hall in a body and begged Lyon Hartwell to take us in.

Bentley had said very little about it, but we all knew what it meant to him to be called home. Each of us knew what it would mean to himself, and each had felt something of that quickened sense of opportunity which comes at seeing another man in any way counted out of the race. Never had the game seemed so enchanting, the chance to play it such a piece of unmerited, unbelievable good fortune.

It must have been, I think, about the middle of October, for I remember that the sycamores were almost bare in the Luxembourg Gardens that morning, and the terraces about the queens of France were strewn with crackling brown leaves. The fat red roses, out the summer long on the stand of the old flower woman at the corner, had given place to dahlias and purple asters. First glimpses of autumn toilettes flashed from the carriages; wonderful little bonnes nodded at one along the Champs Élysées; and in the Quarter an occasional feather boa, red or black or white, brushed one's coat sleeve in the gay twilight of the early evening. The crisp, sunny autumn air was all day full of the stir of people and carriages and of the cheer of salutations; greetings of the students, returned brown and bearded from their holiday, gossip of people come back from Trouville, from St. Valery, from Dieppe, from all over Brittany and the Norman coast. Everywhere was the joyousness of return, the taking up again of life and work and play.

I had felt ever since early morning that this was the saddest of all possible seasons for saying goodbye to that old, old city of youth, and to that little corner of it on the south shore which since the Dark Ages themselves—yes, and before—has been so peculiarly the land of the young.

I can recall our very postures as we lounged about Hartwell's rooms that evening, with Bentley making occasional hurried trips to his desolated workrooms across the hall—as if haunted by a feeling of having forgotten something—or stopping to poke nervously at his *perroquets*, which he had bequeathed to Hartwell, gilt cage and all. Our host himself sat on the couch, his big, bronze-like shoulders backed up against the window, his shaggy head, beaked nose, and long chin cut clean against the gray light.

Our drowsing interest, in so far as it could be said to be fixed upon anything, was centered upon Hartwell's new figure, which stood on the block ready to be cast in bronze, intended as a monument for some American battlefield. He called it *The Color Sergeant*. It was the figure of a young soldier running, clutching the folds of a flag, the staff of which had been shot away. We had known it in all the stages of its growth, and the splendid action and feeling of the thing had come to have a kind of special significance for the half dozen of us who often gathered at Hartwell's rooms—though, in truth, there was as much to dishearten one as to inflame, in the case of a man who had done so much in a field so amazingly difficult; who had thrown up in bronze all the restless, teeming force of that adventurous wave still climbing westward in our own land across the waters. We recalled his *Scout*, his *Pioneer*, his *Gold Seekers*, and those monuments in which he had invested one and another of the heroes of the Civil War with such convincing dignity and power.

"Where in the world does he get the heat to make an idea like that carry?" Bentley remarked morosely, scowling at the clay figure. "Hang me, Hartwell, if I don't think it's just because you're not really an American at all, that you can look at it like that."

The big man shifted uneasily against the window. "Yes," he replied smiling, "perhaps there is something in that. My citizenship was somewhat belated and emotional in its flowering. I've half a mind to tell you about it, Bentley," He rose uncertainly, and, after hesitating a moment, went back into his workroom, where he began fumbling among the litter in the corners.

At the prospect of any sort of personal expression from Hartwell, we glanced questioningly at one another; for although he made us feel that he liked to have us about, we were always held at a distance by a certain diffidence of his. There were rare occasions—when he was in the heat of work or of ideas—when he forgot to be shy, but they were so exceptional that no flattery was quite so seductive as being taken for a moment into Hartwell's confidence. Even in the matter of opinions—the commonest of currency in our circle—he was niggardly and prone to qualify. No man ever guarded his mystery more effectually. There was a singular, intense spell, therefore, about those few evenings when he had broken through this excessive modesty, or shyness, or melancholy, and had, as it were, committed himself.

When Hartwell returned from the back room, he brought with him an unframed canvas which he put on an easel near his clay figure. We drew close about it, for the darkness was rapidly coming on. Despite the dullness of the light, we instantly recognized the boy of Hartwell's *Color Sergeant*. It was the portrait of a very handsome lad in uniform, standing beside a charger impossibly rearing.

Not only in his radiant countenance and flashing eyes, but in every line of his young body there was an energy, a gallantry, a joy of life, that arrested and challenged one.

"Yes, that's where I got the notion," Hartwell remarked, wandering back to his seat in the window. "I've wanted to do it for years, but I've never felt quite sure of myself. I was afraid of missing it. He was an uncle of mine, my father's half brother, and I was named for him. He was killed in one of the big battles of Sixty-four, when I was a child. I never saw him—never knew him until he had been dead for twenty years. And then, one night, I came to know him as we sometimes do living persons—intimately, in a single moment."

He paused to knock the ashes out of his short pipe, refilled it, and puffed at it thoughtfully for a few moments with his hands on his knees. Then, settling back heavily among the cushions and looking absently out of the window, he began his story. As he proceeded further and further into the experience which he was trying to convey to us, his voice sank so low and was sometimes so charged with feeling, that I almost thought he had forgotten our presence and was remembering aloud. Even Bentley forgot his nervousness in astonishment and sat breathless under the spell of the man's thus breathing his memories out into the dusk.

"It was just fifteen years ago this last spring that I first went home, and Bentley's having to cut away like this brings it all back to me.

"I was born, you know, in Italy. My father was a sculptor, though I dare say you've not heard of him. He was one of those first fellows who went over after Story and Powers—went to Italy for 'Art,' quite simply; to lift from its native bough the willing, iridescent bird. Their story is told, informingly enough, by some of those ingenuous marble things at the Metropolitan. My father came over some time before the outbreak of the Civil War, and was regarded as a renegade by his family because he did not go home to enter the army. His half brother, the only child of my grandfather's second marriage, enlisted at fifteen and was killed the next year. I was ten years old when the news of his death reached us. My mother died the following winter, and I was sent away to a Jesuit school, while my father, already ill himself, stayed on at Rome, chipping away at his Indian maidens and marble goddesses, still gloomily seeking the thing for which he had made himself the most unhappy of exiles.

"He died when I was fourteen, but even before that I had been put to work under an Italian sculptor. He had an almost morbid desire that I should carry on his work, under, as he often pointed out to me, conditions so much more auspicious. He left me in the charge of his one intimate friend, an American gentleman in the consulate at Rome, and his instructions were that I was to be educated there and to live there until I was twenty-one. After I was of age, I came to Paris and studied under one master after another until I was nearly thirty. Then, almost for the first time, I was confronted by a duty which was not my pleasure.

"My grandfather's death, at an advanced age, left an invalid maiden sister of my father's quite alone in the world. She had suffered for years from a cerebral disease, a slow decay of the faculties which rendered her almost helpless. I decided to go to America and, if possible, bring her back to Paris, where I seemed on my way toward what my poor father had wished for me.

"On my arrival at my father's birthplace, however, I found that this was not to be thought of. To tear this timid, feeble, shrinking creature, doubly aged by years and illness, from the spot where she had been rooted for a lifetime, would have been little short of brutality. To leave her to the care of strangers seemed equally heartless. There was clearly nothing for me to do but to remain and wait for that slow and painless malady to run its course. I was there something over two years.

"My grandfather's home, his father's homestead before him, lay on the high banks of a river in western Pennsyl-

vania. The little town· twelve miles down the stream,
whither my great-grandfather used to drive his ox-wagon
on market days, had become, in two generations, one of
the largest manufacturing cities in the world. For hundreds of miles about us the gentle hill slopes were
honeycombed with gas wells and coal shafts; oil derricks
creaked in every valley and meadow; the brooks were
sluggish and discolored with crude petroleum, and the air
was impregnated by its searching odor. The great glass
and iron manufactories had come up and up the river
almost to our very door; their smoky exhalations brooded
over us, and their crashing was always in our ears. I was
plunged into the very incandescence of human energy.
But, though my nerves tingled with the feverish, passionate endeavor which snapped in the very air about me,
none of these great arteries seemed to feed me; this tu-
multuous life did not warm me. On every side were the
great muddy rivers, the ragged mountains from which the
timber was being ruthlessly torn away, the vast tracts of
wild country, and the gulches that were like wounds in
the earth; everywhere the glare of that relentless energy
which followed me like a searchlight and seemed to scorch
and consume me. I could only hide my self in the tangled
garden, where the dropping of a leaf or the whistle of a
bird was the only incident.

"The Hartwell homestead had been sold away little by
little, until all that remained of it was garden and orchard.
The house, a square brick structure, stood in the midst of
a great garden which sloped toward the river, ending in a
grassy bank which fell some forty feet to the water's edge.
The garden was now little more than a tangle of neglected
shrubbery; damp, rank, and of that intense blue-green
peculiar to vegetation in smoky places where the sun
shines but rarely, and the mists form early in the evening
and hang late in the morning.

"I shall never forget it as I saw it first, when I arrived
there in the chill of a backward June. The long, rank
grass, thick and soft and falling in billows, was always

wet until midday. The gravel walks were bordered with great lilac bushes, mock orange, and bridal wreath. Back of the house was a neglected rose garden, surrounded by a low stone wall over which the long suckers trailed and matted. They had wound their pink, thorny tentacles, layer upon layer, about the lock and the hinges of the rusty iron gate. Even the porches of the house, and the very windows, were damp and heavy with growth: wistaria, clematis, honeysuckle, and trumpet vine. The garden was grown up with trees, especially that part of it which lay above the river. The bark of the old locusts was blackened by the smoke that crept continually up the valley, and their feathery foliage, so merry in its color, seemed peculiarly precious under that somber sky. There were sycamores and copper beeches; gnarled apple trees, too old to bear; and fall pear trees, hung with a sharp, hard fruit in October; all with a leafage singularly rich and luxuriant, and peculiarly vivid in color. The oaks about the house had been old trees when my great-grandfather built his cabin there, more than a century before, and this garden was almost the only spot for miles along the river where any of the original forest growth still survived. The smoke from the mills was fatal to trees of the larger sort, and even these had the look of doomed things—bent a little toward the town and seemed to wait with head inclined before that oncoming, shrieking force.

"About the river, too, there was a strange hush, a tragic submission—it was so leaden and sullen in its color, and it flowed so soundlessly forever past our door.

"I sat there every evening, on the high veranda overlooking it, watching the dim outlines of the steep hills on the other shore, the flicker of the lights on the island, where there was a boathouse, and listening to the call of the boatmen through the mist. The mist came as certainly as night, whitened by moonshine or starshine. The tin water pipes went splash, splash, with it all evening, and the wind, when it rose at all, was little more than a sighing in the heavy grasses.

"At first it was to think of my distant friends and my old life that I used to sit there; but after awhile it was simply to watch the days and weeks go by, like the river which seemed to carry them away.

"Within the house I was never at home. Month followed month, and yet I could feel no sense of kinship with anything there. Under the roof where my father and grandfather were born, I remained utterly detached. The somber rooms never spoke to me, the old furniture never seemed tinctured with race. This portrait of my boy uncle was the only thing to which I could draw near, the only link with anything I had ever known before.

"There is a good deal of my father in the face, but it is my father transformed and glorified; his hesitating discontent drowned in a kind of triumph. From my first day in that house, I continually turned to this handsome kinsman of mine, wondering in what terms he had lived and had his hope; what he had found there to look like that, to bound at one, after all those years, so joyously out of the canvas.

"From the timid, clouded old woman over whose life I had come to watch, I learned that in the back yard, near the old rose garden, there was a locust tree which my uncle had planted. After his death, while it was still a slender sapling, his mother had a seat built round it, and she used to sit there on summer evenings. His grave was under the apple trees in the old orchard.

"My aunt could tell me little more than this. There were days when she seemed not to remember him at all.

"It was from an old soldier in the village that I learned the boy's story. Lyon was, the old man told me, but fourteen when the first enlistment occurred, but was even then eager to go. He was in the courthouse square every evening to watch the recruits at their drill, and when the home company was ordered off he rode into the city on his pony to see the men board the train and to wave them goodbye. The next year he spent at home with a tutor, but when he was fifteen he held his parents to their promise and went into the army. He was color sergeant of his regiment and fell in a charge upon the breastworks of a fort about a year after his enlistment.

"The veteran showed me an account of this charge which had been written for the village paper by one of my uncle's comrades who had seen his part in the engagement. It seems that as his company were running at full speed across the bottom lands toward the fortified hill, a shell burst over them. This comrade, running beside my uncle, saw the colors waver and sink as if falling, and looked to see that the boy's hand and forearm had been torn away by the exploding shrapnel. The boy, he thought, did not realize the extent of his injury, for he laughed, shouted something which his comrade did not catch, caught the flag in his left hand, and ran on up the hill. They went splendidly up over the breastworks, but just as my uncle, his colors flying, reached the top of the embankment, a second shell carried away his left arm at the armpit, and he fell over the wall with the flag settling about him.

"It was because this story was ever present with me, because I was unable to shake it off, that I began to read such books as my grandfather had collected upon the Civil War. I found that this war was fought largely by boys, that more men enlisted at eighteen than at any other age. When I thought of those battlefields—and I thought of them much in those days—there was always that glory of youth above them, that impetuous, generous passion stirring the long lines on the march, the blue battalions in the plain. The bugle, whenever I have heard it since, has always seemed to me the very golden throat of that boyhood which spent itself so gaily, so incredibly.

"I used often to wonder how it was that this uncle of mine, who seemed to have possessed all the charm and brilliancy allotted to his family and to have lived up its vitality in one splendid hour, had left so little trace in the house where he was born and where he had awaited his destiny. Look as I would, I could find no letters from him, no clothing or books that might have been his. He had been dead but twenty years, and yet nothing seemed to have survived except the tree he had planted. It seemed incredible and cruel that no physical memory of him should linger to be cherished among his kindred—nothing but the dull image in the brain of that aged sister. I used to pace the garden walks in the evening, wondering that no breath of his, no echo of his laugh, of his call to his pony or his whistle to his dogs, should linger about those shaded paths where the pale roses exhaled their dewy, country smell. Sometimes, in the dim starlight, I have thought that I heard on the grasses beside me the stir of a footfall lighter than my own, and under the black arch of the lilacs I have fancied that he bore me company.

"There was, I found, one day in the year for which my old aunt waited, and which stood out from the months that were all of a sameness to her. On the thirtieth of May she insisted that I should bring down the big flag from the attic and run it up upon the tall flagstaff beside Lyon's tree in the garden. Later in the morning she went with me to carry some of the garden flowers to the grave in the orchard—a grave scarcely larger than a child's.

"I had noticed, when I was hunting for the flag in the attic, a leather trunk with my own name stamped upon it, but was unable to find the key. My aunt was all day less apathetic than usual; she seemed to realize more clearly who I was, and to wish me to be with her. I did not have an opportunity to return to the attic until after dinner that evening, when I carried a lamp upstairs and easily forced the lock of the trunk. I found all the things that I had looked for; put away, doubtless, by his mother, and still smelling faintly of lavender and rose leaves; his clothes, his exercise books, his letters from the army, his first boots, his riding whip, some of his toys, even. I took them out and replaced them gently. As I was about to shut the lid, I picked up a copy of the Æneid, on the flyleaf of which was written in a slanting, boyish hand,

Lyon Hartwell, January, 1862.

He had gone to the wars in Sixty-three, I remembered.

"My uncle, I gathered, was none too apt at his Latin, for the pages were dog-eared and rubbed and interlined, the margins mottled with pencil sketches—bugles, stacked bayonets, and artillery carriages. In the act of putting the book down, I happened to run over the pages to the end, and on the flyleaf at the back I saw his name again, and a drawing—with his initials and a date—of the Federal flag; above it, written in a kind of arch and in the same unformed hand:

Oh, say, can you see by the dawn's early light
What so proudly we hailed at the twilight's last gleaming?

It was a stiff, wooden sketch, not unlike a detail from some Egyptian inscription, but, the moment I saw it, wind and color seemed to touch it. I caught up the book, blew out the lamp, and rushed down into the garden.

"I seemed, somehow, at last to have known him; to have been with him in that careless, unconscious moment and to have known him as he was then.

"As I sat there in the rush of this realization, the wind began to rise, stirring the light foliage of the locust over my head and bringing, fresher than before, the woody odor of the pale roses that overran the little neglected garden. Then, as it grew stronger, it brought the sound of something sighing and stirring over my head in the perfumed darkness.

"I thought of that sad one of the Destinies who, as the Greeks believed, watched from birth over those marked for a violent or untimely death. Oh, I could see him, there in the shine of the morning, his book idly on his knee, his flashing eyes looking straight before him, and at his side that grave figure, hidden in her draperies, her eyes following his, but seeing so much farther—seeing what he never saw, that great moment at the end, when he swayed above his comrades on the earthen wall.

"All the while, the bunting I had run up in the morning flapped fold against fold, heaving and tossing softly in the dark—against a sky so black with rain clouds that I could see above me only the blur of something in soft, troubled motion.

"The experience of that night, coming so overwhelmingly to a man so dead, almost rent me in pieces. It was the same feeling that artists know when we, rarely, achieve truth in our work; the feeling of union with some great force, of purpose and security, of being glad that we have lived. For the first time I felt the pull of race and blood and kindred, and felt beating within me things that had not begun with me. It was as if the earth under my feet had grasped and rooted me, and were pouring its essence into me. I sat there until the dawn of morning, and all night long my life seemed to be pouring out of me and running into the ground."

Hartwell drew a long breath that lifted his heavy shoulders, and then let them fall again. He shifted a little and faced more squarely the scattered, silent company before him. The darkness had made us almost invisible to each other, and, except for the occasional red circuit of a cigarette end traveling upward from the arm of a chair, he might have supposed us all asleep.

"And so," Hartwell added thoughtfully, "I naturally feel an interest in fellows who are going home. It's always an experience."

No one said anything, and in a moment there was a loud rap at the door—the concierge, come to take down Bentley's luggage and to announce that the cab was below. Bentley got his hat and coat, enjoined Hartwell to take good care of his *perroquets*, gave each of us a grip of the hand, and went briskly down the long flights of stairs. We followed him into the street, calling our good wishes, and saw him start on his drive across the lighted city to the Gare St. Lazare.

The Profile

The subject of discussion at the Impressionists' Club was a picture, *Circe's Swine*, by a young German painter; a grotesque study showing the enchantress among a herd of bestial things, variously diverging from the human type—furry-eared fauns, shaggy-hipped satyrs, apes with pink palms, snuffing jackals, and thick-jowled swine, all with more or less of human intelligence protesting mutely from their hideous lineaments.

"They are all errors, these freakish excesses," declared an old painter of the Second Empire. "Triboulet, Quasimodo, Gwynplaine, have no proper place in art. Such art belongs to the Huns and Iroquois, who could only be stirred by laceration and dismemberment. The only effects of horror properly within the province of the artist are psychological. Everything else is a mere matter of the abattoir. The body, as Nature has evolved it, is sanctified by her purpose; in any natural function or attitude decent and comely. But lop away so much as a finger, and you have wounded the creature beyond reparation."

Once launched upon this subject, there was no stopping the old lion, and several of his confrères were relieved when Aaron Dunlap quietly rose and left the room. They felt that this was a subject which might well be distasteful to him.

I

Dunlap was a portrait painter—preferably a painter of women. He had the faculty of transferring personalities to his canvas, rather than of putting conceptions there. He was finely sensitive to the merest prettiness, was tender and indulgent of it, careful never to deflower a pretty woman of her little charm, however commonplace.

Nicer critics always discerned, even in his most radiant portraits, a certain quiet element of sympathy, almost of pity, in the treatment. The sharp, flexible profile of Madame R—— of the Française; the worn, but subtle and all-capricious physiognomy of her great Semitic rival; the plump contours of a shopkeeper's pretty wife—Dunlap treated them with equal respect and fidelity. He accepted each as she was, and could touch even obvious prettiness with dignity. Behind the delicate pleasure manifested in his treatment of a beautiful face, one could divine the sadness of knowledge, and one felt that the painter had yearned to arrest what was so fleeting and to hold it back from the cruelty of the years. At an exhibition of Dunlap's pictures, the old painter of the Second Empire had said, with a sigh, that he ought to get together all his portraits of young women and call them "Les Fiançées," so abloom were they with the confidence of their beautiful secret. Then, with that sensitiveness to style, which comes from long and passionate study of form, the old painter had added reflectively, "And, after all, how sad a thing it is to be young."

Dunlap had come from a country where women are hardly used. He had grown up on a farm in the remote mountains of West Virginia, and his mother had died of pneumonia contracted from taking her place at the wash-tub too soon after the birth of a child. When a boy, he had been apprenticed to his grandfather, a country cobbler, who, in his drunken rages, used to beat his wife with odd strips of shoe leather. The painter's hands still bore the mark of that apprenticeship, and the suffering of the mountain women he had seen about him in his childhood had left him almost morbidly sensitive.

Just how or why Dunlap had come to Paris, none of his fellow-painters had ever learned. When he ran away from his grandfather, he had been sent by a missionary fund to some sectarian college in his own state, after which he had taught a country school for three winters and saved money enough for his passage. He arrived in Paris with something less than a hundred dollars, wholly ignorant of the language, without friends, and, apparently, without especial qualifications for study there.

Perhaps the real reason that he never succumbed to want was, that he was never afraid of it. He felt that he could never be really hungry so long as the poplars flickered along the gray quay behind the Louvre; never friendless while the gay busses rolled home across the bridges through the violet twilight, and the barge lights winked above the water.

Little by little his stripes were healed, his agony of ignorance alleviated. The city herself taught him whatever was needful for him to know. She repeated with him that fanciful romance which she has played at with youth for centuries, in which her spontaneity is ever young. She gave him of her best, quickened in him a sense of the more slight and feminine fairness in things; trained his hand and eye to the subtleties of the thousand types of subtle beauty in which she abounds; made him, after a delicate and chivalrous fashion, the expiator of his mountain race. He lived in a bright atmosphere of clear vision and happy associations, delighted at having to do with what was fair and exquisitely brief.

Life went on so during the first ten years of his residence in Paris—a happiness which, despite its almost timorous modesty, tempted fate. It was after Dunlap's name had become somewhat the fashion, that he chanced one day, in a café on the Boulevard St. Michel, to be of some service to an American who was having trouble about his order. After assisting him, Dunlap had some

conversation with the man, a Californian, whose wheat-
lands comprised acres enough for a principality, and whose
enthusiasm was as fresh as a boy's. Several days later, at
the Luxembourg, he met him again, standing in a state of
abject bewilderment before Manet's *Olympe*. Dunlap again
came to his rescue and took him off to lunch, after which
they went to the painter's studio. The acquaintance warmed
on both sides, and, before they separated, Dunlap was
engaged to paint the old gentleman's daughter, agreeing
that the sittings should be at the house on the Boulevard
de Courcelles, which the family had taken for the winter.

When Dunlap called at the house, he went through one
of the most excruciating experiences of his life. He found
Mrs. Gilbert and her daughter waiting to receive him. The
shock of the introduction over, the strain of desultory
conversation began. The only thing that made conversation tolerable—though it added a new element of perplexity—was the girl's seeming unconsciousness, her utter openness and unabashedness. She laughed and spoke,
almost with coquetry, of the honor of sitting to him, of
having heard that he was fastidious as to his subjects.
Dunlap felt that he wanted to rush from the house and
escape the situation which confronted him. The conviction kept recurring that it had just happened, had come
upon her since last she had passed a mirror; that she
would suddenly become conscious of it, and be suffocated
with shame. He felt as if some one ought to tell her and
lead her away.

"Shall we get to work?" she asked presently, apparently curious and eager to begin. "How do you wish me
to sit to you?"

Dunlap murmured something about usually asking his
sitters to decide that for themselves.

"Suppose we try a profile, then?" she suggested carelessly, sitting down in a carved wooden chair.

For the first time since he had entered the room, Dunlap
felt the pressure about his throat relax. For the first time it
was entirely turned from him, and he could not see it at

all. What he did see was a girlish profile, unusually firm for a thing so softly colored; oval, flower-tinted, and shadowed by soft, blonde hair that wound about her head and curled and clung about her brow and neck and ears.

Dunlap began setting up his easel, recovering from his first discomfort and grateful to the girl for having solved his difficulty so gracefully. But no sooner was it turned from him than he felt a strong desire to see it again. Perhaps it had been only a delusion, after all; the clear profile before him so absolutely contradicted it. He went behind her chair to experiment with the window shades, and there, as he drew them up and down, he could look unseen. He gazed long and hard, to blunt his curiosity once and for all, and prevent a further temptation to covert glances. It had evidently been caused by a deep burn, as if from a splash of molten metal. It drew the left eye and the corner of the mouth; made of her smile a grinning distortion, like the shameful conception of some despairing medieval imagination. It was as if some grotesque mask, worn for disport, were just slipping sidewise from her face.

When Dunlap crossed to the right again, he found the same clear profile awaiting him, the same curves of twining, silken hair. "What courage," he thought, "what magnificent courage!" His heart ached at the injustice of it; that her very beauty, the alert, girlish figure, the firm, smooth throat and chin, even her delicate hands, should, through an inch or two of seared flesh, seem tainted and false. He felt that in a plain woman it would have been so much less horrible.

Dunlap left the house overcast by a haunting sense of tragedy, and for the rest of the day he was a prey to distressing memories. All that he had tried to forget seemed no longer dim and faraway—like the cruelties of vanished civilizations—but present and painfully near. He thought of his mother and grandmother, of his little sister, who had died from the bite of a copperhead snake, as if they were creatures yet unreleased from suffering.

II

From the first, Virginia's interest in the portrait never wavered; yet, as the sittings progressed, it became evident to Dunlap that her enthusiasm for the picture was but accessory to her interest in him. By her every look and action she asserted her feeling, as a woman, young and handsome and independent, may sometimes do.

As time went on, he was drawn to her by what had once repelled him. Her courageous candor appealed to his chivalry, and he came to love her, not despite the scar, but, in a manner, for its very sake. He had some indefinite feeling that love might heal her; that in time her hurt might disappear, like the deformities imposed by enchantment to test the hardihood of lovers.

He gathered from her attitude, as well as from that of her family, that the thing had never been mentioned to her, never alluded to by word or look. Both her father and mother had made it their first care to shield her. Had she ever, in the streets of some foreign city, heard a brutal allusion to it? He shuddered to think of such a possibility. Was she not living for the moment when she could throw down the mask and point to it and weep, to be comforted for all time? He looked forward to the hour when there would be no lie of unconsciousness between them. The moment must come when she would give him her confidence; perhaps it would be only a whisper, a gesture, a guiding of his hand in the dark; but, however it might come, it was the pledge he awaited.

During the last few weeks before his marriage, the scar, through the mere strength of his anticipation, had ceased to exist for him. He had already entered to the perfect creature which he felt must dwell behind it; the soul of tragic serenity and twofold loveliness.

They went to the South for their honeymoon, through the Midi and along the coast to Italy. Never, by word or sign, did Virginia reveal any consciousness of what he felt must be said once, and only once, between them. She was spirited, adventurous, impassioned; she exacted much, but she gave magnificently. Her interests in the material world were absorbing, and she demanded continual excitement and continual novelty. Granted these, her good spirits were unfailing.

It was during their wedding journey that he discovered her two all-absorbing interests, which were to become intensified as years went on: her passion for dress and her feverish admiration of physical beauty, whether in men or women or children. This touched Dunlap deeply, as it seemed in a manner an admission of a thing she could not speak.

Before their return to Paris Dunlap had, for the time, quite renounced his hope of completely winning her confidence. He tried to believe his exclusion just; he told himself that it was only a part of her splendid self-respect. He thought of how, from her very childhood, she had been fashioning, day by day, that armor of unconsciousness in which she sheathed her scar. After all, so deep a hurt could, perhaps, be bared to any one rather than the man she loved.

Yet, he felt that their life was enmeshed in falsehood; that he could not live year after year with a woman who shut so deep a part of her nature from him; that since he had married a woman outwardly different from others, he must have that within her which other women did not possess. Until this was granted him, he felt there would be a sacredness lacking in their relation which it peculiarly ought to have. He counted upon the birth of her child to bring this about. It would touch deeper than he could hope to do, and with fingers that could not wound. That would be a tenderness more penetrating, more softening than passion; without pride or caprice; a feeling that would dwell most in the one part of her he had failed to reach. The child, certainly, she could not shut out; whatever hardness or defiant shame it was that held him away from her, her maternity would bring enlightenment; would bring that sad wisdom, that admission of the necessity and destiny to suffer, which is, somehow, so essential in a woman.

Virginia's child was a girl, a sickly baby which cried miserably from the day it was born. The listless, wailing, almost unwilling battle for life that daily went on before his eyes saddened Dunlap profoundly. All his painter's sophistries fell away from him, and more than ever his early destiny seemed closing about him. There was, then, no escaping from the cruelty of physical things—no matter how high and bright the sunshine, how gray and poplar-clad the ways of one's life. The more willing the child seemed to relinquish its feeble hold, the more tenderly he loved it, and the more determinedly he fought to save it.

Virginia, on the contrary, had almost from the first exhibited a marked indifference toward her daughter. She showed plainly that the sight of its wan, aged little face was unpleasant to her; she disliked being clutched by its skeleton fingers, and said its wailing made her head ache. She was always taking Madame de Montebello and her handsome children to drive in the Bois, but she was never to be seen with little Eleanor. If her friends asked to see the child, she usually put them off, saying that she was asleep or in her bath.

When Dunlap once impatiently asked her whether she never intended to permit any one to see her daughter, she replied coldly: "Certainly, when she has filled out and begins to look like something."

Little Eleanor grew into a shy, awkward child, who slipped about the house like an unwelcome dependent. She was four years old when a cousin of Virginia's came from California to spend a winter in Paris. Virginia had known her only slightly at home, but, as she proved to be a charming girl, and as she was ill-equipped to bear the hardships of a winter in a *pension*, the Dunlaps insisted upon her staying with them. The cousin's name was also Eleanor—she had been called so after Virginia's mother—and, from the first, the two Eleanors seemed drawn to each other. Miss Vane was studying, and went out to her lectures every day, but whenever she was at home, little Eleanor was with her. The child would sit quietly in her room while she wrote, playing with anything her cousin happened to give her; or would lie for hours on the hearth rug, whispering to her woolly dog. Dunlap felt a weight lifted from his mind. Whenever Eleanor was at home, he knew that the child was happy.

He had long ceased to expect any solicitude for her from Virginia. That had gone with everything else. It was one of so many disappointments that he took it rather as a matter of course, and it seldom occurred to him that it might have been otherwise. For two years he had been living like a man who knows that some reptile has housed itself and hatched its young in his cellar, and who never cautiously puts his foot out of his bed without the dread of touching its coils. The change in his feeling toward his wife kept him in perpetual apprehension; it seemed to threaten everything he held dear, even his self-respect. His life was a continual effort of self-control, and he found it necessary to make frequent trips to London or sketching tours into Brittany to escape from the strain of the repression he put upon himself. Under this state of things, Dunlap aged perceptibly, and his friends made various and usual conjectures. Whether Virginia was conscious of the change in him, he never knew. Her feeling for him had, in its very nature, been as temporary as it was violent; it had abated naturally, and she probably took for granted that the same readjustment had taken place in him. Perhaps she was too much engrossed in other things to notice it at all.

In Dunlap the change seemed never to be finally established, but forever painfully working. Whereas he had once seen the scar on his wife's face not at all, he now saw it continually. Inch by inch it had crept over her whole countenance. Yet the scar itself seemed now a trivial thing; he had known for a long time that the burn had gone deeper than the flesh.

Virginia's extravagant fondness for gaiety seemed to increase, and her mania for lavish display, doubtless common enough in the Californian wheat empire, was a discordant note in Paris. Dunlap found himself condemned to an existence which daily did violence to his sense of propriety. His wife gave fêtes, the cost of which was noised abroad by the Associated Press and flaunted in American newspapers. Her vanity, the pageantries of her toilet, made them both ridiculous, he felt. She was a woman now, with a husband and child; she had no longer a pretext for keeping up the pitiful bravado under which she had hidden the smarting pride of her girlhood.

He became more and more convinced that she had been shielded from a realization of her disfigurement only to the end of a shocking perversity. Her costumes, her very jewels, blazed defiance. Her confidence became almost insolent, and her laugh was nothing but a frantic denial of a thing so cruelly obvious. The unconsciousness he had once reverenced now continually tempted his brutality, and when he felt himself reduced to the point of actual vituperation, he fled to Normandy or Languedoc to save himself. He had begun, indeed, to feel strangely out of place in Paris. The ancient comfort of the city, never lacking in the days when he had known cold and hunger, failed him now. A certain sordidness had spread itself over ways and places once singularly perfect and pure.

III

One evening when Virginia refused to allow little Eleanor to go down to the music room to see some pantomine performers who were to entertain their guests, Dunlap, to conceal his displeasure, stepped quickly out upon the balcony and closed the window behind him. He stood for some moments in the cold, clear night air.

"God help me," he groaned. "Some day I shall tell her. I shall hold her and tell her."

When he entered the house again, it was by another window, and his anger had cooled. As he stepped into the hallway, he met Eleanor the elder, going upstairs with the little girl in her arms. For the life of him he could not refrain from appealing for sympathy to her kind, grave eyes. He was so hurt, so sick, that he could have put his face down beside the child's and wept.

"Give her to me, little cousin. She is too heavy for you," he said gently, as they went upstairs together.

He remembered with resentment his wife's perfectly candid and careless jests about his fondness for her cousin. After he had put the little girl down in Eleanor's room, as they leaned together above the child's head in the firelight, he became, for the first time, really aware. A sudden tenderness weakened him. He put out his hand and took hers, which was holding the child's, and murmured: "Thank you, thank you, little cousin."

She started violently and caught her hand away from him, trembling all over. Dunlap left the room, thrice more miserable than he had entered it.

After that evening he noticed that Eleanor avoided meeting him alone. Virginia also noticed it, but upon this point she was consistently silent. One morning, as Dunlap was leaving his wife's dressing room, having been to consult her as to whether she intended going to the ball at the Russian Embassy, she called him back. She was carefully arranging her beautiful hair, which she always dressed herself, and said carelessly, without looking up at him:

"Eleanor has a foolish notion of returning home in March. I wish you would speak to her about it. Her family expect her to stay until June, and her going now would be commented upon."

"I scarcely see how I can interfere," he replied coolly. "She doubtless has her reasons."

"Her reasons are not far to seek, I should say," remarked Virginia, carefully slipping the pins into the yellow coils of her hair. "She is pathetically ingenuous about it. I should think you might improve upon the present state of affairs if you were to treat it—well, say a trifle more lightly. That would put her more at ease, at least."

"What nonsense, Virginia," he exclaimed, laughing unnaturally and closing the door behind him with guarded gentleness.

That evening Dunlap joined his wife in her dressing room, his coat on his arm and his hat in his hand. The maid had gone upstairs to hunt for Virginia's last year's fur shoes, as the pair warming before the grate would not fit over her new dancing slippers. Virginia was standing before the mirror, carefully surveying the effect of a new gown, which struck her husband as more than usually conspicuous and defiant. He watched her arranging a pink-and-gold butterfly in her hair and held his peace, but when she put on a pink chiffon collar, with a flaring bow which came directly under her left cheek, in spite of himself he shuddered.

"For heaven's sake, Virginia, take that thing off," he cried. "You ought really to be more careful about such extremes. They only emphasize the scar." He was frightened at the brittleness of his own voice; it seemed to whistle dryly in the air like his grandfather's thong.

She caught her breath and wheeled suddenly about, her face crimson and then gray. She opened her lips twice, but no sound escaped them. He saw the muscles of her throat stiffen, and she began to shudder convulsively, like one who has been plunged into icy water. He started toward her, sick with pity; at last, perhaps—but she pointed him steadily to the door, her eyes as hard as shell, and bright and small, like the sleepless eyes of reptiles.

He went to bed with the sick feeling of a man who has

tortured an animal, yet with a certain sense of relief and finality which he had not known in years.

When he came down to breakfast in the morning, the butler told him that Madame and her maid had left for Nice by the early train. Mademoiselle Vane had gone out to her lectures. Madame requested that Monsieur take Mademoiselle to the opera in the evening, where the widowed sister of Madame de Montebello would join them; she would come home with them to remain until Madame's return. Dunlap accepted these instructions as a matter of course, and announced that he would not dine at home.

When he entered the hall upon his return that evening, he heard little Eleanor sobbing, and she flew to meet him, with her dress burned, and her hands black. Dunlap smelled the sickening odor of ointments. The nurse followed with explanations. The doctor was upstairs. Mademoiselle Vane always used a little alcohol lamp in making her toilet; tonight, when she touched a match to it, it exploded. Little Eleanor was leaning against her dressing table at the time, and her dress caught fire; Mademoiselle Vane had wrapped the rug about her and extinguished it. When the nurse arrived, Mademoiselle Vane was standing in the middle of the floor, plucking at her scorched hair, her face and arms badly burned. She had bent over the lamp in lighting it, and had received the full force of the explosion in her face. The doctor was unable to discover what the explosive had been, as it was entirely consumed. Mademoiselle always filled the little lamp herself; all the servants knew about it, for Madame had sent the nurse to borrow it on several occasions, when little Eleanor had the earache.

The next morning Dunlap received a telegram from his wife, stating that she would go to St. Petersburg for the remainder of the winter. In May he heard that she had sailed for America, and a year later her attorneys wrote that she had begun action for divorce. Immediately after the decree was granted, Dunlap married Eleanor Vane.

He never met or directly heard from Virginia again, though when she returned to Russia and took up her residence in St. Petersburg, the fame of her toilets spread even to Paris.

Society, always prone to crude antitheses, knew of Dunlap only that he had painted many of the most beautiful women of his time, that he had been twice married, and that each of his wives had been disfigured by a scar on the face.

The Willing Muse

Various opinions were held among Kenneth Gray's friends regarding his approaching marriage, but on the whole it was considered a hopeful venture, and, what was with some of us much more to the point, a hopeful indication. From the hour his engagement was an assured relation, he had seemed to gain. There was now a certain intention in his step, an eager, almost confident flash behind his thick glasses, which cheered his friends like indications of recovery after long illness. Even his shoulders seemed to droop less despondently and his head to sit upon them more securely. Those of us who knew him best drew a long sigh of relief that Kenneth had at last managed to get right with the current.

If, on the insecurity of a meager income and a career at its belated dawn, he was to marry at all, we felt that a special indulgence of destiny had allowed him to fix his choice upon Bertha Torrence. If there was anywhere a woman who seemed able to give him what he needed, to play upon him a continual stream of inspiriting confidence, to order the very simple affairs which he had so besottedly bungled, surely Bertha was the woman.

There were certain of his friends in Olympia who held out that it was a mistake for him to marry a woman who followed his own profession; who was, indeed, already much more within the public consciousness than Kenneth himself. To refute such arguments, one had only to ask what was possible between that and a housekeeper. Could any one conceive of Kenneth's living in daily intercourse with a woman who had no immediate and personal interest in letters, bitten to the bone as he was by his slow, consuming passion?

Perhaps, in so far as I was concerned, my personal satisfaction at Kenneth's projected marriage was not without its alloy of selfishness, and I think more than one of us counted upon carrying lighter hearts to his wedding than we had known in his company for some time. It was not that we did not believe in him. Hadn't it become a fixed habit to believe? But we, perhaps, felt slightly aggrieved that our faith had not wrought for him the miracles we could have hoped. We were, we found, willing enough to place the direct administration, the first responsibility, upon Bertha's firm young shoulders.

With Harrison, the musical critic, and me, Kenneth was an old issue. We had been college classmates of his, out in Olympia, Ohio, and even then no one had questioned his calling and election, unless it was Kenneth himself. But he had taxed us all sorely, the town and the college, and he had continued to tax us long afterward. As Harrison put it, he had kept us all holding our breath for years. There was never such a man for getting people into a fever of interest and determination for him, for making people (even people who had very vague surmises as to the particular eminence toward which he might be headed) fervidly desire to push him and for refusing, on any terms, to be pushed. There was nothing more individual about Kenneth than his inability to be exploited. Coercion and encouragement spent themselves upon him like summer rain.

He was thirty-five when his first book, *Charles de Montpensier*, was published, and the work was, to those who knew its author intimately, a kind of record of his inverse development. It was first conceived and written as a prose drama, then amplified into an historical novel, and had finally been compressed into a psychological study of two hundred pages, in which the action was hushed to a whisper and the teeming pageantry of his background, which he had spent years in developing and which had cost him several laborious summers in France and Italy, was reduced to a shadowy atmosphere, suggestive enough, doubtless, but presenting very little that was appreciable to the eyes of the flesh. The majority of Kenneth's readers, even those baptized into his faith, must have recalled the fable of the mouse and the mountain. As for those of us who had travailed with him, confident as we were of the high order of the ultimate production, we had a baffled feeling that there had been a distressing leakage of power. However, when this study of the High Constable of Bourbon was followed by an exquisite prose idyl, *The Wood of Ronsard*, we began to take heart, and when we learned that a stimulus so reassuring as a determination to marry had hurried this charming bit of romance into the world, we felt that Kenneth had at last entered upon the future that had seemed for so long only a step before him.

Since Gray's arrival in New York, Harrison and I had had more than ever the feeling of having him on our hands. He had been so long accustomed to the respectful calm of Olympia that he was unable to find his way about in a new environment. He was incapable of falling in with any of the prevailing attitudes, and even of civilly tolerating them in other people. Commercialism wounded him, flippancy put him out of countenance, and he clung stubbornly to certain fond, Olympian superstitions regarding his profession. One by one his new acquaintances chilled, offended by his arrogant reception of their genial efforts to put him in the way of things. Even those of us who had known him at his best, and who remembered the summer evenings in his garden at Olympia, found his seriousness and punctilious reservations tedious in the broad glare of short, noisy working days.

Some weeks before the day set for Kenneth's marriage, I learned that it might be necessary for me to go to Paris for a time to take the place of our correspondent there, who had fallen into precarious health, and I called at Bertha's apartment for a serious talk with her. I found her in the high tide of work; but she made a point of accepting interruptions agreeably, just as she made a point of looking astonishingly well, of being indispensable in an appalling number of "circles," and of generally nullifying the traditional reproach attaching to clever women.

"In all loyalty to you both," I remarked, "I feel that I ought to remind you that you are accepting a responsibility."

"His uncertainty, you mean?"

"Oh, I mean all of them—the barriers which are so intangible he cannot climb them and so terrifying he can't jump them, which lie between him and everything."

Bertha looked at me thoughtfully out of her candid blue eyes. "But what he needs is, after all, so little compared with what he has."

"What he has," I admitted, "is inestimably precious; but the problem is to keep it from going back into the ground with him."

She shot a glance of alarm at me from under her blond lashes. "But certainly he is endlessly more capable of doing than any of us. With such depth to draw from, how can he possibly fail?"

"Perhaps it's his succeeding that I fear more than anything. I think the fair way to measure Kenneth is by what he simply can't do."

"The cheap, you mean?" she asked reflectively. "Oh, that he will never do. We may just eliminate that from our discussion. The problem is simply to make him mine his vein, even if, from his fanciful angle of vision, it's at first a losing business."

"Ah, my dear young lady, but it's just his fanciful angle, as you so happily term it, that puts a stop to everything, and I've never quite dared to urge him past his scruples, though I'm not saying I could if I would. If there is anything at all in the whole business, any element of chosenness, of a special call, any such value in individual tone as he fancies, then, the question is, dare one urge him?"

"Nonsense!" snapped Bertha, drawing up her slender shoulders with decision—I had purposely set out to exhaust her patience—"you have all put a halo about him until he daren't move for fear of putting it out. What he needs is simply to keep at it. How much satisfaction do you suppose he gets out of hanging back?"

"The point, it seems to me, my dear Bertha, is not that, but the remarkableness of any one's having the conviction, the moral force, just now and under the circumstances, to hang back at all. There must be either very much or very little in a man when he refuses to make the most of his vogue and sell out on a rising market. If he would rather bring up a little water out of the well than turn the river across his lands, has one a right to coerce him?" I put my shaft home steadily, and Bertha caught fire with proper spirit.

"All I can say is, that it's a miracle he's as adaptable as he is. I simply can't understand what you meant, you and Harrison, by keeping him out there in Ohio so long."

"But we didn't," I expostulated. "We didn't keep him there. We only did not succeed in getting him away. We, too, had our scruples. He had his old house there, and his garden, his friends, and the peace of God. And then, Olympia isn't a bad sort of place. It kept his feeling fresh, at least, and in fifteen years or so you'll begin to know the value of that. There everything centers about the college, and every one reads, just as every one goes to church. It's a part of the decent, comely life of the place. In Olympia there is a deep-seated, old-fashioned respect for the printed page, and Kenneth naturally found himself in the place of official sanctity. The townswomen reverently attended his college lectures, along with their sons and daughters, and, had he been corruptible, he might have established a walled supremacy of personal devotion behind which he could have sheltered himself to the end of his days."

"But he didn't, you see," said Bertha, triumphantly;

"which is proof that he was meant for the open waters. Oh, we shall do fine things, I promise you! I can just fancy the hushed breath of the place for wonder at him. And his rose garden! Will people never have done with his rose garden! I remember you and Harrison told me of it, with an air, before I had met Kenneth at all. I wonder that you didn't keep him down there forever from a pure sense of the picturesque. What sort of days and nights do you imagine he passed in his garden, in his miserably uncertain state? I suppose we should all like well enough to grow roses, if we had nothing else to do."

I felt that Bertha was considerately keeping her eyes from the clock, and I rose to go.

"Well, Bertha, I suppose the only reason we haven't brought him to a worse pass than we have, is just the fact that he happens to have been born an anachronism, and such a stubborn one that we leave him pretty much where we found him."

II

After Kenneth's wedding, I left immediately for Paris, and during the next four years I knew of the Grays only what I could sense from Kenneth's labored letters, ever more astonishing in their aridity, and from the parcels I received twice a year by book-post, containing Bertha's latest work. I never picked up an American periodical that Bertha's name was not the first to greet my eye on the advertising pages. She surpassed all legendary accounts of phenomenal productiveness, and I could feel no anxiety for the fortunes of the pair while Bertha's publishers thought her worth such a display of heavy type. There was scarcely a phase of colonial life left untouched by her, and her last, The Maid of Domremy, showed that she had fairly crowded herself out of her own field.

The real wonder was, that, making so many, she could make them so well—should make them, indeed, rather better and better. Even were one so unreasonable as to consider her gain a loss, there was no denying it. I read her latest, one after another, as they arrived, with growing interest and amazement, wholly unable to justify my first suspicion. There was every evidence that she had absorbed from Kenneth like a water plant, but none that she had used him more violently than a clever woman may properly use her husband. Knowing him as I did, I could never accredit him with having any hand in Bertha's intrepid, wholehearted, unimpeachable conventionality. One could not exactly call her unscrupulous; one could observe only that no predicament embarrassed her; that she went ahead and pulled it off.

When I returned to New York, I found a curious state of feeling prevalent concerning the Grays. Bertha was *la fille du régiment* more than ever. Every one championed her, every one went to her teas, every one was smilingly and conspicuously present in her triumph. Even those who had formerly stood somewhat aloof, now found no courage to dissent. With Bertha herself so gracious, so eager to please, the charge of pettiness, of jealousy, even, could be too easily incurred. She quite floated the sourest and heaviest upon her rising tide.

There was, however, the undertow. I felt it even before I had actually made sure of it—in the peculiar warmth with which people spoke of Kenneth. In him they saw their own grievances magnified until he became symbolic. Publicly every one talkèd of Bertha; but behind closed doors it was of Kenneth they spoke—*sotto voce* and with a shake of the head. As he had published nothing since his marriage, this smothered feeling had resulted in a new and sumptuous edition of *Montpensier* and *The Wood of Ronsard*; one of those final, votive editions, suggestive of the bust and the catafalque.

I called upon the Grays at the first opportunity. They had moved from their downtown flat into a new apartment house on Eighty-fifth street. The servant who took my card did not return, but Kenneth himself stumbled into the reception hall, overturning a gilt chair in his haste, and gripped my hands as if he would never let them go. He held on to my arm as he took me to his study, telling me again and again that I couldn't possibly know what pleasure it gave him to see me. When he dropped limply into his desk chair, he seemed really quite overcome with excitement. It was not until I asked him about his wife that he collected himself and began to talk coherently.

"I'm sorry I can't speak to her now," he explained, rapidly twirling a paper cutter between his long fingers. "She won't be free until four o'clock. She will be so pleased that I'm almost tempted to call her at once. But she's so overworked, poor girl, and she will go out so much."

"My dear Kenneth, how does she ever manage it all? She must have nerves of iron."

"Oh, she's wonderful, wonderful!" he exclaimed, brushing his limp hair back from his forehead with a perplexed gesture. "As to how she does it, I really don't know much more than you. It all gets done, somehow." He glanced quickly toward the partition, through which we heard the steady clicking of a typewriter. "I scarcely know what she is up to until her proofs come in. I usually go at those with her." He darted a piercing look at me, and I wondered whether he had got a hint of the malicious stories which found their way about concerning his varied usefulness to Bertha.

"If you'll excuse me for a moment, Philip," he went on, "I'll finish a letter that must go out this afternoon, and then I shall be quite free."

He turned in his revolving chair to a desk littered deep with papers, and began writing hurriedly. I could see that the simplest kind of composition still perplexed and disconcerted him. He stopped, hesitated, bit his nails, then scratched desperately ahead, darting an annoyed glance at the partition as if the sharp, regular click of the machine bewildered him.

He had grown older, I noticed, but it was good to see

him again—his limp, straight hair, which always hung down in a triangle over his high forehead; his lean cheek, loose under lip, and long whimsical chin; his faded, serious eyes, which were always peering inquiringly from behind his thick glasses; his long, tremulous fingers, which handled a pen as uncertainly as ever. There was a general looseness of articulation about his gaunt frame that made his every movement seem more or less haphazard.

On the desk lay a heap of letters, the envelopes marked "answered" in Kenneth's small, irregular hand, and all of them, I noticed, addressed to Bertha. In the open drawer at his left were half a dozen manuscript envelopes, addressed to her in as many different hands.

"What on earth!" I gasped. "Does Bertha conduct a literary agency as well?"

Kenneth swung round in his chair, and made a wry face as he glanced at the contents of the drawer. "It's almost as bad as that. Really, it's the most abominable nuisance. But we're the victims of success, as Bertha says. Sometimes a dozen manuscripts come in to her for criticism in one week. She dislikes to hurt any one's feelings, so one of us usually takes a look at them."

"Bertha's correspondence must be something of a responsibility in itself," I ventured.

"Oh, it is, I assure you. People are most inconsiderate. I'm rather glad, though, when it piles up like this and I can take a hand at it. It gives me an excuse for putting off my own work, and you know how I welcome any pretext," he added, with a flushed, embarrassed smile.

"What are you doing, anyhow? I don't know where you'll ever learn industry if Bertha can't teach you."

"I'm working, I'm working," he insisted, hurriedly crossing out the last sentence of his letter and blotting it carefully. "You know how reprehensibly slow I am. It seems to grow on me. I'm finishing up some studies in the French Renaissance. They'll be ready by next fall, I think." As he spoke, he again glanced hurriedly over the closely written page before him; then, stopping abruptly, he tore the sheet across the middle. "Really, you've quite upset me. Tell me about yourself, Philip. Are you going out to Olympia?"

"That depends upon whether I remain here or decamp immediately for China, which prospect is in the cards. Olympia is greatly changed, Harrison tells me."

Kenneth sighed and sank deeper into his chair, reaching again for the paper cutter. "Ruined completely. Capital and enterprise have broken in even there. They've all sorts of new industries, and the place is black with smoke and thick with noise from sunrise to sunset. I still own my house there, but I seldom go back. I don't know where we're bound for, I'm sure. There must be places, somewhere in the world, where a man can take a book or two and drop behind the procession for an hour; but they seem impossibly far from here."

I could not help smiling at the deeply despondent gaze which he fixed upon the paper cutter. "But the procession itself is the thing we've got to enjoy," I suggested, "the mere sense of speed."

"I suppose so, I suppose so," he reiterated, wiping his forehead with his handkerchief. "The six-day bicycle race seems to be what we've all come to, and doubtless one form of it's as much worth while as another. We don't get anywhere, but we go. We certainly go; and that's what we're after. You'll be lucky if you are sent to China. There must be calm there as yet, I imagine."

Our conversation went on fitfully, with interruptions, irrelevant remarks, and much laughter, as talk goes between two persons who have once been frank with each other, and who find that frankness has become impossible. My coming had clearly upset him, and his agitation of manner visibly increased when he spoke of his wife. He wiped his forehead and hands repeatedly, and finally opened a window. He fairly wrested the conversation out of my hands and was continually interrupting and forestalling me, as if he were apprehensive that I might say something he did not wish to hear. He started and leaned forward in his chair whenever I approached a question.

At last we were aware of a sudden slack in the tension; the typewriter had stopped. Kenneth looked at his watch, and disappeared through a door into his wife's study. When he returned, Bertha was beside him, her hand on his shoulder, taller, straighter, younger than I had left her—positively childlike in her freshness and candor.

"Didn't I tell you," she cried, "that we should do fine things?"

III

A few weeks later I was sent to Hong Kong, where I remained for two years. Before my return to America, I was ordered into the interior for eight months, during which time my mail was to be held for me at the consul's office in Canton, the port where I was to take ship for home. Once in the Sze Chuen province, floods and bad roads delayed me to such an extent that I barely reached Canton on the day my vessel sailed. I hurried on board with all my letters unread, having had barely time to examine the instructions from my paper.

We were well out at sea when I opened a letter from Harrison in which he gave an account of Kenneth Gray's disappearance. He had, Harrison stated, gone out to Olympia to dispose of his property there which, since the development of the town, had greatly increased in value. He completed his business after a week's stay, and left for New York by the night train, several of his friends accompanying him to the station. Since that night he had not been seen or heard of. Detectives had been at work; hospitals and morgues had been searched without result.

The date of this communication put me beside myself. It had awaited me in Canton for nearly seven months, and Gray had last been seen on the tenth of November, four months before the date of Harrison's letter, which was written as soon as the matter was made public. It was eleven months, then, since Kenneth Gray had been seen in America. During my long voyage I went through an accumulated bulk of American newspapers, but found nothing more reassuring than occasional items to the effect that the mystery surrounding Gray's disappearance remained unsolved. In a "literary supplement" of comparatively recent date, I came upon a notice to the effect that the new novel by Bertha Torrence Gray, announced for spring publication, would, owing to the excruciating experience through which the young authoress had lately passed, be delayed until the autumn.

I bore my suspense as best I could across ocean and continent. When I arrived in New York, I went from the ferry to the *Messenger* office, and, once there, directly to Harrison's room.

"What's all this," I cried, "about Kenneth Gray? I tell you I saw Gray in Canton ten months ago."

Harrison sprang to his feet and put his finger to his lip.

"Hush! Don't say another word! There are leaky walls about here. Go and attend to your business, and then come back and go to lunch with me. In the meantime, be careful not to discuss Gray with any one."

Four hours later, when we were sitting in a quiet corner of a café, Harrison dismissed the waiter and turned to me: "Now," he said, leaning across the table, "if you can be sufficiently guarded, you may tell me what you know about our friend."

"Well," I replied, "it would have been, under ordinary circumstances, a commonplace thing enough. On the day before I started for the interior, I was in Canton, making some last purchases to complete my outfit. I stepped out of a shop on one of the crooked streets in the old part of the city, and I saw him as plainly as I see you, being trundled by in a jinrikisha, got up in a helmet and white duck, a fat white umbrella across his knees, peering hopefully out through his glasses. He was so like himself, his look and attitude, his curious chin poked forward, that I simply stood and stared until he had passed me and turned a corner, vanishing like a stereopticon picture traveling across the screen. I hurried to the banks, the big hotels, to the consul's, getting no word of him, but leaving letters for him everywhere. My party started the next day, and I was compelled to leave for an eight-months' nightmare in the interior. I got back to Canton barely in time to catch my steamer, and did not open your letter until we were down the river and losing sight of land. Either I saw Kenneth, or I am a subject for the Society for Psychical Research."

"Just so," said Harrison, peering mysteriously above his coffee cup. "And now forget it. Simply disabuse yourself of any notion that you've seen him since we crossed the ferry with you three years ago. It's your last service to him, probably."

"Speak up," I cried, exasperated. "I've had about all of this I can stand. I came near wiring the story in from San Francisco. I don't know why I didn't."

"Well, here's to whatever withheld you! When a man comes to the pass where he wants to wipe himself off the face of the earth, when it's the last play he can make for his self-respect, the only decent thing is to let him do it. You know the yielding stuff he's made of well enough to appreciate the amount of pressure it must have taken to harden him to such an exit. I'm sure I never supposed he had it in him."

"But what, short of insanity—"

"Insanity? Nonsense! I wonder that people don't do it oftener. The pressure simply got past the bearing-point. His life was going, and going for nothing—worse than nothing. His future was chalked out for him, and whichever way he turned he was confronted by his unescapable destiny. In the light of Bertha's splendid success, he couldn't be churlish or ungracious; he had to play his little part along with the rest of us. And Bertha, you know, has passed all the limits of nature, not to speak of decorum. They come as certainly as the seasons, her new ones, each cleverer and more damnable than the last. And yet there is nothing that one can actually put one's finger on—not, at least, without saying the word that would lay us open to a charge which as her friends we are none of us willing to incur, and which no one would listen to if it were said.

"I tell you," Harrison continued, "the whole thing sickened him. He had dried up like a stockfish. His brain was beaten into torpidity by the mere hammer of her machine, as by so many tiny mallets. He had lived to help lessen the value of all that he held precious, to disprove all that he wanted to believe. Having ridden to victory under the banners of what he most despised, there was nothing for him but to live in the blaze of her conquest, and that was the very measure of his fall. His usefulness to the world was over when he had done what he did for Bertha. I don't believe he even knew where he stood; the thing had gone so, seemed to answer the purpose so wonderfully well, and there was never anything that one could really put one's finger on—except all of it. It was a trial of faith, and Bertha had won out so beautifully. He had proved the fallacy of his own position. There was nothing left for him to say. I'm sure I don't know whether he had anything left to think."

"Do you remember," I said slowly, "I used to hold that, in the end, Kenneth would be measured by what he didn't do, by what he couldn't do? What a wonder he was at not being able to do it. Surely, if Bertha couldn't convince him, fire and faggots couldn't."

"For, after all," sighed Harrison, as we rose to go, "Bertha is a wonderful woman—a woman of her time and people; and she has managed, in spite of her fatal facility, to be enough sight better than most of us."

Eleanor's House

"Shall you, then," Harriet ventured, "go to Fortuney?" The girl threw a startled glance toward the corner of the garden where Westfield and Harold were examining a leak in the basin of the little fountain, and Harriet was sorry that she had put the question so directly. Ethel's reply, when it came, seemed a mere emission of breath rather than articulation.

"I think we shall go later. It's very trying for him there, of course. He hasn't been there since." She relapsed into silence—indeed, she had never come very far out of it—and Harriet called to Westfield. She found that she couldn't help resenting Ethel's singular ineptness at keeping herself in hand.

"Come, Robert. Harold is tired after his journey, and he and Ethel must have much to say to each other."

Both Harold and his wife, however, broke into hurried random remarks with an eagerness which seemed like a protest.

"It is delightful to be near you here at Arques, with only a wall between our gardens," Ethel spurred herself to say. "It will mean so much to Harold. He has so many old associations with you, Mrs. Westfield."

The two men had come back to the tea table, and as the younger one overheard his wife's last remark, his handsome brown face took on the blackness of disapproval.

Ethel glanced at him furtively, but Harriet was unable to

detect whether she realized just why or to what extent her remark had been unfortunate. She certainly looked as if she might not be particularly acute, drooping about in her big garden hat and her limp white frock, which had not been very well put on. However, some sense of maladroitness certainly penetrated her vagueness, for she shrank behind the tea table, gathering her scarf about her shoulders as if she were mysteriously blown upon by a chilling current.

The Westfields drew together to take their leave. Harold stepped to his wife's side as they went toward the gate with their guests, and put his hand lightly on her shoulder, at which she waveringly emerged from her eclipse and smiled.

Harriet could not help looking back at them from under her sunshade as they stood there in the gateway; the man with his tense brown face and abstracted smile, the girl drooping, positively swaying in her softness and uncertainty.

When they reached the sunny square of their own garden, Harriet sank into a wicker chair in the deep shadow of the stucco wall and addressed her husband with conviction:

"I know now, my dear, why he wished so much to come. I sensed it yesterday, when I first met her. But now that I've seen them together, it's perfectly clear. He brought her here to keep her away from Fortuney, and he's counting on us to help him."

Westfield, who was carefully examining his rose trees, looked at his wife with interest and frank bewilderment, a form of interrogation with which she was perfectly familiar.

"If there is one thing that's plainer even than his misery," Harriet continued, "it is that she is headed toward Fortuney. They've been married over two years, and he couldn't, I suppose, keep her across the Channel any longer. So he has simply deflected her course, and we are the pretext."

"Certainly," Westfield admitted, as he looked up from

his pruning, "one feels something not altogether comfortable with them, but why should it be Fortuney any more than a hundred other things? There are opportunities enough for people who wish to play at cross-purposes."

"Ah! But Fortuney," sighed his wife, "Fortuney's the summing up of all his past. It's Eleanor herself. How could he, Robert, take this poor girl there? It would be cruelty. The figure she'd cut in a place of such distinction!"

"I should think that if he could marry her, he could take her to Fortuney," Westfield maintained bluntly.

"Oh, as to his marrying her! But I suppose we are all to blame for that—all his and Eleanor's old friends. We certainly failed him. We fled at the poor fellow's approach. We simply couldn't face the extent of his bereavement. He seemed a mere fragment of a man dragged out from under the wreckage. They had so grown together that when she died there was nothing in him left whole. We dreaded him, and were glad enough to get him off to India. I even hoped he would marry out there. When the news came that he had, I supposed that would end it; that he would become merely a chapter in natural history. But, you see, he hasn't; he's more widowed than before. He can't do anything well without her. You see, he couldn't even do this."

"This?" repeated Westfield, quitting his gardening abruptly. "Am I to understand that she would have been of assistance in selecting another wife for him?"

Harriet preferred to ignore that his tone implied an enormity. "She would certainly have kept him from getting into such a box as he's in now. She could at least have found him some one who wouldn't lacerate him by her every movement. Oh, that poor, limp, tactless, terrified girl! Have you noticed the exasperating way in which she walks, even? It's as if she were treading pain, forbearing and forgiving, when she but steps to the tea table. There was never a person so haunted by the notion of her own untidy picturesqueness. It wears her thin and consumes her, like her unhappy passion. I know how he feels; he hates the way she likes what she likes, and he hates the way she dislikes what she doesn't like. And, mark my words, she is bent upon Fortuney. That, at least, Robert, he certainly can't permit. At Fortuney, Eleanor is living still. The place is so intensely, so rarely personal. The girl has fixed her eye, made up her mind. It's symbolic to her, too, and she's circling about it; she can't endure to be kept out. Yesterday, when I went to see her, she couldn't wait to begin explaining her husband to me. She seemed to be afraid I might think she hadn't poked into everything."

While his wife grew more and more vehement, Westfield lay back in a garden chair, half succumbing to the drowsy warmth of the afternoon.

"It seems to me," he remarked, with a discreet yawn, "that the poor child is only putting up a good fight against the tormenting suspicion that she hasn't got into anything. She may be just decently trying to conceal her uncertainty."

Harriet looked at him intently for a moment, watching the shadows of the sycamore leaves play across his face, and then laughed indulgently. "The idea of her decently trying to conceal anything amuses me. So that's how much you know of her!" she sighed. "She's taken you in just as she took him. He doubtless thought she wouldn't poke; that she would go on keeping the door of the chamber, breathing faint benedictions and smiling her moonbeam smile as he came and went. But, under all her meekness and air of poetically foregoing, she has a forthcomingness and an outputtingness which all the brutality he's driven to can't discourage. I've known her kind before! You may clip their tendrils every day of your life only to find them renewed and sweetly taking hold the next morning. She'd find the crevices in polished alabaster. Can't you see what she wants?" Mrs. Westfield sat up with flashing eyes. "She wants to be to him what Eleanor was; she sees no reason why she shouldn't be!"

Westfield rubbed the stiff blond hair above his ear in

perplexity. "Well, why, in Heaven's name, shouldn't she be? He married her. What less can she expect?"

"Oh, Robert!" cried Harriet, as if he had uttered something impious. "But then, you never knew them. Why, Eleanor made him. He is the work of her hands. She saved him from being something terrible."

Westfield smiled ironically.

"Was he, then, in his natural state, so—so very much worse?"

"Oh, he was better than he is now, even then. But he was somehow terribly off the key. He was the most immature thing ever born into the world. Youth was a disease with him; he almost died of it. He was so absorbed in his own waking up, and he so overestimated its importance. He made such a clamor about it and so thrust it upon one that I used to wonder whether he would ever get past the stage of opening packages under the Christmas tree and shouting. I suppose he did know that his experiences were not unique, but I'm sure he felt that the degree of them was peculiarly his.

"When he met Eleanor he lost himself, and that was what he needed. She happened to be born tempered and poised. There never was a time when she wasn't discriminating. She could enjoy all kinds of things and people, but she was never, never mistaken in the kind. The beauty of it was that her distinctions had nothing to do with reason; they were purely shades of feeling.

"Well, you can conjecture what followed. She gave him the one thing which made everything else he had pertinent and dignified. He simply had better fiber than any of us realized, and she saw it. She was infallible in detecting quality.

"Two years after their marriage, I spent six weeks with them at Fortuney, and even then I saw their possibilities, what they would do for each other. And they went on and on. They had all there is—except children. I suppose they were selfish. As Eleanor once said to me, they needed only eternity and each other. But, whatever it was, it was Olympian."

II

Harriet was walking one morning on the green hill that rises, topped by its sprawling feudal ruin, behind Arques-la-Bataille. The sunlight still had the magical golden hue of early day, and the dew shone on the smooth, grassy folds and clefts that mark the outlines of the old fortifications. Below lay the delicately colored town—seen through a grove of glistening white birches—the shining, sinuous curves of the little river, and the green, open stretches of the pleasant Norman country.

As she skirted the base of one of the thick towers on the inner edge of the moat, her sunshade over her shoulder and her white shoes gray with dew, she all but stepped upon a man who lay in a shaded corner within the elbow of the wall and the tower, his straw hat tilted over his eyes.

"Why, Harold Forscythe!" she exclaimed breathlessly.

He sprang to his feet, baring his head in the sun.

"Sit down, do," he urged. "It's quite dry there—the masonry crops out—and the view's delightful."

"You didn't seem to be doing much with the view as I came up." Harriet put down her sunshade and stood looking at him, taking in his careless morning dress, his gray, unshaven face and heavy eyes. "But I shall sit down," she affectionately assured him, "to look at you, since I have so few opportunities. Why haven't you been to see me?"

Forscythe gazed attentively at her canvas shoes, hesitating and thrusting out his lower lip, an impetuous mannerism she had liked in him as a boy. "Perhaps—perhaps I haven't quite dared," he suggested.

"Which means," commented Harriet reproachfully, "that you accredit me with a very disagreeable kind of stupidity."

"You? Oh, dear, no! I didn't—I don't. How could you

suppose it?" He helped her to her seat on the slant of gray rock, moving about her solicitously, but avoiding her eyes.

"Then why do you stand there, hesitating?"

"I was just thinking"—he shot her a nervous glance from under a frown—"whether I ought not to cut away now, on your account. I'm in the devil of a way in the early morning sometimes."

Mrs. Westfield looked at him compassionately as he stood poking the turf with his stick. She wondered how he could have reached eight-and-thirty without growing at all older than he had been in his twenties. And yet, that was just what their happiness had done for them. If it had kept them young, gloriously and resplendently young, it had also kept them from arriving anywhere. It had prolonged his flowering time, but it hadn't mellowed him. Growing older would have meant making concessions. He had never made any; had not even learned how, and was still striking back like a boy.

Harriet pointed to the turf beside her, and he dropped down suddenly.

"I'm really not fit to see any one this morning. These first hours—" He shrugged his shoulders and began to pull the grass blades swiftly, one at a time.

"Are hard for you?"

He nodded.

"Because they used to be your happiest?" Harriet continued, feeling her way.

"It's queer," he said quietly, "but in the morning I often feel such an absurd certainty of finding her. I suppose one has more vitality at this time of day, a keener sense of things."

"My poor boy! Is it still as hard as that?"

"Did you for a moment suppose that it would ever be any—easier?" he asked, with a short laugh.

"I hoped so. Oh, I hoped so."

Forscythe shook his head. "You know why I haven't been to see you," he brought out abruptly.

Harriet touched his arm. "You ought not to be afraid

with me. If I didn't love her as much as you did, at least I
never loved anything else so well."

"I know. That's one reason I came here. You were
always together when I first knew her, and it's easy to see
her beside you. Sometimes I think the image of her—coming
down the stairs, crossing the garden, holding out her
hand—is growing dimmer, and that terrifies me. Some
people and some places give me the feeling of her." He
stopped with a jerk, and threw a pebble across the moat,
where the sloping bank, softened and made shallower by
the slow centuries, was yellow with buttercups.

"But that feeling, Harold, must be more in you than
anywhere. There's where she willed it and breathed it and
stored it for years."

Harold was looking fixedly at the bare spot under his
hand and pulling the grass blades out delicately. When he
spoke, his voice fairly startled her with its sound of water
working underground.

"It was like that once, but now I lose it sometimes—for
weeks together. It's like trying to hold some delicate scent
in your nostrils, and heavier odors come in and blur it "

"My poor boy, what can I say to you?" Harriet's eyes
were so dim that she could only put out a hand to be sure
that he was there. He pressed it and held it a moment.

"You don't have to say anything. Your thinking reaches
me. It's extraordinary how we can be trained down, how
little we can do with. If she could only have written to
me—if there could have been a sign, a shadow on the
grass or in the sky, to show that she went on with me, it
would have been enough. And now—I wouldn't ask anything but to be left alone with my hurt. It's all that's left
me. It's the most precious thing in the world."

"Oh, but that, my dear Harold, is too terrible! She
couldn't have endured your doing it," murmured Harriet,
overcome.

"Yes, she could. She'd have done it. She'd have kept
me alive in her anguish, in her incompleteness."

Mrs. Westfield put out her hand entreatingly to stop

him. He had lain beside her on the grass so often in the days of his courtship, of his first tempestuous happiness. It was incredible that he should have changed so little. He hadn't grown older, or wiser, or, in himself, better. He had simply grown more and more to be Eleanor. The misery of his entanglement touched her afresh, and she put her hands to her eyes and murmured, "Oh, that poor little Ethel! How could you do it?"

She heard him bound up, and when she lifted her face he was half the length of the wall away. She called to him, but he waved his hat meaninglessly, and she watched him hurry across the smooth green swell of the hill. Harriet leaned back into the warm angle of masonry and tried to settle into the deep peace of the place, where so many follies and passions had spent themselves and ebbed back into the stillness of the grass. But a sense of pain kept throbbing about her. It seemed to come from the spot where poor Forscythe had lain, and to rise like a miasma between her and the farms and orchards and the gray-green windings of the river. When at last she rose with a sigh, she murmured to herself, "Oh, my poor Eleanor! If you know, I pity you. Wherever you are, I pity you."

III

The silence once broken, Forscythe came often to Mrs. Westfield's garden. He spent whole mornings there, watching her embroider, or walked with her about the ruins on the hilltop, or along the streams that wound through the fertile farm country. Though he said little himself, he made it supremely easy for her to talk. He followed her about in grateful silence while she told him, freely and almost lightly, of her girlhood with Eleanor Sanford; of their life at a convent-school in Paris; of the copy of *Manon Lescaut* which they kept sewed up in the little pine pillow they had brought from Schenectady; of the adroit machinations by which, on her fête-day, under the guardianship of an innocent aunt from Albany, Eleanor had managed to convey all her birthday roses out to Père-la-Chaise and arrange them under de Musset's willow.

Harriet even found a quiet happiness in being with him. She felt that he was making amends; that she could trust him not to renew the terrible experience which had crushed her at their first meeting on the hill. When he spoke of Eleanor at all, it was only to recall the beauty of their companionship, a thing she loved to reflect upon. For if they had been selfish, at least their selfishness had never taken the form of comfortable indolence. They had kept the edge of their zest for action; their affection had never grown stocky and middle-aged. How, Harriet often asked herself, could two people have crowded so much into ten circumscribed mortal years? And, of course, the best of it was that all the things they did and the places they went to and the people they knew didn't in the least matter, were only the incidental music of their drama.

The end, when it came, had, by the mercy of Heaven, come suddenly. An illness of three days at Fortuney, their own place on the Oise, and it was over. He was flung out into space to find his way alone; to keep fighting about in his circle, forever yearning toward the center.

One morning, when Harold asked her to go for a long walk into the country, Harriet felt from the moment they left the town behind them that he had something serious to say to her. They were having their déjeuner in the garden of a little auberge, sitting at a table beside a yellow clay wall overgrown with wall peaches, when he told her that he was going away.

"I don't know for just how long. Perhaps a week; perhaps two. I'd hate to have you misunderstand. I don't want you to underestimate the good you've done me these last weeks. But, you see, this is a sort of—a sort of tryst," he explained, smiling faintly. "We got stranded once in an absurd little town down on the Mediterranean, not far from Hyères. We liked it and stayed for days, and when we left, Eleanor said we'd go back every year when the grapes were ripe. We never did go back, for that was the last year. But I've been there that same week every autumn. The people there all remember her. It's a little bit of a place."

Harriet looked at him, holding her breath. The black kitten came up and brushed against him, tapping his arm with its paw and mewing to be fed.

"Is that why you go away so much? Ethel has told me. She said there was some business, but I doubted that."

"I'm sorry it has to be so. Of course, I feel despicable—do all the time, for that matter." He wiped his face and hands miserably with his napkin and pushed back his chair. "You see," he went on, beginning to make geometrical figures in the sand with his walking stick, "you see, I can't settle down to anything, and I'm so driven. There are times when places pull me—places where things happened, you know. Not big things, but just our own things." He stopped, and then added thoughtfully, "Going to miss her is almost what going to meet her used to be. I get in such a state of impatience."

Harriet couldn't, she simply couldn't, altogether despise him, and it was because, as he said, she did know. They sat in the quiet, sunny little garden, full of dahlias and sunflowers and the hum of bees, and she remembered what Eleanor had told her about this fishing village where they had lived on figs and goat's milk and watched the meager vintage being gathered; how, when they had to leave it, got into their compartment and flashed away along the panoramic Mediterranean shore, she had cried— she who never wept for pain or weariness, Harriet put in fondly. It was not the blue bay and the lavender and the pine hills they were leaving, but some peculiar shade of being together. Yet they were always leaving that. Every day brought colors in the sky, on the sea, in the heart, which could not possibly come just so again. That tomorrow's would be just as beautiful never quite satisfied them. They wanted it all. Yes, whatever they were, those two, they were Olympian.

As they were nearing home in the late afternoon,

Forscythe turned suddenly to Harriet. "I shall have to count on you for something while I am away, you know."

"About the business? Oh, yes, I'll understand."

"And you'll do what you can for her, won't you?" he asked shakily. "It's such a hellish existence for her. I'd do anything if I could undo what I've done—anything."

Harriet paused a moment. "It simply can't, you know, go on like this."

"Yes, yes, I know that," he replied abstractedly. "But that's not the worst of it. The worst is that sometimes I feel as if Eleanor wants me to give her up; that she can't stand it any longer and is begging me to let her rest."

Harriet tried to look at him, but he had turned away his face.

IV

Forscythe's absence stretched beyond a fortnight, and no one seemed very definitely informed as to when he might return. Meanwhile, Mrs. Westfield had his wife considerably upon her hands. She could not, indeed, account for the degree to which she seemed responsible. It was always there, groping for her and pulling at her, as she told Westfield. The garden wall was not high enough to shut out entirely the other side; the girl pacing the gravel paths with the meek, bent step which poor Harriet found so exasperating, her wistful eyes peering from under her garden hat, her preposterous skirts trailing behind her like the brier-torn gown of some wandering Griselda.

During the long, dull hours in which they had their tea together, Harriet realized more and more the justice of the girl's position—of her claim, since she apparently had no position that one could well define. The reasonableness of it was all the more trying since Harriet felt so compelled to deny it. They read and walked and talked, and the subject to which they never alluded was always in the air. It was in the girl's long, silent, entreating looks; in her thin hands, nervously clasping and unclasping; in her ceaseless pacing about. Harriet distinctly felt that she was working herself up to something, and she declared to Westfield every morning that, whatever it was, she wouldn't be a party to it.

"I can understand perfectly," she insisted to her husband, "how he did it. He married her to talk to her about Eleanor. Eleanor had been the theme of their courtship. The rest of the world went on attending to its own business and shaking him off, and she stopped and sympathized and let him pour himself out. He didn't see, I suppose, why he shouldn't have just a wife like other men, for it didn't occur to him that he couldn't be just a husband. He thought she'd be content to console; he never dreamed she'd try to heal."

As for Ethel, Harriet had to admit that she, too, could be perfectly accounted for. She had gone into it, doubtless, in the spirit of self-sacrifice, a mood she was romantically fond of permitting herself and humanly unable to live up to. She had married him in one stage of feeling, and had inevitably arrived at another—had come, indeed, to the place where she must be just one thing to him. What she was, or was not, hung on the throw of the dice in a way that savored of trembling captives and barbarous manners, and Harriet had to acknowledge that almost anything might be expected of a woman who had let herself go to such lengths and had yet got nowhere worth mentioning.

"She is certainly going to do something," Harriet declared. "But whatever can she hope to do now? What weapon has she left? How is she, after she's poured herself out so, ever to gather herself up again? What she'll do is the horror. It's sure to be ineffectual, and it's equally sure to have distinctly dramatic aspects."

Harriet was not, however, quite prepared for the issue which confronted her one morning. She sat down shaken and aghast when Ethel, pale and wraith-like, glided somnambulantly into her garden and asked whether Mrs.

Westfield would accompany her to Fortuney on the following day.

"But, my dear girl, ought you to go there alone?"

"Without Harold, you mean?" the other inaudibly suggested. "Yes, I think I ought. He has such a dread of going back there, and yet I feel that he'll never be satisfied until he gets among his own things. He would be happier if he took the shock and had done with it. And my going there first might make it easier for him."

Harriet stared. "Don't you think he should be left to decide that for himself?" she reasoned mildly. "He may wish to forget the place in so far as he can."

"He doesn't forget," Ethel replied simply. "He thinks about it all the time. He ought to live there; it's his home. He ought not," she brought out, with a fierce little burst, "to be kept away."

"I don't know that he or any one else can do much in regard to that," commented Harriet dryly.

"He ought to live there," Ethel repeated automatically; "and it might make it easier for him if I went first."

"How?" gasped Mrs. Westfield.

"It might," she insisted childishly, twisting her handkerchief around her fingers. "We can take an early train and get there in the afternoon. It's but a short drive from the station. I am sure"—she looked pleadingly at Harriet—"I'm sure he'd like it better if you went with me."

Harriet made a clutch at herself and looked pointedly at the ground. "I really don't see how I could, Ethel. It doesn't seem to me a proper thing to do."

Ethel sat straight and still. Her liquid eyes brimmed over and the tears rolled mildly down her cheeks. "I'm sorry it seems wrong to you. Of course you can't go if it does. I shall go alone, then, tomorrow." She rose and stood poised in uncertainty, her hand on the back of the chair.

Harriet moved quickly toward her. The girl's infatuate obstinacy carried a power with it.

"But why, dear child, do you wish me to go with you? What good could that possibly do?"

There was a long silence, trembling and gentle tears. At last Ethel murmured: "I thought, because you were her friend, that would make it better. If you were with me, it couldn't seem quite so—indelicate." Her shoulders shook with a sudden wrench of feeling and she pressed her hands over her face. "You see," she faltered, "I'm so at a loss. I haven't—any one."

Harriet put an arm firmly about her drooping slenderness. "Well, for this venture, at least, you shall have me. I can't see it, but I'm willing to go; more willing than I am that you should go alone. I must tell Robert and ask him to look up the trains for us."

The girl drew gently away from her and stood in an attitude of deep dejection. "It's difficult for you, too, our being here. We ought never to have come. And I must not take advantage of you. Before letting you go with me, I must tell you the real reason why I am going to Fortuney."

"The real reason?" echoed Harriet.

"Yes. I think he's there now."

"Harold? At Fortuney?"

"Yes. I haven't heard from him for five days. Then it was only a telegram, dated from Pontoise. That's very near Fortuney. Since then I haven't had a word."

"You poor child, how dreadful! Come here and tell me about it." Harriet drew her to a chair, into which she sank limply.

"There's nothing to tell, except what one fears. I've lost sleep until I imagine all sorts of horrible things. If he has been alone there for days, shut up with all those memories, who knows what may have happened to him? I shouldn't, you know, feel like this if he were with—any one. But this—oh, you are all against me! You none of you understand. You think I am trying to make him—inconstant" (for the first time her voice broke into passionate scorn). "But there's no other way to save him. It's simply killing him. He's been frightfully ill twice, once in

London and once before we left India. The London doctors told me that unless he was got out of this state he might do almost anything. They even wanted me to leave him. So, you see, I must do something."

Harriet sat down on the stool beside her and took her hand.

"Why don't you, then, my dear, do it—leave him?"

The girl looked wildly toward the garden wall. "I can't—not now. I might have once, perhaps. Oh!" with a burst of trembling, "don't, please don't talk about it. Just help me to save him if you can."

"Had you rather, Ethel, that I went to Fortuney alone?" Harriet suggested hopefully.

The girl shook her head. "No; he'd know I sent you, and he'd think I was afraid. I am, of course, but not in the way he thinks. I've never crossed him in anything, but we can't go on like this any longer. I'll go, and he'll just have to—choose."

Having seen Ethel safely to her own door, Harriet went to her husband, who was at work in the library, and told him to what she had committed herself. Westfield received the intelligence with marked discouragement. He disliked her being drawn more and more into the Forscythes' affairs, which he found very depressing and disconcerting, and he flatly declared that he wanted nothing so much as to get away from all that hysteria next door and finish the summer in Switzerland.

"It's an obsession with her to get to Fortuney," Harriet explained. "To her it somehow means getting into everything she's out of. I really can't have her thinking I'm against her in that definite, petty sort of way. So I've promised to go. Besides, if she is going down there, where all Eleanor's things are—"

"Ah, so it's to keep her out, and not to help her in, that you're going," Westfield deduced.

"I declare to you, I don't know which it is. I'm going for both of them—for her and for Eleanor."

V

Fortuney stood in its cluster of cool green, halfway up the hillside and overlooking the green loop of the river. Harriet remembered, as she approached it, how Eleanor used to say that after the South, it was good to come back and rest her eyes there. Nowhere were skies so gray, streams so clear, or fields so pleasantly interspersed with woodland. The hill on which the house stood overlooked an island where the haymakers were busy cutting a second crop, swinging their bright scythes in the long grass and stopping to hail the heavy lumber barges as they passed slowly up the glassy river.

Ethel insisted upon leaving the carriage by the roadside, so the two women alighted and walked up the long driveway that wound under the linden trees. An old man who was clipping the hedge looked curiously at them as they passed. Except for the snipping of his big shears and occasional halloos from the island, a pale, sunny quiet lay over the place, and their approach, Harriet reflected, certainly savored all too much of a reluctance to break it. She looked at Ethel with all the exasperation of fatigue, and felt that there was something positively stealthy about her soft, driven tread.

The front door was open, but, as they approached, a bent old woman ran out from the garden behind the house, her apron full of gourds, calling to them as she ran. Ethel addressed her without embarrassment: "I am Madame Forscythe. Monsieur is awaiting me. Yes, I know that he is ill. You need not announce me."

The old woman tried to detain her by salutations and questions, tried to explain that she would immediately get rooms ready for Madame and her friend. Why had she not been told?

But Ethel brushed past her, seeming to float over the threshold and up the staircase, while Harriet followed her, protesting. They went through the salon, the library, into Harold's study, straight toward the room which had been Eleanor's.

"Let us wait for him here in his study, please, Ethel," Harriet whispered. "We've no right to steal upon any one like this."

But Ethel seemed drawn like the victim of mesmerism. The door opening from the study into Eleanor's room was hung with a heavy curtain. She lifted it, and there they paused, noiselessly. It was just as Harriet remembered it; the tapestries, the prie-Dieu, the Louis Seize furniture—absolutely unchanged, except that her own portrait, by Constant, hung where Harold's used to be. Across the foot of the bed, in a tennis shirt and trousers, lay Harold himself, asleep. He was lying on his side, his face turned toward the door and one arm thrown over his head. The habit of being on his guard must have sharpened his senses, for as they looked at him he awoke and sprang up, flushed and disordered.

"Ethel, what on earth—?" he cried hotly.

She was frightened enough now. She trembled from head to foot and pressed her hands tightly over her breast. "You never told me not to come," she panted. "You only said," with a wild burst of reproach, "that you couldn't."

Harold gripped the foot of the bed with both hands and his voice shook with anger. "Please go downstairs and wait in the reception room, while I ask Mrs. Westfield to enlighten me."

Something leaped into Ethel's eyes as she took another step forward into the room and let the curtain fall behind her. "I won't go, Harold, until you go with me," she cried. Drawing up her frail shoulders, she glanced desperately about her—at the room, at her husband, at Harriet, and finally at her, the handsome, disdainful face which glowed out of the canvas. "You have no right to come here secretly," she broke out. "It's shameful to her as well as to me. I'm not afraid of her. She couldn't but loathe you for what you do to me. She couldn't have been so contemptible as you all make her—so jealous!"

Forscythe swung round on his heel, his clenched hands hanging at his side, and, throwing back his head, faced the picture.

"Jealous? Of whom—my God!"

"Harold!" cried Mrs. Westfield entreatingly.

But she was too late. The girl had slipped to the floor as if she had been cut down.

VI

One rainy night, four weeks after her visit to Fortuney, Forscythe stood at Mrs. Westfield's door, his hat in his hand, bidding her good night. Harriet looked worn and troubled, but Forscythe himself was calm.

"I'm so glad you gave me a chance at Fortuney, Harold. I couldn't bear to see it go to strangers. I'll keep it just as it is—as it was; you may be sure of that, and if ever you wish to come back—"

Forscythe spoke up quickly: "I don't think I shall be coming back again, Mrs. Westfield. And please don't hesitate to make any changes. As I've tried to tell you, I don't feel the need of it any longer. She has come back to me as much as she ever can."

"In another person?"

Harold smiled a little and shook his head. "In another way. She lived and died, dear Harriet, and I'm all there is to show for it. That's pitiful enough, but I must do what I can. I shall die very far short of the mark—but she was always generous."

He held out his hand to Mrs. Westfield and took hers resolutely, though she hesitated as if to detain him.

"Tell Ethel I shall go over to see her in the morning before you leave, and thank her for her message," Harriet murmured.

"Please come. She has been seeing to the packing in spite of me, and is quite worn out. She'll be herself again, once I get her back to Surrey, and she's very keen about going to America. Good night, dear lady," he called after him as he crossed the veranda.

Harriet heard him splash down the gravel walk to the gate and then closed the door. She went slowly through the hall and into her husband's study, where she sat quietly down by the wood fire.

Westfield rose from his work and looked at her with concern.

"Why didn't you send that madman home long ago, Harriet? It's past midnight, and you're completely done out. You look like a ghost." He opened a cabinet and poured her a glass of wine.

"I feel like one, dear. I'm beginning to feel my age. I've no spirit to hold it off any longer. I'm going to buy Fortuney and give up to it. It will be pleasant to grow old there in that atmosphere of lovely things past and forgotten."

Westfield sat down on the arm of her chair and drew her head to him. "He is really going to sell it, then? He has come round sure enough, hasn't he?"

"Oh, he melts the heart in me, Robert. He makes me feel so old and lonely; that he and I are left over from another age—a lovely time that's gone. He's giving up everything. He's going to take her home to America after her child is born."

"Her child?"

"Yes. He didn't know until after that dreadful day at Fortuney. She had never told any one. He says he's so glad—that it will make up to her for everything. Oh, Robert! if only Eleanor had left him children all this wouldn't have been."

"Do you think," Westfield asked after a long silence, "that he is glad?"

"I know it. He's been so gentle and comprehending with her." Harriet stopped to dry the tears on her cheek, and put her head down on her husband's shoulder. "And oh, Robert, I never would have believed that he could be so splendid about it. It's as if he had come up to his possibilities for the first time, through this silly, infatuated girl, while Eleanor, who gave him kingdoms—"

She cried softly on his shoulder for a long while, and then he felt that she was thinking. When at last she looked up, she smiled gratefully into his eyes.

"Well, we'll have Fortuney, dearest. We'll have all that's left of them. He'll never turn back; I feel such a strength in him now. He'll go on doing it and being finer and finer. And do you know, Robert," her lips trembled again, but she still smiled from her misty eyes, "if Eleanor knows, I believe she'll be glad; for—oh, my Eleanor!—she loved him beyond anything, beyond even his love."

On the Gulls' Road

The Ambassador's Story

It often happens that one or another of my friends stops before a red chalk drawing in my study and asks me where I ever found so lovely a creature. I have never told the story of that picture to any one, and the beautiful woman on the wall, until yesterday, in all these twenty years has spoken to no one but me. Yesterday a young painter, a countryman of mine, came to consult me on a matter of business, and upon seeing my drawing of Alexandra Ebbling, straightway forgot his errand. He examined the date upon the sketch and asked me, very earnestly, if I could tell him whether the lady were still living. When I answered him, he stepped back from the picture and said slowly:

"So long ago? She must have been very young. She was happy?"

"As to that, who can say—about any one of us?" I replied. "Out of all that is supposed to make for happiness, she had very little."

He shrugged his shoulders and turned away to the window, saying as he did so: "Well, there is very little use in troubling about anything, when we can stand here and look at her, and you can tell me that she has been dead all these years, and that she had very little."

We returned to the object of his visit, but when he bade

229

me goodbye at the door his troubled gaze again went back to the drawing, and it was only by turning sharply about that he took his eyes away from her.

I went back to my study fire, and as the rain kept away less impetuous visitors, I had a long time in which to think of Mrs. Ebbling. I even got out the little box she gave me, which I had not opened for years, and when Mrs. Hemway brought my tea I had barely time to close the lid and defeat her disapproving gaze.

My young countryman's perplexity, as he looked at Mrs. Ebbling, had recalled to me the delight and pain she gave me when I was of his years. I sat looking at her face and trying to see it through his eyes—freshly, as I saw it first upon the deck of the *Germania*, twenty years ago. Was it her loveliness, I often ask myself, or her loneliness, or her simplicity, or was it merely my own youth? Was her mystery only that of the mysterious North out of which she came? I still feel that she was very different from all the beautiful and brilliant women I have known; as the night is different from the day, or as the sea is different from the land. But this is our story, as it comes back to me.

For two years I had been studying Italian and working in the capacity of clerk to the American legation at Rome, and I was going home to secure my first consular appointment. Upon boarding my steamer at Genoa, I saw my luggage into my cabin and then started for a rapid circuit of the deck. Everything promised well. The boat was thinly peopled, even for a July crossing; the decks were roomy; the day was fine; the sea was blue; I was sure of my appointment, and, best of all, I was coming back to Italy. All these things were in my mind when I stopped sharply before a *chaise longue* placed sidewise near the stern. Its occupant was a woman, apparently ill, who lay with her eyes closed, and in her open arm was a chubby little red-haired girl, asleep. I can still remember that first glance at Mrs. Ebbling, and how I stopped as a wheel does when the band slips. Her splendid, vigorous body lay still and relaxed under the loose folds of her clothing, her white throat and arms and red-gold hair were drenched with sunlight. Such hair as it was: wayward as some kind of gleaming seaweed that curls and undulates with the tide. A moment gave me her face; the high cheekbones, the thin cheeks, the gentle chin, arching back to a girlish throat, and singular loveliness of the mouth. Even then it flashed through me that the mouth gave the whole face its peculiar beauty and distinction. It was proud and sad and tender, and strangely calm. The curve of the lips could not have been cut more cleanly with the most delicate instrument, and whatever shade of feeling passed over them seemed to partake of their exquisiteness.

But I am anticipating. While I stood stupidly staring (as if, at twenty-five, I had never before beheld a beautiful woman) the whistles broke into a hoarse scream, and the deck under us began to vibrate. The woman opened her eyes, and the little girl struggled into a sitting position, rolled out of her mother's arm, and ran to the deck rail. After putting my chair near the stern, I went forward to see the gangplank up and did not return until we were dragging out to sea at the end of a long towline.

The woman in the *chaise longue* was still alone. She lay there all day, looking at the sea. The little girl, Carin, played noisily about the deck. Occasionally she returned and struggled up into the chair, plunged her head, round and red as a little pumpkin, against her mother's shoulder in an impetuous embrace, and then struggled down again with a lively flourishing of arms and legs. Her mother took such opportunities to pull up the child's socks or to smooth the fiery little braids; her beautiful hands, rather large and very white, played about the riotous little girl with a quieting tenderness. Carin chattered away in Italian and kept asking for her father, only to be told that he was busy.

When any of the ship's officers passed, they stopped for a word with my neighbor, and I heard the first mate address her as Mrs. Ebbling. When they spoke to her, she smiled appreciatively and answered in low, faltering Italian, but I fancied that she was glad when they passed on and left her to her fixed contemplation of the sea. Her eyes seemed to drink the color of it all day long, and after every interruption they went back to it. There was a kind of pleasure in watching her satisfaction, a kind of excitement in wondering what the water made her remember or forget. She seemed not to wish to talk to any one, but I knew I should like to hear whatever she might be thinking. One could catch some hint of her thoughts, I imagined, from the shadows that came and went across her lips, like the reflection of light clouds. She had a pile of books beside her, but she did not read, and neither could I. I gave up trying at last, and watched the sea, very conscious of her presence, almost of her thoughts. When the sun dropped low and shone in her face, I rose and asked if she would like me to move her chair. She smiled and thanked me, but said the sun was good for her. Her yellow-hazel eyes followed me for a moment and then went back to the sea.

After the first bugle sounded for dinner, a heavy man in uniform came up the deck and stood beside the *chaise longue*, looking down at its two occupants with a smile of satisfied possession. The breast of his trim coat was hidden by waves of soft blond beard, as long and heavy as a woman's hair, which blew about his face in glittering profusion. He wore a large turquoise ring upon the thick hand that he rubbed good-humoredly over the little girl's head. To her he spoke Italian, but he and his wife conversed in some Scandinavian tongue. He stood stroking his fine beard until the second bugle blew, then bent stiffly from his hips, like a soldier, and patted his wife's hand as it lay on the arm of her chair. He hurried down the deck, taking stock of the passengers as he went, and stopped before a thin girl with frizzed hair and a lace coat, asking her a facetious question in thick English. They began to talk about Chicago and went below. Later I saw him at the head of his table in the dining room, the befrizzed Chicago lady on his left. They must have got a famous start at luncheon, for by the end of the dinner Ebbling was peeling figs for her and presenting them on the end of a fork.

The Doctor confided to me that Ebbling was the chief engineer and the dandy of the boat; but this time he would have to behave himself, for he had brought his sick wife along for the voyage. She had a bad heart valve, he added, and was in a serious way.

After dinner Ebbling disappeared, presumably to his engines, and at ten o'clock, when the stewardess came to put Mrs. Ebbling to bed, I helped her to rise from her chair, and the second mate ran up and supported her down to her cabin. About midnight I found the engineer in the card room, playing with the Doctor, an Italian naval officer, and the commodore of a Long Island yacht club. His face was even pinker than it had been at dinner, and his fine beard was full of smoke. I thought a long while about Ebbling and his wife before I went to sleep.

The next morning we tied up at Naples to take on our cargo, and I went on shore for the day. I did not, however, entirely escape the ubiquitous engineer, whom I saw lunching with the Long Island commodore at a hotel in the Santa Lucia. When I returned to the boat in the early evening, the passengers had gone down to dinner, and I found Mrs. Ebbling quite alone upon the deserted deck. I approached her and asked whether she had had a dull day. She looked up smiling and shook her head, as if her Italian had quite failed her. I saw that she was flushed with excitement, and her yellow eyes were shining like two clear topazes.

"Dull? Oh, no! I love to watch Naples from the sea, in this white heat. She has just lain there on her hillside among the vines and laughed for me all day long. I have been able to pick out many of the places I like best."

I felt that she was really going to talk to me at last. She had turned to me frankly, as to an old acquaintance, and seemed not to be hiding from me anything of what she felt. I sat down in a glow of pleasure and excitement and asked her if she knew Naples well.

"Oh, yes! I lived there for a year after I was first married. My husband has a great many friends in Naples. But he was at sea most of the time, so I went about alone. Nothing helps one to know a city like that. I came first by sea, like this. Directly to Naples from Finmark, and I had never been south before." Mrs. Ebbling stopped and looked over my shoulder. Then, with a quick, eager glance at me, she said abruptly: "It was like a baptism of fire. Nothing has ever been quite the same since. Imagine how this bay looked to a Finmark girl. It seemed like the overture to Italy."

I laughed. "And then one goes up the country—song by song and wine by wine."

Mrs. Ebbling sighed. "Ah, yes. It must be fine to follow it. I have never been away from the seaports myself. We live now in Genoa."

The deck steward brought her tray, and I moved forward a little and stood by the rail. When I looked back, she smiled and nodded to let me know that she was not missing anything. I could feel her intentness as keenly as if she were standing beside me.

The sun had disappeared over the high ridge behind the city, and the stone pines stood black and flat against the fires of the afterglow. The lilac haze that hung over the long, lazy slopes of Vesuvius warmed with golden light, and films of blue vapor began to float down toward Baiæ. The sky, the sea, and the city between them turned a shimmering violet, fading grayer as the lights began to glow like luminous pearls along the water-front—the necklace of an irreclaimable queen. Behind me I heard a low exclamation; a slight, stifled sound, but it seemed the perfect vocalization of that weariness with which we at last let go of beauty, after we have held it until the senses are darkened. When I turned to her again, she seemed to have fallen asleep.

That night, as we were moving out to sea and the tail

lights of Naples were winking across the widening stretch of black water, I helped Mrs. Ebbling to the foot of the stairway. She drew herself up from her chair with effort and leaned on me wearily. I could have carried her all night without fatigue.

"May I come and talk to you tomorrow?" I asked. She did not reply at once. "Like an old friend?" I added. She gave me her languid hand, and her mouth, set with the exertion of walking, softened altogether. "*Grazia*," she murmured.

I returned to the deck and joined a group of my countrywomen, who, primed with inexhaustible information, were discussing the baseness of Renaissance art. They were intelligent and alert, and as they leaned forward in their deck chairs under the circle of light, their faces recalled to me Rembrandt's picture of a clinical lecture. I heard them through, against my will, and then went to the stern to smoke and to see the last of the island lights. The sky had clouded over, and a soft, melancholy wind was rushing over the sea. I could not help thinking how disappointed I would be if rain should keep Mrs. Ebbling in her cabin tomorrow. My mind played constantly with her image. At one moment she was very clear and directly in front of me; the next she was far away. Whatever else I thought about, some part of my consciousness was busy with Mrs. Ebbling; hunting for her, finding her, losing her, then groping again. How was it that I was so conscious of whatever she might be feeling? That when she sat still behind me and watched the evening sky, I had had a sense of speed and change, almost of danger; and when she was tired and sighed, I had wished for night and loneliness.

II

Though when we are young we seldom think much about it, there is now and again a golden day when we feel a sudden, arrogant pride in our youth; in the light-

ness of our feet and the strength of our arms, in the warm
fluid that courses so surely within us; when we are conscious of something powerful and mercurial in our breasts,
which comes up wave after wave and leaves us irrespon-
sible and free. All the next morning I felt this flow of life,
which continually impelled me toward Mrs. Ebbling. After the merest greeting, however, I kept away. I found it
pleasant to thwart myself, to measure myself against a
current that was sure to carry me with it in the end. I was
content to let her watch the sea—the sea that seemed now
to have come into me, warm and soft, still and strong. I
played shuffleboard with the Commodore, who was anxious to keep down his figure, and ran about the deck with
the stout legs of the little pumpkin-colored Carin about
my neck. It was not until the child was having her afternoon nap below that I at last came up and stood beside
her mother.

"You are better today," I exclaimed, looking down at
her white gown. She colored unreasonably, and I laughed
with a familiarity which she must have accepted as the
mere foolish noise of happiness, or it would have seemed
impertinent.

We talked at first of a hundred trivial things, and we
watched the sea. The coast of Sardinia had lain to our port
for some hours and would lie there for hours to come,
now advancing in rocky promontories, now retreating
behind blue bays. It was the naked south coast of the
island, and though our course held very near the shore,
not a village or habitation was visible; there was not even
a goatherd's hut hidden away among the low pinkish
sand hills. Pinkish sand hills and yellow headlands; with
dull-colored scrubby bushes massed about their bases and
following the dried watercourses. A narrow strip of beach
glistened like white paint between the purple sea and the
umber rocks, and the whole island lay gleaming in the
yellow sunshine and translucent air. Not a wave broke on
that fringe of white sand, not the shadow of a cloud
played across the bare hills. In the air about us there was

no sound but that of a vessel moving rapidly through absolutely still water. She seemed like some great sea-animal, swimming silently, her head well up. The sea before us was so rich and heavy and opaque that it might have been lapis lazuli. It was the blue of legend, simply; the color that satisfies the soul like sleep.

And it was of the sea we talked, for it was the substance of Mrs. Ebbling's story. She seemed always to have been swept along by ocean streams, warm or cold, and to have hovered about the edge of great waters. She was born and had grown up in a little fishing town on the Arctic Ocean. Her father was a doctor, a widower, who lived with his daughter and who divided his time between his books and his fishing rod. Her uncle was skipper on a coasting vessel, and with him she had made many trips along the Norwegian coast. But she was always reading and thinking about the blue seas of the South.

"There was a curious old woman in our village, Dame Ericson, who had been in Italy in her youth. She had gone to Rome to study art, and had copied a great many pictures there. She was well connected, but had little money, and as she grew older and poorer she sold her pictures one by one, until there was scarcely a well-to-do family in our district that did not own one of Dame Ericson's paintings. But she brought home many other strange things; a little orange tree which she cherished until the day of her death, and bits of colored marble, and sea shells and pieces of coral, and a thin flask full of water from the Mediterranean. When I was a little girl she used to show me her things and tell me about the South; about the coral fishers, and the pink islands, and the smoking mountains, and the old, underground Naples. I suppose the water in her flask was like any other, but it never seemed so to me. It looked so elastic and alive, that I used to think if one unsealed the bottle something penetrating and fruitful might leap out and work an enchantment over Finmark."

Lars Ebbling, I learned, was one of her father's friends. She could remember him from the time when she was a

little girl and he a dashing young man who used to come
home from the sea and make a stir in the village. After he
got his promotion to an Atlantic liner and went South, she
did not see him until the summer she was twenty, when
he came home to marry her. That was five years ago. The
little girl, Carin, was three. From her talk, one might have
supposed that Ebbling was proprietor of the Mediterranean and its adjacent lands, and could have kept her
away at his pleasure. Her own rights in him she seemed
not to consider.

But we wasted very little time on Lars Ebbling. We
talked, like two very young persons, of arms and men, of
the sea beneath us and the shores it washed. We were
carried a little beyond ourselves, for we were in the presence of the things of youth that never change; fleeing past
them. Tomorrow they would be gone, and no effort of
will or memory could bring them back again. All about us
was the sea of great adventure, and below us, caught
somewhere in its gleaming meshes, were the bones of
nations and navies . . . nations and navies that gave youth
its hope and made life something more than a hunger of
the bowels. The unpeopled Sardinian coast unfolded gently
before us, like something left over out of a world that was
gone; a place that might well have had no later news since
the corn ships brought the tidings of Actium.

"I shall never go to Sardinia," said Mrs. Ebbling. "It
could not possibly be as beautiful as this."

"Neither shall I," I replied.

As I was gong down to dinner that evening, I was
stopped by Lars Ebbling, freshly brushed and scented,
wearing a white uniform, and polished and glistening as
one of his own engines. He smiled at me with his own
kind of geniality. "You have been very kind of talk to my
wife," he explained. "It is very bad for her this trip that
she speaks no English. I am indebted to you."

I told him curtly that he was mistaken, but my acri-
mony made no impression upon his blandness. I felt that
I should certainly strike the fellow if he stood there much

longer, running his blue ring up and down his beard. I should probably have hated any man who was Mrs. Ebbling's husband, but Ebbling made me sick.

III

The next day I began my drawing of Mrs. Ebbling. She seemed pleased and a little puzzled when I asked her to sit for me. It occurred to me that she had always been among dull people who took her looks as a matter of course, and that she was not at all sure that she was really beautiful. I can see now her quick, confused look of pleasure. I thought very little about the drawing then, except that the making of it gave me an opportunity to study her face; to look as long as I pleased into her yellow eyes, at the noble lines of her mouth, at her splendid, vigorous hair.

"We have a yellow vine at home," I told her, "that is very like your hair. It seems to be growing while one looks at it, and it twines and tangles about itself and throws out little tendrils in the wind."

"Has it any name?"

"We call it love vine."

How little a thing could disconcert her!

As for me, nothing disconcerted me. I awoke every morning with a sense of speed and joy. At night I loved to hear the swish of the water rushing by. As fast as the pistons could carry us, as fast as the water could bear us, we were going forward to something delightful; to something together. When Mrs. Ebbling told me that she and her husband would be five days in the docks in New York and then return to Genoa, I was not disturbed, for I did not believe her. I came and went, and she sat still all day, watching the water. I heard an American lady say that she watched it like one who is going to die, but even that did not frighten me: I somehow felt that she had promised me to live.

All those long blue days when I sat beside her talking

about Finmark and the sea, she must have known that I loved her. I sat with my hands idle on my knees and let the tide come up in me. It carried me so swiftly that, across the narrow space of deck between us, it must have swayed her, too, a little. I had no wish to disturb or distress her. If a little, a very little of it reached her, I was satisfied. If it drew her softly, but drew her, I wanted no more. Sometimes I could see that even the light pressure of my thoughts made her paler. One still evening, after a long talk, she whispered to me, "You must go and walk now, and—don't think about me." She had been held too long and too closely in my thoughts, and she begged me to release her for a little while. I went out into the bow and put her far away, at the skyline, with the faintest star, and thought of her gently across the water. When I went back to her, she was asleep.

But even in those first days I had my hours of misery. Why, for instance, should she have been born in Finmark, and why should Lars Ebbling have been her only door of escape? Why should she be silently taking leave of the world at the age when I was just beginning it, having had nothing, nothing of whatever is worth while?

She never talked about taking leave of things and yet I sometimes felt that she was counting the sunsets. One yellow afternoon, when we were gliding between the shores of Spain and Africa, she spoke of her illness for the first time. I had got some magnolias at Gibraltar, and she wore a bunch of them in her girdle and the rest lay on her lap. She held the cool leaves against her cheek and fingered the white petals. "I can never," she remarked, "get enough of the flowers of the South. They make me breathless, just as they did at first. Because of them I should like to live a long while—almost forever."

I leaned forward and looked at her. "We could live almost forever if we had enough courage. It's of our lives that we die. If we had the courage to change it all, to run away to some blue coast like that over there, we could live on and on, until we were tired."

She smiled tolerantly and looked southward through half-shut eyes. "I am afraid I should never have courage enough to go behind that mountain, at least. Look at it, it looks as if it hid horrible things."

A sea mist, blown in from the Atlantic, began to mask the impassive African coast, and above the fog, the gray mountain peak took on the angry red of the sunset. It burned sullen and threatening until the dark land drew the night about her and settled back into the sea. We watched it sink, while under us, slowly but ever increasing, we felt the throb of the Atlantic come and go, the thrill of the vast, untamed waters of that lugubrious and passionate sea. I drew Mrs. Ebbling's wraps about her and shut the magnolias under her cloak. When I left her, she slipped me one warm, white flower.

IV

From the Straits of Gibraltar we dropped into the abyss, and by morning we were rolling in the trough of a sea that drew us down and held us deep, shaking us gently back and forth until the timbers creaked, and then shooting us out on the crest of a swelling mountain. The water was bright and blue, but so cold that the breath of it penetrated one's bones, as if the chill of the deep underfathoms of the sea were being loosed upon us. There were not more than a dozen people upon the deck that morning, and Mrs. Ebbling was sheltered behind the stern, muffled in a sea jacket, with drops of moisture upon her long lashes and on her hair. When a shower of icy spray beat back over the deck rail, she took it gleefully.

"After all," she insisted, "this is my own kind of water; the kind I was born in. This is first cousin to the Pole waters, and the sea we have left is only a kind of fairy tale. It's like the burnt-out volcanoes; its day is over. This is the real sea now, where the doings of the world go on."

"It is not our reality, at any rate," I answered.

"Oh, yes, it is! These are the waters that carry men to their work, and they will carry you to yours."

I sat down and watched her hair grow more alive and iridescent in the moisture. "You are pleased to take an attitude," I complained.

"No, I don't love realities any more than another, but I admit them, all the same."

"And who are you and I to define the realities?"

"Our minds define them clearly enough, yours and mine, everybody's. Those are the lines we never cross, though we flee from the equator to the Pole. I have never really got out of Finmark, of course. I shall live and die in a fishing town on the Arctic Ocean, and the blue seas and the pink islands are as much a dream as they ever were. All the same, I shall continue to dream them."

The Gulf Stream gave us warm blue days again, but pale, like sad memories. The water had faded, and the thin, tepid sunshine made something tighten about one's heart. The stars watched us coldly, and seemed always to be asking me what I was going to do. The advancing line on the chart, which at first had been mere foolishness, began to mean something, and the wind from the west brought disturbing fears and forebodings. I slept lightly, and all day I was restless and uncertain except when I was with Mrs. Ebbling. She quieted me as she did little Carin, and soothed me without saying anything, as she had done that evening at Naples when we watched the sunset. It seemed to me that every day her eyes grew more tender and her lips more calm. A kind of fortitude seemed to be gathering about her mouth, and I dreaded it. Yet when, in an involuntary glance, I put to her the question that tortured me, her eyes always met mine steadily, deep and gentle and full of reassurance. That I had my word at last, happened almost by accident.

On the second night out from shore there was the concert for the Sailors' Orphanage, and Mrs. Ebbling dressed and went down to dinner for the first time, and sat on her husband's right. I was not the only one who was glad to see her. Even the women were pleased. She wore a pale green gown, and she came up out of it regally white and gold. I was so proud that I blushed when any one spoke of her. After dinner she was standing by her deck chair talking to her husband when people began to go below for the concert. She took up a long cloak and attempted to put it on. The wind blew the light thing about, and Ebbling chatted and smiled his public smile while she struggled with it. Suddenly his roving eye caught sight of the Chicago girl, who was having a similar difficulty with her draperies, and he pranced half the length of the deck to assist her. I had been watching from the rail, and when she was left alone I threw my cigar away and wrapped Mrs. Ebbling up roughly.

"Don't go down," I begged. "Stay up here. I want to talk to you."

She hesitated a moment and looked at me thoughtfully. Then, with a sigh, she sat down. Every one hurried down to the saloon, and we were absolutely alone at last, behind the shelter of the stern, with the thick darkness all about us and a warm east wind rushing over the sea. I was too sore and angry to think. I leaned toward her, holding the arm of her chair with both hands, and began anywhere.

"You remember those two blue coasts out of Gibraltar? It shall be either one you choose, if you will come with me. I have not much money, but we shall get on somehow. There has got to be an end of this. We are neither one of us cowards, and this is humiliating, intolerable."

She sat looking down at her hands, and I pulled her chair impatiently toward me.

"I felt," she said at last, "that you were going to say something like this. You are sorry for me, and I don't wish to be pitied. You think Ebbling neglects me, but you are mistaken. He has had his disappointments, too. He wants children and a gay, hospitable house, and he is tied to a sick woman who cannot get on with people. He has more to complain of than I have, and yet he bears with me. I am grateful to him, and there is no more to be said."

"Oh, isn't there?" I cried, "and I?"

She laid her hand entreatingly upon my arm. "Ah, you! you! Don't ask me to talk about that. *You*——" Her fingers slipped down my coat sleeve to my hand and pressed it. I caught her two hands and held them, telling her I would never let them go.

"And you meant to leave me day after tomorrow, to say goodbye to me as you will to the other people on this boat? You meant to cut me adrift like this, with my heart on fire and all my life unspent in me?"

She sighed despondently. "I am willing to suffer—whatever I must suffer—to have had you," she answered simply. "I was ill—and so lonely—and it came so quickly and quietly. Ah, don't begrudge it to me! Do not leave me in bitterness. If I have been wrong, forgive me." She bowed her head and pressed my fingers entreatingly. A warm tear splashed on my hand. It occurred to me that she bore my anger as she bore little Carin's importunities, as she bore Ebbling. What a circle of pettiness she had about her! I fell back in my chair and my hands dropped at my side. I felt like a creature with its back broken. I asked her what she wished me to do.

"Don't ask me," she whispered. "There is nothing that we can do. I thought you knew that. You forget that—that I am too ill to begin my life over. Even if there were nothing else in the way, that would be enough. And that is what has made it all possible, our loving each other, I mean. If I were well, we couldn't have had even this much. Don't reproach me. Hasn't it been at all pleasant to you to find me waiting for you every morning, to feel me thinking of you when you went to sleep? Every night I have watched the sea for you, as if it were mine and I had made it, and I have listened to the water rushing by you, full of sleep and youth and hope. And everything you had done or said during the day came back to me, and when I went to sleep it was only to feel you more. You see there was never any one else; I have never thought of any one in the dark but you." She spoke pleadingly, and her voice had sunk so low that I could scarcely hear her.

"And yet you will do nothing," I groaned. "You will dare nothing. You will give me nothing."

"Don't say that. When I leave you day after tomorrow, I shall have given you all my life. I can't tell you how, but it is true. There is something in each of us that does not belong to the family or to society, not even to ourselves. Sometimes it is given in marriage, and sometimes it is given in love, but oftener it is never given at all. We have nothing to do with giving or withholding it. It is a wild thing that sings in us once and flies away and never comes back, and mine has flown to you. When one loves like that, it is enough, somehow. The other things can go if they must. That is why I can live without you, and die without you."

I caught her hands and looked into her eyes that shone warm in the darkness. She shivered and whispered in a tone so different from any I ever heard from her before or afterward: "Do you grudge it to me? You are so young and strong, and you have everything before you. I shall have only a little while to want you in—and I could want you forever and not weary." I kissed her hair, her cheeks, her lips, until her head fell forward on my shoulder and she put my face away with her soft, trembling fingers. She took my hand and held it close to her, in both her own. We sat silent, and the moments came and went, bringing us closer and closer, and the wind and water rushed by us, obliterating our tomorrows and all our yesterdays.

The next day Mrs. Ebbling kept her cabin, and I sat stupidly by her chair until dark, with the rugged little girl to keep me company, and an occasional nod from the engineer.

I saw Mrs. Ebbling again only for a few moments, when we were coming into the New York harbor. She wore a street dress and a hat, and these alone would have made

her seem far away from me. She was very pale and looked
down when she spoke to me, as if she had been guilty of
a wrong toward me. I have never been able to remember
that interview without heartache and shame, but then I
was too desperate to care about anything. I stood like a
wooden post and let her approach me, let her speak to
me, let her leave me. She came up to me as if it were a
hard thing to do, and held out a little package, timidly,
and her gloved hand shook as if she were afraid of me.

"I want to give you something," she said. "You will not
want it now, so I shall ask you to keep it until you hear
from me. You gave me your address a long time ago,
when you were making that drawing. Some day I shall
write to you and ask you to open this. You must not come
to tell me goodbye this morning, but I shall be watching
you when you go ashore. Please don't forget that."

I took the little box mechanically and thanked her. I
think my eyes must have filled, for she uttered an exclamation of pity, touched my sleeve quickly, and left me. It
was one of those strange, low, musical exclamations which
meant everything and nothing, like the one that had thrilled
me that night at Naples, and it was the last sound I ever
heard from her lips.

An hour later I went on shore, one of those who crowded
over the gangplank the moment it was lowered. But the
next afternoon I wandered back to the docks and went on
board the *Germania*. I asked for the engineer, and he came
up in his shirt sleeves from the engine room. He was red
and dishevelled, angry and voluble; his bright eye had a
hard glint, and I did not once see his masterful smile.
When he heard my inquiry he became profane. Mrs.
Ebbling had sailed for Bremen on the *Hohenstauffen* that
morning at eleven o'clock. She had decided to return by
the northern route and pay a visit to her father in Finmark. She was in no condition to travel alone, he said. He
evidently smarted under her extravagance. But who, he
asked, with a blow of his fist on the rail, could stand
between a woman and her whim? She had always been a

wilful girl, and she had a doting father behind her. When she set her head with the wind, there was no holding her; she ought to have married the Arctic Ocean. I think Ebbling was still talking when I walked away.

I spent that winter in New York. My consular appointment hung fire (indeed, I did not pursue it with much enthusiasm), and I had a good many idle hours in which to think of Mrs. Ebbling. She had never mentioned the name of her father's village, and somehow I could never quite bring myself to go to the docks when Ebbling's boat was in and ask for news of her. More than once I made up my mind definitely to go to Finmark and take my chance at finding her; the shipping people would know where Ebbling came from. But I never went. I have often wondered why. When my resolve was made and my courage high, when I could almost feel myself approaching her, suddenly everything crumbled under me, and I fell back as I had done that night when I dropped her hands, after telling her, only a moment before, that I would never let them go.

In the twilight of a wet March day, when the gutters were running black outside and the Square was liquefying under crusts of dirty snow, the housekeeper brought me a damp letter which bore a blurred foreign postmark. It was from Niels Nannestad, who wrote that it was his sad duty to inform me that his daughter, Alexandra Ebbling, had died on the second day of February, in the twenty-sixth year of her age. Complying with her request, he inclosed a letter which she had written some days before her death.

I at last brought myself to break the seal of the second letter. It read thus:

> My Friend:—You may open now the little package I gave you. May I ask you to keep it? I gave it to you because there is no one else who would care about it in just that way. Ever since I left you I have been thinking what it would be like to live a lifetime caring and being cared for like that. It was not the life I was meant to live,

and yet, in a way, I have been living it ever since I first knew you.

Of course you understand now why I could not go with you. I would have spoiled your life for you. Besides that, I was ill—and I was too proud to give you the shadow of myself. I had much to give you, if you had come earlier. As it was, I was ashamed. Vanity sometimes saves us when nothing else will, and mine saved you. Thank you for everything. I hold this to my heart, where I once held your hand.

Alexandra

The dusk had thickened into night long before I got up from my chair and took the little box from its place in my desk drawer. I opened it and lifted out a thick coil, cut from where her hair grew thickest and brightest. It was tied firmly at one end, and when it fell over my arm it curled and clung about my sleeve like a living thing set free. How it gleamed, how it still gleams in the firelight! It was warm and softly scented under my lips, and stirred under my breath like seaweed in the tide. This, and a withered magnolia flower, and two pink sea shells; nothing more. And it was all twenty years ago!

The Enchanted Bluff

We had our swim before sundown, and while we were cooking our supper the oblique rays of light made a dazzling glare on the white sand about us. The translucent red ball itself sank behind the brown stretches of corn field as we sat down to eat, and the warm layer of air that had rested over the water and our clean sand bar grew fresher and smelled of the rank ironweed and sunflowers growing on the flatter shore. The river was brown and sluggish, like any other of the half-dozen streams that water the Nebraska corn lands. On one shore was an irregular line of bald clay bluffs where a few scrub oaks with thick trunks and flat, twisted tops threw light shadows on the long grass. The western shore was low and level, with corn fields that stretched to the sky-line, and all along the water's edge were little sandy coves and beaches where slim cottonwoods and willow saplings flickered.

The turbulence of the river in springtime discouraged milling, and, beyond keeping the old red bridge in repair, the busy farmers did not concern themselves with the stream; so the Sandtown boys were left in undisputed possession. In the autumn we hunted quail through the miles of stubble and fodder land along the flat shore, and, after the winter skating season was over and the ice had gone out, the spring freshets and flooded bottoms gave us our great excitement of the year. The channel was never the same for two successive seasons. Every spring the swollen stream undermined a bluff to the east, or bit out a few acres of corn field to the west and whirled the soil away to deposit it in spumy mud banks somewhere else. When the water fell low in midsummer, new sand bars were thus exposed to dry and whiten in the August sun. Sometimes these were banked so firmly that the fury of the next freshet failed to unseat them; the little willow seedlings emerged triumphantly from the yellow froth, broke into spring leaf, shot up into summer growth, and with their mesh of roots bound together the moist sand beneath them against the batterings of another April. Here and there a cottonwood soon glittered among them, quivering in the low current of air that, even on breathless days when the dust hung like smoke above the wagon road, trembled along the face of the water.

It was on such an island, in the third summer of its yellow green, that we built our watch fire; not in the thicket of dancing willow wands, but on the level terrace of fine sand which had been added that spring; a little new bit of world, beautifully ridged with ripple marks, and strewn with the tiny skeletons of turtles and fish, all as white and dry as if they had been expertly cured. We had been careful not to mar the freshness of the place, although we often swam to it on summer evenings and lay on the sand to rest.

This was our last watch fire of the year, and there were reasons why I should remember it better than any of the others. Next week the other boys were to file back to their old places in the Sandtown High School, but I was to go up to the Divide to teach my first country school in the Norwegian district. I was already homesick at the thought of quitting the boys with whom I had always played; of leaving the river, and going up into a windy plain that was all windmills and corn fields and big pastures; where there was nothing wilful or unmanageable in the landscape, no new islands, and no chance of unfamiliar birds— such as often followed the watercourses.

Other boys came and went and used the river for fishing or skating, but we six were sworn to the spirit of the stream, and we were friends mainly because of the river. There were the two Hassler boys, Fritz and Otto, sons of the little German tailor. They were the youngest of us; ragged boys of ten and twelve, with sunburned hair, weather-stained faces, and pale blue eyes. Otto, the elder, was the best mathematician in school, and clever at his books, but he always dropped out in the spring term as if the river could not get on without him. He and Fritz caught the fat, horned catfish and sold them about the town, and they lived so much in the water that they were as brown and sandy as the river itself.

There was Percy Pound, a fat, freckled boy with chubby cheeks, who took half a dozen boys' story-papers and was always being kept in for reading detective stories behind his desk. There was Tip Smith, destined by his freckles and red hair to be the buffoon in all our games, though he walked like a timid little old man and had a funny, cracked laugh. Tip worked hard in his father's grocery store every afternoon, and swept it out before school in the morning. Even his recreations were laborious. He collected cigarette cards and tin tobacco-tags indefatigably, and would sit for hours humped up over a snarling little scroll-saw which he kept in his attic. His dearest possessions were some little pill bottles that purported to contain grains of wheat from the Holy Land, water from the Jordan and the Dead Sea, and earth from the Mount of Olives. His father had bought these dull things from a Baptist missionary who peddled them, and Tip seemed to derive great satisfaction from their remote origin.

The tall boy was Arthur Adams. He had fine hazel eyes that were almost too reflective and sympathetic for a boy, and such a pleasant voice that we all loved to hear him read aloud. Even when he had to read poetry aloud at school, no one ever thought of laughing. To be sure, he was not at school very much of the time. He was seventeen and should have finished the High School the year before, but he was always off somewhere with his gun.

Arthur's mother was dead, and his father, who was fever-ishly absorbed in promoting schemes, wanted to send the boy away to school and get him off his hands; but Arthur always begged off for another year and promised to study. I remember him as a tall, brown boy with an intelligent face, always lounging among a lot of us little fellows, laughing at us oftener than with us, but such a soft, satisfied laugh that we felt rather flattered when we pro-voked it. In after-years people said that Arthur had been given to evil ways even as a lad, and it is true that we often saw him with the gambler's sons and with old Spanish Fanny's boy, but if he learned anything ugly in their company he never betrayed it to us. We would have followed Arthur anywhere, and I am bound to say that he led us into no worse places than the cattail marshes and the stubble fields. These, then, were the boys who camped with me that summer night upon the sand bar.

After we finished our supper we beat the willow thicket for driftwood. By the time we had collected enough, night had fallen, and the pungent, weedy smell from the shore increased with the coolness. We threw ourselves down about the fire and made another futile effort to show Percy Pound the Little Dipper. We had tried it often before, but he could never be got past the big one.

"You see those three big stars just below the handle, with the bright one in the middle?" said Otto Hassler; "that's Orion's belt, and the bright one is the clasp." I crawled behind Otto's shoulder and sighted up his arm to the star that seemed perched upon the tip of his steady forefinger. The Hassler boys did seine-fishing at night, and they knew a good many stars.

Percy gave up the Little Dipper and lay back on the sand, his hands clasped under his head. "I can see the North Star," he announced, contentedly, pointing toward it with his big toe. "Anyone might get lost and need to know that."

We all looked up at it.

"How do you suppose Columbus felt when his compass didn't point north any more?" Tip asked.

Otto shook his head. "My father says that there was another North Star once, and that maybe this one won't last always. I wonder what would happen to us down here if anything went wrong with it?"

Arthur chuckled. "I wouldn't worry, Ott. Nothing's apt to happen to it in your time. Look at the Milky Way! There must be lots of good dead Indians."

We lay back and looked, meditating, at the dark cover of the world. The gurgle of the water had become heavier. We had often noticed a mutinous, complaining note in it at night, quite different from its cheerful daytime chuckle, and seeming like the voice of a much deeper and more powerful stream. Our water had always these two moods: the one of sunny complaisance, the other of inconsolable, passionate regret.

"Queer how the stars are all in sort of diagrams," remarked Otto. "You could do most any proposition in geometry with 'em. They always look as if they meant something. Some folks say everybody's fortune is all written out in the stars, don't they?"

"They believe so in the old country," Fritz affirmed.

But Arthur only laughed at him. "You're thinking of Napoleon, Fritzey. He had a star that went out when he began to lose battles. I guess the stars don't keep any close tally on Sandtown folks."

We were speculating on how many times we could count a hundred before the evening star went down behind the corn fields, when someone cried, "There comes the moon, and it's as big as a cart wheel!"

We all jumped up to greet it as it swam over the bluffs behind us. It came up like a galleon in full sail; an enormous, barbaric thing, red as an angry heathen god.

"When the moon came up red like that, the Aztecs used to sacrifice their prisoners on the temple top," Percy announced.

"Go on, Perce. You got that out of *Golden Days*. Do you believe that, Arthur?" I appealed.

Arthur answered, quite seriously: "Like as not. The moon was one of their gods. When my father was in Mexico City he saw the stone where they used to sacrifice their prisoners."

As we dropped down by the fire again some one asked whether the Mound-Builders were older than the Aztecs. When we once got upon the Mound-Builders we never willingly got away from them, and we were still conjecturing when we heard a loud splash in the water.

"Must have been a big cat jumping," said Fritz. "They do sometimes. They must see bugs in the dark. Look what a track the moon makes!"

There was a long, silvery streak on the water, and where the current fretted over a big log it boiled up like gold pieces.

"Suppose there ever *was* any gold hid away in this old river?" Fritz asked. He lay like a little brown Indian, close to the fire, his chin on his hand and his bare feet in the air. His brother laughed at him, but Arthur took his suggestion seriously.

"Some of the Spaniards thought there was gold up here somewhere. Seven cities chuck full of gold, they had it, and Coronado and his men came up to hunt it. The Spaniards were all over this country once."

Percy looked interested. "Was that before the Mormons went through?"

We all laughed at this.

"Long enough before. Before the Pilgrim Fathers, Perce. Maybe they came along this very river. They always followed the watercourses."

"I wonder where this river really does begin?" Tip mused. That was an old and a favorite mystery which the map did not clearly explain. On the map the little black line stopped somewhere in western Kansas; but since rivers generally rose in mountains, it was only reasonable to suppose that ours came from the Rockies. Its destination, we knew, was the Missouri, and the Hassler boys always maintained that we could embark at Sandtown in floodtime, follow our noses, and eventually arrive at New Orleans. Now they took up their old argument. "If us boys had grit enough to try it, it wouldn't take no time to get to Kansas City and St. Joe."

We began to talk about the places we wanted to go to. The Hassler boys wanted to see the stockyards in Kansas City, and Percy wanted to see a big store in Chicago. Arthur was interlocutor and did not betray himself.

"Now it's your turn, Tip."

Tip rolled over on his elbow and poked the fire, and his eyes looked shyly out of his queer, tight little face. "My place is awful far away. My Uncle Bill told me about it."

Tip's Uncle Bill was a wanderer, bitten with mining fever, who had drifted into Sandtown with a broken arm, and when it was well had drifted out again.

"Where is it?"

"Aw, it's down in New Mexico somewhere. There aren't no railroads or anything. You have to go on mules, and you run out of water before you get there and have to drink canned tomatoes."

"Well, go on, kid. What's it like when you do get there?"

Tip sat up and excitedly began his story.

"There's a big red rock there that goes right up out of the sand for about nine hundred feet. The country's flat all around it, and this here rock goes up all by itself, like a monument. They call it the Enchanted Bluff down there, because no white man has ever been on top of it. The sides are smooth rock, and straight up, like a wall. The Indians say that hundreds of years ago, before the Spaniards came, there was a village away up there in the air. The tribe that lived there had some sort of steps, made out of wood and bark, hung down over the face of the bluff, and the braves went down to hunt and carried water up in big jars swung on their backs. They kept a big supply of water and dried meat up there, and never went down except to hunt. They were a peaceful tribe that made cloth and pottery, and they went up there to get out of the wars. You see, they could pick off any war party that tried to get up their little steps. The Indians say they were a handsome people, and they had some sort of queer religion. Uncle Bill thinks they were Cliff-Dwellers who had got into trouble and left home. They weren't fighters, anyhow.

"One time the braves were down hunting and an awful storm came up—a kind of waterspout—and when they got back to their rock they found their little staircase had been all broken to pieces, and only a few steps were left hanging away up in the air. While they were camped at the foot of the rock, wondering what to do, a war party from the north came along and massacred 'em to a man, with all the old folks and women looking on from the rock. Then the war party went on south and left the village to get down the best way they could. Of course they never got down. They starved to death up there, and when the war party came back on their way north, they could hear the children crying from the edge of the bluff where they had crawled out, but they didn't see a sign of a grown Indian, and nobody has ever been up there since."

We exclaimed at this dolorous legend and sat up.

"There couldn't have been many people up there," Percy demurred. "How big is the top, Tip?"

"Oh, pretty big. Big enough so that the rock doesn't look nearly as tall as it is. The top's bigger than the base. The bluff is sort of worn away for several hundred feet up. That's one reason it's so hard to climb."

I asked how the Indians got up, in the first place.

"Nobody knows how they got up or when. A hunting party came along once and saw that there was a town up there, and that was all."

Otto rubbed his chin and looked thoughtful. "Of course there must be some way to get up there. Couldn't people get a rope over someway and pull a ladder up?"

Tip's little eyes were shining with excitement. "I know a way. Me and Uncle Bill talked it all over. There's a kind of rocket that would take a rope over—life-savers use 'em—and then you could hoist a rope ladder and peg it down at the bottom and make it tight with guy ropes on the other side. I'm going to climb that there bluff, and I've got it all planned out."

Fritz asked what he expected to find when he got up there.

"Bones, maybe, or the ruins of their town, or pottery, or some of their idols. There might be 'most anything up there. Anyhow, I want to see."

"Sure nobody else has been up there, Tip?" Arthur asked.

"Dead sure. Hardly anybody ever goes down there. Some hunters tried to cut steps in the rock once, but they didn't get higher than a man can reach. The Bluff's all red granite, and Uncle Bill thinks it's a boulder the glaciers left. It's a queer place, anyhow. Nothing but cactus and desert for hundreds of miles, and yet right under the Bluff there's good water and plenty of grass. That's why the bison used to go down there."

Suddenly we heard a scream above our fire, and jumped up to see a dark, slim bird floating southward far above us—a whooping crane, we knew by her cry and her long neck. We ran to the edge of the island, hoping we might see her alight, but she wavered southward along the rivercourse until we lost her. The Hassler boys declared that by the look of the heavens it must be after midnight, so we threw more wood on our fire, put on our jackets, and curled down in the warm sand. Several of us pretended to doze, but I fancy we were really thinking about Tip's Bluff and the extinct people. Over in the wood the ring doves were calling mournfully to one another, and once we heard a dog bark, far away. "Somebody getting into old Tommy's melon patch," Fritz murmured sleepily, but nobody answered him. By and by Percy spoke out of the shadows.

"Say, Tip, when you go down there will you take me with you?"

"Maybe."

"Suppose one of us beats you down there, Tip?"

"Whoever gets to the Bluff first has got to promise to tell the rest of us exactly what he finds," remarked one of the Hassler boys, and to this we all readily assented.

Somewhat reassured, I dropped off to sleep. I must have dreamed about a race for the Bluff, for I awoke in a kind of fear that other people were getting ahead of me and that I was losing my chance. I sat up in my damp clothes and looked at the other boys, who lay tumbled in uneasy attitudes about the dead fire. It was still dark, but the sky was blue with the last wonderful azure of night. The stars glistened like crystal globes, and trembled as if they shone through a depth of clear water. Even as I watched, they began to pale and the sky brightened. Day came suddenly, almost instantaneously. I turned for another look at the blue night, and it was gone. Everywhere the birds began to call, and all manner of little insects began to chirp and hop about in the willows. A breeze sprang up from the west and brought the heavy smell of ripened corn. The boys rolled over and shook themselves. We stripped and plunged into the river just as the sun came up over the windy bluffs.

When I came home to Sandtown at Christmas time, we skated out to our island and talked over the whole project of the Enchanted Bluff, renewing our resolution to find it.

Although that was twenty years ago, none of us have ever climbed the Enchanted Bluff. Percy Pound is a stock-broker in Kansas City and will go nowhere that his red touring car cannot carry him. Otto Hassler went on the railroad and lost his foot braking; after which he and Fritz succeeded their father as the town tailors.

Arthur sat about the sleepy little town all his life—he died before he was twenty-five. The last time I saw him, when I was home on one of my college vacations, he was sitting in a steamer chair under a cottonwood tree in the little yard behind one of the two Sandtown saloons. He was very untidy and his hand was not steady, but when he rose, unabashed, to greet me, his eyes were as clear and warm as ever. When I had talked with him for an hour and heard him laugh again, I wondered how it was that when Nature had taken such pains with a man, from his hands to the arch of his long foot, she had ever lost him in Sandtown. He joked about Tip Smith's Bluff, and declared he was going down there just as soon as the weather got cooler; he thought the Grand Canyon might be worth while, too.

I was perfectly sure when I left him that he would never get beyond the high plank fence and the comfortable shade of the cottonwood. And, indeed, it was under that very tree that he died one summer morning.

Tip Smith still talks about going to New Mexico. He married a slatternly, unthrifty country girl, has been much tied to a perambulator, and has grown stooped and gray from irregular meals and broken sleep. But the worst of his difficulties are now over, and he has, as he says, come into easy water. When I was last in Sandtown I walked home with him late one moonlight night, after he had balanced his cash and shut up his store. We took the long way around and sat down on the schoolhouse steps, and between us we quite revived the romance of the lone red rock and the extinct people. Tip insisted that he still means to go down there, but he thinks now he will wait until his boy Bert is old enough to go with him. Bert has been let into the story, and thinks of nothing but the Enchanted Bluff.

The Joy of
Nelly Deane

Nell and I were almost ready to go on for the last act of *Queen Esther*, and we had for the moment got rid of our three patient dressers, Mrs. Dow, Mrs. Freeze, and Mrs. Spinny. Nell was peering over my shoulder into the little cracked looking glass that Mrs. Dow had taken from its nail on her kitchen wall and brought down to the church under her shawl that morning. When she realized that we were alone, Nell whispered to me in the quick, fierce way she had:

"Say, Peggy, won't you go up and stay with me tonight? Scott Spinny's asked to take me home, and I don't want to walk up with him alone."

"I guess so, if you'll ask my mother."

"Oh, I'll fix her!" Nell laughed, with a toss of her head which meant that she usually got what she wanted, even from people much less tractable than my mother.

In a moment our tiring-women were back again. The three old ladies—at least they seemed old to us—fluttered about us, more agitated than we were ourselves. It seemed as though they would never leave off patting Nell and touching her up. They kept trying things this way and that, never able in the end to decide which way was best. They wouldn't hear to her using rouge, and as they powered her neck and arms, Mrs. Freeze murmured that she hoped we wouldn't get into the habit of using such things. Mrs. Spinny divided her time between pulling up and tucking down the "illusion" that filled in the square neck of Nelly's dress. She didn't like things much low, she said; but after she had pulled it up, she stood back and looked at Nell thoughtfully through her glasses. While the excited girl was reaching for this and that, buttoning a slipper, pinning down a curl, Mrs. Spinny's smile softened more and more until, just before Esther made her entrance, the old lady tiptoed up to her and softly tucked the illusion down as far as it would go.

"She's so pink; it seems a pity not," she whispered apologetically to Mrs. Dow.

Every one admitted that Nelly was the prettiest girl in Riverbend, and the gayest—oh, the gayest! When she was not singing, she was laughing. When she was not laid up with a broken arm, the outcome of a foolhardy coasting feat, or suspended from school because she ran away at recess to go buggy-riding with Guy Franklin, she was sure to be up to mischief of some sort. Twice she broke through the ice and got soused in the river because she never looked where she skated or cared what happened so long as she went fast enough. After the second of these duckings our three dressers declared that she was trying to be a Baptist despite herself.

Mrs. Spinny and Mrs. Freeze and Mrs. Dow, who were always hovering about Nelly, often whispered to me their hope that she would eventually come into our church and not "go with the Methodists"; her family were Wesleyans. But to me these artless plans of theirs never wholly explained their watchful affection. They had good daughters themselves—except Mrs. Spinny, who had only the sullen Scott—and they loved their plain girls and thanked God for them. But they loved Nelly differently. They were proud of her pretty figure and yellow-brown eyes, which dilated so easily and sparkled with a kind of golden effervescence. They were always making pretty things for her, always coaxing her to come to the sewing circle, where she knotted her thread, and put in the wrong sleeve, and laughed and chattered and said a great many things that she should not have said, and somehow always warmed their hearts. I think they loved her for her unquenchable joy.

All the Baptist ladies liked Nell, even those who criticized her most severely, but the three who were first in fighting the battles of our little church, who held it together by their prayers and the labor of their hands, watched over her as they did over Mrs. Dow's century plant before it blossomed. They looked for her on Sunday morning and smiled at her as she hurried, always a little late, up to the choir. When she rose and stood behind the organ and sang "There Is a Green Hill," one could see Mrs. Dow and Mrs. Freeze settle back in their accustomed seats and look up at her as if she had just come from that hill and had brought them glad tidings.

It was because I sang contralto, or, as we said, alto, in the Baptist choir that Nell and I became friends. She was so gay and grown up, so busy with parties and dances and picnics, that I would scarcely have seen much of her had we not sung together. She liked me better than she did any of the older girls, who tried clumsily to be like her, and I felt almost as solicitous and admiring as did Mrs. Dow and Mrs. Spinny. I think even then I must have loved to see her bloom and glow, and I loved to hear her sing, in "The Ninety and Nine,"

But one was out on the hills away

in her sweet, strong voice. Nell had never had a singing lesson, but she had sung from the time she could talk, and Mrs. Dow used fondly to say that it was singing so much that made her figure so pretty.

After I went into the choir it was found to be easier to get Nelly to choir practice. If I stopped outside her gate on my way to church and coaxed her, she usually laughed, ran in for her hat and jacket, and went along with me. The three old ladies fostered our friendship, and because I was "quiet," they esteemed me a good influence for Nelly. This view was propounded in a sewing-circle discussion and, leaking down to us through our mothers, greatly amused us. Dear old ladies! It was so manifestly for what Nell was that they loved her, and yet they were always looking for "influences" to change her.

The *Queen Esther* performance had cost us three months of hard practice, and it was not easy to keep Nell up to attending the tedious rehearsals. Some of the boys we knew were in the chorus of Assyrian youths, but the solo cast was made up of older people, and Nell found them very poky. We gave the cantata in the Baptist church on Christmas Eve, "to a crowded house," as the Riverbend *Messenger* truly chronicled. The country folk for miles about had come in through a deep snow, and their teams and wagons stood in a long row at the hitch-bars on each side of the church door. It was certainly Nelly's night, for however much the tenor—he was her schoolmaster, and naturally thought poorly of her—might try to eclipse her in his dolorous solos about the rivers of Babylon, there would be no doubt as to whom the people had come to hear—and to see.

After the performance was over, our fathers and mothers came back to the dressing rooms—the little rooms behind the baptistry where the candidates for baptism were robed—to congratulate us, and Nell persuaded my mother to let me go home with her. This arrangement may not have been wholly agreeable to Scott Spinny, who stood glumly waiting at the baptistry door; though I used to think he dogged Nell's steps not so much for any pleasure he got from being with her as for the pleasure of keeping other people away. Dear little Mrs. Spinny was perpetually in a state of humiliation on account of his bad manners, and she tried by a very special tenderness to make up to Nelly for the remissness of her ungracious son.

Scott was a spare, muscular fellow, good-looking, but with a face so set and dark that I used to think it very like the castings he sold. He was taciturn and domineering, and Nell rather liked to provoke him. Her father was so easy with her that she seemed to enjoy being ordered about now and then. That night, when every one was praising her and telling her how well she sang and how pretty she looked, Scott only said, as we came out of the dressing room:

"Have you got your high shoes on?"

"No; but I've got rubbers on over my low ones. Mother doesn't care."

"Well, you just go back and put 'em on as fast as you can."

Nell made a face at him and ran back, laughing. Her mother, fat, comfortable Mrs. Deane, was immensely amused at this.

"That's right, Scott," she chuckled. "You can do enough more with her than I can. She walks right over me an' Jud."

Scott grinned. If he was proud of Nelly, the last thing he wished to do was to show it. When she came back he began to nag again. "What are you going to do with all those flowers? They'll freeze stiff as pokers."

"Well, there won't none of *your* flowers freeze, Scott Spinny, so there!" Nell snapped. She had the best of him that time, and the Assyrian youths rejoiced. They were most of them high-school boys, and the poorest of them had "chipped in" and sent all the way to Denver for Queen Esther's flowers. There were bouquets from half a dozen townspeople, too, but none from Scott. Scott was a prosperous hardware merchant and notoriously penurious, though he saved his face, as the boys said, by giving liberally to the church.

"There's no use freezing the fool things, anyhow. You get me some newspapers, and I'll wrap 'em up." Scott took from his pocket a folded copy of the Riverbend *Messenger* and began laboriously to wrap up one of the bouquets. When we left the church door he bore three large newspaper bundles, carrying them as carefully as if they had been so many newly frosted wedding cakes, and left Nell and me to shift for ourselves as we floundered along the snow-burdened sidewalk.

Although it was after midnight, lights were shining from many of the little wooden houses, and the roofs and shrubbery were so deep in snow that Riverbend looked as if it had been tucked down into a warm bed. The companies of people, all coming from church, tramping this way and that toward their homes and calling "Good night" and "Merry Christmas" as they parted company, all seemed to us very unusual and exciting.

When we got home, Mrs. Deane had a cold supper ready, and Jud Deane had already taken off his shoes and fallen to on his fried chicken and pie. He was so proud of his pretty daughter that he must give her her Christmas presents then and there, and he went into the sleeping chamber behind the dining room and from the depths of his wife's closet brought out a short sealskin jacket and a round cap and made Nelly put them on.

Mrs. Deane, who sat busy between a plate of spice cake and a tray piled with her famous whipped cream tarts, laughed inordinately at his behavior.

"Ain't he worse than any kid you ever see? He's been running to that closet like a cat shut away from her kittens. I wonder Nell ain't caught on before this. I did think he'd make out now to keep 'em till Christmas morning; but he's never made out to keep anything yet."

That was true enough, and fortunately Jud's inability to keep anything seemed always to present a highly humorous aspect to his wife. Mrs. Deane put her heart into her cooking, and said that so long as a man was a good provider she had no cause to complain. Other people were not so charitable toward Jud's failing. I remember how many strictures were passed upon that little sealskin and how he was censured for his extravagance. But what a public-spirited thing, after all, it was for him to do! How, the winter through, we all enjoyed seeing Nell skating on the river or running about the town with the brown collar turned up about her bright cheeks and her

hair blowing out from under the round cap!· "No seal,"
Mrs. Dow said, "would have begrudged it to her. Why
should we?" This was at the sewing circle, when the new
coat was under grave discussion.

At last Nelly and I got upstairs and undressed, and the
pad of Jud's slippered feet about the kitchen premises—
where he was carrying up from the cellar things that
might freeze—ceased. He called "Good night, daughter,"
from the foot of the stairs, and the house grew quiet. But
one is not a prima donna the first time for nothing, and it
seemed as if we could not go to bed. Our light must have
burned long after every other in Riverbend was out. The
muslin curtains of Nell's bed were drawn back; Mrs. Deane
had turned down the white counterpane and taken off the
shams and smoothed the pillows for us. But their fair
plumpness offered no temptation to two such hot young
heads. We could not let go of life even for a little while.
We sat and talked in Nell's cozy room, where there was a
tiny, white fur rug—the only one in Riverbend—before
the bed; and there were white sash curtains, and the
prettiest little desk and dressing table I had ever seen. It
was a warm, gay little room, flooded all day long with
sunlight from east and south windows that had climbing
roses all about them in summer. About the dresser were
photographs of adoring high school boys; and one of Guy
Franklin, much groomed and barbered, in a dress coat
and a boutonnière. I never liked to see that photograph
there. The home boys looked properly modest and bash-
ful on the dresser, but he seemed to be staring impu-
dently all the time.

I knew nothing definite against Guy, but in Riverbend
all "traveling men" were considered worldly and wicked.
He traveled for a Chicago dry-goods firm, and our fathers
didn't like him because he put extravagant ideas into our
mothers' heads. He had very smooth and flattering ways,
and he introduced into our simple community a great
variety of perfumes and scented soaps, and he always
reminded me of the merchants in Caesar, who brought

into Gaul "those things which effeminate the mind," as we translated that delightfully easy passage.

Nell was sitting before the dressing table in her nightgown, holding the new fur coat and rubbing her cheek against it, when I saw a sudden gleam of tears in her eyes. "You know, Peggy," she said in her quick, impetuous way, "this makes me feel bad. I've got a secret from my daddy."

I can see her now, so pink and eager, her brown hair in two springy braids down her back, and her eyes shining with tears and with something even softer and more tremulous.

"I'm engaged, Peggy," she whispered, "really and truly."

She leaned forward, unbuttoning her nightgown, and there on her breast, hung by a little gold chain about her neck, was a diamond ring—Guy Franklin's solitaire; every one in Riverbend knew it well.

"I'm going to live in Chicago, and take singing lessons, and go to operas, and do all those nice things—oh, everything! I know you don't like him, Peggy, but you know you *are* a kid. You'll see how it is yourself when you grow up. He's so *different* from our boys, and he's just terribly in love with me. And then, Peggy,"—flushing all down over her soft shoulders,—"I'm awfully fond of him, too. Awfully."

"Are you, Nell, truly?" I whispered. She seemed so changed to me by the warm light in her eyes and that delicate suffusion of color. I felt as I did when I got up early on picnic mornings in summer, and saw the dawn come up in the breathless sky above the river meadows and make all the corn fields golden.

"Sure I do, Peggy; don't look so solemn. It's nothing to look that way about, kid. It's nice." She threw her arms about me suddenly and hugged me.

"I hate to think about your going so far away from us all, Nell."

"Oh, you'll love to come and visit me. Just you wait."

She began breathlessly to go over things Guy Franklin

had told her about Chicago, until I seemed to see it all looming up out there under the stars that kept watch over our little sleeping town. We had neither of us ever been to a city, but we knew what it would be like. We heard it throbbing like great engines, and calling to us, that far-away world. Even after we had opened the windows and scurried into bed, we seemed to feel a pulsation across all the miles of snow. The winter silence trembled with it, and the air was full of something new that seemed to break over us in soft waves. In that snug, warm little bed I had a sense of imminent change and danger. I was somehow afraid for Nelly when I heard her breathing so quickly beside me, and I put my arm about her protectingly as we drifted toward sleep.

In the following spring we were both graduated from the Riverbend high school, and I went away to college. My family moved to Denver, and during the next four years I heard very little of Nelly Deane. My life was crowded with new people and new experiences, and I am afraid I held her little in mind. I heard indirectly that Jud Deane had lost what little property he owned in a luckless venture in Cripple Creek, and that he had been able to keep his house in Riverbend only through the clemency of his creditors. Guy Franklin had his route changed and did not go to Riverbend any more. He married the daughter of a rich cattleman out near Long Pine, and ran a dry-goods store of his own. Mrs. Dow wrote me a long letter about once a year, and in one of these she told me that Nelly was teaching in the sixth grade in the Riverbend school.

Dear Nelly does not like teaching very well. The children try her, and she is so pretty it seems a pity for her to be tied down to uncongenial employment. Scott is still very attentive, and I have noticed him look up at the window of Nelly's room in a very determined way as he goes home to dinner. Scott continues prosperous; he has made money during these hard times and now owns both our hardware stores. He is close, but a very honorable fellow. Nelly seems to hold off, but I think Mrs. Spinny has hopes. Nothing would please her more. If Scott were more careful about his appearance, it would help. He of course gets black about his business, and Nelly, you know, is very dainty. People do say his mother does his courting for him, she is so eager. If only Scott does not turn out hard and penurious like his father! We must all have our schooling in this life, but I don't want Nelly's to be too severe. She is a dear girl, and keeps her color.

Mrs. Dow's own schooling had been none too easy. Her husband had long been crippled with rheumatism, and was bitter and faultfinding. Her daughters had married poorly, and one of her sons had fallen into evil ways. But her letters were always cheerful, and in one of them she gently remonstrated with me because I "seemed inclined to take a sad view of life."

In the winter vacation of my senior year I stopped on my way home to visit Mrs. Dow. The first thing she told me when I got into her old buckboard at the station was that "Scott had at last prevailed," and that Nelly was to marry him in the spring. As a preliminary step, Nelly was about to join the Baptist church. "Just think, you will be here for her baptizing! How that will please Nell! She is to be immersed tomorrow night."

I met Scott Spinny in the post office that morning and he gave me a hard grip with one black hand. There was something grim and saturnine about his powerful body and bearded face and his strong, cold hands. I wondered what perverse fate had driven him for eight years to dog the footsteps of a girl whose charm was due to qualities naturally distasteful to him. It still seems strange to me that in easygoing Riverbend, where there were so many boys who could have lived contentedly enough with my little grasshopper, it was the pushing ant who must have her and all her careless ways.

By a kind of unformulated etiquette one did not call upon candidates for baptism on the day of the ceremony, so I had my first glimpse of Nelly that evening. The baptistry was a cemented pit directly under the pulpit rostrum, over which we had our stage when we sang *Queen Esther*. I sat through the sermon somewhat nervously. After the minister, in his long, black gown, had gone down into the water and the choir had finished singing, the door from the dressing room opened, and, led by one of the deacons, Nelly came down the steps into the pool. Oh, she looked so little and meek and chastened! Her white cashmere robe clung about her, and her brown hair was brushed straight back and hung in two soft braids from a little head bent humbly. As she stepped down into the water I shivered with the cold of it, and I remembered sharply how much I had loved her. She went down until the water was well above her waist, and stood white and small, with her hands crossed on her breast, while the minister said the words about being buried with Christ in baptism. Then, lying in his arm, she disappeared under the dark water. "It will be like that when she dies," I thought, and a quick pain caught my heart. The choir began to sing "Washed in the Blood of the Lamb" as she rose again, the door behind the baptistry opened, revealing those three dear guardians, Mrs. Dow, Mrs. Freeze, and Mrs. Spinny, and she went up into their arms.

I went to see Nell next day, up in the little room of many memories. Such a sad, sad visit! She seemed changed—a little embarrassed and quietly despairing. We talked of many of the old Riverbend girls and boys, but she did not mention Guy Franklin or Scott Spinny, except to say that her father had got work in Scott's hardware store. She begged me, putting her hands on my shoulders with something of her old impulsiveness, to come and stay a few days with her. But I was afraid—afraid of what she might tell me and of what I might say. When I sat in that room with all her trinkets, the foolish harvest of her girlhood, lying about, and the white curtains and the little white rug, I thought of Scott Spinny with positive terror and could feel his hard grip on my hand again. I made the best excuse I could about having to hurry on to Denver; but she gave me one quick look, and her eyes ceased to plead. I saw that she understood me perfectly. We had known each other so well. Just once, when I got up to go and had trouble with my veil, she laughed her old merry laugh and told me there were some things I would never learn, for all my schooling.

The next day, when Mrs. Dow drove me down to the station to catch the morning train for Denver, I saw Nelly hurrying to school with several books under her arm. She had been working up her lessons at home, I thought. She was never quick at her books, dear Nell.

It was ten years before I again visited Riverbend. I had been in Rome for a long time, and had fallen into bitter homesickness. One morning, sitting among the dahlias and asters that bloom so bravely upon those gigantic heaps of earth-red ruins that were once the palaces of the Caesars, I broke the seal of one of Mrs. Dow's long yearly letters. It brought so much sad news that I resolved then and there to go home to Riverbend, the only place that had ever really been home to me. Mrs. Dow wrote me that her husband, after years of illness, had died in the cold spell last March. "So good and patient toward the last," she wrote, "and so afraid of giving extra trouble." There was another thing she saved until the last. She wrote on and on, dear woman, about new babies and village improvements, as if she could not bear to tell me; and then it came:

> You will be sad to hear that two months ago our dear Nelly left us. It was a terrible blow to us all. I cannot write about it yet, I fear. I wake up every morning feeling that I ought to go to her. She went three days after her little boy was born. The baby is a fine child and will live, I think, in spite of everything. He and her little girl, now eight years old, whom she named Margaret, after you, have gone to Mrs. Spinny's. She loves them more than if they were her own. It seems as if already they had made her quite young again. I wish you could see Nelly's children.

Ah, that was what I wanted, to see Nelly's children! The wish came aching from my heart along with the bitter homesick tears; along with a quick, torturing recollection that flashed upon me, as I looked about and tried to collect myself, of how we two had sat in our sunny seat in the corner of the old bare schoolroom one September afternoon and learned the names of the seven hills together. In that place, at that moment, after so many years, how it all came back to me—the warm sun on my back, the chattering girl beside me, the curly hair, the laughing yellow eyes, the stubby little finger on the page! I felt as if even then, when we sat in the sun with our heads together, it was all arranged, written out like a story, that at this moment I should be sitting among the crumbling bricks and drying grass, and she should be lying in the place I knew so well, on that green hill far away.

Mrs. Dow sat with her Christmas sewing in the familiar sitting room, where the carpet and the wall paper and the tablecover had all faded into soft, dull colors, and even the chromo of Hagar and Ishmael had been toned to the sobriety of age. In the bay window the tall wire flowerstand still bore its little terraces of potted plants, and the big fuchsia and the Martha Washington geranium had blossomed for Christmastide. Mrs. Dow herself did not look greatly changed to me. Her hair, thin ever since I could remember it, was now quite white, but her spare, wiry little person had all its old activity, and her eyes gleamed with the old friendliness behind her silver-bowed glasses. Her gray house dress seemed just like those she used to wear when I ran in after school to take her angelfood cake down to the church supper.

The house sat on a hill, and from behind the geraniums I could see pretty much all of Riverbend, tucked down in the soft snow, and the air above was full of big, loose flakes, falling from a gray sky which betokened settled weather. Indoors the hard-coal burner made a tropical temperature, and glowed a warm orange from its isinglass sides. We sat and visited, the two of us, with a great sense of comfort and completeness. I had reached Riverbend only that morning, and Mrs. Dow, who had been haunted by thoughts of shipwreck and suffering upon wintery seas, kept urging me to draw nearer to the fire and suggesting incidental refreshment. We had chattered all through the winter morning and most of the afternoon, taking up one after another of the Riverbend girls and boys, and agreeing that we had reason to be well satisfied with most of them. Finally, after a long pause in which I had listened to the contented ticking of the clock and the crackle of the coal, I put the question I had until then held back:

"And now, Mrs. Dow, tell me about the one we loved best of all. Since I got your letter I've thought of her every day. Tell me all about Scott and Nelly."

The tears flashed behind her glasses, and she smoothed the little pink bag on her knee.

"Well, dear, I'm afraid Scott proved to be a hard man, like his father. But we must remember that Nelly always had Mrs. Spinny. I never saw anything like the love there was between those two. After Nelly lost her own father and mother, she looked to Mrs. Spinny for everything. When Scott was too unreasonable, his mother could 'most always prevail upon him. She never lifted a hand to fight her own battles with Scott's father, but she was never afraid to speak up for Nelly. And then Nelly took great comfort of her little girl. Such a lovely child!"

"Had she been very ill before the little baby came?"

"No, Margaret; I'm afraid 't was all because they had the wrong doctor. I feel confident that either Doctor Tom or Doctor Jones could have brought her through. But, you see, Scott had offended them both, and they'd stopped trading at his store, so he would have young Doctor Fox, a boy just out of college and a stranger. He got scared and didn't know what to do. Mrs. Spinny felt he wasn't doing right, so she sent for Mrs. Freeze and me. It seemed like Nelly had got discouraged. Scott would move into their big new house before the plastering was dry, and though 't was summer, she had taken a terrible cold that seemed to have drained her, and she took no interest in fixing the place up. Mrs. Spinny had been down with her back again and wasn't able to help, and things was just anyway. We won't talk about that, Margaret; I think 't would hurt Mrs. Spinny to have you know. She nearly died of mortification when she sent for us, and blamed her poor back. We did get Nelly fixed up nicely before she died. I prevailed upon Doctor Tom to come in at the last, and it 'most broke his heart. 'Why, Mis' Dow,' he said, 'if you'd only have come and told me how 't was, I'd have come and carried her right off in my arms.' "

"Oh, Mrs. Dow," I cried, "then it needn't have been?"

Mrs Dow dropped her needle and clasped her hands quickly. "We mustn't look at it that way, dear," she said tremulously and a little sternly; "we mustn't let ourselves. We must just feel that our Lord wanted her *then*, and took her to Himself. When it was all over, she did look so like a child of God, young and trusting, like she did on her baptizing night, you remember?"

I felt that Mrs. Dow did not want to talk any more about Nelly then, and, indeed, I had little heart to listen; so I told her I would go for a walk, and suggested that I might stop at Mrs. Spinny's to see the children.

Mrs. Dow looked up thoughtfully at the clock. "I doubt if you'll find little Margaret there now. It's half-past four, and she'll have been out of school an hour and more. She'll be most likely coasting on Lupton's Hill. She usually makes for it with her sled the minute she is out of the schoolhouse door. You know, it's the old hill where you all used to slide. If you stop in at the church about six o'clock, you'll likely find Mrs. Spinny there with the baby. I promised to go down and help Mrs. Freeze finish up the tree, and Mrs. Spinny said she'd run in with the baby, if 't wasn't too bitter. She won't leave him alone with the Swede girl. She's like a young woman with her first."

Lupton's Hill was at the other end of town, and when I

got there the dusk was thickening, drawing blue shadows over the snowy fields. There were perhaps twenty children creeping up the hill or whizzing down the packed sled track. When I had been watching them for some minutes, I heard a lusty shout, and a little red sled shot past me into the deep snowdrift beyond. The child was quite buried for a moment, then she struggled out and stood dusting the snow from her short coat and red woolen comforter. She wore a brown fur cap, which was too big for her and of an old-fashioned shape, such as girls wore long ago, but I would have known her without the cap. Mrs. Dow had said a beautiful child, and there would not be two like this in Riverbend. She was off before I had time to speak to her, going up the hill at a trot, her sturdy little legs plowing through the trampled snow. When she reached the top she never paused to take breath, but threw herself upon her sled and came down with a whoop that was quenched only by the deep drift at the end.

"Are you Margaret Spinny?" I asked as she struggled out in a cloud of snow.

"Yes, 'm." She approached me with frank curiosity, pulling her little sled behind her. "Are you the strange lady staying at Mrs. Dow's?" I nodded, and she began to look my clothes over with respectful interest.

"Your grandmother is to be at the church at six o'clock, isn't she?"

"Yes, 'm."

"Well, suppose we walk up there now. It's nearly six, and all the other children are going home." She hesitated, and looked up at the faintly gleaming track on the hill slope. "Do you want another slide? Is that it?" I asked.

"Do you mind?" she asked shyly.

"No. I'll wait for you. Take your time; don't run."

Two little boys were still hanging about the slide, and they cheered her as she came down, her comforter streaming in the wind.

"Now," she announced, getting up out of the drift, "I'll show you where the church is."

"Shall I tie your comforter again?"

"No, 'm, thanks. I'm plenty warm." She put her mittened hand confidingly in mine and trudged along beside me.

Mrs. Dow must have heard us tramping up the snowy steps of the church, for she met us at the door. Every one had gone except the old ladies. A kerosene lamp flickered over the Sunday school chart, with the lesson-picture of the Wise Men, and the little barrel stove threw out a deep glow over the three white heads that bent above the baby. There the three friends sat, patting him, and smoothing his dress, and playing with his hands, which made theirs look so brown.

"You ain't seen nothing finer in all your travels," said Mrs. Spinny, and they all laughed.

They showed me his full chest and how strong his back was; had me feel the golden fuzz on his head, and made him look at me with his round, bright eyes. He laughed and reared himself in my arms as I took him up and held him close to me. He was so warm and tingling with life, and he had the flush of new beginnings, of the new morning and the new rose. He seemed to have come so lately from his mother's heart! It was as if I held her youth and all her young joy. As I put my cheek down against his, he spied a pink flower in my hat, and making a gleeful sound, he lunged at it with both fists.

"Don't let him spoil it," murmured Mrs. Spinny. "He loves color so—like Nelly."

Behind the
Singer Tower

It was a hot, close night in May, the night after the burning of the Mont Blanc Hotel, and some half dozen of us who had been thrown together, more or less, during that terrible day, accepted Fred Hallet's invitation to go for a turn in his launch, which was tied up in the North River. We were all tired and unstrung and heartsick, and the quiet of the night and the coolness on the water relaxed our tense nerves a little. None of us talked much as we slid down the river and out into the bay. We were in a kind of stupor. When the launch ran out into the harbor, we saw an Atlantic liner come steaming up the big sea road. She passed so near to us that we could see her crowded steerage decks.

"It's the *Re di Napoli*," said Johnson of the *Herald*. "She's going to land her first cabin passengers tonight, evidently. Those people are terribly proud of their new docks in the North River; feel they've come up in the world."

We ruffled easily along through the bay, looking behind us at the wide circle of lights that rim the horizon from east to west and from west to east, all the way round except for that narrow, much-traveled highway, the road to the open sea. Running a launch about the harbor at night is a good deal like bicycling among the motors on Fifth Avenue. That night there was probably no less activity than usual; the turtle-backed ferry boats swung to and fro, the tugs screamed and panted beside the freight cars they were towing on barges, the Coney Island boats threw out their streams of light and faded away. Boats of every shape and purpose went about their business and made noise enough as they did it, doubtless. But to us, after what we had been seeing and hearing all day long, the place seemed unnaturally quiet and the night unnaturally black. There was a brooding mournfulness over the harbor, as if the ghost of helplessness and terror were abroad in the darkness. One felt a solemnity in the misty spring sky where only a few stars shone, pale and far apart, and in the sighs of the heavy black water that rolled up into the light. The city itself, as we looked back at it, seemed enveloped in a tragic self-consciousness. Those incredible towers of stone and steel seemed, in the mist, to be grouped confusedly together, as if they were confronting each other with a question. They looked positively lonely, like the great trees left after a forest is cut away. One might fancy that the city was protesting, was asserting its helplessness, its irresponsibility for its physical conformation, for the direction it had taken. It was an irregular parallelogram pressed between two hemispheres, and, like any other solid squeezed in a vise, it shot upward.

There were six of us in the launch: two newspapermen—Johnson and myself; Fred Hallet, the engineer, and one of his draftsmen; a lawyer from the District Attorney's office; and Zablowski, a young Jewish doctor from the Rockefeller Institute. We did not talk; there was only one thing to talk about, and we had had enough of that. Before we left town the death list of the Mont Blanc had gone above three hundred.

The Mont Banc was the complete expression of the New York idea in architecture; a thirty-five story hotel which made the Plaza look modest. Its prices, like its proportions, as the newspapers had so often asseverated, outscaled everything in the known world. And it was still standing there, massive and brutally unconcerned, only a little blackened about its thousand windows and with the foolish fire escapes in its court melted down. About the fire itself nobody knew much. It had begun on the twelfth story, broken out through the windows, shot up long streamers that had gone in at the windows above, and so on up to the top. A high wind and much upholstery and oiled wood had given it incredible speed.

On the night of the fire the hotel was full of people from everywhere, and by morning half a dozen trusts had lost their presidents, two states had lost their governors, and one of the great European powers had lost its ambassador. So many businesses had been disorganized that Wall Street had shut down for the day. They had been snuffed out, these important men, as lightly as the casual guests who had come to town to spend money, or as the pampered opera singers who had returned from an overland tour and were waiting to sail on Saturday. The lists were still vague, for whether the victims had jumped or not, identification was difficult, and in either case, they had met with obliteration, absolute effacement, as when a drop of water falls into the sea.

Out of all I had seen that day, one thing kept recurring to me; perhaps because it was so little in the face of a destruction so vast. In the afternoon, when I was going over the building with the firemen, I found, on the ledge of a window on the fifteenth floor, a man's hand snapped off at the wrist as cleanly as if it had been taken off by a cutlass—he had thrown out his arm in falling.

It had belonged to Graziani, the tenor, who had occupied a suite on the thirty-second floor. We identified it by a little-finger ring, which had been given to him by the German Emperor. Yes, it was the same hand. I had seen it often enough when he placed it so confidently over his chest as he began his "Celeste Aida," or when he lifted— much too often, alas!—his little glasses of white arrack at Martin's. When he toured the world he must have whatever was most costly and most characteristic in every city; in New York he had the thirty-second floor, poor fellow! He had plunged from there toward the cobwebby life nets stretched five hundred feet below on the asphalt. Well, at any rate, he would never drag out an obese old age in the English country house he had built near Naples.

Heretofore fires in fireproof buildings of many stories had occurred only in factory lofts, and the people who perished in them, fur workers and garment workers, were obscure for more reasons than one; most of them bore names unpronounceable to the American tongue; many of them had no kinsmen, no history, no record anywhere.

But we realized that, after the burning of the Mont Blanc, the New York idea would be called to account by every state in the Union, by all the great capitals of the world. Never before, in a single day, had so many of the names that feed and furnish the newspapers appeared in their columns all together, and for the last time.

In New York the matter of height was spoken of jocularly and triumphantly. The very window cleaners always joked about it as they buckled themselves fast outside your office in the forty-fifth story of the Wertheimer tower, though the average for window cleaners, who, for one reason or another, dropped to the pavement was something over one a day. In a city with so many millions of windows that was not perhaps an unreasonable percentage. But we felt that the Mont Blanc disaster would bring our particular type of building into unpleasant prominence, as the cholera used to make Naples and the conditions of life there too much a matter of discussion, or as the earthquake of 1906 gave such undesirable notoriety to the affairs of San Francisco.

For once we were actually afraid of being too much in the public eye, of being overadvertised. As I looked at the great incandescent signs along the Jersey shore, blazing across the night the names of beer and perfumes and corsets, it occurred to me that, after all, that kind of thing could be overdone; a single name, a single question, could be blazed too far. Our whole scheme of life and progress and profit was perpendicular.

There was nothing for us but height. We were whipped up the ladder. We depended upon the ever-growing possibilities of girders and rivets as Holland depends on her dikes.

"Did you ever notice," Johnson remarked when we were about halfway across to Staten Island, "what a Jewy-looking thing the Singer Tower is when it's lit up? The fellow who placed those incandescents must have had a sense of humor. It's exactly like the Jewish high priest in the old Bible dictionaries."

He pointed back, outlining with his forefinger the jeweled miter, the high, sloping shoulders, and the hands pressed together in the traditional posture of prayer.

Zablowski, the young Jewish doctor, smiled and shook his head. He was a very handsome fellow, with sad, thoughtful eyes, and we were all fond of him, especially Hallet, who was always teasing him. "No, it's not Semitic, Johnson," he said. "That high-peaked turban is more apt to be Persian. He's a Magi or a fire-worshiper of some sort, your high priest. When you get nearer he looks like a Buddha, with two bright rings in his ears."

Zablowski pointed with his cigar toward the blurred Babylonian heights crowding each other on the narrow tip of the island. Among them rose the colossal finger of the Singer Tower, watching over the city and the harbor like a presiding Genius. He had come out of Asia quietly in the night, no one knew just when or how, and the Statue of Liberty, holding her feeble taper in the gloom off to our left, was but an archeological survival.

"Who could have foreseen that she, in her high-mindedness, would ever spawn a great heathen idol like that?" Hallet exclaimed. "But that's what idealism comes to in the end, Zablowski."

Zablowski laughed mournfully. "What did you expect, Hallet? You've used us for your ends—waste for your machine, and now you talk about infection. Of course we brought germs from over there," he nodded toward the northeast.

"Well, you're all here at any rate, and I won't argue with you about all that tonight," said Hallet wearily. "The fact is," he went on as he lit a cigar and settled deeper into his chair, "when we met the *Re di Napoli* back there, she set me thinking. She recalled something that happened when I was a boy just out of Tech; when I was working under Merryweather on the Mont Blanc foundation."

We all looked up. Stanley Merryweather was the most successful manipulator of structural steel in New York, and Hallet was the most intelligent; the enmity between them was one of the legends of the Engineers' Society.

Hallet saw our interest and smiled. "I suppose you've heard yarns about why Merryweather and I don't even pretend to get on. People say we went to school together and then had a terrible row of some sort. The fact is, we never did get on, and back there in the foundation work of the Mont Blanc our ways definitely parted. You know how Merryweather happened to get going? He was the only nephew of old Hughie Macfarlane, and Macfarlane was the pioneer in steel construction. He dreamed the dream. When he was a lad working for the Pennsylvania Bridge Company, he saw Manhattan just as it towers there tonight. Well, Macfarlane was aging and he had no children, so he took his sister's son to make an engineer of him. Macfarlane was a thoroughgoing Scotch Presbyterian, sound Pittsburgh stock, but his sister had committed an indiscretion. She had married a professor of languages in a theological seminary out there; a professor who knew too much about some Oriental tongues I needn't name to be altogether safe. It didn't show much in the old professor, who looked like a Baptist preacher except for his short, thick hands, and of course it is very much veiled in Stanley. When he came up to the Massachusetts Tech he was a big, handsome boy, but there was something in his moist, bright blue eye—well, something that you would recognize, Zablowski."

Zablowski chuckled and inclined his head delicately forward.

Hallet continued: "Yes, in Stanley Merryweather there

were racial characteristics. He was handsome and jolly and glitteringly frank and almost insultingly cordial, and yet he was never really popular. He was quick and superficial, built for high speed and a light load. He liked to come it over people, but when you had him, he always crawled. Didn't seem to hurt him one bit to back down. If you made a fool of him tonight—well, 'Tomorrow's another day,' he'd say lightly, and tomorrow he'd blossom out in a new suit of clothes and a necktie of some unusual weave and haunting color. He had the feeling for color and texture. The worst of it was that, as truly as I'm sitting here, he never bore a grudge toward the fellow who'd called his bluff and shown him up for a lush growth; no ill feeling at all, Zablowski. He simply didn't know what that meant—"

Hallet's sentence trailed and hung wistfully in the air, while Zablowski put his hand penitently to his forehead.

"Well, Merryweather was quick and he had plenty of spurt and a talking manner, and he didn't know there had ever been such a thing as modesty or reverence in the world. He got all round the old man, and old Mac was perfectly foolish about him. It was always: 'Is it well with the young man Absalom?' Stanley was a year ahead of me in school, and when he came out of Tech the old man took him right into the business. He married a burgeoning Jewish beauty, Fanny Reizenstein, the daughter of the importer, and he hung her with the jewels of the East until she looked like the Song of Solomon done into motion pictures. I will say for Stanley that he never pretended that anything stronger than Botticelli hurt his eyes. He opened like a lotus flower to the sun and made a streak of color, even in New York. Stanley always felt that Boston hadn't done well by him, and he enjoyed throwing jobs to old Tech men. 'Largess, largess, Lord Marmion, all as he lighted down.' When they began breaking ground for the Mont Blanc I applied for a job because I wanted experience in deep foundation work. Stanley beamed at me across his mirror-finish mahogany and offered me something better, but it was foundation work I wanted, so early in the spring I went into the hole with a gang of twenty dagos.

"It was an awful summer, the worst New York can do in the way of heat, and I guess that's the worst in the world, excepting India maybe. We sweated away, I and my twenty dagos, and I learned a good deal—more than I ever meant to. Now there was one of those men I liked, and it's about him I must tell you. His name was Caesaro, but he was so little that the other dagos in the hole called him Caesarino, Little Caesar. He was from the island of Ischia, and I had been there when a young lad with my sister who was ill. I knew the particular goat track Caesarino hailed from, and maybe I had seen him there among all the swarms of eager, panting little animals that roll around in the dust and somehow worry through famine and fever and earthquake, with such a curiously hot spark of life in them and such delight in being allowed to live at all.

"Caesarino's father was dead and his older brother was married and had a little swarm of his own to look out for. Caesarino and the next two boys were coral divers and went out with the fleet twice a year; when they were at home they worked about by the day in the vineyards. He couldn't remember ever having had any clothes on in summer until he was ten; spent all his time swimming and diving and sprawling about among the nets on the beach. I've seen 'em, those wild little water dogs; look like little seals with their round eyes and their hair always dripping. Caesarino thought he could make more money in New York than he made diving for coral, and he was the mainstay of the family. There were ever so many little water dogs after him; his father had done the best he could to insure the perpetuity of his breed before he went under the lava to begin all over again by helping to make the vines grow in that marvelously fruitful volcanic soil. Little Caesar came to New York, and that is where we begin.

"He was one of the twenty crumpled, broken little men

who worked with me down in that big hole. I first noticed him because he was so young, and so eager to please, and because he was so especially frightened. Wouldn't you be at all this terrifying, complicated machinery, after sun and happy nakedness and a goat track on a volcanic island? Haven't you ever noticed how, when a dago is hurt on the railroad and they trundle him into the station on a truck, another dago always runs alongside him, holding his hand and looking the more scared of the two? Little Caesar ran about the hole looking like that. He was afraid of everything he touched. He never knew what might go off. Suppose we went to work for some great and powerful nation in Asia that had a civilization built on sciences we knew nothing of, as ours is built on physics and chemistry and higher mathematics; and suppose we knew that to these people we were absolutely meaningless as social beings, were waste to clean their engines, as Zablowski says; that we were there to do the dangerous work, to be poisoned in caissons under rivers, blown up by blasts, drowned in coal mines, and that these masters of ours were as indifferent to us individually as the Carthaginians were to their mercenaries? I'll tell you we'd guard the precious little spark of life with trembling hands."

"But I say—" sputtered the lawyer from the District Attorney's office.

"I know, I know, Chambers." Hallet put out a soothing hand. "*We* don't want 'em, God knows. They come. But why do they come? It's the pressure of their time and ours. It's not rich pickings they've got where I've worked with them, let me tell you. Well, Caesarino, with the others, came. The first morning I went on my job he was there, more scared of a new boss than any of the others; literally quaking. He was only twenty-three and lighter than the other men, and he was afraid I'd notice that. I thought he would pull his shoulder blades loose. After one big heave I stopped beside him and dropped a word: '*Buono soldato.*' In a moment he was grinning with all his teeth, and he squeaked out: '*Buono soldato, da boss he talka dago!*' That was the beginning of our acquaintance."

Hallet paused a moment and smoked thoughtfully. He was a soft man for the iron age, I reflected, and it was easy enough to see why Stanley Merryweather had beaten him in the race. There is a string to every big contract in New York, and Hallet was always tripping over the string.

"From that time on we were friends. I knew just six words of Italian, but that summer I got so I could understand his fool dialect pretty well. I used to feel ashamed of the way he'd look at me, like a girl in love. You see, I was the only thing he wasn't afraid of. On Sundays we used to poke off to a beach somewhere, and he'd lie in the water all day and tell me about the coral divers and the bottom of the Mediterranean. I got very fond of him. It was my first summer in New York and I was lonesome, too. The game down here looked pretty ugly to me. There were plenty of disagreeable things to think about, and it was better fun to see how much soda water Caesarino could drink. He never drank wine. He used to say: 'At home—oh, yes-a! At New York,' making that wise little gesture with the forefinger between his eyes, '*niente*. Sav'-a da mon'.' But even his economy had its weak spots. He was very fond of candy, and he was always buying 'pop-a corn off-a da push-a cart.'

"However, he had sent home a good deal of money, and his mother was ailing and he was so frightened about her and so generally homesick that I urged him to go back to Ischia for the winter. There was a poor prospect for steady work, and if he went home he wouldn't be out much more than if he stayed in New York working on half time. He backed and filled and agonized a good deal, but when I at last got him to the point of engaging his passage he was the happiest dago on Manhattan Island. He told me about it all a hundred times.

"His mother, from the *piccola casa* on the cliff, could see all the boats go by to Naples. She always watched for them. Possibly he would be able to see her from the steamer, or at least the *casa*, or certainly the place where the *casa* stood.

"All this time we were making things move in the hole. Old Macfarlane wasn't around much in those days. He passed on the results, but Stanley had a free hand as to ways and means. He made amazing mistakes, harrowing blunders. His path was strewn with hairbreadth escapes, but they never dampened his courage or took the spurt out of him. After a close shave he'd simply duck his head and smile brightly and say: 'Well, I got *that* across, old Persimmons!' I'm not underestimating the value of dash and intrepidity. He made the wheels go round. One of his maxims was that men are cheaper than machinery. He smashed up a lot of hands, but he always got out under the fellow-servant act. 'Never been caught yet, huh?' he used to say with his pleasant, confiding wink. I'd been complaining to him for a long while about the cabling, but he always put me off; sometimes with a surly insinuation that I was nervous about my own head, but oftener with fine good humor. At last something did happen in the hole.

"It happened one night late in August, after a stretch of heat that broke the thermometers. For a week there hadn't been a dry human being in New York. Your linen went down three minutes after you put it on. We moved about insulated in moisture, like the fishes in the sea. That night I couldn't go down into the hole right away. When you once got down there the heat from the boilers and the steam from the diamond drills made a temperature that was beyond anything the human frame was meant to endure. I stood looking down for a long while, I remember. It was a hole nearly three acres square, and on one side the Savoyard rose up twenty stories, a straight blank, brick wall. You know what a mess such a hole is; great boulders of rock and deep pits of sand and gulleys of water, with drills puffing everywhere and little crumpled men crawling about like tumblebugs under the stream from the searchlight. When you got down into the hole,

that wall of the Savoyard seemed to go clear up the sky;
the pale blue enamel sky of a midsummer New York
night. Six of my men were moving a diamond drill and
settling it into a new place, when one of the big clamshells
that swung back and forth over the hole fell with its load
of sand—the worn cabling, of course. It was directly over
my men when it fell. They couldn't hear anything for the
noise of the drill; didn't know anything had happened
until it struck them. They were bending over, huddled
together, and the thing came down on them like a brick
dropped on an ant hill. They were all buried, Caesarino
among them. When we got them out, two were dead and
the others were dying. My boy was the first we reached.
The edge of the clamshell had struck him, and he was all
broken to pieces. The moment we got his head out he
began chattering like a monkey. I put my ear down to his
lips—the other drills were still going—and he was talking
about what I had forgotten, that his steamer ticket was in
his pocket and that he was to sail next Saturday. '*È
necessario, signore, è necessario,*' he kept repeating. He had
written his family what boat he was coming on, and his
mother would be at the door, watching it when it went by
to Naples. '*È necessario, signore, è necessario.*'

"When the ambulances got there the orderlies lifted two
of the men and had them carried up to the street, but
when they turned to Caesarino they dismissed him with a
shrug, glancing at him with the contemptuous expression
that ambulance orderlies come to have when they see that
a man is too much shattered to pick up. He saw the look,
and a boy who doesn't know the language learns to read
looks. He broke into sobs and began to beat the rock with
his hands. '*Curs-a da hole, curs-a da hole, curs-a da
build*'!' he screamed, bruising his fists on the shale. I
caught his hands and leaned over him. '*Buono soldato,
buono soldato,*' I said in his ear. His shrieks stopped, and
his sobs quivered down. He looked at me—'*Buono soldato,*'
he whispered '*ma, perchè?*' Then the hemorrhage from his

mouth shut him off, and he began to choke. In a few minutes it was all over with Little Caesar.

"About that time Merryweather showed up. Some one had telephoned him, and he had come down in his car. He was a little frightened and pleasurably excited. He has the truly journalistic mind—saving your presence, gentlemen—and he likes anything that bites on the tongue. He looked things over and ducked his head and grinned good-naturedly. 'Well, I guess you've got your new cabling out of me now, huh, Freddy?' he said to me. I went up to the car with him. His hand shook a little as he shielded a match to light his cigarette. 'Don't get shaky, Freddy. That wasn't so worse,' he said, as he stepped into his car.

"For the next few days I was busy seeing that the boy didn't get buried in a trench with a brass tag around his neck. On Saturday night I got his pay envelope, and he was paid for only half of the night he was killed; the accident happened about eleven o'clock. I didn't fool with any paymaster. On Monday morning I went straight to Merryweather's office, stormed his bower of rose and gold, and put that envelope on the mahogany between us. 'Merryweather,' said I, 'this is going to cost you something. I hear the relatives of the other fellows have all signed off for a few hundred, but this little dago hadn't any relatives here, and he's going to have the best lawyers in New York to prosecute his claim for him.'

"Stanley flew into one of his quick tempers. 'What business is it of yours, and what are you out to do us for?'

" 'I'm out to get every cent that's coming to this boy's family.'

" 'How in hell is that any concern of yours?'

" 'Never mind that. But we've got one awfully good case, Stanley. I happen to be the man who reported to you on that cabling again and again. I have a copy of the letter I wrote you about it when you were at Mount Desert, and I have your reply.'

"Stanley whirled around in his swivel chair and reached

for his checkbook. 'How much are you gouging for?' he asked with his baronial pout.

" 'Just all the courts will give me. I want it settled there,' I said, and I got up to go.

" 'Well, you've chosen your class, sir,' he broke out, ruffling up red. 'You can stay in a hole with the guineas till the end of time for all of me. That's where you've put yourself.'

"I got my money out of that concern and sent it off to the old woman in Ischia, and that's the end of the story. You all know Merryweather. He's the first man in my business since his uncle died, but we manage to keep clear of each other. The Mont Blanc was a milestone for me; one road ended there and another began. It was only a little accident, such as happens in New York every day in the year, but that one happened near me. There's a lot of waste about building a city. Usually the destruction all goes on in the cellar; it's only when it hits high, as it did last night, that it sets us thinking. Wherever there is the greatest output of energy, wherever the blind human race is exerting itself most furiously, there's bound to be tumult and disaster. Here we are, six men, with our pitiful few years to live and our one little chance for happiness, throwing everything we have into that conflagration on Manhattan Island, helping, with every nerve in us, with everything our brain cells can generate, with our very creature heat, to swell its glare, its noise, its luxury, and its power. Why do we do it? And why, in heaven's name, do *they* do it? *Ma, perchè?* as Caesarino said that night in the hole. Why did he, from that lazy volcanic island, so tiny, so forgotten, where life is simple and pellucid and tranquil, shaping itself to tradition and ancestral manners as water shapes itself to the jar, why did he come so far to cast his little spark in the bonfire? And the thousands like him, from islands even smaller and more remote, why do they come, like iron dust to the magnet, like moths to the flame? There must be something wonderful coming. When the frenzy is over, when the furnace has cooled, what marvel will be left on Manhattan Island?"

"What has been left often enough before," said Zablowski dreamily. "What was left in India, only not half so much."

Hallet disregarded him. "What it will be is a new idea of some sort. That's all that ever comes, really. That's what we are all the slaves of, though we don't know it. It's the whip that cracks over us till we drop. Even Merryweather—and that's where the gods have the laugh on him—every firm he crushes to the wall, every deal he puts through, every cocktail he pours down his throat, he does it in the service of this unborn Idea, that he will never know anything about. Some day it will dawn, serene and clear, and your Moloch on the Singer Tower over there will get down and do it Asian obeisance."

We reflected on this while the launch, returning toward the city, ruffled through the dark furrows of water that kept rolling up into the light. Johnson looked back at the black sea road and said quietly:

"Well, anyhow, we are the people who are doing it, and whatever it is, it will be ours."

Hallet laughed. "Don't call anything ours, Johnson, while Zablowski is around."

"Zablowski," Johnson said irritably, "why don't you *ever* hit back?"

The Bohemian Girl

The transcontinental express swung along the windings of the Sand River Valley, and in the rear seat of the observation car a young man sat greatly at his ease, not in the least discomfited by the fierce sunlight which beat in upon his brown face and neck and strong back. There was a look of relaxation and of great passivity about his broad shoulders, which seemed almost too heavy until he stood up and squared them. He wore a pale flannel shirt and a blue silk necktie with loose ends. His trousers were wide and belted at the waist, and his short sack coat hung open. His heavy shoes had seen good service. His reddish-brown hair, like his clothes, had a foreign cut. He had deep-set, dark blue eyes under heavy reddish eyebrows. His face was kept clean only by close shaving, and even the sharpest razor left a glint of yellow in the smooth brown of his skin. His teeth and the palms of his hands were very white. His head, which looked hard and stubborn, lay indolently in the green cushion of the wicker chair, and as he looked out at the ripe summer country a teasing, not unkindly smile played over his lips. Once, as he basked thus comfortably, a quick light flashed in his eyes, curiously dilating the pupils, and his mouth became a hard, straight line, gradually relaxing into its former smile of rather kindly mockery. He told himself, apparently, that there was no point in getting excited; and he seemed a master hand at taking his ease when he could.

Neither the sharp whistle of the locomotive nor the brakeman's call disturbed him. It was not until after the train had stopped that he rose, put on a Panama hat, took from the rack a small valise and a flute case, and stepped deliberately to the station platform. The baggage was already unloaded, and the stranger presented a check for a battered sole-leather steamer trunk.

"Can you keep it here for a day or two?" he asked the agent. "I may send for it, and I may not."

"Depends on whether you like the country, I suppose?" demanded the agent in a challenging tone.

"Just so."

The agent shrugged his shoulders, looked scornfully at the small trunk, which was marked "N.E.," and handed out a claim check without further comment. The stranger watched him as he caught one end of the trunk and dragged it into the express room. The agent's manner seemed to remind him of something amusing. "Doesn't seem to be a very big place," he remarked, looking about.

"It's big enough for us," snapped the agent, as he banged the trunk into a corner.

That remark, apparently, was what Nils Ericson had wanted. He chuckled quietly as he took a leather strap from his pocket and swung his valise around his shoulder. Then he settled his Panama securely on his head, turned up his trousers, tucked the flute case under his arm, and started off across the fields. He gave the town, as he would have said, a wide berth, and cut through a great fenced pasture, emerging, when he rolled under the barbed wire at the farther corner, upon a white dusty road which ran straight up from the river valley to the high prairies, where the ripe wheat stood yellow and the tin roofs and weathercocks were twinkling in the fierce sunlight. By the time Nils had done three miles, the sun was sinking and the farm wagons on their way home from town came rattling by, covering him with dust and making him sneeze. When one of the farmers pulled up and offered to give him a lift, he clambered in willingly. The driver was a thin, grizzled old man with a long lean neck and a foolish sort of beard, like a goat's. "How fur ye goin'?" he asked, as he clucked to his horses and started off.

"Do you go by the Ericson place?"

"Which Ericson?" The old man drew in his reins as if he expected to stop again.

"Preacher Ericson's."

"Oh, the Old Lady Ericson's!" He turned and looked at Nils. "La, me! If you're goin' out there you might 'a' rid out in the automobile. That's a pity, now. The Old Lady Ericson was in town with her auto. You might 'a' heard it snortin' anywhere about the post office er the butcher shop."

"Has she a motor?" asked the stranger absently.

"'Deed an' she has! She runs into town every night about this time for her mail and meat for supper. Some folks say she's afraid her auto won't get exercise enough, but I say that's jealousy."

"Aren't there any other motors about here?"

"Oh, yes! we have fourteen in all. But nobody else gets around like the Old Lady Ericson. She's out, rain er shine, over the whole county, chargin' into town and out amongst her farms, an' up to her sons' places. Sure you ain't goin' to the wrong place?" He craned his neck and looked at Nils' flute case with eager curiosity. "The old woman ain't got any piany that I knows on. Olaf, he has a grand. His wife's musical; took lessons in Chicago."

"I'm going up there tomorrow," said Nils imperturbably. He saw that the driver took him for a piano tuner.

"Oh, I see!" The old man screwed up his eyes mysteriously. He was a little dashed by the stranger's noncommunicativeness, but he soon broke out again.

"I'm one o' Mis' Ericson's tenants. Look after one of her places. I did own the place myself oncet, but I lost it a while back, in the bad years just after the World's Fair. Just as well, too, I say. Lets you out o' payin' taxes. The Ericsons do own most of the county now. I remember the old preacher's fav'rite text used to be, 'To them that hath shall be given.' They've spread something wonderful—run over this here country like bindweed. But I ain't one that begretches it to 'em. Folks is entitled to what they kin git; and they're hustlers. Olaf, he's in the Legislature now, and a likely man fur Congress. Listen, if that ain't the old woman comin' now. Want I should stop her?"

Nils shook his head. He heard the deep chug-chug of a motor vibrating steadily in the clear twilight behind them. The pale lights of the car swam over the hill, and the old man slapped his reins and turned clear out of the road, ducking his head at the first of three angry snorts from behind. The motor was running at a hot, even speed, and passed without turning an inch from its course. The driver was a stalwart woman who sat at ease in the front seat and drove her car bareheaded. She left a cloud of dust and a trail of gasoline behind her. Her tenant threw back his head and sneezed.

"Whew! I sometimes say I'd as lief be *before* Mrs. Ericson as behind her. She does beat all! Nearly seventy, and never lets another soul touch that car. Puts it into commission herself every morning, and keeps it tuned up by the hitch-bar all day. I never stop work for a drink o' water that I don't hear her a-churnin' up the road. I reckon her darter-in-laws never sets down easy nowadays. Never know when she'll pop in. Mis' Otto, she says to me: 'We're so afraid that thing'll blow up and do Ma some injury yet, she's so turrible venturesom.' Says I: 'I wouldn't stew, Mis' Otto; the old lady'll drive that car to the funeral of every darter-in-law she's got.' That was after the old woman had jumped a turrible bad culvert."

The stranger heard vaguely what the old man was saying. Just now he was experiencing something very much like homesickness, and he was wondering what had brought it about. The mention of a name or two, perhaps; the rattle of a wagon along a dusty road; the rank, resinous smell of sunflowers and ironweed, which the night damp brought up from the draws and low places; perhaps, more than all, the dancing lights of the motor that had plunged by. He squared his shoulders with a comfortable sense of strength.

The wagon, as it jolted westward, climbed a pretty steady upgrade. The country, receding from the rough river valley, swelled more and more gently, as if it had been smoothed out by the wind. On one of the last of the rugged ridges, at the end of a branch road, stood a grim square house with a tin roof and double porches. Behind the house stretched a row of broken, wind-racked poplars, and down the hill slope to the left straggled the sheds and stables. The old man stopped his horses where the Ericsons' road branched across a dry sand creek that wound about the foot of the hill.

"That's the old lady's place. Want I should drive in?"

"No, thank you. I'll roll out here. Much obliged to you. Good night."

His passenger stepped down over the front wheel, and the old man drove on reluctantly, looking back as if he would like to see how the stranger would be received.

As Nils was crossing the dry creek he heard the restive tramp of a horse coming toward him down the hill. Instantly he flashed out of the road and stood behind a thicket of wild plum bushes that grew in the sandy bed. Peering through the dusk, he saw a light horse, under tight rein, descending the hill at a sharp walk. The rider was a slender woman—barely visible against the dark hillside—wearing an old-fashioned derby hat and a long riding skirt. She sat lightly in the saddle, with her chin high, and seemed to be looking into the distance. As she passed the plum thicket her horse snuffed the air and shied. She struck him, pulling him in sharply, with an angry exclamation, "*Blázne!*" in Bohemian. Once in the main road, she let him out into a lope, and they soon emerged upon the crest of high land, where they moved along the skyline, silhouetted against the band of faint color that lingered in the west. This horse and rider, with their free, rhythmical gallop, were the only moving things to be seen on the face of the flat country. They seemed, in the last sad light of evening, not to be there accidentally, but as an inevitable detail of the landscape.

Nils watched them until they had shrunk to a mere moving speck against the sky, then he crossed the sand creek and climbed the hill. When he reached the gate the front of the house was dark, but a light was shining from the side windows. The pigs were squealing in the hog corral, and Nils could see a tall boy, who carried two big wooden buckets, moving about among them. Halfway between the barn and the house, the windmill wheezed lazily. Following the path that ran around to the back porch, Nils stopped to look through the screen door into the lamplit kitchen. The kitchen was the largest room in the house; Nils remembered that his older brothers used to give dances there when he was a boy. Beside the stove stood a little girl with two light yellow braids and a broad, flushed face, peering anxiously into a frying pan. In the dining room beyond, a large, broad-shouldered woman was moving about the table. She walked with an active, springy step. Her face was heavy and florid, almost without wrinkles, and her hair was black at seventy. Nils felt proud of her as he watched her deliberate activity; never a momentary hesitation, or a movement that did not tell. He waited until she came out into the kitchen and, brushing the child aside, took her place at the stove. Then he tapped on the screen door and entered.

"It's nobody but Nils, Mother. I expect you weren't looking for me."

Mrs. Ericson turned away from the stove and stood staring at him. "Bring the lamp, Hilda, and let me look."

Nils laughed and unslung his valise. "What's the matter, Mother? Don't you know me?"

Mrs. Ericson put down the lamp. "You must be Nils. You don't look very different, anyway."

"Nor you, Mother. You hold your own. Don't you wear glasses yet?"

"Only to read by. Where's your trunk, Nils?"

"Oh, I left that in town. I thought it might not be convenient for you to have company so near threshing-time."

"Don't be foolish, Nils." Mrs. Ericson turned back to the stove. "I don't thresh now. I hitched the wheat land onto the next farm and have a tenant. Hilda, take some hot water up to the company room, and go call little Eric."

The tow-haired child, who had been standing in mute amazement, took up the tea kettle and withdrew, giving Nils a long, admiring look from the door of the kitchen stairs.

"Who's the youngster?" Nils asked, dropping down on the bench behind the kitchen stove.

"One of your Cousin Henrik's."

"How long has Cousin Henrik been dead?"

"Six years. There are two boys. One stays with Peter and one with Anders. Olaf is their guardeen."

There was a clatter of pails on the porch, and a tall, lanky boy peered wonderingly in through the screen door. He had a fair, gentle face and big gray eyes, and wisps of soft yellow hair hung down under his cap. Nils sprang up and pulled him into the kitchen, hugging him and slapping him on the shoulders. "Well, if it isn't my kid! Look at the size of him! Don't you know me, Eric?"

The boy reddened under his sunburn and freckles, and hung his head. "I guess it's Nils," he said shyly.

"You're a good guesser," laughed Nils giving the lad's hand a swing. To himself he was thinking: "That's why the little girl looked so friendly. He's taught her to like me. He was only six when I went away, and he's remembered for twelve years."

Eric stood fumbling with his cap and smiling. "You look just like I thought you would," he ventured.

"Go wash your hands, Eric," called Mrs. Ericson. "I've got cob corn for supper, Nils. You used to like it. I guess you don't get much of that in the old country. Here's Hilda; she'll take you up to your room. You'll want to get the dust off you before you eat."

Mrs. Ericson went into the dining room to lay another plate, and the little girl came up and nodded to Nils as if to let him know that his room was ready. He put out his hand and she took it, with a startled glance up at his face. Little Eric dropped his towel, threw an arm about Nils and one about Hilda, gave them a clumsy squeeze, and then stumbled out to the porch.

During supper Nils heard exactly how much land each of his eight grown brothers farmed, how their crops were coming on, and how much live stock they were feeding. His mother watched him narrowly as she talked. "You've got better looking, Nils," she remarked abruptly, whereupon he grinned and the children giggled. Eric, although he was eighteen and as tall as Nils, was always accounted a child, being the last of so many sons. His face seemed childlike, too, Niles thought, and he had the open, wandering eyes of a little boy. All the others had been men at his age.

After supper Nils went out to the front porch and sat down on the step to smoke a pipe. Mrs. Ericson drew a rocking chair up near him and began to knit busily. It was one of the few Old World customs she had kept up, for she could not bear to sit with idle hands.

"Where's little Eric, Mother?"

"He's helping Hilda with the dishes. He does it of his own will; I don't like a boy to be too handy about the house."

"He seems like a nice kid."

"He's very obedient."

Nils smiled a little in the dark. It was just as well to shift the line of conversation. "What are you knitting there, Mother?"

"Baby stockings. The boys keep me busy." Mrs. Ericson chuckled and clicked her needles.

"How many grandchildren have you?"

"Only thirty-one now. Olaf lost his three. They were sickly, like their mother."

"I supposed he had a second crop by this time!"

"His second wife has no children. She's too proud. She tears about on horseback all the time. But she'll get caught up with, yet. She sets herself very high, though nobody knows what for. They were low enough Bohemians she came of. I never thought much of Bohemians; always drinking."

Nils puffed away at his pipe in silence, and Mrs. Ericson knitted on. In a few moments she added grimly: "She was down here tonight, just before you came. She'd like to quarrel with me and come between me and Olaf, but I don't give her the chance. I suppose you'll be bringing a wife home some day."

"I don't know. I've never thought much about it."

"Well, perhaps it's best as it is," suggested Mrs. Ericson hopefully. "You'd never be contented tied down to the land. There was roving blood in your father's family, and it's come out in you. I expect your own way of life suits you best." Mrs. Ericson had dropped into a blandly agreeable tone which Nils well remembered. It seemed to amuse him a good deal and his white teeth flashed behind his pipe. His mother's strategies had always diverted him, even when he was a boy—they were so flimsy and patent, so illy proportioned to her vigor and force. "They've been waiting to see which way I'd jump," he reflected. He felt that Mrs. Ericson was pondering his case deeply as she sat clicking her needles.

"I don't suppose you've ever got used to steady work," she went on presently. "Men ain't apt to if they roam around too long. It's a pity you didn't come back the year after the World's Fair. Your father picked up a good bit of land cheap then, in the hard times, and I expect maybe he'd have give you a farm. It's too bad you put off comin' back so long, for I always thought he meant to do something by you."

Nils laughed and shook the ashes out of his pipe. "I'd have missed a lot if I had come back then. But I'm sorry I didn't get back to see father."

"Well, I suppose we have to miss things at one end or

the other. Perhaps you are as well satisfied with your own doings, now, as you'd have been with a farm," said Mrs. Ericson reassuringly.

"Land's a good thing to have," Nils commented, as he lit another match and sheltered it with his hand.

His mother looked sharply at his face until the match burned out. "Only when you stay on it!" she hastened to say.

Eric came round the house by the path just then, and Nils rose, with a yawn. "Mother, if you don't mind, Eric and I will take a little tramp before bedtime. It will make me sleep."

"Very well; only don't stay long. I'll sit up and wait for you. I like to lock up myself."

Niles put his hand on Eric's shoulder, and the two tramped down the hill and across the sand creek into the dusty highroad beyond. Neither spoke. They swung along at an even gait, Nils puffing at his pipe. There was no moon, and the white road and the wide fields lay faint in the starlight. Over everything was darkness and thick silence, and the smell of dust and sunflowers. The brothers followed the road for a mile or more without finding a place to sit down. Finally, Nils perched on a stile over the wire fence, and Eric sat on the lower step.

"I began to think you never would come back, Nils," said the boy softly.

"Didn't I promise you I would?"

"Yes; but people don't bother about promises they make to babies. Did you really know you were going away for good when you went to Chicago with the cattle that time?"

"I thought it very likely, if I could make my way."

"I don't see how you did it, Nils. Not many fellows could." Eric rubbed his shoulder against his brother's knee.

"The hard thing was leaving home—you and father. It was easy enough, once I got beyond Chicago. Of course I got awful homesick; used to cry myself to sleep. But I'd burned my bridges."

"You had always wanted to go, hadn't you?"

"Always. Do you still sleep in our little room? Is that cottonwood still by the window?"

Eric nodded eagerly and smiled up at his brother in the gray darkness.

"You remember how we always said the leaves were whispering when they rustled at night? Well, they always whispered to me about the sea. Sometimes they said names out of the geography books. In a high wind they had a desperate sound, like something trying to tear loose."

"How funny, Nils," said Eric dreamily, resting his chin on his hand. "That tree still talks like that, and 'most always it talks to me about you."

They sat a while longer, watching the stars. At last Eric whispered anxiously: "Hadn't we better go back now? Mother will get tired waiting for us." They rose and took a short cut home, through the pasture.

II

The next morning Nils woke with the first flood of light that came with dawn. The white-plastered walls of his room reflected the glare that shone through the thin window shades, and he found it impossible to sleep. He dressed hurriedly and slipped down the hall and up the back stairs to the half-story room which he used to share with his little brother. Eric, in a skimpy nightshirt, was sitting on the edge of the bed, rubbing his eyes, his pale yellow hair standing up in tufts all over his head. When he saw Nils, he murmured something confusedly and hustled his long legs into his trousers. "I didn't expect you'd be up so early, Nils," he said, as his head emerged from his blue shirt.

"Oh, you thought I was a dude, did you?" Nils gave him a playful tap which bent the tall boy up like a clasp knife. "See here; I must teach you to box." Nils thrust his hands into his pockets and walked about. "You haven't changed things much up here. Got most of my old traps, haven't you?"

He took down a bent, withered piece of sapling that hung over the dresser. "If this isn't the stick Lou Sandberg killed himself with!"

The boy looked up from his shoe-lacing.

"Yes; you never used to let me play with that. Just how did he do it, Nils? You were with father when he found Lou, weren't you?"

"Yes. Father was going off to preach somewhere, and, as we drove along, Lou's place looked sort of forlorn, and we thought we'd stop and cheer him up. When we found him father said he'd been dead a couple of days. He'd tied a piece of binding twine round his neck, made a noose in each end, fixed the nooses over the ends of a bent stick, and let the stick spring straight; strangled himself."

"What made him kill himself such a silly way?"

The simplicity of the boy's question set Nils laughing. He clapped little Eric on the shoulder. "What made him such a silly as to kill himself at all, I should say!"

"Oh, well! But his hogs had the cholera, and all up and died on him, didn't they?"

"Sure they did; but he didn't have cholera; and there were plenty of hogs left in the world, weren't there?"

"Well, but, if they weren't his, how could they do him any good?" Eric asked, in astonishment.

"Oh, scat! He could have had lots of fun with other people's hogs. He was a chump, Lou Sandberg. To kill yourself for a pig—think of that, now!" Nils laughed all the way downstairs, and quite embarrassed little Eric, who fell to scrubbing his face and hands at the tin basin. While he was parting his wet hair at the kitchen looking glass, a heavy tread sounded on the stairs. The boy dropped his comb. "Gracious, there's Mother. We must have talked too long." He hurried out to the shed, slipped on his overalls, and disappeared with the milking pails.

Mrs. Ericson came in, wearing a clean white apron, her black hair shining from the application of a wet brush.

"Good morning, Mother. Can't I make the fire for you?"

"No, thank you, Nils. It's no trouble to make a cob fire, and I like to manage the kitchen stove myself." Mrs. Ericson paused with a shovel full of ashes in her hand. "I expect you will be wanting to see your brothers as soon as possible. I'll take you up to Anders' place this morning. He's threshing, and most of our boys are over there."

"Will Olaf be there?"

Mrs. Ericson went on taking out the ashes, and spoke between shovels. "No; Olaf's wheat is all in, put away in his new barn. He got six thousand bushel this year. He's going to town today to get men to finish roofing his barn."

"So Olaf is building a new barn?" Nils asked absently.

"Biggest one in the county, and almost done. You'll likely be here for the barn-raising. He's going to have a supper and a dance as soon as everybody's done threshing. Says it keeps the voters in a good humor. I tell him that's all nonsense; but Olaf has a long head for politics."

"Does Olaf farm all Cousin Henrik's land?"

Mrs. Ericson frowned as she blew into the faint smoke curling up about the cobs. "Yes; he holds it in trust for the children, Hilda and her brothers. He keeps strict account of everything he raises on it, and puts the proceeds out at compound interest for them."

Nils smiled as he watched the little flames shoot up. The door of the back stairs opened, and Hilda emerged, her arms behind her, buttoning up her long gingham apron as she came. He nodded to her gaily, and she twinkled at him out of her little blue eyes, set far apart over her wide cheekbones.

"There, Hilda, you grind the coffee—and just put in an extra handful; I expect your Cousin Nils likes his strong," said Mrs. Ericson, as she went out to the shed.

Nils turned to look at the little girl, who gripped the coffee grinder between her knees and ground so hard that her two braids bobbed and her face flushed under its broad spattering of freckles. He noticed on her middle finger something that had not been there last night, and that had evidently been put on for company: a tiny gold ring with a clumsily set garnet stone. As her hand went round and round he touched the ring with the tip of his finger, smiling.

Hilda glanced toward the shed door through which Mrs. Ericson had disappeared. "My Cousin Clara gave me that," she whispered bashfully. "She's Cousin Olaf's wife."

III

Mrs. Olaf Ericson—Clara Vavrika, as many people still called her—was moving restlessly about her big bare house that morning. Her husband had left for the county town before his wife was out of bed—her lateness in rising was one of the many things the Ericson family had against her. Clara seldom came downstairs before eight o'clock, and this morning she was even later, for she had dressed with unusual care. She put on, however, only a tight-fitting black dress, which people thereabouts thought very plain. She was a tall, dark woman of thirty, with a rather sallow complexion and a touch of dull salmon red in her cheeks, where the blood seemed to burn under her brown skin. Her hair, parted evenly above her low forehead, was so black that there were distinctly blue lights in it. Her black eyebrows were delicate half-moons and her lashes were long and heavy. Her eyes slanted a little, as if she had a strain of Tartar or gypsy blood, and were sometimes full of fiery determination and sometimes dull and opaque. Her expression was never altogether amiable; was often, indeed, distinctly sullen, or, when she was animated, sarcastic. She was most attractive in profile, for then one saw to advantage her small, well-shaped head and delicate ears, and felt at once that here was a very positive, if not an altogether pleasing, personality.

The entire management of Mrs. Olaf's household devolved upon her aunt, Johanna Vavrika, a superstitious, doting woman of fifty. When Clara was a little girl her mother died, and Johanna's life had been spent in ungrudging service to her niece. Clara, like many self-willed and discontented persons, was really very apt, without knowing it, to do as other people told her, and to let her destiny be decided for her by intelligences much below her own. It was her Aunt Johanna who had humored and spoiled her in her girlhood, who had got her off to Chicago to study piano, and who had finally persuaded her to marry Olaf Ericson as the best match she would be likely to make in that part of the country. Johanna Vavrika had been deeply scarred by smallpox in the old country. She was short and fat, homely and jolly and sentimental. She was so broad, and took such short steps when she walked, that her brother, Joe Vavrika, always called her his duck. She adored her niece because of her talent, because of her good looks and masterful ways, but most of all because of her selfishness.

Clara's marriage with Olaf Ericson was Johanna's particular triumph. She was inordinately proud of Olaf's position, and she found a sufficiently exciting career in managing Clara's house, in keeping it above the criticism of the Ericsons, in pampering Olaf to keep him from finding fault with his wife, and in concealing from every one Clara's domestic infelicities. While Clara slept of a morning, Johanna Vavrika was bustling about, seeing that Olaf and the men had their breakfast, and that the cleaning or the butter-making or the washing was properly begun by the two girls in the kitchen. Then, at about eight o'clock, she would take Clara's coffee up to her, and chat with her while she drank it, telling her what was going on in the house. Old Mrs. Ericson frequently said that her daughter-in-law would not know what day of the week it was if Johanna did not tell her every morning. Mrs. Ericson despised and pitied Johanna, but did not wholly dislike her. The one thing she hated in her daughter-in-law above everything else was the way in which Clara could come it over people. It enraged her that the affairs of her son's big, barnlike house went on as well as they did, and she used to feel that in this world we have to wait overlong to see the guilty punished. "Suppose Johanna Vavrika died or got sick?" the old lady used to say to Olaf. "Your wife wouldn't know where to look for her own dishcloth." Olaf only shrugged his shoulders. The fact remained that Johanna did not die, and, although Mrs. Ericson often told her she was looking poorly, she was never ill. She seldom left the house, and she slept in a little room off the kitchen. No Ericson, by night or day, could come prying about there to find fault without her knowing it. Her one weakness was that she was an incurable talker, and she sometimes made trouble without meaning to.

This morning Clara was tying a wine-colored ribbon about her throat when Johanna appeared with her coffee. After putting the tray on a sewing table, she began to make Clara's bed, chattering the while in Bohemian.

"Well, Olaf got off early, and the girls are baking. I'm going down presently to make some poppy-seed bread for Olaf. He asked for prune preserves at breakfast, and I told him I was out of them, and to bring some prunes and honey and cloves from town."

Clara poured her coffee. "Ugh! I don't see how men can eat so much sweet stuff. In the morning, too!"

Her aunt chuckled knowingly. "Bait a bear with honey, as we say in the old country."

"Was he cross?" her niece asked indifferently.

"Olaf? Oh, no! He was in fine spirits. He's never cross if you know how to take him. I never knew a man to make so little fuss about bills. I gave him a list of things to get a yard long, and he didn't say a word; just folded it up and put it in his pocket."

"I can well believe he didn't say a word," Clara remarked with a shrug. "Some day he'll forget how to talk."

"Oh, but they say he's a grand speaker in the Legislature. He knows when to keep quiet. That's why he's got such influence in politics. The people have confidence in him." Johanna beat up a pillow and held it under her fat chin while she slipped on the case. Her niece laughed.

"Maybe we could make people believe we were wise, Aunty, if we held our tongues. Why did you tell Mrs. Ericson that Norman threw me again last Saturday and turned my foot? She's been talking to Olaf."

Johanna fell into great confusion. "Oh, but, my precious, the old lady asked for you, and she's always so angry if I can't give an excuse. Anyhow, she needn't talk; she's always tearing up something with that motor of hers."

When her aunt clattered down to the kitchen, Clara went to dust the parlor. Since there was not much there to dust, this did not take very long. Olaf had built the house new for her before their marriage, but her interest in furnishing it had been short-lived. It went, indeed, little beyond a bathtub and her piano. They had disagreed about almost every other article of furniture, and Clara had said she would rather have her house empty than full of things she didn't want. The house was set in a hillside, and the west windows of the parlor looked out above the kitchen yard thirty feet below. The east windows opened directly into the front yard. At one of the latter, Clara, while she was dusting, heard a low whistle. She did not turn at once, but listened intently as she drew her cloth slowly along the round of a chair. Yes, there it was:

I dreamt that I dwelt in ma-a-arble halls.

She turned and saw Nils Ericson laughing in the sunlight, his hat in his hand, just outside the window. As she crossed the room he leaned against the wire screen. "Aren't you at all surprised to see me, Clara Vavrika?"

"No; I was expecting to see you. Mother Ericson telephoned Olaf last night that you were here."

Nils squinted and gave a long whistle. "Telephoned? That must have been while Eric and I were out walking. Isn't she enterprising? Lift this screen, won't you?"

Clara lifted the screen, and Nils swung his leg across the window sill. As he stepped into the room she said: "You didn't think you were going to get ahead of your mother, did you?"

He threw his hat on the piano. "Oh, I do sometimes. You see, I'm ahead of her now. I'm supposed to be in Anders' wheat field. But, as we were leaving, Mother ran her car into a soft place beside the road and sank up to the hubs. While they were going for horses to pull her out, I cut away behind the stacks and escaped." Nils chuckled. Clara's dull eyes lit up as she looked at him admiringly.

"You've got them guessing already. I don't know what your mother said to Olaf over the telephone, but he came back looking as if he'd seen a ghost, and he didn't go to bed until a dreadful hour—ten o'clock, I should think. He sat out on the porch in the dark like a graven image. It had been one of his talkative days, too." They both laughed, easily and lightly, like people who have laughed a great deal together; but they remained standing.

"Anders and Otto and Peter looked as if they had seen ghosts, too, over in the threshing field. What's the matter with them all?"

Clara gave him a quick, searching look. "Well, for one thing, they've always been afraid you have the other will."

Nils looked interested. "The other will?"

"Yes. A later one. They knew your father made another, but they never knew what he did with it. They almost tore the old house to pieces looking for it. They always suspected that he carried on a clandestine correspondence with you, for the one thing he would do was to get his own mail himself. So they thought he might have sent the new will to you for safekeeping. The old one, leaving everything to your mother, was made long before you went away, and it's understood among them that it cuts you out—that she will leave all the property to the others. Your father made the second will to prevent that. I've been hoping you had it. It would be such fun to spring it on them." Clara laughed mirthfully, a thing she did not often do now.

Nils shook his head reprovingly. "Come, now, you're malicious."

"No, I'm not. But I'd like something to happen to stir them all up, just for once. There never was such a family for having nothing ever happen to them but dinner and threshing. I'd almost be willing to die, just to have a funeral. *You* wouldn't stand it for three weeks."

Nils bent over the piano and began pecking at the keys with the finger of one hand. "I wouldn't? My dear young lady, how do you know what I can stand? *You* wouldn't wait to find out."

Clara flushed darkly and frowned. "I didn't believe you would ever come back—" she said defiantly.

"Eric believed I would, and he was only a baby when I went away. However, all's well that ends well, and I haven't come back to be a skeleton at the feast. We mustn't quarrel. Mother will be here with a search warrant pretty soon." He swung round and faced her, thrusting his hands into his coat pockets. "Come, you ought to be glad to see me, if you want something to happen. I'm something, even without a will. We can have a little fun, can't we? I think we can!"

She echoed him, "I think we can!" They both laughed and their eyes sparkled. Clara Vavrika looked ten years younger than when she had put the velvet ribbon about her throat that morning.

"You know, I'm so tickled to see mother," Nils went on. "I didn't know I was so proud of her. A regular pile driver. How about little pigtails, down at the house? Is Olaf doing the square thing by those children?"

Clara frowned pensively. "Olaf has to do something that looks like the square thing, now that he's a public man!" She glanced drolly at Nils. "But he makes a good commission out of it. On Sundays they all get together here and figure. He lets Peter and Anders put in big bills for the keep of the two boys, and he pays them out of the estate. They are always having what they call account-ings. Olaf gets something out of it, too. I don't know just how they do it, but it's entirely a family matter, as they say. And when the Ericsons say that—" Clara lifted her eyebrows.

Just then the angry *honk-honk* of an approaching motor sounded from down the road. Their eyes met and they began to laugh. They laughed as children do when they can not contain themselves, and can not explain the cause of their mirth to grown people, but share it perfectly together. When Clara Vavrika sat down at the piano after he was gone, she felt that she had laughed away a dozen years. She practised as if the house were burning over her head.

When Nils greeted his mother and climbed into the front seat of the motor beside her, Mrs. Ericson looked grim, but she made no comment upon his truancy until she had turned her car and was retracing her revolutions along the road that ran by Olaf's big pasture. Then she remarked dryly:

"If I were you I wouldn't see too much of Olaf's wife while you are here. She's the kind of woman who can't see much of men without getting herself talked about. She was a good deal talked about before he married her."

"Hasn't Olaf tamed her?" Nils asked indifferently.

Mrs. Ericson shrugged her massive shoulders. "Olaf don't seem to have much luck, when it comes to wives. The first one was meek enough, but she was always ailing. And this one has her own way. He says if he quarreled with her she'd go back to her father, and then he'd lose the Bohemian vote. There are a great many Bohunks in this district. But when you find a man under his wife's thumb you can always be sure there's a soft spot in him somewhere."

Nils thought of his own father, and smiled. "She brought him a good deal of money, didn't she, besides the Bohemian vote?"

Mrs. Ericson sniffed. "Well, she has a fair half section in

her own name, but I can't see as that does Olaf much good. She will have a good deal of property some day, if old Vavrika don't marry again. But I don't consider a saloonkeeper's money as good as other people's money."

Nils laughed outright. "Come, Mother, don't let your prejudices carry you that far. Money's money. Old Vavrika's a mighty decent sort of saloonkeeper. Nothing rowdy about him."

Mrs. Ericson spoke up angrily: "Oh, I know you always stood up for them! But hanging around there when you were a boy never did you any good, Nils, nor any of the other boys who went there. There weren't so many after her when she married Olaf, let me tell you. She knew enough to grab her chance."

Nils settled back in his seat. "Of course I liked to go there, Mother, and you were always cross about it. You never took the trouble to find out that it was the one jolly house in this country for a boy to go to. All the rest of you were working yourselves to death, and the houses were mostly a mess, full of babies and washing and flies. Oh, it was all right—I understand that; but you are young only once, and I happened to be young then. Now, Vavrika's was always jolly. He played the violin, and I used to take my flute, and Clara played the piano, and Johanna used to sing Bohemian songs. She always had a big supper for us—herrings and pickles and poppy-seed bread, and lots of cake and preserves. Old Joe had been in the army in the old country, and he could tell lots of good stories. I can see him cutting bread, at the head of the table, now. I don't know what I'd have done when I was a kid if it hadn't been for the Vavrikas, really."

"And all the time he was taking money that other people had worked hard in the fields for," Mrs. Ericson observed.

"So do the circuses, Mother, and they're a good thing. People ought to get fun for some of their money. Even father liked old Joe."

"Your father," Mrs. Ericson said grimly, "liked everybody."

As they crossed the sand creek and turned into her own place, Mrs. Ericson observed, "There's Olaf's buggy. He's stopped on his way from town." Nils shook himself and prepared to greet his brother, who was waiting on the porch.

Olaf was a big, heavy Norwegian, slow of speech and movement. His head was large and square, like a block of wood. When Nils, at a distance, tried to remember what his brother looked like, he could recall only his heavy head, high forehead, large nostrils, and pale blue eyes, set far apart. Olaf's features were rudimentary: the thing one noticed was the face itself, wide and flat and pale, devoid of any expression, betraying his fifty years as little as it betrayed anything else, and powerful by reason of its very stolidness. When Olaf shook hands with Nils he looked at him from under his light eyebrows, but Nils felt that no one could ever say what that pale look might mean. The one thing he had always felt in Olaf was a heavy stubbornness, like the unyielding stickiness of wet loam against the plow. He had always found Olaf the most difficult of his brothers.

"How do you do, Nils? Expect to stay with us long?"

"Oh, I may stay forever," Nils answered gaily. "I like this country better than I used to."

"There's been some work put into it since you left," Olaf remarked.

"Exactly. I think it's about ready to live in now—and I'm about ready to settle down." Nils saw his brother lower his big head. ("Exactly like a bull," he thought.) "Mother's been persuading me to slow down now, and go in for farming," he went on lightly.

Olaf made a deep sound in his throat. "Farming ain't learned in a day," he brought out, still looking at the ground.

"Oh, I know! But I pick things up quickly." Nils had not meant to antagonize his brother, and he did not know

now why he was doing it. "Of course," he went on, "I shouldn't expect to make a big success, as you fellows have done. But then, I'm not ambitious. I won't want much. A little land, and some cattle, maybe."

Olaf still stared at the ground, his head down. He wanted to ask Nils what he had been doing all these years, that he didn't have a business somewhere he couldn't afford to leave; why he hadn't more pride than to come back with only a little sole-leather trunk to show for himself, and to present himself as the only failure in the family. He did not ask one of these questions, but he made them all felt distinctly.

"Humph!" Nils thought. "No wonder the man never talks, when he can butt his ideas into you like that without ever saying a word. I suppose he used that kind of smokeless powder on his wife all the time. But I guess she has her innings." He chuckled, and Olaf looked up. "Never mind me, Olaf. I laugh without knowing why, like little Eric. He's another cheerful dog."

"Eric," said Olaf slowly, "is a spoiled kid. He's just let his mother's best cow go dry because he don't milk her right. I was hoping you'd take him away somewhere and put him into business. If he don't do any good among strangers, he never will." This was a long speech for Olaf, and as he finished it he climbed into his buggy.

Nils shrugged his shoulders. "Same old tricks," he thought. "Hits from behind you every time. What a whale of a man!" He turned and went round to the kitchen, where his mother was scolding little Eric for letting the gasoline get low.

IV

Joe Vavrika's saloon was not in the county seat, where Olaf and Mrs. Ericson did their trading, but in a cheerfuller place, a little Bohemian settlement which lay at the other end of the county, ten level miles north of Olaf's farm. Clara rode up to see her father almost every day. Vavrika's house was, so to speak, in the back yard of his saloon. The garden between the two buildings was inclosed by a high board fence as tight as a partition, and in summer Joe kept beer tables and wooden benches among the gooseberry bushes under his little cherry tree. At one of these tables Nils Ericson was seated in the late afternoon, three days after his return home. Joe had gone in to serve a customer, and Nils was lounging on his elbows, looking rather mournfully into his half-emptied pitcher, when he heard a laugh across the little garden. Clara, in her riding habit, was standing at the back door of the house, under the grapevine trellis that old Joe had grown there long ago. Nils rose.

"Come out and keep your father and me company. We've been gossiping all afternoon. Nobody to bother us but the flies."

She shook her head. "No, I never come out here any more. Olaf doesn't like it. I must live up to my position, you know."

"You mean to tell me you never come out and chat with the boys, as you used to? He *has* tamed you! Who keeps up these flower beds?"

"I come out on Sundays, when father is alone, and read the Bohemian papers to him. But I am never here when the bar is open. What have you two been doing?"

"Talking, as I told you. I've been telling him about my travels. I find I can't talk much at home, not even to Eric."

Clara reached up and poked with her riding-whip at a white moth that was fluttering in the sunlight among the vine leaves. "I suppose you will never tell me about all those things."

"Where can I tell them? Not in Olaf's house, certainly. What's the matter with our talking here?" He pointed persuasively with his hat to the bushes and the green table, where the flies were singing lazily above the empty beer glasses.

Clara shook her head weakly. "No, it wouldn't do. Besides, I am going now."

"I'm on Eric's mare. Would you be angry if I overtook you?"

Clara looked back and laughed. "You might try and see. I can leave you if I don't want you. Eric's mare can't keep up with Norman."

Nils went into the bar and attempted to pay his score. Big Joe, six feet four, with curly yellow hair and mustache, clapped him on the shoulder. "Not a God-damn a your money go in my drawer, you hear? Only next time you bring your flute, te-te-te-te-te-ty." Joe wagged his fingers in imitation of the flute player's position. "My Clara, she come all-a-time Sundays an' play for me. She not like to play at Ericson's place." He shook his yellow curls and laughed. "Not a God-damn a fun at Ericson's. You come a Sunday. You like-a fun. No forget de flute." Joe talked very rapidly and always tumbled over his English. He seldom spoke it to his customers, and had never learned much.

Nils swung himself into the saddle and trotted to the west end of the village, where the houses and gardens scattered into prairie land and the road turned south. Far ahead of him, in the declining light, he saw Clara Vavrika's slender figure, loitering on horseback. He touched his mare with the whip, and shot along the white, level road, under the reddening sky. When he overtook Olaf's wife he saw that she had been crying. "What's the matter, Clara Vavrika?" he asked kindly.

"Oh, I get blue sometimes. It was awfully jolly living there with father. I wonder why I ever went away."

Nils spoke in a low, kind tone that he sometimes used with women: "That's what I've been wondering these many years. You were the last girl in the country I'd have picked for a wife for Olaf. What made you do it, Clara?"

"I suppose I really did it to oblige the neighbors"—Clara tossed her head. "People were beginning to wonder."

"To wonder?"

"Yes—why I didn't get married. I suppose I didn't like

to keep them in suspense. I've discovered that most girls marry out of consideration for the neighborhood."

Nils bent his head toward her and his white teeth flashed. "I'd have gambled that one girl I knew would say, 'Let the neighborhood be damned.' "

Clara shook her head mournfully. "You see, they have it on you, Nils; that is, if you're a woman. They say you're beginning to go off. That's what makes us get married: we can't stand the laugh."

Nils looked sidewise at her. He had never seen her head droop before. Resignation was the last thing he would have expected of her. "In your case, there wasn't something else?"

"Something else?"

"I mean, you didn't do it to spite somebody? Somebody who didn't come back?"

Clara drew herself up. "Oh, I never thought you'd come back. Not after I stopped writing to you, at least. *That* was all over, long before I married Olaf."

"It never occurred to you, then, that the meanest thing you could do to me was to marry Olaf?"

Clara laughed. "No; I didn't know you were so fond of Olaf."

Nils smoothed his horse's mane with his glove. "You know, Clara Vavrika, you are never going to stick it out. You'll cut away some day, and I've been thinking you might as well cut away with me."

Clara threw up her chin. "Oh, you don't know me as well as you think. I won't cut away. Sometimes, when I'm with father, I feel like it. But I can hold out as long as the Ericsons can. They've never got the best of me yet, and one can live, so long as one isn't beaten. If I go back to father, it's all up with Olaf in politics. He knows that, and he never goes much beyond sulking. I've as much wit as the Ericsons. I'll never leave them unless I can show them a thing or two."

"You mean unless you can come it over them?"

"Yes—unless I go away with a man who is cleverer than they are, and who has more money."

Nils whistled. "Dear me, you are demanding a good deal. The Ericsons, take the lot of them, are a bunch to beat. But I should think the excitement of tormenting them would have worn off by this time."

"It has, I'm afraid," Clara admitted mournfully.

"Then why don't you cut away? There are more amusing games than this in the world. When I came home I thought it might amuse me to bully a few quarter sections out of the Ericsons; but I've almost decided I can get more fun for my money somewhere else."

Clara took in her breath sharply. "Ah, you have got the other will! That was why you came home!"

"No, it wasn't. I came home to see how you were getting on with Olaf."

Clara struck her horse with the whip, and in a bound she was far ahead of him. Nils dropped one word, "Damn!" and whipped after her; but she leaned forward in her saddle and fairly cut the wind. Her long riding skirt rippled in the still air behind her. The sun was just sinking behind the stubble in a vast, clear sky, and the shadows drew across the fields so rapidly that Nils could scarcely keep in sight the dark figure on the road. When he overtook her he caught her horse by the bridle. Norman reared, and Nils was frightened for her; but Clara kept her seat.

"Let me go, Nils Ericson!" she cried. "I hate you more than any of them. You were created to torture me, the whole tribe of you—to make me suffer in every possible way."

She struck her horse again and galloped away from him. Nils set his teeth and looked thoughtful. He rode slowly home along the deserted road, watching the stars come out in the clear violet sky. They flashed softly into the limpid heavens, like jewels let fall into clear water. They were a reproach, he felt, to a sordid world. As he turned across the sand creek, he looked up at the North Star and smiled, as if there were an understanding be-

tween them. His mother scolded him for being late for
supper.

V

On Sunday afternoon Joe Vavrika, in his shirtsleeves and
carpet slippers, was sitting in his garden, smoking a long-
tasseled porcelain pipe with a hunting scene painted on
the bowl. Clara sat under the cherry tree, reading aloud to
him from the weekly Bohemian papers. She had worn a
white muslin dress under her riding habit, and the leaves
of the cherry tree threw a pattern of sharp shadows over
her skirt. The black cat was dozing in the sunlight at her
feet, and Joe's dachshund was scratching a hole under the
scarlet geraniums and dreaming of badgers. Joe was filling his pipe for the third time since dinner, when he
heard a knocking on the fence. He broke into a loud
guffaw and unlatched the little door that led into the
street. He did not call Nils by name, but caught him by
the hand and dragged him in. Clara stiffened and the
color deepened under her dark skin. Nils, too, felt a little
awkward. He had not seen her since the night when she
rode away from him and left him alone on the level road
between the fields. Joe dragged him to the wooden bench
beside the green table.

"You bring de flute," he cried, tapping the leather case
under Nils' arm. "Ah, das-a good! Now we have some
liddle fun like old times. I got somet'ing good for you."
Joe shook his finger at Nils and winked his blue eye, a
bright clear eye, full of fire, though the tiny bloodvessels
on the ball were always a little distended. "I got
somet'ing for you from"—he paused and waved his hand—
"Hongarie. You know Hongarie? You wait!" He pushed
Nils down on the bench, and went through the back door
of his saloon.

Nils looked at Clara, who sat frigidly with her white
skirts drawn tight about her. "He didn't tell you he had

asked me to come, did he? He wanted a party and proceeded to arrange it. Isn't he fun? Don't be cross; let's give him a good time."

Clara smiled and shook out her skirt. "Isn't that like father? And he has sat here so meekly all day. Well, I won't pout. I'm glad you came. He doesn't have very many good times now any more. There are so few of his kind left. The second generation are a tame lot."

Joe came back with a flask in one hand and three wine glasses caught by the stems between the fingers of the other. These he placed on the table with an air of ceremony, and going behind Nils, held the flask between him and the sun, squinting into it admiringly. "You know dis, Tokai? A great friend of mine, he bring dis to me, a present out of Hongarie. You know how much it cost, dis wine? Chust so much what it weigh in gold. Nobody but de nobles drink him in Bohemie. Many, many years I save him up, dis Tokai." Joe whipped out his official corkscrew and delicately removed the cork. "De old man die what bring him to me, an' dis wine he lay on his belly in my cellar an' sleep. An' now," carefully pouring out the heavy yellow wine, "an' now he wake up; and maybe he wake us up, too!" He carried one of the glasses to his daughter and presented it with great gallantry.

Clara shook her head, but seeing her father's disappointment, relented. "You taste it first. I don't want so much."

Joe sampled it with a beatific expression, and turned to Nils. "You drink him slow, dis wine. He very soft, but he go down hot. You see!"

After a second glass Nils declared that he couldn't take any more without getting sleepy. "Now get your fiddle, Vavrika," he said as he opened his flute case.

But Joe settled back in his wooden rocker and wagged his big carpet slipper. "No-no-no-no-no-no-no! No play fiddle now any more: too much ache in de finger," waving them, "all-a-time rheumatiz. You play de flute, te-tety-te-tety-te. Bohemie songs."

"I've forgotten all the Bohemian songs I used to play with you and Johanna. But here's one that will make Clara pout. You remember how her eyes used to snap when we called her the Bohemian Girl?" Nils lifted his flute and began "When Other Lips and Other Hearts," and Joe hummed the air in a husky baritone, waving his carpet slipper. "Oh-h-h, das-a fine music," he cried, clapping his hands as Nils finished. "Now 'Marble Halls, Marble Halls'! Clara, you sing him."

Clara smiled and leaned back in her chair, beginning softly:

> "I dreamt that I dwelt in ma-a-arble halls,
>   With vassals and serfs at my knee,"

and Joe hummed like a big bumblebee.

"There's one more you always played," Clara said quietly: "I remember that best." She locked her hands over her knee and began "The Heart Bowed Down," and sang it through without groping for the words. She was singing with a good deal of warmth when she came to the end of the old song:

> For memory is the only friend
>   That grief can call its own.

Joe flashed out his red silk handkerchief and blew his nose, shaking his head. "No-no-no-no-no-no-no! Too sad, too sad! I not like-a dat. Play quick somet'ing gay now."

Nils put his lips to the instrument, and Joe lay back in his chair, laughing and singing, "Oh, Evelina, Sweet Evelina!" Clara laughed, too. Long ago, when she and Nils went to high school, the model student of their class was a very homely girl in thick spectacles. Her name was Evelina Oleson; she had a long, swinging walk which somehow suggested the measure of that song, and they used mercilessly to sing it at her.

"Dat ugly Oleson girl, she teach in de school," Joe gasped, "an' she still walk chust like dat, yup-a, yup-a, yup-a, chust like a camel she go! Now, Nils, we have some more li'l drink. Oh, yes-yes-yes-yes-yes-yes-*yes*! Dis time you haf to drink, and Clara she haf to, so she show she not jealous. So, we all drink to your girl. You not tell her name, eh? No-no-no, I no make you tell. She pretty, eh? She make good sweetheart? I bet!" Joe winked and lifted his glass. "How soon you get married?"

Nils screwed up his eyes. "That I don't know. When she says."

Joe threw out his chest. "Das-a way boys talks. No way for mans. Mans say, 'You come to de church, an' get a hurry on you.' Das-a way mans talks."

"Maybe Nils hasn't got enough to keep a wife," put in Clara ironically. "How about that, Nils?" she asked him frankly, as if she wanted to know.

Nils looked at her coolly, raising one eyebrow. "Oh, I can keep her, all right."

"The way she wants to be kept?"

"With my wife, I'll decide that," replied Nils calmly. "I'll give her what's good for her."

Clara made a wry face. "You'll give her the strap, I expect, like old Peter Oleson gave his wife."

"When she needs it," said Nils lazily, locking his hands behind his head and squinting up through the leaves of the cherry tree. "Do you remember the time I squeezed the cherries all over your clean dress, and Aunt Johanna boxed my ears for me? My gracious, weren't you mad! You had both hands full of cherries, and I squeezed 'em and made the juice fly all over you. I liked to have fun with you; you'd get so mad."

"We *did* have fun, didn't we? None of the other kids ever had so much fun. We knew how to play."

Nils dropped his elbows on the table and looked steadily across at her. "I've played with lots of girls since, but I haven't found one who was such good fun."

Clara laughed. The late afternoon sun was shining full in her face, and deep in the back of her eyes there shone something fiery, like the yellow drops of Tokai in the brown glass bottle. "Can you still play, or are you only pretending?"

"I can play better than I used to, and harder."

"Don't you ever work, then?" She had not intended to say it. It slipped out because she was confused enough to say just the wrong thing.

"I work between times." Nils' steady gaze still beat upon her. "Don't you worry about my working, Mrs. Ericson. You're getting like all the rest of them." He reached his brown, warm hand across the table and dropped it on Clara's, which was cold as an icicle. "Last call for play, Mrs. Ericson!" Clara shivered, and suddenly her hands and cheeks grew warm. Her fingers lingered in his a moment, and they looked at each other earnestly. Joe Vavrika had put the mouth of the bottle to his lips and was swallowing the last drops of the Tokai, standing. The sun, just about to sink behind his shop, glistened on the bright glass, on his flushed face and curly yellow hair. "Look," Clara whispered; "that's the way I want to grow old."

VI

On the day of Olaf Ericson's barn-raising, his wife, for once in a way, rose early. Johanna Vavrika had been baking cakes and frying and boiling and spicing meats for a week beforehand, but it was not until the day before the party was to take place that Clara showed any interest in it. Then she was seized with one of her fitful spasms of energy, and took the wagon and little Eric and spent the day on Plum Creek, gathering vines and swamp golden-rod to decorate the barn.

By four o'clock in the afternoon buggies and wagons began to arrive at the big unpainted building in front of Olaf's house. When Nils and his mother came at five, there were more than fifty people in the barn, and a great drove of children. On the ground floor stood six long tables, set with the crockery of seven flourishing Ericson families, lent for the occasion. In the middle of each table was a big yellow pumpkin, hollowed out and filled with woodbine. In one corner of the barn, behind a pile of green-and-white-striped watermelons, was a circle of chairs for the old people: the younger guests sat on bushel measures or barbed-wire spools, and the children tumbled about in the haymow. The box stalls Clara had converted into booths. The framework was hidden by goldenrod and sheaves of wheat, and the partitions were covered with wild grapevines full of fruit. At one of these Johanna Vavrika watched over her cooked meats, enough to provision an army; and at the next her kitchen girls had ranged the ice-cream freezers, and Clara was already cutting pies and cakes against the hour of serving. At the third stall, little Hilda, in a bright pink lawn dress, dispensed lemonade throughout the afternoon. Olaf, as a public man, had thought it inadvisable to serve beer in his barn; but Joe Vavrika had come over wilth two demijohns concealed in his buggy, and after his arrival the wagon shed was much frequented by the men.

"Hasn't Cousin Clara fixed things lovely?" little Hilda whispered, when Nils went up to her stall and asked for lemonade.

Nils leaned against the booth, talking to the excited little girl and watching the people. The barn faced the west, and the sun, pouring in at the big doors, filled the whole interior with a golden light, through which filtered fine particles of dust from the haymow, where the children were romping. There was a great chattering from the stall where Johanna Vavrika exhibited to the admiring women her platters heaped with fried chicken, her roasts of beef, boiled tongues, and baked hams with cloves stuck in the crisp brown fat and garnished with tansy and parsley. The older women, having assured themselves that there were twenty kinds of cake, not counting cookies, and three dozen fat pies, repaired to the corner behind the pile of watermelons, put on their white aprons, and fell to their knitting and fancywork. They were a fine company of old women, and a Dutch painter would have loved to find them there together, where the sun made bright patches on the floor and sent long, quivering shafts of gold through the dusky shade up among the rafters. There were fat, rosy old women who looked hot in their best black dresses; spare, alert old women with brown, dark-veined hands; and several of almost heroic frame, not less massive than old Mrs. Ericson herself. Few of them wore glasses, and old Mrs. Svendsen, a Danish woman, who was quite bald, wore the only cap among them. Mrs. Oleson, who had twelve big grandchildren, could still show two braids of yellow hair as thick as her own wrists. Among all these grandmothers there were more brown heads than white. They all had a pleased, prosperous air, as if they were more than satisfied with themselves and with life. Nils, leaning against Hilda's lemonade stand, watched them as they sat chattering in four languages, their fingers never lagging behind their tongues.

"Look at them over there," he whispered, detaining Clara as she passed him. "Aren't they the Old Guard? I've just counted thirty hands. I guess they've wrung many a chicken's neck and warmed many a boy's jacket for him in their time."

In reality he fell into amazement when he thought of the Herculean labors those fifteen pairs of hands had performed: of the cows they had milked, the butter they had made, the gardens they had planted, the children and grandchildren they had tended, the brooms they had worn out, the mountains of food they had cooked. It made him dizzy. Clara Vavrika smiled a hard, enigmatical smile at him and walked rapidly away. Nils' eyes followed her white figure as she went toward the house. He watched her walking alone in the sunlight, looked at her slender, defiant shoulders and her little hard-set head with its coils of blue-black hair. "No," he reflected; "she'd never be like them, not if she lived here a hundred years. She'd only grow more bitter. You can't tame a wild thing; you can only chain it. People aren't all alike. I mustn't lose my nerve." He gave Hilda's pigtail a parting tweak and set out after Clara. "Where to?" he asked, as he came upon her in the kitchen.

"I'm going to the cellar for preserves."

"Let me go with you. I never get a moment alone with you. Why do you keep out of my way?"

Clara laughed. "I don't usually get in anybody's way."

Nils followed her down the stairs and to the far corner of the cellar, where a basement window let in a stream of light. From a swinging shelf Clara selected several glass jars, each labeled in Johanna's careful hand. Nils took up a brown flask. "What's this? It looks good."

"It is. It's some French brandy father gave me when I was married. Would you like some? Have you a corkscrew? I'll get glasses."

When she brought them, Nils took them from her and put them down on the window sill. "Clara Vavrika, do you remember how crazy I used to be about you?"

Clara shrugged her shoulders. "Boys are always crazy about somebody or other. I dare say some silly has been crazy about Evelina Oleson. You got over it in a hurry."

"Because I didn't come back, you mean? I had to get on, you know, and it was hard sledding at first. Then I heard you'd married Olaf."

"And then you stayed away from a broken heart," Clara laughed.

"And then I began to think about you more than I had since I first went away. I began to wonder if you were really as you had seemed to me when I was a boy. I thought I'd like to see. I've had lots of girls, but no one ever pulled me the same way. The more I thought about you, the more I remembered how it used to be—like hearing a wild tune you can't resist, calling you out at night. It had been a long while since anything had pulled me out of my boots, and I wondered whether anything ever could again." Nils thrust his hands into his coat pockets and squared his shoulders, as his mother sometimes squared hers, as Olaf, in a clumsier manner, squared his. "So I thought I'd come back and see. Of course the family have tried to do me, and I rather thought I'd bring out father's will and make a fuss. But they can have their old land; they've put enough sweat into it." He took the flask and filled the two glasses carefully to the brim. "I've found out what I want from the Ericsons. Drink *skoal*, Clara." He lifted his glass, and Clara took hers with downcast eyes. "Look at me, Clara Vavrika. *Skoal!*"

She raised her burning eyes and answered fiercely: "*Skoal!*"

The barn supper began at six o'clock and lasted for two hilarious hours. Yense Nelson had made a wager that he could eat two whole fried chickens, and he did. Eli Swanson stowed away two whole custard pies, and Nick Hermanson ate a chocolate layer cake to the last crumb. There was even a cooky contest among the children, and one thin, slablike Bohemian boy consumed sixteen and won the prize, a gingerbread pig which Johanna Vavrika had carefully decorated with red candies and burnt sugar. Fritz Sweiheart, the German carpenter, won in the pickle contest, but he disappeared soon after supper and was not seen for the rest of the evening. Joe Vavrika said that Fritz could have managed the pickles all right, but he had sampled the demijohn in his buggy too often before sitting down to the table.

While the supper was being cleared away the two fiddlers began to tune up for the dance. Clara was to accompany them on her old upright piano, which had been brought down from her father's. By this time Nils had renewed old acquaintances. Since his interview with Clara in the cellar, he had been busy telling all the old women how young they looked, and all the young ones how pretty they were, and assuring the men that they had here the best farmland in the world. He had made himself so agreeable that old Mrs. Ericson's friends began to come up to her and tell how lucky she was to get her smart son back again, and please to get him to play his flute. Joe Vavrika, who could still play very well when he forgot that he had rheumatism, caught up a fiddle from Johnny Oleson and played a crazy Bohemian dance tune that set the wheels going. When he dropped the bow every one was ready to dance.

Olaf, in a frock coat and a solemn made-up necktie, led the grand march with his mother. Clara had kept well out of *that* by sticking to the piano. She played the march with a pompous solemnity which greatly amused the prodigal son, who went over and stood behind her.

"Oh, aren't you rubbing it into them, Clara Vavrika? And aren't you lucky to have me here, or all your wit would be thrown away."

"I'm used to being witty for myself. It saves my life."

The fiddles struck up a polka, and Nils convulsed Joe Vavrika by leading out Evelina Oleson, the homely schoolteacher. His next partner was a very fat Swedish girl, who, although she was an heiress, had not been asked for the first dance, but had stood against the wall in her tight, high-heeled shoes, nervously fingering a lace handkerchief. She was soon out of breath, so Nils led her, pleased and panting, to her seat, and went over to the piano, from which Clara had been watching his gallantry. "Ask Olena Yenson," she whispered. "She waltzes beautifully."

Olena, too, was rather inconveniently plump, handsome in a smooth, heavy way, with a fine color and good-natured, sleepy eyes. She was redolent of violet sachet powder, and had warm, soft, white hands, but she danced divinely, moving as smoothly as the tide coming in. "There, that's something like," Nils said as he released her. "You'll give me the next waltz, won't you? Now I must go and dance with my little cousin."

Hilda was greatly excited when Nils went up to her stall and held out his arm. Her little eyes sparkled, but she declared that she could not leave her lemonade. Old Mrs. Ericson, who happened along at this moment, said she would attend to that, and Hilda came out, as pink as her pink dress. The dance was a schottische, and in a moment her yellow braids were fairly standing on end. "Bravo!" Nils cried encouragingly. "Where did you learn to dance so nicely?"

"My Cousin Clara taught me," the little girl panted.

Nils found Eric sitting with a group of boys who were too awkward or too shy to dance, and told him that he must dance the next waltz with Hilda.

The boy screwed up his shoulders. "Aw, Nils, I can't dance. My feet are too big; I look silly."

"Don't be thinking about yourself. It doesn't matter how boys look."

Nils had never spoken to him so sharply before, and Eric made haste to scramble out of his corner and brush the straw from his coat.

Clara nodded approvingly. "Good for you, Nils. I've been trying to get hold of him. They dance very nicely together; I sometimes play for them."

"I'm obliged to you for teaching him. There's no reason why he should grow up to be a lout."

"He'll never be that. He's more like you than any of them. Only he hasn't your courage." From her slanting eyes Clara shot forth one of those keen glances, admiring and at the same time challenging, which she seldom bestowed on any one, and which seemed to say, "Yes, I admire you, but I am your equal."

Clara was proving a much better host than Olaf, who, once the supper was over, seemed to feel no interest in anything but the lanterns. He had brought a locomotive headlight from town to light the revels, and he kept skulking about it as if he feared the mere light from it might set his new barn on fire. His wife, on the contrary, was cordial to every one, was animated and even gay. The deep salmon color in her cheeks burned vividly, and her eyes were full of life. She gave the piano over to the fat Swedish heiress, pulled her father away from the corner where he sat gossiping with his cronies, and made him dance a Bohemian dance with her. In his youth Joe had been a famous dancer, and his daughter got him so limbered up that every one sat round and applauded them. The old ladies were particularly delighted, and made them go through the dance again. From their corner where they watched and commented, the old women kept time with their feet and hands, and whenever the fiddles struck up a new air old Mrs. Svendsen's white cap would begin to bob.

Clara was waltzing with little Eric when Nils came up to them, brushed his brother aside, and swung her out among the dancers. "Remember how we used to waltz on rollers at the old skating rink in town? I suppose people don't do that any more. We used to keep it up for hours. You know, we never did moon around as other boys and girls did. It was dead serious with us from the beginning. When we were most in love with each other, we used to fight. You were always pinching people; your fingers were like little nippers. A regular snapping turtle, you were. Lord, how you'd like Stockholm! Sit out in the streets in front of cafés and talk all night in summer. Just like a reception—officers and ladies and funny English people. Jolliest people in the world, the Swedes, once you get them going. Always drinking things—champagne and stout mixed, half-and-half; serve it out of big pitchers, and serve plenty. Slow pulse, you know; they can stand a lot. Once they light up, they're glowworms, I can tell you."

"All the same, you don't really like gay people."

"I don't?"

"No; I could see that when you were looking at the old women there this afternoon. They're the kind you really admire, after all; women like your mother. And that's the kind you'll marry."

"Is it, Miss Wisdom? You'll see who I'll marry, and she won't have a domestic virtue to bless herself with. She'll be a snapping turtle, and she'll be a match for me. All the same, they're a fine bunch of old dames over there. You admire them yourself."

"No, I don't; I detest them."

"You won't, when you look back on them from Stock-holm or Budapest. Freedom settles all that. Oh, but you're the real Bohemian Girl, Clara Vavrika!" Nils laughed down at her sullen frown and began mockingly to sing:

> "Oh, how could a poor gypsy maiden like me
> Expect the proud bride of a baron to be?"

Clara clutched his shoulder. "Hush, Nils; every one is looking at you."

"I don't care. They can't gossip. It's all in the family, as the Ericsons say when they divide up little Hilda's patri-mony amongst them. Besides, we'll give them something to talk about when we hit the trail. Lord, it will be a godsend to them! They haven't had anything so interest-ing to chatter about since the grasshopper year. It'll give them a new lease of life. And Olaf won't lose the Bohemian vote, either. They'll have the laugh on him so that they'll vote two apiece. They'll send him to Congress. They'll never forget his barn party, or us. They'll always remem-ber us as we're dancing together now. We're making a legend. Where's my waltz, boys?" he called as they whirled past the fiddlers.

The musicians grinned, looked at each other, hesitated, and began a new air; and Nils sang with them, as the couples fell from a quick waltz to a long, slow glide:

> "When other lips and other hearts
> Their tale of love shall tell,
> In language whose excess imparts
> The power they feel so well."

The old women applauded vigorously. "What a gay one he is, that Nils!" And old Mrs. Svendsen's cap lurched dreamily from side to side to the flowing measure of the dance.

> Of days that have as ha-a-p-py been,
> And you'll remember me.

VII

The moonlight flooded that great, silent land. The reaped fields lay yellow in it. The straw stacks and poplar windbreaks threw sharp black shadows. The roads were white rivers of dust. The sky was a deep, crystalline blue, and the stars were few and faint. Everything seemed to have succumbed, to have sunk to sleep, under the great, golden, tender, midsummer moon. The splendor of it seemed to transcend human life and human fate. The senses were too feeble to take it in, and every time one looked up at the sky one felt unequal to it, as if one were sitting deaf under the waves of a great river of melody. Near the road, Nils Ericson was lying against a straw stack in Olaf's wheat field. His own life seemed strange and unfamiliar to him, as if it were something he had read about, or dreamed, and forgotten. He lay very still, watching the white road that ran in front of him, lost itself among the fields, and then, at a distance, reappeared over a little hill. At last, against this white band he saw something moving rapidly, and he got up and walked to the edge of the field. "She is passing the row of poplars now," he thought. He heard the padded beat of hoofs along the dusty road, and as she came into sight he stepped out and waved his arms. Then, for fear of frightening the horse, he drew back and waited. Clara had seen him, and she came up at a walk. Nils took the horse by the bit and stroked his neck.

"What are you doing out so late, Clara Vavrika? I went to the house, but Johanna told me you had gone to your father's."

"Who can stay in the house on a night like this? Aren't you out yourself?"

"Ah, but that's another matter."

Nils turned the horse into the field.

"What are you doing. Where are you taking Norman?"

"Not far, but I want to talk to you tonight; I have something to say to you. I can't talk to you at the house, with Olaf sitting there on the porch, weighing a thousand tons."

Clara laughed. "He won't be sitting there now. He's in bed by this time, and asleep—weighing a thousand tons."

Nils plodded on across the stubble. "Are you really going to spend the rest of your life like this, night after night, summer after summer? Haven't you anything better to do on a night like this than to wear yourself and Norman out tearing across the country to your father's and back? Besides, your father won't live forever, you know. His little place will be shut up or sold, and then you'll have nobody but the Ericsons. You'll have to fasten down the hatches for the winter then."

Clara moved her head restlessly. "Don't talk about that. I try never to think of it. If I lost father I'd lose everything, even my hold over the Ericsons."

"Bah! You'd lose a good deal more than that. You'd lose your race, everything that makes you yourself. You've lost a good deal of it now."

"Of what?"

"Of your love of life, your capacity for delight."

Clara put her hands up to her face. "I haven't, Nils Ericson, I haven't! Say anything to me but that. I won't have it!" she declared vehemently.

Nils led the horse up to a straw stack, and turned to Clara, looking at her intently, as he had looked at her that Sunday afternoon at Vavrika's. "But why do you fight for that so? What good is the power to enjoy, if you never enjoy? Your hands are cold again; what are you afraid of all the time? Ah, you're afraid of losing it; that's what's the matter with you! And you will, Clara Vavrika, you will! When I used to know you—listen; you've caught a wild bird in your hand, haven't you, and felt its heart beat so hard that you were afraid it would shatter its little body to pieces? Well, you used to be just like that, a slender, eager thing with a wild delight inside you. That is how I remembered you. And I come back and find you—a bitter woman. This is a perfect ferret fight here; you live by biting and being bitten. Can't you remember what life used to be? Can't you remember that old delight? I've never forgotten it, or known its like, on land or sea."

He drew the horse under the shadow of the straw stack. Clara felt him take her foot out of the stirrup, and she slid softly down into his arms. He kissed her slowly. He was a deliberate man, but his nerves were steel when he wanted anything. Something flashed out from him like a knife out of a sheath. Clara felt everything slipping away from her; she was flooded by the summer night. He thrust his hand into his pocket, and then held it out at arm's length. "Look," he said. The shadow of the straw stack fell sharp across his wrist, and in the palm of his hand she saw a silver dollar shining. "That's my pile," he muttered; "will you go with me?"

Clara nodded, and dropped her forehead on his shoulder.

Nils took a deep breath. "Will you go with me tonight?"

"Where?" she whispered softly.

"To town, to catch the midnight flyer."

Clara lifted her head and pulled herself together. "Are you crazy, Nils? We couldn't go away like that."

"That's the only way we ever will go. You can't sit on the bank and think about it. You have to plunge. That's the way I've always done, and it's the right way for people like you and me. There's nothing so dangerous as sitting still. You've only got one life, one youth, and you can let it slip through your fingers if you want to; nothing easier. Most people do that. You'd be better off tramping the roads with me than you are here." Nils held back her head and looked into her eyes. "But I'm not that kind of a tramp, Clara. You won't have to take in sewing. I'm with a Norwegian shipping line; came over on business with the New York offices, but now I'm going straight back to Bergen. I expect I've got as much money as the Ericsons. Father sent me a little to get started. They never knew about that. There, I hadn't meant to tell you; I wanted you to come on your own nerve."

Clara looked off across the fields. "It isn't that, Nils, but something seems to hold me. I'm afraid to pull against it. It comes out of the ground, I think."

"I know all about that. One has to tear loose. You're not needed here. Your father will understand; he's made like us. As for Olaf, Johanna will take better care of him than ever you could. It's now or never, Clara Vavrika. My bag's at the station; I smuggled it there yesterday."

Clara clung to him and hid her face against his shoulder. "Not tonight," she whispered. "Sit here and talk to me tonight. I don't want to go anywhere tonight. I may never love you like this again."

Nils laughed through his teeth. "You can't come that on me. That's not my way, Clara Vavrika. Eric's mare is over there behind the stacks, and I'm off on the midnight. It's goodbye, or off across the world with me. My carriage won't wait. I've written a letter to Olaf; I'll mail it in town. When he reads it he won't bother us—not if I know him. He'd rather have the land. Besides, I could demand an investigation of his administration of Cousin Henrik's estate, and that would be bad for a public man. You've no clothes, I know; but you can sit up tonight, and we can get everything on the way. Where's your old dash, Clara Vavrika? What's become of your Bohemian blood? I used to think you had courage enough for anything. Where's your nerve—what are you waiting for?"

Clara drew back her head, and he saw the slumberous fire in her eyes. "For you to say one thing, Nils Ericson."

"I never say that thing to any woman, Clara Vavrika." He leaned back, lifted her gently from the ground, and whispered through his teeth: "But I'll never, never let you go, not to any man on earth but me! Do you understand me? Now, wait here."

Clara sank down on a sheaf of wheat and covered her face with her hands. She did not know what she was going to do—whether she would go or stay. The great, silent country seemed to lay a spell upon her. The ground seemed to hold her as if by roots. Her knees were soft under her. She felt as if she could not bear separation from her old sorrows, from her old discontent. They were dear to her, they had kept her alive, they were a part of her. There would be nothing left of her if she were wrenched away from them. Never could she pass beyond that skyline against which her restlessness had beat so many times. She felt as if her soul had built itself a nest there on that horizon at which she looked every morning and every evening, and it was dear to her, inexpressibly dear. She pressed her fingers against her eyeballs to shut it out. Beside her she heard the tramping of horses in the soft earth. Nils said nothing to her. He put his hands under her arms and lifted her lightly to her saddle. Then he swung himself into his own.

"We shall have to ride fast to catch the midnight train. A last gallop, Clara Vavrika. Forward!"

There was a start, a thud of hoofs along the moonlit road, two dark shadows going over the hill; and then the great, still land stretched untroubled under the azure night. Two shadows had passed.

VIII

A year after the flight of Olaf Ericson's wife, the night train was steaming across the plains of Iowa. The conductor was hurrying through one of the day coaches, his lantern on his arm, when a lank, fair-haired boy sat up in one of the plush seats and tweaked him by the coat.

"What is the next stop, please, sir?"

"Red Oak, Iowa. But you go through to Chicago, don't you?" He looked down, and noticed that the boy's eyes were red and his face was drawn, as if he were in trouble.

"Yes. But I was wondering whether I could get off at the next place and get a train back to Omaha."

"Well, I suppose you could. Live in Omaha?"

"No. In the western part of the State. How soon do we get to Red Oak?"

"Forty minutes. You'd better make up your mind, so I can tell the baggageman to put your trunk off."

"Oh, never mind about that! I mean, I haven't got any," the boy added, blushing.

"Run away," the conductor thought, as he slammed the coach door behind him.

Eric Ericson crumpled down in his seat and put his brown hand to his forehead. He had been crying, and he had had no supper, and his head was aching violently. "Oh, what shall I do?" he thought, as he looked dully down at his big shoes. "Nils will be ashamed of me; I haven't got any spunk."

Ever since Nils had run away with his brother's wife, life at home had been hard for little Eric. His mother and Olaf both suspected him of complicity. Mrs. Ericson was harsh and faultfinding, constantly wounding the boy's pride; and Olaf was always setting her against him.

Joe Vavrika heard often from his daughter. Clara had always been fond of her father, and happiness made her kinder. She wrote him long accounts of the voyage to Bergen, and of the trip she and Nils took through Bohemia to the little town where her father had grown up and where she herself was born. She visited all her kinsmen there, and sent her father news of his brother, who was a priest; of his sister, who had married a horsebreeder—of their big farm and their many children. These letters Joe always managed to read to little Eric. They contained messages for Eric and Hilda. Clara sent presents, too, which Eric never dared to take home and which poor little Hilda never even saw, though she loved to hear Eric tell about them when they were out getting the eggs together. But Olaf once saw Eric coming out of Vavrika's house— the old man had never asked the boy to come into his saloon—and Olaf went straight to his mother and told her. That night Mrs. Ericson came to Eric's room after he was in bed and made a terrible scene. She could be very terrifying when she was really angry. She forbade him ever to speak to Vavrika again, and after that night she would not allow him to go to town alone. So it was a long while before Eric got any more news of his brother. But old Joe suspected what was going on, and he carried Clara's letters about in his pocket. One Sunday he drove out to see a German friend of his, and chanced to catch sight of Eric, sitting by the cattle pond in the big pasture. They went together into Fritz Oberlies' barn, and read the letters and talked things over. Eric admitted that things were getting hard for him at home. That very night old Joe sat down and laboriously penned a statement of the case to his daughter.

Things got no better for Eric. His mother and Olaf felt that, however closely he was watched, he still, as they said, "heard." Mrs. Ericson could not admit neutrality. She had sent Johanna Vavrika packing back to her brother's, though Olaf would much rather have kept her than Anders' eldest daughter, whom Mrs. Ericson installed in her place. He was not so highhanded as his mother, and he once sulkily told her that she might better have taught her granddaughter to cook before she sent Johanna away. Olaf could have borne a good deal for the sake of prunes spiced in honey, the secret of which Johanna had taken away with her.

At last two letters came to Joe Vavrika: one from Nils, inclosing a postal order for money to pay Eric's passage to Bergen, and one from Clara, saying that Nils had a place for Eric in the offices of his company, that he was to live with them, and that they were only waiting for him to come. He was to leave New York on one of the boats of Nils' own line; the captain was one of their friends, and Eric was to make himself known at once.

Nils' directions were so explicit that a baby could have followed them, Eric felt. And here he was, nearing Red Oak, Iowa, and rocking backward and forward in despair. Never had he loved his brother so much, and never had the big world called to him so hard. But there was a lump in his throat which would not go down. Ever since nightfall he had been tormented by the thought of his mother, alone in that big house that had sent forth so many men. Her unkindness now seemed so little, and her loneliness so great. He remembered everything she had ever done for him: how frightened she had been when he tore his hand in the cornsheller, and how she wouldn't let Olaf scold him. When Nils went away he didn't leave his mother all alone, or he would never have gone. Eric felt sure of that.

The train whistled. The conductor came in, smiling not unkindly. "Well, young man, what are you going to do? We stop at Red Oak in three minutes."

"Yes, thank you. I'll let you know." The conductor went out, and the boy doubled up with misery. He couldn't let his one chance go like this. He felt for his breast pocket and crackled Nils' kind letter to give him courage. He didn't want Nils to be ashamed of him. The train stopped. Suddenly he remembered his brother's kind, twinkling eyes, that always looked at you as if from far away. The lump in his throat softened. "Ah, but Nils, Nils would *understand*!" he thought. "That's just it about Nils; he always understands."

A lank, pale boy with a canvas telescope stumbled off the train to the Red Oak siding, just as the conductor called, "All aboard!"

The next night Mrs. Ericson was sitting alone in her wooden rocking chair on the front porch. Little Hilda had been sent to bed and had cried herself to sleep. The old woman's knitting was in her lap, but her hands lay motionless on top of it. For more than an hour she had not moved a muscle. She simply sat, as only the Ericsons and the mountains can sit. The house was dark, and there was no sound but the croaking of the frogs down in the pond of the little pasture.

Eric did not come home by the road, but across the fields, where no one could see him. He set his telescope down softly in the kitchen shed, and slipped noiselessly along the path to the front porch. He sat down on the step without saying anything. Mrs. Ericson made no sign, and the frogs croaked on. At last the boy spoke timidly.

"I've come back, Mother."

"Very well," said Mrs. Ericson.

Eric leaned over and picked up a little stick out of the grass.

"How about the milking?" he faltered.

"That's been done, hours ago."

"Who did you get?"

"Get? I did it myself. I can milk as good as any of you."

Eric slid along the step near to her. "Oh, Mother, why did you?" he asked sorrowfully. "Why didn't you get one of Otto's boys?"

"I didn't want anybody to know I was in need of a boy," said Mrs. Ericson bitterly. She looked straight in front of her and her mouth tightened. "I always meant to give you the home farm," she added.

The boy started and slid closer. "Oh, Mother," he faltered, "I don't care about the farm. I came back because I thought you might be needing me, maybe." He hung his head and got no further.

"Very well,'" said Mrs. Ericson. Her hand went out from her suddenly and rested on his head. Her fingers twined themselves in his soft, pale hair. His tears splashed down on the boards; happiness filled his heart.

SELECTED BIBLIOGRAPHY

April Twilights, 1903 *Poems*

The Troll Garden, 1905 *Stories*
    (Meridian Classic 0452-00714-3)

Alexander's Bridge, 1912 *Novel*
    (Meridian Classic 0452-008751)

O Pioneers! 1913 *Novel*

The Song of the Lark, 1915 *Novel*

My Ántonia, 1918 *Novel*

Youth and the Bright Medusa, 1920 *Stories*

One of Ours, 1922 *Novel*

A Lost Lady, 1923 *Novel*

The Professor's House, 1925 *Novel*

My Mortal Enemy, 1926 *Novel*

Death Comes for the Archbishop, 1927 *Novel*

Shadows on the Rock, 1931 *Novel*

Obscure Destinies, 1932 *Stories*

Lucy Gayheart, 1935 *Novel*

Not Under Forty, 1936 *Essays*

Sapphira and the Slave Girl, 1940 *Novel*

The Old Beauty and Others, 1948 *Stories*

On Writing: Critical Studies on Writing as an Art,
    1949 *Eassays and Letters*

Willa Cather: 24 Stories, 1987 *Stories*
    (Meridian Classic 0452-008743)

SELECTED BIOGRAPHY
AND CRITICISM

Arnold, Marilyn. *Willa Cather's Short Fiction*. Athens: Ohio University Press, 1984.

Brown, Edward K., and Edel, Leon. *Willa Cather: A Critical Biography*. New York: Avon, 1980.

Daiches, David. *Willa Cather: A Critical Introduction*. Ithaca, N.Y.: Cornell University Press, 1951.

Fryer, Judith. *Felicitous Space: The Imaginative Structures of Edith Wharton and Willa Cather*. Chapel Hill: University of North Carolina Press, 1986.

Lewis, Edith. *Willa Cather Living: A Personal Record*. New York: Alfred A. Knopf, 1953.

O'Brien, Sharon. *Willa Cather: The Emerging Voice*. New York: Oxford University Press, 1987.

Robinson, Phylis C. *Willa: The Life of Willa Cather*. New York: Doubleday, 1983.

Rosowski, Susan J. *The Voyage Perilous: Willa Cather's Romanticism*. Lincoln: University of Nebraska Press, 1986.

Sergeant, Elizabeth. *Willa Cather: A Memoir*. Lincoln: University of Nebraska Press [Bison ed.], 1963.

Stouck, David. *Willa Cather's Imagination*. Lincoln: University of Nebraska Press, 1975.

Woodress, James. *Willa Cather: A Literary Life*. Lincoln: University of Nebraska Press, 1987.

EARLY WORKS OF WILLA CATHER

☐ **THE TROLL GARDEN.** In her first book, Willa Cather evokes the dreams that haunt men and women torn between the desire to confess and the need to conceal their private fantastical aspirations. These stories, including the reknowned "Paul's Case," are about dreamers and artists whose spiritual yearnings are in conflict with the meager reality of their lives. (007143—$3.95)

☐ **WILLA CATHER: 24 STORIES.** This superb collection of Willa Cather's early stories shows the full scope and richness of her developing craft in the important years from 1892 until 1912. The collection opens with her very first published story, "Peter," which draws on the Nebraskan landscape and immigrant culture and ends with the breakthrough work that led to her famous novel *O Pioneers!*

(008743—$5.95)*

☐ **ALEXANDER'S BRIDGE.** Her first published novel will delight readers who know Cather best as poet of the prairie and immigrant American life. Set in the sophisticated drawing rooms of Boston and London, is the forceful story of rugged bridge-builder Bartley Alexander, fighting with a divided self that leaves him torn between two women—his elegant wife and an Irish actress. (008751—$4.95)*

*Not available in Canada.

Buy them at your local bookstore or use this convenient coupon for ordering.

NEW AMERICAN LIBRARY
P.O. Box 999, Bergenfield, New Jersey 07621

Please send me the books I have checked above. I am enclosing
$_____ (please add $1.00 to this order to cover postage and handling). Send check or money order—no cash or C.O.D.'s. Prices and numbers are subject to change without notice.

Name _____

Address _____

City _____ State _____ Zip Code _____

Allow 4-6 weeks for delivery.
This offer subject to withdrawal without notice.

STORIES BY MARK TWAIN

**Buy them at your local
bookstore or use coupon
on next page for ordering.**